J.B.'s Daughter

John Sherlock

McGraw-Hill Book Company

New York
St. Louis
San Francisco
Toronto

1 2 3 4 5 6 7 8 9 DO DO 8 7 6 5 4 3 2 1 0

LIBRARY OF CONGRESS CATALOGING IN PUBLICATION DATA

Sherlock, John, 1932-
J. B.'s daughter.
I. Title.
PS3569·H3997J3   813'.54   80-23955
ISBN 0-07-056750-6

Book design by Roberta Rezk

For Peter,
my son,
with fondest love

 **1**

SWEATING, heart palpitations, a rapid pulse: Ceetra Rampling recognized the symptoms. She had suffered from claustrophobia for as long as she could remember. She knew that if she didn't leave soon the walls of the room where she sat alone in the darkness would begin closing in on her.

But how could she walk out on a party being held in her honor? It was a surprise celebration arranged by Andrea Cooper, her partner in the fashion business they operated out of an elegant Georgian mansion on Cheyne Walk in London's Chelsea district, and Andrea had obviously put a lot of work into planning it. Ceetra's only suspicion that something out of the ordinary was under way had come around five o'clock, when the staff showed no signs of wanting to go home. This would have been unusual any time, but on a Friday evening, when most of them tried to get away early in order to make the most of the weekend, it was downright puzzling.

Before Ceetra could probe, Andrea had insisted she needed her in the small room at the top of the house which served as their office. Her pretext was a long discussion about the costs of various fabrics they had recently ordered. By the time they emerged the employees had decorated the three main work areas with balloons and streamers, and a crew of caterers from Fortnum and Mason's had set up tables of food and champagne. A combo that had just finished a long engagement at Annabel's, the smartest discotheque in London, struck up the chords of "Happy Birthday" as a cake inscribed with the date—20 April 1984—was carried into the room.

Now it was almost 9:30 p.m. and Ceetra still hadn't thought of a way to leave without offending everybody. At first she had planned on slipping away after she'd opened her gifts, but a young shipping clerk who fancied himself as an English John Travolta had brashly invited her to dance, and rather than appear snobbish she had embarked on what quickly turned into a marathon contest of skills. She matched her partner's flashy gyrations move for move, stubbornly refusing to yield the floor to somebody still in his teens, and experienced a perverse satisfaction when lack of stamina forced him to quit. It had left her exhausted, but rather than show her fatigue, she'd excused herself on the pretense of having to make a telephone call, and sought respite in the small upstairs office.

"Are you all right?"

Ceetra turned and saw Andrea standing in the doorway. She was small and plain, a total contrast to Ceetra's high-fashion model's body and stunningly beautiful face. But her ordinary appearance hid an extraordinary ability as an administrator, a skill that perfectly complemented Ceetra's talent for creating designs that were so original they were the hit of leading fashion shows in the world's major capitals year after year.

"Fine," Ceetra said. "Just trying to get myself back in one piece."

"You were wonderful."

"My muscles aren't as impressed. I think they're trying to tell me I'm going to regret it in the morning."

Andrea laughed. "You're not as young as you used to be."

"Twenty-six does have an ominous ring, doesn't it? Maybe that's why I'm sitting up here like a recluse."

"Are you sure that's all?"

Ceetra hesitated. "You want the truth?"

"Of course."

"I've been trying to think of a way to leave that won't offend you."

"Don't you like the party?" The question was edged with hurt.

"It's wonderful." Ceetra got up and put her arms around Andrea. "I couldn't have asked for a nicer surprise."

"But—?"

"You can still read me like a book, can't you?"

"I've had a lot of practice."

Ceetra walked to the window. Her friend's words triggered the realization that they had known each other since they were both thirteen. Thirteen years. God, how quickly the time had gone. Suddenly she wondered if the future would bring anything to fill the void that seemed to loom ahead. She looked out at a tug pulling a string of barges down the Thames. It had started to rain a fine mist, and the moisture created a blurred nimbus around the lights on the boats. The sight only heightened her sense of desolation.

"It's just that I'd made other plans for this evening," she said lamely.

"Can't you change them?"

"Not now. It's too late. Paul's probably already on his way—"

"Paul Mayhew?"

Ceetra nodded.

"I thought you'd stopped seeing him."

"I have," she said. "At least a dozen times. But it never seems to stick."

Andrea stepped into the room, switched on a light, and closed the door. "It's none of my business, but I care what happens to you, so I'm going to stick my nose in anyway."

"Please—"

"No, I want to say it. Paul Mayhew is one of the few real bastards I've ever met."

"You don't know him the way—"

"Know him? Aren't you forgetting I introduced the two of you? Jesus, if only I'd known then what I was getting you into."

"You're overlooking something."

"Tell me."

"We love each other."

Andrea laughed. "Love? You must be joking. Paul doesn't know the meaning of the word."

"I do," Ceetra said quietly.

"No. What you feel for that man isn't love. It's a sickness. God knows, I've seen it eating away at you for years. Well, I'm not going to stand by and say nothing any more. Paul Mayhew is a cancer, and unless you cut him out of your life completely he's going to kill you."

Ceetra didn't answer. The only sound was the noise of laughter from the party downstairs. Finally she said, "I appreciate your concern, but this is something I have to work out for myself."

Andrea shrugged. "I've had my say. If you still want to leave it's all right with me. Everybody's high on either booze or dope. I doubt if they'll know you've gone."

"It's your feelings I'm concerned about."

"Well, don't be. I understand a lot better than you think. Why else would I risk losing the best friend I've got by shooting off my mouth that way?"

The two women were silent for a moment, and then they smiled.

"Thanks," Ceetra murmured.

"For what?"

"The party and—well, being you."

"Listen, I'm no bargain. If I could look like you I'd trade places any time." Andrea crossed to the door. "Just remember what I told you. All right?"

Ceetra nodded. When Andrea left she sat for a long time watching the rain spatter against the window. The suffocating sense of being trapped had passed, and she wondered how, in such a short space of time, an emotion that was nearly paralyzing in its intensity could so easily dissolve. Dr. Carlin, the psychiatrist she'd been seeing for the last two years, attributed her claustrophobia to childhood fears of not measuring up to the expectations of her father, and had often told her that she would only be rid of it when she became convinced of her own self-worth. But that did little to explain why her brief conversation with Andrea had succeeded, while her twice-weekly sessions on Dr. Carlin's couch had so far produced only a series of exorbitant bills.

It was nearly 10:15 p.m. by the time Ceetra made her way downstairs. She'd expected a chorus of disappointment at her early departure, and had readied the excuse that she was coming down with the flu. But she needn't have worried. The main workroom was in darkness except for a shaft of light coming from a projector. It shone on a large screen that had been set up against the far wall. A pornographic film was being shown and the audience was too preoccupied by what they were seeing to notice Ceetra making her way across the room.

Her white Rolls-Royce convertible was parked in a private mews behind the house. She turned the key in the ignition and guided the car up Beaufort Street toward King's Road.

Only a short distance separated Chelsea and Mayfair, but the difference in character between the two places was so great it seemed impossible they could be part of one country, let alone neighboring boroughs in the same city. The former was a place of bold individualism and defiant eccentricity, while the latter reflected the faded elegance of a more genteel time. Its image of exclusivity had been somewhat tarnished in recent years by the influx of oil-rich Middle Easterners eager to invest their massive wealth in some of the most expensive real estate in the world, and the Dorchester Hotel had lost a considerable amount of prestige when it was purchased by a syndicate of Arabs. But Ceetra had lived in

Mayfair since she first arrived in England with her mother at the age of five, and although born in Texas, she now looked upon this fashionable district of London as home.

Her apartment occupied the entire ground floor of a stately old house at the end of Hill Street nearest to Park Lane.

After letting herself in, she switched on the stereo and looked at her watch. It was 11:08 p.m. Paul had promised to be at the apartment an hour ago, but his lateness didn't surprise her. Last-minute changes in plans were a requisite part of having an affair with a married man, and she had long ago learned to accept them. This time she was even glad of his tardiness; it gave her the chance to make sure everything would be ready by the time he arrived.

Going into the kitchen she checked the refrigerator to make sure the champagne was on ice. Estelle, the cook/housekeeper who came in for three hours every morning, had fixed an assortment of hors d'oeuvres which only needed to be reheated, and prepared the chopped onions and hard-boiled eggs Ceetra liked to serve with caviar. There was also a cold veal and ham pie, salad and an assortment of cheeses. But the pièce de résistance was the cake: a torte covered with rich chocolate frosting. Estelle had baked it herself, and had left a small note which read, "Happy Birthday, Miss R. I bought two dozen candles. They're in the drawer next to the sink. See you on Monday. Estelle."

Ceetra smiled. Two dozen candles weren't enough to mark the passing of twenty-six years, but it pleased her to know that her housekeeper thought she couldn't be more than twenty-four. Suddenly buoyed, she went into the bedroom, undressed and stepped into the shower in the adjoining bathroom.

Back in the bedroom she opened the doors of a huge walk-in closet. All her clothes were designer originals, and more than a few bore the distinctive label of her own firm. She sorted through them looking for something that would match her mood. Various possibilities presented themselves:

a long, flowing garment that was intended as a dress but looked more like a filmy negligee; pure silk lounging pajamas; a kaftan made of a gossamer material that was so sheer it was almost transparent. But for some reason none of them triggered a visceral response.

Then she glimpsed something she thought she'd thrown away years ago. It was the blue serge skirt and white blouse that she'd been required to wear at the boarding school she'd attended on the chalk cliffs overlooking the Sussex coast. The only time she'd had the uniform on since she was eighteen was when she'd worn it to a fancy dress party. Now she wondered if it still fit. Yielding to the impulse to find out, she took the clothes into the bedroom and put them on. It pleased her to discover they were slightly large for her. Apparently, she was trimmer now than she had been eight years ago. When she looked at herself in the full-length mirror she was surprised to see how young the outfit made her appear. The effect was heightened by the fact that she had removed her makeup before showering, and the steam had made her skin glow.

Suddenly she decided to keep the uniform on. Paul was so accustomed to seeing her in gorgeous clothes it would be a surprise for him to find her in something different. Maybe even a turn-on.

It was after midnight when Ceetra finished setting the table in the dining room. She went into the living room and poured herself a drink. But she hesitated before putting the glass to her lips. If she was going to be drinking champagne, a vodka and tonic wasn't such a good idea. She experienced the first stirrings of irritation at Paul's tardiness. The least he could have done was call. It occurred to her that he might have telephoned earlier in the evening, but when she checked her answering service there were no messages. Annoyed, she swallowed the drink and poured herself another, which she took with her as she crossed to the sofa.

She stretched out on the deep pillows and closed her eyes. The strains of Beethoven's Ninth Symphony flowed from the speakers of the stereo. It was a piece she loved, but she found it difficult to concentrate on the music. Her mind kept drifting back to Andrea's warning: "Paul Mayhew is a cancer . . . unless you cut him out of your life completely he's going to kill you."

Her psychiatrist had put it a different way: "You're caught between two emotions: idealization of your father, and a terrible anger at him for abandoning you. It has produced an ambivalence that manifests itself sexually in your seeking out men, like Paul, who constantly put you in situations which make you feel humiliated. It allows you to feel justified in hating them."

The smell of something burning jolted her out of her reverie, and she remembered the hors d'oeuvres she'd put in the oven. By the time she got to the kitchen they were burnt to a crisp, and the room was filled with smoke. Furious, she threw the remains in the garbage, and opened the windows to let in some fresh air.

When she returned to the living room she was still angry. Finishing what was left of her second drink, she refilled her glass and crossed to the window. There was no sign of Paul's car. It was 1:30 a.m. He was over four hours late. If there had been any way of contacting him she would have called and told him to forget their date, but there wasn't, and it left her even more frustrated.

Beethoven's Ninth had ended and the speakers were silent. She crossed to the stereo to put on another record, then pulled a huge leatherbound scrapbook from the shelf, carried it back with her to the sofa and opened the cover. It contained page after page of clippings from newspapers and magazines. Looking at them triggered memories of the hundreds of hours she had spent as a child finding the items and lovingly pasting them into the book. Every item concerned her father in some way or other, and they comprised the sum total of everything she knew about him. Now, as she leafed through the pages, she was astonished at the extensiveness of the collection. It covered almost every phase of his life, some of it relating to a time long before she was born, and she realized how much dedication had been required to put such a collection together.

Headlines on the items shared the common denominator of a single name: Jake Rampling. And the articles under them established him as a larger-than-life man who had turned a small business in Dallas, Texas, into the largest construction company in the world.

But at what cost?

Ceetra put her head back and closed her eyes. She willed herself not to think. She was too tired and the memories were too painful. For twenty years she had tried to piece together fragments that would enable her to understand her father, but so many didn't fit or were missing.

The night stillness was broken by the hollow sound of footsteps crossing the marble porch, then the slightly sharp metallic clink of a key being inserted into the lock of her front door.

 **2** DAN BLAKE sensed danger. In-
stincts honed by years as the top
troubleshooter for Rampling Inter-
national warned him that something was wrong, but when he
strained to identify the sound that had jolted him out of
sleep, all he heard was the incessant roar of the wind.

At the camp that had sprung up around the main shaft a
hundred thirty miles northeast of Amarillo the wind scoured
paint from bulldozers and every other piece of equipment
that was denied shelter. It pitted their windshields and
turned the glass in them translucent. Despite the most careful efforts to seal buildings in which parts were stored, dust
forced its way inside, leaving little piles on the window sills.
Even when the air was clear and there was no dust, the wind
still blew.

After nearly a year on the project Dan had come to hate
the way it leached moisture from his skin, and its constant
roar had nearly driven him insane. He had worked in some
of the least hospitable places on earth and prided himself on
having learned to live with hardship in its many forms, from
Saudi Arabia's enervating heat to the lung-searing cold of
Alaska's North Slope. All had marked his thirty-six years in
their own way. But none so profoundly as the endless wind
that angrily buffeted the thirty-six-foot aluminum trailer in
which he now lay.

Eleven months of its constant presence had left him irritable and quick-tempered. At first he'd attributed his displays of impatience to the pressures of the job: the digging of the deepest section of a transcontinental tunnel 5,000 feet below ground. The 3,000-mile commuter tunnel was the longest ever attempted, and keeping the project on schedule made demands on him that increased with each passing day. His displays of temper were so completely out of character that he'd begun to wonder if he'd simply become less pliant than he had been when he became Jake Rampling's personal assistant twelve years earlier. But finally his hard-headed pragmatism had laid the blame where it properly belonged: on the wind, the unceasing wind.

He had gone to bed early. His day had started at 4:30 a.m. when he went underground to check on the progress being made by the graveyard shift, and it had been filled with problems. None of any major importance, but still enough to run him ragged for the next sixteen hours. An inspector from the Occupational Safety and Health Administration office in Lubbock had made an unannounced spot check of the tunnel the previous day, and found a number of small violations. Not sufficient to red-tag the operation, but enough to warrant the issuance of a few simple, explicit orders aimed at preventing any possibility of disaster. He wanted continuous testing at the tunnel face for flammable gases. If the gas in the tunnel atmosphere reached a concentration of one percent by volume, steps should be taken to improve the ventilation system. Prior to starting excavation machines, or advancing them, holes were to be drilled ahead of the face to test for flammable gases. Self-contained breathing apparatus were to be provided for all personnel working underground, and training set up to ensure they knew how to use the oxygen units.

Dan had spent a long day making sure the OSHA inspector's instructions were carried out, and by the time he finally finished he was exhausted. It was dark when he emerged from the man trip. Too tired to wait in line for dinner at the cafeteria, he had picked up a ham sandwich and taken it back to his trailer. There he had taken a bottle of Pearl beer from the small refrigerator and, seated on the edge of the iron cot that served as his bed, had eaten his solitary meal with such disinterest that he was barely conscious of what he was swallowing. Afterward, despite his fatigue, he'd taken a hot shower at a nearby change house. Only then did he wearily climb under the rough blankets and let himself sleep.

Now the noise that had awakened him came again. This time it was louder and easier to identify. A deep-throated rumble like thunder before a storm. The earth trembled. Then an ominous silence in which the only sound was the moan of the wind. Dan swung his legs over the side of his cot and grabbed his clothes. He reached for his hard hat, but it wasn't on the nail where he usually hung it over his bed. Irritated, he flicked on the light, flooding the trailer with harsh illumination from the naked 100-watt bulb. It revealed an interior equipped with the barest essentials: a metal footlocker that doubled as a chair, a section of steel pipe across one end of the trailer that supported work clothes hung on cheap wire hangers, a sheet of half-inch plywood set across two sawhorses which served as a work table.

The yellow hard hat was on a narrow shelf just inside the door. Dan remembered putting it there while he got the beer from the refrigerator, and he experienced a prickle of annoyance at not having hung it in its usual place over the bed. Another lapse in routine. One of many in recent weeks. Angrily he adjusted the identity card that was clipped to the front of the hat. It was a laminated green plastic card bearing his name, payroll number, and a small Polaroid photograph. It showed a face with strong, even features that could have been handsome if it weren't for the nose. Badly broken in a brawl when he was still in his teens, it had been improperly set, and was flatter than traditional good looks demanded.

The picture dated from a year ago, when Dan was assigned to the project by James Bowen Rampling ("Jake" to his friends, "J. B." to others; Dan was counted among the former). When Jake had called him in and told him the magnitude of the project he'd found it difficult to comprehend. "Washington's decided to underwrite the construction of an underground rapid transit system between New York and Los Angeles," Jake had announced. "It's based on a concept the Rand Corporation came up with about ten years ago . . . huge vacuum tubes that will contain gondolas floating on magnetic fields at speeds in excess of ten thousand miles an hour . . . coast-to-coast in less than thirty minutes. It'll be the biggest tunneling job ever attempted, and I aim to get a piece of it." When contracts for the 200-billion-dollar undertaking were finally awarded, the job of digging the deepest part of the tunnel, a section running under the northern tip of the Panhandle, had gone to Rampling International.

Dan was one of the few people who knew the extent of the gamble Jake had taken in submitting his bid. The firm was already involved in numerous other projects in at least half a dozen countries around the world, all of them huge jobs that required massive investments of capital, and it was in no position to extend itself any further. But Jake was obsessed by the desire to be an essential part of the largest construction job ever undertaken, and in order to ensure the financial guarantees necessary to such an undertaking he had convinced a consortium of bankers to back him. Impressed by Rampling's reputation for getting jobs done on time and under budget, they had agreed to extend J. B. the line of credit he needed, but only on the understanding they could reassess their involvement every ninety days, and withdraw any time they felt the risks to their investment were too great. As further protection they had insisted that in the event of a default the consortium was to be allowed to foreclose on any equity Rampling International held in any of its other projects.

In effect, Jake had gambled the future of the firm it had taken him a lifetime to build on the successful outcome of a single job. It was a risk few other men would have been willing to take. But Jake was different. He had made the company the biggest of its kind in the world by taking chances, and he saw no reason to back off from a challenge just because it meant mortgaging everything he owned. Rampling International was a privately held company and he owned nearly sixty percent of its stock. That gave him the right to make whatever decisions he wished, and when he announced his intention of constructing the deepest section of the nation's first transcontinental rapid transit system, nobody on the board of directors questioned the wisdom of J. B.'s action.

But the project had been plagued with problems from the very beginning. Part of the trouble lay in the man Jake assigned the job of project supervisor. David Seymour was a brilliant engineer, and his conceptual approach to the staggering technical difficulties of constructing a tunnel a mile underground bordered on genius. While the tunnel was still in the planning stages, it seemed he was the most logical person to put in charge of implementing his own ideas. But when it came to translating theory into practice it quickly became apparent that his expertise lay in working with blueprints and not with the kind of men such a huge operation attracted. Miners were a tough, independent breed who needed a firm hand to control them, and Seymour had lived too long in an ivory tower to know what made them tick. As a result the project experienced endless labor troubles and costly delays while they were resolved. Within months it began slipping behind schedule, and Jake Rampling realized he must act quickly if he was to avoid losing everything he had risked.

The simplest solution would have been to replace Seymour with somebody who had more experience in dealing with miners, but removing the engineer in the critical early stages of a project he had conceived would mean more delays, and that was something Jake knew he couldn't afford. Instead, he had called in Dan Blake, and given him instructions that were simple and to the point: "Put fear in their pants. That's the only language they understand." It was a phrase Dan had heard from his boss many times before, and he knew precisely what was expected of him. Less than a month later the project was back on schedule.

The shrill wail of a siren rose above the steady moan of the wind as Dan opened the door of his trailer. It had rained the previous evening, and now the wind had shifted and was coming from the northern quarter. It brought with it a cold front that had a raw, bitter edge. Dan guessed the temperature must have fallen twenty degrees or more in the few hours since he went to bed, and knew from experience that it could go much lower before dawn. Even in April the temperature could fall to near freezing on the flat plains of this part of Texas.

Slapping his arms against the sides of his body in an effort to generate some warmth, he strode briskly toward the main shaft. The wind was steady, and, despite the cold, was touched with the scent of verbena and crimson clover. The land surrounding the camp had once been cattle country, but was now one of the largest irrigated farming areas in the world. Everything about it was vast. Men tilled thousands of acres and raised bumper crops of grain sorghum, vegetables and cotton. During the season gins operated night and day.

But that world lay beyond the camp and didn't concern Dan. His only interest was the area illuminated by floodlights which cast their harsh, white glare over neatly arranged tiers of bunkhouses that housed the three hundred workers involved in the project. To one side of the bunkhouses was a massive dirt lot where the heavy-duty equipment used in operations above ground was parked. Wind-whipped dust swirled around bulldozers and forklifts, mobile cranes and compressors, dump trucks and drag lines. Row after row of yellow machines crouched like huge predators, ready to spring to life at the touch of a button. They exuded an aura of brute strength that still awed Dan as much as it had on his first construction job fifteen years earlier.

That had been on a tunnel for the U.S. Bureau of Reclamation near Provo, Utah. Dan was twenty-one and fresh from working as a roughneck in the oil fields of East Texas. His experience in drilling enabled him to get a job with Rampling International, which had been awarded the contract to build the tunnel. Within a year he had been promoted to foreman of the swing shift. He had also developed a reputation for toughness and efficiency. He displayed an instinctive ability to drive men to limits even they didn't think themselves capable of achieving. It was a talent that won him grudging respect, and few friends. But it did make him noticed by the project engineer, who made frequent mention of Dan's accomplishments in his weekly reports to company headquarters.

By 1969 Rampling International had outgrown both Brown & Root and the Bechtel Corporation, but despite the vast scope of its operations Jake Rampling kept his finger on the pulse of everything that was going on in his firm. Nothing was too small to escape his notice. When he read the work progress reports submitted from Provo, Utah, and noticed that one shift was constantly outperforming all the others, he made it his business to find out why.

A week later Dan was summoned to an interview with his boss at Rampling's new international headquarters in Dallas. The two men didn't say much. Jake asked Dan about his background and the younger man summarized it in a few terse sentences. But they were enough to establish that the two of them had a lot in common. Both had learned through firsthand experience how to get the most out of the men working under them. Jake prided himself on being able to accurately assess a man's character within minutes of meeting him, and before the interview ended had offered Dan the job of working directly with him as a personal assistant. The fact that Dan had very little experience in the construction business didn't faze him. "I can buy all the men I want who have fancy diplomas," he said. "But what you've got is worth more to me than all those bastards rolled into one!"

17

Dan never received a specific title. It wasn't necessary. Everybody in the company quickly learned he was J. B. Rampling's right-hand man, and that was more of an identity than any job description could possibly have provided. Whenever a problem arose on a project the firm was involved in anywhere in the world, Dan Blake was assigned to solve it. He had carte blanche to use whatever methods he deemed necessary to resolve the situation. Many of the techniques he used were so unorthodox that they were talked about throughout the construction industry, and over the twelve years he had worked for Jake he had become something of a legendary figure. Many considered him an unfeeling taskmaster who achieved results by milking men's fear. Others saw him as a brilliant motivator who knew precisely what buttons to push in order to get the best out of his workers. Only a few understood that Dan's unique skill lay in his intuitive ability to sense the precise limits to which a man could be pushed without breaking.

It was this characteristic that Jake most admired about Dan, and the closeness between the two men slowly grew to a point where he treated him more like a son than an employee. Jake did have two children of his own: a daughter, Ceetra, and his son Bromley. After he divorced his wife, the girl, who was only five at the time, had accompanied her mother to Europe and remained there ever since. But the boy stayed with Jake. Getting custody of him had triggered a bitter legal battle. Jake was obsessed by the desire for a male heir, and was willing to go to any lengths to ensure that Bromley was raised in a way that would equip him to run the company when it was time for him to take over the reins from his father.

The boy was now almost twenty-one, and on the surface it appeared that Jake's efforts to mold the youngster in his own image had succeeded. Rather than going to college, Bromley had elected to enter the firm and learn the business by working for a short time in each of its numerous departments. Nothing could have pleased Jake more. He had focused all his hopes on the boy and worked unceasingly at turning his dreams for Bromley's future into a reality.

But he rarely talked of either his ex-wife, Mary, or his daughter. Dan had heard that Mary was confined to a private sanatorium somewhere in the south of England which specialized in treating patients whose wealth was sufficient to keep them out of mental institutions. But the cause of her emotional instability, and its degree, remained shrouded in as much mystery as the events which precipitated the divorce. There had been rumors that Ed Morley, a former partner of Jake's in the days when the company was still in its infancy, had been involved in some way, but the few who knew remained silent, and Dan had never learned whether there was any substance to the vague innuendoes he'd heard from time to time.

Ceetra Rampling was much less of a mystery. Now a strikingly beautiful woman in her mid-twenties, her activities were frequently chronicled in the gossip columns of newspapers and magazines around the world. Adding to the interest editors normally showed in the children of enormously wealthy people was the fact that Ceetra had also established herself as a successful fashion designer. The combination of riches, good looks, and business acumen had proved an irresistible lure to publishers, and Ceetra's photograph had appeared on the covers of dozens of glossy magazines. The articles accompanying them portrayed her as an arrogant, self-willed woman whose uninhibited behavior and numerous affairs, many with prominent men who were already married, made it apparent that she lived by her own rules. Candid pictures taken in such playgrounds of the rich as St.-Tropez, Sardinia and the Greek Islands showed her free-spiritedly water-skiing in the nude and browsing bare-breasted in sunsplashed boutiques. Without hearing a single word about Ceetra from Jake, Dan felt he both knew and disliked her. She was the antithesis of everything he respected in a woman.

The sudden, earsplitting shriek of a steam whistle jolted

Dan out of his reverie. As he strode swiftly toward the project control center he wondered why he felt no particular sense of unease. Perhaps, he thought, it was because there had been so many false alarms in recent months. Most of them were the result of actions taken by inexperienced workers the company had been obliged to hire in recent months. The country was in the midst of its worst depression since the early '30s, and one of the prime reasons the government had decided to go ahead with the transcontinental tunnel was to provide jobs for the huge numbers of people who were unemployed. A condition of being awarded a contract to build a section of the project was that the firm agreed to offer on-the-job training for men who could no longer find work in their regular professions. The scheme was an updated version of the WPA of the '30s, and to the bureaucrats in Washington who had enacted the legislation to put it into effect, it seemed like a simple solution to one of the worst problems the nation faced. But to the experienced miners who had to train the newcomers it was a concept that literally threatened their lives. They knew that an essential part of survival underground was being able to depend on the skills of the men working next to them, and they bitterly resented having their safety jeopardized. It was a situation that had produced mounting conflict between the two factions, and one that Dan knew must sooner or later erupt in open violence.

He studied the faces of the men who were pouring out of the bunkhouses to take up the positions they had been assigned in the event of an emergency. In the glare of the floodlights their faces looked pale, and the eyes of many were clouded with fear. Yet they moved with a sureness that reflected the effectiveness of the crisis training they had undergone immediately after their arrival, and he experienced a quick surge of pride at the success of the system he had implemented.

"Emergency crews to the main shaft." The voice coming over the loudspeaker system had a hollow, metallic ring. "Stand by fire and medical personnel."

Now the wind carried sounds that quickened Dan's blood: blaring sirens, engines coughing to life, the muted roar of heavy equipment being moved from the dirt parking area toward the main shaft. He watched as a lift crane with a 110-foot boom crawled forward, its cable swaying under the weight of special hoisting devices. It was closely followed by track drills and mobile compressors, front-end shovels, crawler loaders, scrapers, backhoes, and bulldozers with counterrotational tracks that enabled them to turn within their own length. All were headed for positions their operators had been ordered to take up in the event of an emergency. The smell of newly turned earth rose up around him, and he tasted the dust the grinding steel tracks churned up in the chill night air. The ground shook at the massive weight of their passing. It started the adrenaline flowing. This was where he belonged, his natural milieu, the environment he knew best, and where he had spent a lifetime learning to survive.

He quickened his step and moved up the ramp leading to the project control center. It was situated to one side of the glistening steel superstructure that straddled the main shaft. Double doors protected its interior from the dust raised by the constant wind, and helped insulate it from the roar of machines moving directly below. Going through them was like entering a church from the teeming sidewalks of a busy city: one moment there was a din that was almost tangible, the next a quiet that contained its own special sanctity. The walls were lined with consoles, each of which served a different function. Some were linked to computers at the firm's Dallas headquarters, and were capable of displaying inventory and equipment availability charts at the touch of a button. Others contained large rolls of microfilm, each of which was coded in such a way that any of the thousands of blueprints necessary to a project this size could be summoned up in a matter of seconds.

But the equipment that immediately caught Dan's attention was an enormous fluorescent screen on which the main shaft and tunnel were outlined in cross section by green lines. It showed the whole work area at a glance. At a point near the bottom of the shaft a tiny red light flashed on and off.

"Jesus!" His south Texas accent softened the word, but only partially hid the anxiety it contained.

David Seymour was hunched over a computer. At the sound of Dan's voice he looked up.

"I didn't hear you come in—"

"What the hell happened?"

"The damned shaft blew."

"When?"

The other man tore a printout from one of the computers and handed it to Dan. "The sensors registered blast about twenty minutes ago, but I didn't hear anything—"

"How deep?"

"About forty-seven hundred feet."

"How many are down there?"

Seymour's voice carried an audible tremble. "Eighty at least." He hesitated. "And that's not all."

"What?"

"Jake Rampling went down with his son when the swing shift changed."

Now it was Dan who sounded unsteady. "Jake? That's impossible—"

"I saw them boarding the man trip."

"He would have told me—"

"Not if he wanted to make a spot check."

Dan knew this was true. Jake often turned up at his projects unannounced so he could see for himself how work was progressing.

"But he's never taken Bromley."

Seymour shrugged. He was a pale, fleshy man in his late fifties, and his skin glistened with sweat. "Maybe he figured it was time for the boy to learn a few tricks."

Dan looked at the red light that was still flashing on the fluorescent screen.

"Is there a damage estimate yet?"

22

"Only a preliminary report, and it's pretty sketchy."

"I want everything you've got."

"There's a cave-in at the forty-seven-hundred-foot level."

"What about the main shaft?"

"Hard to say. It looks clear."

"And the man trip?"

"It's working, but there's no telling whether the blast damaged the cables or hoist mechanism."

Dan turned and started toward the door.

"Where the hell do you think you're going?" Seymour snapped.

"To organize a rescue crew—"

"I've been through to Dallas. They're flying in a specially trained group—"

"There are men at camp with enough experience to blast through that cave-in."

"It could trigger more slides."

"Not with Gallagher setting the charges. He's the best damned powder man in the country."

"Most of the fan lines are down, and there could be gas down there. A single spark would set it off."

Dan looked at the electric clock to one side of the fluorescent screen. It was 12:25 a.m. "Somebody better get to those guys fast. With the fan lines down and the blowers out they've got ten or twelve hours at the most. Less for those who don't have any breathing equipment."

Seymour stared at the red light marking the site of the disaster. He seemed momentarily hypnotized by its repeated flashing. "I can't risk it," he murmured finally. "Not with Jake and his son down there. If anything went wrong—" He left the sentence unfinished. "I've asked Mule Barnes to get in touch with Ceetra in London," he added.

"Why, for chris'sake?"

"She *is* his daughter."

"They haven't seen each other in twenty years," Dan said. "I doubt if she cares whether he lives or dies."

"She should. If her father and brother don't make it she's the only next of kin."

The statement jolted Dan. Jake had invested so much of himself in grooming Bromley as his heir that it had never occurred to him that anybody else could inherit control of Rampling International.

"All the more reason to make our move now," he said.

"I'm in charge of this project." Seymour's tone turned stubborn. "Getting them out is my responsibility, and I think the safest course of action is to wait for the rescue team to arrive from Dallas."

The two men faced each other in silence. The tension between them was almost visible. It was heightened by an angry clamor of unrest from the workers clustered around the main shaft who couldn't understand why an attempt to reach the trapped men wasn't already underway.

"You'd better be right," Dan said. "You're gambling with a lot of lives, and time's running out."

 **3**

IN FASHIONABLE Georgetown, in Washington, D.C., a party was still in full swing even though it was nearly 1:30 a.m. It was being held at an elegant, colonial-style mansion not far from stately Dumbarton Oaks, where representatives of the victorious Allies had met after World War II to draft the forerunner of the United Nations Charter.

Indeed, the house itself had witnessed much of the history of the years since the city's beginning in 1751, as a 60-acre tract authorized by the Maryland Assembly. The community fell on hard times around the end of the nineteenth century, and the house had become dilapidated after standing empty for some years. But wealth had come back to the area, and the house had been purchased by a millionaire industrialist who had dedicated himself, and his money, to restoring the building and the five acres on which it stood to their original splendor.

Now it belonged to the tall, impeccably tailored man who was carrying on a loud, animated conversation with a group of his guests at an antique mahogany bar in an alcove to one side of the huge ballroom. Although in his late fifties, Ed Morley had an ebullience that made him seem younger, an impression that was heightened by his smooth, pink-skinned face, and a forehead that had somehow largely escaped the lines of aging. Only the grey in his thick hair betrayed his age, and it added a touch of distinction that befitted a lobbyist who represented the interests of many of the country's largest corporations.

His accounts included major oil companies, automobile manufacturers and two of the world's largest airlines. Even the A.F.L.-C.I.O., which maintained its own 300-member staff at its impressive stone and marble headquarters near the White House, retained Morley as a special consultant. His hiring had been bitterly opposed by their own lobbyists, but after years of contesting him in the corridors of Congress, even they had been obliged to admit that when it came to pulling strings at the highest level of government, they couldn't begin to compete.

When Morley had first seen the house in the fall of 1980, the leaves on the maples that dotted its grounds had begun to turn, transforming their branches into arches of gold. But it wasn't their beauty that had convinced him to buy the place. Nor was it the graceful dignity of its perfectly proportioned columns which fronted a bow-shaped center, flanked by wings on both sides. What had made him willing to pay the exorbitant price that was being asked for the mansion was the fact that it looked very much like the White House.

Appearances were important to Morley. His success as a lobbyist hinged on the image he projected to his clients, and he had long ago learned that men of power preferred to do business with people whose lifestyle most closely approximated their own. This was particularly true when it came to selecting a lobbyist. The heads of multibillion-dollar firms, increasingly aware that government wasn't going to retreat from its intrusion into their corporate lives, now frequently pleaded their cases personally in Washington. It was vital for them to gain access to whatever congressman held the key to the outcome of the particular piece of legislation that most interested them, and experience had taught them this could most easily be arranged by somebody who made it his business to navigate the shoals of Capitol Hill.

This need, added to the fact that he projected an image of success which inspired confidence in even the most wary, is what ultimately brought them to Ed Morley's mansion in Georgetown. He was the best in the business. Even his opponents openly admired him. "He's always on the wrong side," another top lobbyist had told a reporter doing a profile on Morley, "but he's good for his client. He delivers."

Combining the old-time lobbying techniques of banter, broads and booze with a sophisticated computerized information system that enabled him to explain even the most complex issues in relatively simple terms, had made it possible for him to establish a remarkable record. It had begun ten years ago, in the early '70s, with his work on the passing of a bill reorganizing seven railroads in the Northeast and Midwest. Since then he had helped persuade Congress to increase the investment tax credit and to turn down a proposed boycott of trade with the Arabs.

Whatever the project, he applied a personal philosophy that he was fond of repeating whenever reporters interviewed him. "My priorities are easy to define," he'd say with a broad, easy smile. "I take what I can get." And that was considerable. An income in excess of $500,000 a year, a chauffeured Mercedes limousine, long-standing membership in the ultra-exclusive Burning Tree Golf Club, and a private table at Sans Souci, where the most powerful men in Washington met to eat and swap gossip over lunch. All of which, when added to the splendor of his opulent mansion in Georgetown, enabled him to impress the giants of industry who were his clients.

Three such giants were with him this evening. He smiled to himself as Bonnie Oliver, his "social coordinator" and girlfriend, introduced a pert blonde and a slender redhead to two men standing near the French windows that opened onto the terrace which overlooked a large artificial lake. The oldest, Beecher Curtis, was a distinguished-looking white-haired man in his early sixties who was president of one of the nation's largest airlines. His companion, Tyrone Richardson, was about five years younger. A small, dynamic man, he was the major stockholder in a company that brokered more crude oil than any other firm in the world. He also headed a syndicate of Middle East oil-producing countries that were vitally interested in finding ways to best wield their considerable power to influence legislation in Washington.

Moments later they were joined by a thickset, blunt-featured man who was so obviously uncomfortable in his ill-fitting evening dress that he looked like a circus bear decked out in a costume. But Morley knew it would have been a big mistake to think that Robert Grimwood's lack of social graces made him a fool. Starting as a furnace tender in the steel mills of Pittsburgh, Grimwood had obtained a law degree by attending night school, and had gone to work on the legal staff of the International Brotherhood of Teamsters at their headquarters on Louisiana Avenue in downtown Washington. After proving himself a tough negotiator with a natural flair for mediation, he had worked his way up through the ranks to become senior legal counsel to Frank Fitzsimmons, the union's general president.

Although Curtis, Richardson and Grimwood represented vastly different worlds, they shared a common interest: all were deeply concerned about the coast-to-coast tunnel that was presently under construction between Los Angeles and New York. The concept of gondolas floating on magnetic fields at speeds in excess of 10,000 miles per hour had stirred the imagination of the public, particularly as it promised fares as low as fifty dollars one-way, and travel times of less than thirty minutes. They also welcomed the jobs the 200-billion-dollar project had provided at a time when the United States was undergoing its worst depression since the 1930s. But to the factions Curtis, Richardson and Grimwood represented, the Very-High-Speed-Transit (VHST) posed a serious threat.

The airlines were worried about VHST's high speeds and low fares. They couldn't begin to compete. Although more supersonic passenger jets were in use now than there had been in the late '70s, they were expensive to buy and costly to operate. Any aircraft traveling faster than the speed of sound used up a large part of its available energy supply just climbing to an altitude where it could function efficiently at the speeds for which it was designed. And the energy crisis had become so severe that the cost of air travel had risen sharply since the beginning of the '80s. Short routes, such as those within states or between them, were the least profitable of all for the airlines because of the added number of takeoffs and landings they required. Most major companies depended on coast-to-coast flights to make a profit, and it was doubtful if they could survive the loss of revenue that was bound to result from passengers using the cheaper and faster VHST.

The Teamsters were alarmed because they anticipated huge losses in revenues when the VHST began transporting freight between Los Angeles and New York. Experts had estimated that as much as ten million tons of freight a day would be shipped from one side of the nation to the other in special containers designed to travel at the same speeds as passenger-carrying gondolas. The effect on long-distance trucking would be crippling, and when branch lines were added to the main tube even the trucking of goods between states would be radically reduced.

The oil industry was more worried by the VHST concept than any other business. It had continued to reap massive profits ever since President Carter removed price controls in 1979, and the idea of giving up any part of this bonanza was not something they accepted easily. But it was an undeniable fact that once the VHST was in operation and branch lines were established to service every state in the nation, there was going to be far less demand for oil. Fewer aircraft and trucks to consume fuel was bad enough, but when the increased number of subway-style rapid transit systems were linked to the VHST network, people were going to begin using their cars less. The price of gas had already risen to a point where an automobile had become more of a liability than an asset, and the American public was ready for an alternative way of getting around. They were tired of being beholden to a small group like the politically unstable Middle East countries, which had wielded power for so many years by squeezing the pocketbook of the average working person.

The looming prospect of lost revenues had made bedfellows of industries that had frequently been the bitterest of enemies in the past. It was the common bond that linked Curtis, Richardson and Grimwood, and brought them to Washington in search of help for the interests they represented. Because of Morley's reputation for being able to pull strings in high places, they had approached him with a proposal he'd found impossible to refuse: a $250,000 retainer to make his "best effort" on their behalf.

Precisely what they meant by this wasn't spelled out. The men who had made the offer were too cagey to put anything specific in writing. But all of them knew they wanted the lobbyist to lay groundwork on Capitol Hill for legislation that would limit the effectiveness of the VHST system. They acknowledged that it was too late to prevent the cross-country tunnel from being constructed, but there was still plenty of time to sow seeds that would grow into forests of legislative red tape that would severely limit the effectiveness of the VHST once it went into operation.

Morley took his drink and went out onto the terrace. The night air was heavy with the scent of winter jasmine, and lights hidden around the grounds turned banks of azaleas and flowering dogwoods into islands of brilliant color among the still-bare Yoshino cherry trees. In about two weeks the blossoms would break forth in clouds of deep pink. It was a sight he looked forward to every spring, but this year his anticipation was tinged with sadness, for he knew there was a strong possibility it might be the last year he would occupy the mansion he had come to love.

Now that he was alone the desperateness of his situation

settled on him with new intensity. His accountants had warned him months ago that his cash reserves were dangerously low, and that he faced bankruptcy unless he found ways of replenishing them quickly. The $250,000 he had received as a retainer from Grimwood, Curtis and Richardson had helped to alleviate the situation, but it had largely gone to pay off loans he'd taken out over the previous four years to keep himself in business.

The root of his problem lay in his propensity for gambling. Not on horses or at the casino in Atlantic City, but on the commodities market. For as long as he could remember he had been unable to resist the urge to speculate on the future of such items as pork bellies, sugar and wheat, and for years he had made a handsome profit. Much of his success was due to the inside information he received from the people he came into contact with as part of his job. They often made him privy to facts not available to the general public, and he capitalized on them by investing huge sums in the rise and fall of future prices. But the past year had been a disaster. He had gambled heavily on the price of coffee going down, and lost when unseasonably cold weather wiped out crops in Colombia and Brazil. In an effort to recoup he had invested heavily in silver futures, and taken another beating when they didn't rise as quickly as he had expected.

Now, unless something entirely unexpected happened, Morley knew it was only a matter of time before his creditors closed in and foreclosed on everything he owned. The house was already heavily mortgaged, and it would go first. Then his expensive office equipment, his cars, and any other thing of value they could lay their hands on. Without the facade of success, he would no longer be able to function effectively as a lobbyist, and at his age it was too late to begin all over again.

He heard footsteps approaching and turned to see Bonnie Oliver walking toward him. She was wearing a green silk dress that clung to her body, emphasizing the firm fullness of her breasts and the sensuous curve of her buttocks. Her long blonde hair was pulled back in a chignon, but wisps of it had sprung free over her ears to give a soft frame to her face. Morley wondered what would happen to Bonnie when he went under. She was the only person who knew about the trouble he was in, and had continued to work for him even though it was three months since she had received any salary.

"Are you okay?" Her voice was tinged with a southern drawl.

"Just thinking," he said.

"Sure?"

He nodded. "How are our guests of honor doing?"

"Fine. They were looking for you."

"That figures."

She laid her hand gently on his arm. "Is there anything I can do?"

"I'm all right, really."

"There's a call for you. From Dallas. It's Mule Barnes."

"What the hell does he want?"

"He wouldn't say anything, except it's urgent."

"Must be to keep him up this late."

"They're an hour behind us down there."

"Still a long way past Mule's bedtime."

"I can tell him to call back," she said.

"It doesn't matter. Why don't you put it through to the library. I'll take it there."

Morley made his way through the guests, exchanging banter along the way with cabinet members, senators, columnists and diplomats. He stopped in the large entry hall to say goodnight to Katherine Graham who, as owner of the *Washington Post, Newsweek,* and Washington's Channel 9, as well as sundry other news outlets, was one of the most powerful women in the world.

"Hurry back, ya hear?" he said as she waved to him from the door.

He didn't feel as flippant as he sounded, and to a large extent his banter was simply a delay tactic to allow him to gather his thoughts. It wasn't like Mule Barnes to phone at all, let alone at this time of the night, and Morley knew him well enough to be aware that he didn't use the word "urgent" lightly. After twenty-five years as Jake Rampling's attorney, Barnes had learned to cope with almost any emergency, and had obtained the nickname "Mule" by stubbornly refusing to be flustered by any turn of events.

The library in which Morley took the call was the only room in the house that was strictly off-limits to guests. Only he possessed a key to the heavy oak door. Although the walls were lined with volume-filled shelves, it was fitted out more as an office than a place to browse through books, and most of the space was devoted to business equipment. Prime among these was an elaborate computer terminal that was linked to the two IBM storage banks in his downtown office. It gave him immediate access to the reams of data he needed at his fingertips at all times. He considered summoning up a readout on Rampling International, but decided it wasn't necessary. He knew from firsthand experience all there was to know about that company, and unless anything had changed very recently, rechecking the information would be a pointless exercise. Instead, he sat down in the deep leather chair behind his huge mahogany desk, and pressed the button that was lit on the call-control console.

"Mule?"

"Yeah." The voice at the other end of the line had a harsh, raspy edge. "That you, Ed?"

"None other."

Morley tried to remember when he had last talked to Barnes. Two, maybe three years. Not since Barnes approached him on behalf of Jake Rampling to grease the right wheels in Washington at the time contracts were being awarded for the VHST tunnel project.

"Bonnie tells me you're in the middle of a party."

"That's right."

"You work late hours."

"Just part of the job."

Barnes was normally a blunt, straight-to-the-point talker,

33

and these preliminaries suggested he was trying to feel Morley out. But Morley was determined to wait him out. He and Jake had been partners over twenty years ago. When Jake abruptly decided he wanted to end the relationship, it was Barnes who had acted as his hatchet man. The wily lawyer tried every trick in his repertoire before finally inducing Morley to sell back the stock he owned in Rampling International. His trump card was undeniable evidence that he had the judge who was going to adjudicate the issue in his pocket. Morley knew that fighting a protracted legal battle would be hopeless, so he had reluctantly given in, and had set about building a new career for himself with the money he received from the sale of the stock. But it had left him with a residue of bitterness.

"Some woman, Bonnie," Barnes said.

He sounded reflective, and Morley knew why. When Barnes had come to Washington to enlist the lobbyist's skills in ensuring that Rampling International got the contract for building the deepest section of the tunnel, he had been a guest at a number of parties at the Georgetown mansion. And Bonnie had given him the red-carpet treatment. It was her duty to make sure Morley's clients got what they wanted, and in this case it was her. By the time Morley discovered that Bonnie had gone to bed with Barnes it was too late for him to tell her it wasn't necessary.

"That why you called," Morley asked, "to reminisce about old times?"

"Not exactly."

There was a long silence during which the only sound was Barnes's deep breathing.

"There's been an accident in the tunnel. An explosion. Jake and his son are trapped with about eighty other men over four thousand feet underground."

Morley had hated Jake for more than twenty years, yet the news still left him feeling numb.

"Are they okay?" he asked.

"Too early to tell," Barnes said. "They're flying in a special rescue team from Dallas."

"That could take hours. There must be enough men at camp with experience to get a crew together—"

"Dave Seymour's project engineer, and he doesn't want to risk it."

"How much air have they got?"

"Nobody knows for sure. Dan Blake figures ten, maybe twelve hours."

"If they're lucky."

"That's why I called." There was a taut silence. "They may not make it, Ed."

Suddenly the pieces fell into place. Barnes hadn't phoned just to pass along information that would be in the headlines of the morning papers. He had some other reason, and Morley was pretty sure he knew what it was.

If privately held firms in the United States were listed among *Fortune's* 500, Rampling International would rank twenty-fourth, just above the Bechtel Corporation. Jake owned nearly sixty percent of the company's common stock, and an even larger amount of its preferred stock. All the other shareholders, fewer than twenty at last count, were company vice presidents. The only exception to this was Barnes who, as corporate legal counsel, had been allowed to retain the stock he obtained when he joined the firm. After Morley parted company with Jake, having put up such a struggle before relinquishing his stock, Jake determined he would never again be put in a position where he didn't have absolute control over his own firm.

He had forced the board of directors to adopt a ruling that each shareholder agree to sell his stock back to the company when he died or left the firm. In effect this meant that any shareholder who didn't do as Jake told him could be fired and forced to sell his stock back, at a price determined behind closed doors by the half-dozen people who were major stockholders. From time to time these people had attempted to persuade Jake to go public, but he had always resisted them, even though it would have vastly increased the worth of the stock. He didn't need the money, and the last thing he wanted to do was relinquish control. His answer to these suggestions was always the same: "As long as there's breath in me this company is mine. And when I'm gone I want my son to take over where I left off."

It had never occurred to Jake that Bromley might die with him. If this proved to be the case it meant the company was going to be up for grabs.

"You hear what I said?" the voice at the other end of the line asked irritably.

"Loud and clear," Morley replied. "The only thing I don't understand is what you want of me."

"I'll get to that," the other man said. "But not on the phone. I'm taking a plane out of here at noon. I have some business in New York. We can discuss it there."

Barnes kept a penthouse in New York and spent much of his time there. Morley suspected he could have postponed this business engagement long enough to see him in Washington, but he decided to play the game Barnes's way. "We can meet at the Plaza," he said.

"That's where you can send Bonnie. I'll see you at the Trattoria Roma for a late supper around midnight." Barnes didn't bother with farewells. He simply hung up.

The buzzer sounded. Morley flipped a switch on the intercom and heard the sound of Bonnie's voice.

"Our guests of honor look like they're getting ready to leave," she said.

"Ask them to come in here. I'd like to talk with them for a few minutes before they go."

He flipped the speaker off and crossed to the computer terminal. His instinct before every meeting was to get a read-out on the participants, but this time it wasn't necessary. He'd already spent more time than usual researching their backgrounds, and knew it was going to take a lot more than Bonnie Oliver's girls to impress them.

As Bonnie ushered Richardson, Grimwood and Curtis into the library, he resumed his role as genial host.

"Gentlemen! I didn't want you to leave without trying some very special brandy."

He took a bottle of hundred-year-old Camus cognac out of the liquor cabinet. It had cost over a thousand dollars five years ago, when money had been worth a lot more, and he kept it for guests he particularly wanted to impress.

"Are we celebrating something?" Richardson asked.

"Could be," Morley said, pausing to pour four glasses.

"Are you going to tell us," Grimwood asked. "Or do we have to guess?"

"There's been an accident," the lobbyist said.

"Where?"

"Near Amarillo. At the section of the VHST tunnel Rampling International is working on."

"Jake's operation." Curtis put his glass down. "Jesus, I've known him for years. He isn't going to be one damned bit—"

"Jake and his son are among the men trapped underground," Morley said.

"Jesus!" Curtis sounded genuinely shocked. "When did this happen?"

"About an hour ago. I just got word from Dallas."

"What happened?" Richardson asked.

"An explosion in the main shaft. The rest is pretty vague. They're flying in a special rescue crew."

"What are their chances?"

"Not good."

"Then what the hell are we doing standing around here like we were drinking a toast to something?" he asked sharply.

"Because it could be the best thing that ever happened for you guys." Morley replied quietly.

"I don't understand how," Curtis said. "Sure, it'll delay completion of the project for a while, but that isn't going to help our cause a hell of a lot. A dozen such accidents, maybe—"

"Do you remember what happened back in seventy-nine when all those DC-10s started crashing?" Morley asked.

"How could I forget? The public got scared. Figured they weren't safe, and nothing we could do would persuade them otherwise. My firm lost a bundle."

"What do you think would happen if the VHST system encountered the same kind of problems?"

"You mean accidents after it's in operation?"

"To gondolas traveling at over ten thousand miles an hour."

"The public would quit using it so goddam fast—"

Grimwood broke in. "I don't see how a tunnel cave-in during the construction phase is going to affect the system once it's in operation."

"It isn't," Morley replied. "But it wouldn't be hard for the company doing that construction to build in weaknesses that would result in an accident at some later date. Improperly placed sets, fracture areas in the rock that aren't properly bolted, flawed welding of the tube seams . . . there's no end to the possibilities."

"That's why they have safety inspectors."

"But they make mistakes. Why else would there have been an explosion at Amarillo?"

"If you're suggesting we try and bribe Jake Rampling to build in flaws you can forget it," Curtis said. "He'll do anything to get a contract, but once it's got his name on it you'd better believe it's gonna be the best goddam job possible. He may be a sonofabitch, but he's a proud one, and he'd rather die than have any failure in the section of tunnel his firm is doing."

"And what if he's already dead?" Morley asked.

The three other men looked at each other silently. None of them seemed to know how to respond, so the lobbyist answered his own question.

"Rampling International is a privately held company," he said. "Jake owns at least sixty percent of the stock. He's always refused to go public because he didn't want to relinquish any of his power. He built an empire and wanted to pass it along intact to his son. But if Bromley dies with him, the controlling interest in the firm is suddenly going to be up for grabs."

"I thought Jake had a daughter," Richardson said. "She used to play with my kid when they were both in preschool down in Dallas. What the hell was her name?"

"Ceetra," Morley said.

"That's right. What happened to her?"

"She's living in London."

"What makes you think she won't claim the estate?"

"My guess is Jake made damned sure in his will that she doesn't get a dime. He wasn't exactly what you'd call close to either his daughter or her mother."

"She could still contest it," Richardson persisted.

"And if she wins, what's she gonna do with the firm, run it?" Morley laughed. "If what I read in the glossy magazines is true she's more interested in lolling around the Riviera flashing her ass than operating the largest construction company in the world."

"Where do we fit into all of this?" Grimwood asked.

"You hired me to make my best efforts on your behalf, right?" Morley said.

"That's true," Grimwood acknowledged.

"If Jake and his son don't come out of that cave-in alive, I intend to get controlling interest of Rampling International. It's going to take a lot of money any way you slice it. That's where you guys come in. I'll set up a corporation and serve as a front. People will think I'm just trying to get back what was once mine. Nobody has to know you are involved. But if everything goes the way I figure it should, you can count on there being more than one disaster once the VHST system gets under way."

"It's a clever idea," Richardson said.

"The best you're likely to get."

Richardson looked at the other two men. They nodded.

"All right," he said. "Let us know what you'll need, and we'll find it."

They stood up and shook hands.

"The only part of your plan that worries me is the girl," the other man said. "Are you sure you can handle her?"

"I'll stake my life on it," Morley replied.

 **4**

IN LONDON, where it was 6:30 a.m., Ceetra Rampling heard the telephone ring, but made no attempt to answer it. She wondered if it would awaken Paul. Part of her wished it would, but rather than making sure by reaching across him to pick up the receiver on the far side of the bed, she decided to let Providence make the decision. Lying back against the pillow, she picked up the cadence and began to count silently under her breath: " . . . four, five, six, seven, eight, nine. . . ." When the ringing finally stopped, the man lying next to her still hadn't moved.

The heavy velvet drapes were drawn, but there was a space where the two halves didn't quite come together, and it allowed enough cold, grey morning light to filter into the room for her to see his eyes were closed. She raised herself on one arm and examined his features. Thick, close-cropped grey hair, straight nose, firm mouth, and a chiseled chin. No doubt about it, she thought, even in his late forties Paul Mayhew was a very handsome man. The only visible evidence that he was in his middle years lay in the deeply etched lines at the sides of his nostrils, and a slight blurring of his jawline. Even in his sleep he emanated an aura of strength. Ceetra felt again the sensation she'd experienced when he finally arrived four hours earlier: a blend of excitement, anger and fear, not unlike that she remembered undergoing in childhood whenever she was in her father's presence.

"You could have called," she had said when he finally appeared.

He stood at the door smiling. "Love your outfit."

She had been half asleep when he let himself in, and had forgotten about the school uniform she'd put on. Suddenly, she wished she hadn't. The situation called for a display of cool reserve.

"It was intended as a joke," she said. "I'll change."

"No, don't. You look wonderful. Reminds me of the time I first met you. Remember?"

Every detail of that day was clearly etched in her memory, but she was damned if she was going to give him the satisfaction of knowing it.

"That was a long time ago."

"You haven't changed," he said.

"I'm not eighteen anymore."

"But you're more beautiful than ever." He closed the door and took her in his arms. His clothes were damp from the rain, and his breath smelled strongly of whiskey. But the warmth of his kiss made her oblivious to everything else, and by the time he released her, her anger had begun to dissolve.

She took his hand and led him into the living room. "My friends keep telling me I'm insane to go on seeing you."

"Andrea?"

"She and others."

"What do you think?"

"Evenings like this I think they may be right."

"All you have to do is say the word."

Her anger flared again. He sounded so goddamned sure of himself. But when she spoke her voice betrayed no sign of the frustration churning inside her.

"I think we should talk," she said.

"Can we do it over a drink?"

"There's some champagne in the fridge."

"Great! Why don't you sit there and rehearse what it is you want to tell me, while I get the bubbly."

She watched as he disappeared into the kitchen. Her fists were clenched so hard the knuckles showed white under the skin, and tears welled in her eyes. His nonchalance was a deliberate slap in the face. He knew how much she cared for him and was using it as a weapon against her. Whenever she expressed her feelings he always managed to respond in a way that enabled him to avoid making any kind of emotional commitment to her. The truth was that Paul was quite content to keep their relationship on a strictly sexual level, and she was sick of it.

"Did you know there's a gorgeous cake in here?" His voice came from the kitchen, and moments later he appeared carrying a large silver tray with the chocolate torte Estelle had baked. He had decorated it with candles, and the light from them shimmered in the cut glass of two iced wine goblets. "I want you to close your eyes and make a wish."

"I wish," she said, her eyes wide open, "that we could have a more normal relationship."

"It doesn't work unless you close your eyes," he said.

"All right." She sighed and closed her eyes. "I wish that we—"

The sentence was only half-finished when he kissed her gently on the lips.

"Happy birthday, darling," he murmured.

She pulled back and looked at him. "Is it too much to ask?"

"A normal relationship?"

"Yes."

"I don't know." He trailed the tip of his finger down her cheek. "Probably expensive. Everything is, nowadays."

"Jesus! Just once I'd like to get a straight answer to a simple question!"

"Shall we fuck?"

"That's not what—"

"Simple question," he said. "How about a straight answer?"

"All you think about is—"

"You lying in my arms while I make wild, passionate love to you."

"Listen, Paul—"

He didn't wait for her to finish, but picked her up and carried her into the bedroom. She struggled, but he was too strong for her, and when he unbuttoned her blouse and began kissing her nipples, the anger was replaced by an overwhelming urge to be enveloped by him. She wanted him to blot out her capacity to think, and knew the sure way to this oblivion was to give herself up to him completely.

"Lie still," he said.

"Let me take off these clothes."

"No. I like you with them on."

She watched as he undressed. He had a lean, well-muscled body that was kept supple by daily workouts in the indoor pool of his house. It was eight years since the first time she'd seen it, and it hadn't appreciably changed in all that time. His stomach was board-flat, and there wasn't an ounce of excess fat anywhere. He left his bikini-style undershorts on, but she could see the bulge of his swollen penis when he emerged from the bathroom carrying a large jar of Nivea cream. It had become an essential part of their sexual ritual.

"Turn over," he said.

She buried her face in the pillow and waited. She never knew where he would begin, or what to expect once he had started. It depended entirely on his mood. For him a woman's body was an instrument that he used to express feelings he seemed incapable of verbalizing. They ran the gamut from tenderness to outright anger. And at one time or another she had experienced them all.

This time he started gently, smoothing the cream on her feet, and working it slowly between her toes. Sensuous, tantalizing, it evoked tremors inside her thighs and across her buttocks. Gradually he worked his way to the back of her knees, where he trailed his fingers across the skin, lightly scratching her with his nails. She quivered.

"Relax," he said. "Just let yourself go."

He slid the palms of both hands along the inside of her thighs until they rested on the mounds of her buttocks. She half raised her hips, and he pulled her panties down. Then he smeared her with Nivea while rubbing his thumb over her clitoris. It went on and on. Her body responded with a rhythmic movement of its own, backwards and forwards. Her breathing quickened, and she began to moan.

"I want you to kneel over me," he said.

She straddled his waist, and he pulled her up over his chest until she was directly over his mouth.

She touched herself. Now her excitement came from watching his eyes. They were riveted on her fingers, and filled with desire.

"When was the first time?"

"I was twelve."

"Go on."

"It was a boarding school. There was this other girl—"

"Yes?"

"When there was a storm I'd creep into her bed—"

It was a game they'd played before, and the fantasy excited them both. He lifted his head and pressed his mouth against the lips of her vagina. He pulled her lower, spreading her legs wide, parting the lips until he could see her engorged clitoris. His tongue made gentle circles as he felt her clitoris harden.

She spread her legs wider, trying to prolong the moment, feeling the exquisite pressure of his mouth envelop her. Finally she could hold back no longer. With a deep groan she shuddered and sank back to lie beside him.

As she listened to the pounding of her heart, she thought she had never been so satisfied. But of course, she reminded herself, she had. If nothing else, Paul was a superb lover.

She began kissing his neck and chest, sliding her hand down to feel the hardness of his erection. He moved toward her, but she took her hand away.

"Not yet. Lie still," she said.

He put his head back on the pillows and closed his eyes. She ran her nails lightly down both sides of his chest and across his belly. His flesh quivered.

"Feel good?" she asked.

"Don't stop."

She wet each of his nipples with her tongue, and squeezed them.

"Too hard?"

"No."

She lowered her body onto him and began to move with a sensuousness that made him groan.

She quickened her movements until his body arched and he finally sank back against the bed, completely drained.

"Hold me," she said. But already she felt him drawing away.

"Wait a few minutes."

"Lie close. Don't turn your back." She pressed against him, attempting to recapture the closeness that only sex seemed to bring.

"All I need is some rest." His voice was edged with annoyance.

"It doesn't matter." She moved away and stood up. "Get some sleep."

"Half an hour. That's all I need."

"Sure," she said.

But she knew she was defeated. The evening had begun with so much promise, but ended as so many others: in a guarded encounter that masqueraded as making love.

She went into the bathroom and closed the door. Her anger had given way to a feeling of disgust. At herself, at the absurd illusions she'd woven around a relationship which was really nothing but a sickness in them both. For a long time she sat on the edge of the tub, her head in her hands, wishing she could cry. But tears didn't come. All she wanted now was to be cleansed. She stepped into the shower. The water was hot and the needle-sharp spray made her skin sting. But even though it hurt, she let it beat on her breasts and run into her mouth. Only after she had soaped every inch of her body did she finally turn off the faucet.

By the time she had dried herself and returned to the bedroom, Paul was asleep. He stirred as she got into bed, but didn't open his eyes, and moments later resumed deep, even breathing. She envied him his ability to find oblivion. Such a sanctuary was much harder for her to discover.

She had been plagued by insomnia for as long as she could remember. Sleeping pills had become as much a part of her nightly ritual as cleaning the makeup off her face. When her doctor warned that she was in danger of becoming addicted to them, she had tried to find other ways: yoga, deep-breathing exercises, herb teas, even self-hypnosis. But nothing worked. She knew that sleep would only come when it began to get light. Until then all she could do was try not to think.

5 DAN'S BODY ACHED. He had been on his feet for five and a half hours, and the rescue team David Seymour had summoned from Dallas still hadn't arrived.

"This is crazy!" He looked at the electric clock on the wall of the project control center. It was almost 6:00 a.m. "Those bastards should have been here hours ago."

The phone rang and Seymour answered it. He frowned, listening intently. Finally he replaced the receiver. "The plane had engine trouble. It had to turn back."

"Why didn't they let us know, for chris'sake?"

Seymour didn't answer. His face glistened with sweat, and there were huge damp patches under both armpits.

"Well, I've waited long enough," Dan said.

"Another plane's on the way. It should be landing in Amarillo any minute."

"What's wrong with the camp strip?"

"Too short for the size of aircraft they need to bring in the special equipment."

"Jesus!" Dan shook his head. "It'll take 'em another four hours at least."

Seymour wiped his face with a large handkerchief and nervously pulled at the front of his shirt, which was clinging damply to his chest.

"The police are providing an escort . . . "

His words trailed away, and the only sound in the stale-smelling room was the clatter of a teletype machine, which stopped as abruptly as it had started. Dan tore off the sheet and read the message.

"Estimated air supply eleven hours." He looked at the project director. "I asked the computer guys in Dallas to run a check."

"Without checking with me?"

"You've had your head up your ass ever since this whole goddam mess started."

"I've followed what I consider to be the safest procedures," Seymour said.

"Safe for you and your goddam job, or for those poor bastards? Why don't you go outside and tell that crowd gathered at the main shaft that you're playing by the book? They're so fucking mad at nobody doing anything there's going to be a riot if something doesn't happen—fast!"

"I can't risk Jake's life, or his son's, by attempting anything that isn't guaranteed—"

"It's too late for guarantees," Dan snapped. "It'll be a miracle if we get through to them before noon, and that's cutting it pretty fine."

"You said they've got eleven hours."

"From the time of the explosion."

Seymour turned away and stared out of the massive window that overlooked the entrance to the main shaft. It was already dawn, but the floodlights around the perimeter of camp were still on, and the wind-whipped dust swirled in opaque clouds around the heavy-duty equipment that had been moved into position in readiness for a rescue attempt. Miners stood around them in clusters, eyes glazed and faces drawn, the dew on their yellow hard hats reflecting the first rays of the sun as they bobbed their heads in angry conversation. It created an almost surrealistic effect that was heightened by the glare of television lamps set up by news crews who were already taping interviews with some of the workers.

"Why the hell did he have to take Bromley down there

with him?" It was a rhetorical question, but uttered so bitterly that Dan suddenly realized why Seymour had waited so long. It wasn't indecision or fear of making the wrong move. He had a much more personal stake. Seymour was closer to the boy than his father. They shared a common interest in the arts: music, painting, the ballet. It was a bond that had brought them together in recent months.

"I'm moving now whether you like it or not," Dan announced.

"Okay." Seymour turned away from the window. "Get a crew and take your best shot. I'll take full responsibility."

Dan nodded. For the first time since he'd known Seymour he felt genuine empathy toward him. It was obvious from his face that he was hurting inside. But there wasn't time to talk about it. He opened the outer door of the control center and started down the steps, but was forced to stop when a throng of reporters suddenly converged on him, all screaming at once.

" . . . Is it true that J. B. Rampling's down there? . . . What about his son? . . . Can you give us an accurate estimate of their chances? . . . "

Dan started elbowing his way through the crowd.

"This is a federal project," a woman holding a microphone shouted. "The public has a right to know . . . "

Dan looked at the security guards. "Will ya get these jerks outa here?"

The guards began herding the reporters back.

" . . . What the hell is this? . . . Hey, look out for my goddam camera! . . . Take it easy, okay? . . . "

The protests continued as Dan forced his way through the clearing the guards had made. Hands plucked at his quilted jacket in a desperate effort to get his attention. One man tried forcibly to block his way, but fell back as Dan pushed him to one side.

"Who the fuck d'ya think ya are, buddy?" The man hauled himself to his feet and grabbed Dan's shoulder. "I've got a good mind to punch you in the—"

Without breaking step, Dan pulled himself free. But the other man wasn't about to be put off that easily. He caught hold of Dan's arm and tried to swing him around, but before he completed the motion a hand reached out from behind, grabbed him by the back of his jacket, and lifted him clear off the ground. The reporter turned with startled eyes to look into the face of the man who was holding him in mid-air. He was huge, well over seven feet tall and weighing at least 280 pounds. His features had the ill-formed, slightly off-kilter look of a mongoloid child: slanting eyes, a broad flat skull, and massive hands with short, blunt fingers. He wore a vacant expression, as if now that he had lifted the man off the ground he didn't quite know what to do with him. He looked at Dan for instructions.

"It's okay, Sid. Put him down." Dan spoke with a quiet, patient tone he might have used with a child. "I'm all right. He wasn't trying to hurt me."

"You heard him, for chris'sake—" The reporter's bluster had a hollow ring.

Other members of the press had crowded around and were watching in awe. When a photographer aimed his camera and triggered a flashbulb in the big man's face, he flinched.

"Try that again," Dan snapped at the photographer, "and he's liable to break your back."

"Christ, I didn't mean—"

Dan turned to Sid. "Come on, we've got work to do."

The big man let go of the reporter and loped after Dan as he walked toward a row of trailers parked in neat lines on the far side of camp.

"Goddam gorilla!" the reporter muttered, straightening his jacket and dusting himself off.

"Hey, man," one of the security guards said. "Wouldn't say that too loud if I was you. Big Sid may be a little light in the head, but I've seen him step on guys twice your size."

"Crazy bastard!" The reporter's voice measurably lower. "He belongs in a cage."

"What does a hulk like that do around here?" the woman with the microphone asked.

"He's a construction clown," the guard said.

"You're kidding!"

The security man shook his head. "Most troubleshooters use 'em. Sid's been with Dan for years."

Sensing a story, the woman flicked on her tape recorder. "Is that what a construction clown does—strong-arm stuff around camp?"

The guard sensed he was getting himself into a situation that might cost him his job, and backed off. "Sorry," he said. "You people will have to move back behind the barrier. Come on now, all the way back. I've got my orders."

A hundred yards away Dan turned and looked back at where the reporters were being herded away from the project control center.

"Assholes," he muttered. Then he turned and addressed Sid. "Find Gallagher. Tell him to meet me at the main shaft. And I want you there, too."

Sid ambled away toward a corrugated steel warehouse on the opposite side of camp. Dan watched him go and shook his head. A sudden cold gust of wind flapped the canvas covering over the cockpit of a front-end loader. It made a loud cracking sound, like a whip being snapped. He took a deep breath. The raw morning air tasted gritty, and the swirling dust had a damp, musty odor that he knew would vanish as the day grew warmer.

"Edmonds!" He slapped the side of the nearest trailer, raising his voice to make himself heard over the wind. "You in there?"

When there was no answer, he pushed open the door and thrust his head inside. He saw four metal cots. Three of them had their mattresses neatly rolled, blankets folded and piled on the bare springs in quasi-military fashion. The fourth cot, the one farthest from the door, was occupied by a squat, dark-skinned man with thinning black hair, and the finely chiseled features of an Arapaho Indian.

"I'm goin' in, Russ," Dan said. "And I want you with me."

The man remained motionless for a moment, as if in a trance.

"Russ, listen to me for chris'sake. We got more'n eighty men trapped down there, and it's gonna take more than those goddam prayers of yours to get 'em out!"

The other man suddenly opened his eyes and nodded. Without questions or protest, he silently put on his hard hat.

"Let's go," he said.

There was a flatness to his voice which betrayed no emotion. But it didn't bother Dan. After years of working with Edmonds, he had come to realize that belief in predestination was a natural part of the Indian character. If he hadn't wanted to go, nothing on earth could have persuaded him.

Gallagher, the powder man, was waiting with Sid at the main shaft. They were watching a scuffle between two miners. Dan recognized the fighters: one was an experienced driller he had worked with on other jobs, the other an on-the-job trainee.

"What the hell's going on?" he asked.

Gallagher shrugged. "Bound to happen," he said. "Just a matter of time."

A muscular man in his late forties, Gallagher still had a solid body, although it was beginning to show signs of softening around the belly, and there were streaks of grey in his thick hair. He was with Rampling International when Dan joined the firm. Prior to that he'd been with Brown & Root, where he worked under Ed Morley. The two men had been close friends, and despite the differences in their positions, had spent a lot of time together before Morley went to Washington after his split with Jake. A dedicated union man, he was an outspoken critic of on-the-job training. Tunneling was too dangerous to risk the mistakes inexperienced workers were likely to make.

"That what they're fighting about?" Dan asked.

"The guys figure this whole mess wouldn't have happened if it hadn't been for the goddam trainees. They don't know their ass from a hole in the ground."

"Shit!" Dan strode to where the men were fighting. "Okay, you two, break it up."

He pried the men apart. They were covered in dust but neither appeared hurt. The experienced miner recognized Dan.

"You gotta tell these lousy bastards once and for all we ain't gonna milk feed 'em anymore."

"Just back off," Dan replied quietly. "We got more important things on our hands than your dumb squabbles."

"You goin' in?"

Dan nodded.

"We tried earlier. Those lousy fire department guys wouldn't let us."

He motioned to where a group of helmeted firemen were standing beside unhooked ladders and coiled hoses. They weren't company men, and Dan guessed they must have responded to news of the accident and come out from Amarillo. He went over to the fire chief.

"I'm assuming control," he announced.

"There may be a fire down there," the man replied. "That makes it our jurisdiction—"

"You got five thousand feet of hose?"

"Other units are on the way."

"If there is a fire it's gas that's burning. You aren't gonna put that out with water."

"We got our set procedures—"

Dan thrust a blunt finger in the other man's face. "I want breathing apparatus, and I want it now. Understood?"

"The Bureau of Mines directive states that anybody using breathing apparatus has to be screened—"

"See those guys?" He motioned toward the miners who were angrily milling around the main shaft. "Either you do what I say, fast, or they come over here and beat the shit out of your fireboys. Now what's it gonna be?"

The man turned to an assistant. "Bring the breathing units."

Dan walked back to where Gallagher was standing.

"Sid told me you wanted me to bring my stuff." He nodded toward a large canvas duffle bag that bulged with various protruding shapes.

"That all you're gonna need?"

"It's the way you use it that counts."

Dan didn't argue. Gallagher was the best powder man he had ever known. He trusted his judgment completely.

"Okay," he said. "Let's get this show on the road."

Sid grabbed the duffle bag and loaded it into the man trip. Then he stacked Edmonds's drilling equipment to one side of it. It was heavy, but the big man handled it with ease. Even the portable generator they were taking to use in the event the power below was out presented no problem.

Seymour arrived. He looked pale and drawn.

"They're lowering a power line," he said.

"I've got an auxiliary unit," Dan replied.

"You may need it. There's no guarantee we'll get the line all the way down." He handed Dan a walkie-talkie. "It may not work with all that steel around. But it's worth a try."

Fatigue made his voice hoarse, and there was an undertone of hopelessness he made no effort to hide.

"What's the word on the man trip cable?" Dan asked.

"Good, so far as we can tell." Seymour looked up at where the massive flywheel was built into the steel superstructure. "Christ, I don't know—the blast could have weakened it."

"We'll find out soon enough."

Seymour nodded. "Good luck."

Dan looked across to where the reporters were standing behind a barrier of yellow trestles. There were now several television cameras pointed at the man trip. Gallagher, Edmonds and Sid were already aboard the huge steel cage. Dan turned and stepped in. Pulling the gate closed, he signaled the switchman, who eased in the lever controlling the hoist mechanism. The massive flywheel high in the steel super-structure started to turn, and the man trip slowly disappeared underground.

The lights set in the upper part of the shaft were still working, but he knew they were powered from the surface. As the descent quickened, they cast bright splotches across the faces of the men standing alongside him. The flickering effect was like that of early silent films: it created the eerie sensation of their being animated images.

"Take it slower," he said into the mouthpiece of the walkie-talkie.

"Slower it is," Seymour replied.

The rate of descent was reduced appreciably. When they reached the 2,000-foot marker, the air rising from below had an acid stench. The elevator had been loaded with breathing equipment: masks that were linked by rubber hoses to aluminum cylinders designed to be strapped on the back. And there were four large battery-operated flashlights. The atmosphere became so foul by the time they reached the 4,000-foot level that Dan issued the order to put on the masks. But they seemed to pass through the worst of it, and by the time the man trip came to a stop moments after they had passed the 4,500-foot marker, the air was quite breathable again.

"Looks like we're down as far as we can go," Dan announced, pressing the rubber mouthpiece of the walkie-talkie over his lips.

"See anything?" Seymour's voice sounded disembodied and very far away.

"Negative. I'll keep you informed. Over and out."

He put the walkie-talkie inside his jacket, and tried to raise the metal gate of the man trip. It wouldn't move.

"Probably still locked," he said. "It works automatically. I guess we stopped too high to make contact with the breakers."

He tried again, but the gate wouldn't budge.

"Sid?"

The big man squeezed past the other two men and grasped the steel bars. Bending his knees he went into a crouch, and then slowly began to stand. For a moment the only sound was his grunting. Then something snapped, and the gate slid open.

"Bring the lights and stay close," Dan said.

They emerged to find themselves on a narrow platform which normally served as a place for workers to wait when shifts changed. It was an area that looked very much like a subway, except that the gallery leading away from it was hewn from living rock. It was unbearably hot, and the stink of the burned-out tunnel filled their nostrils. Ribs made of molded steel H-beams were placed in sets at four-foot intervals, and stretched in a steep incline toward the work-face. Lights surrounded by wire-mesh baskets were still working, and provided enough illumination for them to see some of the damage the explosion had done.

"Jesus," Gallagher murmured. "It must have been one hell of a blast."

His eyes were fixed on a mass of twisted metal that had once been a low-profile loader. About a hundred yards away was a jumbled pile of massive boulders that blocked the gallery. It was evident even from where they stood that the passage leading to where the men were trapped was completely sealed.

"What do you think, Russ?" Dan asked.

Edmonds walked nearer the rock fall and examined the debris more closely. He stood for a long time without saying anything. It seemed he was making some kind of mental calculation only he understood.

"Must be a couple of hundred feet thick, at least," he said finally.

"Blasting's the only way we're gonna get through that lot," Gallagher added.

Dan didn't answer. But the men knew what he was thinking. With the huge air-vent fan lines now a mess of crushed sheet metal, there was a strong possibility that pockets of highly flammable methane gas were still around. Their portable gas-testing meters showed minimal readings, but there was no way of knowing what concentrations had been trapped in the air spaces between the fallen boulders. That would require more careful testing, and they hadn't time for such a procedure. The crew coming in from Dallas were experts, and it was possible they'd have more sophisticated equipment, but meanwhile the men trapped behind that wall of rock were slowly suffocating.

"We've gotta risk it," Dan said after a long silence. "Now let's move ass."

They returned to the man trip and carefully unloaded their equipment. Sid shouldered the portable generator, carried it down the gallery, and positioned it near the cave-in. Then he hauled the drills to the same spot before returning to help Gallagher with his duffle bag.

"Any sign of the crew from Dallas?" Dan asked into the walkie-talkie.

"None," Seymour replied. "Has the power line reached you?"

"No. It must have got caught in the hoist cables. We'll have to use the generator."

"That could be real dangerous."

"Now you tell me."

The sound of a nervous chuckle came from the surface. "Any sounds of life?"

"None so far."

There was a long silence during which the only sound was the crackle of static.

"You'll have to . . . "

Suddenly the walkie-talkie went dead. Dan held it to his ear but heard nothing. Then the lights began to flicker. They faded and went on again.

"Shit!" Gallagher said. "That's all we need."

As he spoke the lights took on an unnatural intensity, and then went out.

"Get the flashlights," Dan said.

Moments later a beam of light cut through the humid darkness as Edmonds made his way toward the jumble of rocks. He was followed by Gallagher, who had attached his flashlight to his belt. It swayed with each movement of his body, slicing swaths in the surrounding gloom like a giant scythe. Sid brought up the rear, carrying additional lights which he held steady as the other men made their preparations.

"I'll need holes here and here," Gallagher said, pointing to spots in the fallen debris.

"How deep?" Edmonds asked.

"Ten—maybe twelve feet."

Edmonds fitted a tungsten bit into his drill and put it against the rock.

"Give me some juice," he said.

Dan pressed the button on the portable generator, and it burst into life. The confined space acted as an echo chamber, and made the noise deafening. They went to work instantly. The quicker they got on with it, the sooner the risk of sparks igniting pockets of trapped gas would be over.

The tension was clearly visible in the men's faces. The drill writhed in Edmonds' hands like a living thing. He grunted as the bit hit a hard spot, and twisted the drill so savagely it was almost wrenched out of his hands.

"How much further?" Dan shouted to make himself heard over the stuttering roar.

"Six or eight feet," Edmonds yelled.

"Try and get—"

An ear-shattering screech cut Dan's sentence short. The high-pitched whine continued for ten or twelve seconds. Then the bit suddenly buckled, jolting the drill out of Edmonds' grasp with a force that slammed him into a metal wall plate that was bolted to the flanges between two H-beams. The drill jerked loose from the bit and began snaking crazily at the end of the cable linking it to the generator. Gallagher saw it coming and tried to get out of the way, but didn't move fast enough. The drill whipped into the side of his right leg.

"Grab it!" Dan bellowed at Sid.

But it was a full two or three seconds before the words registered in the big man's brain. Enough time for the bitless drill to flail in a wicked arc that sent it thudding into Gallagher's stomach, driving the air out of his lungs in a gasp that was clearly audible in spite of the thunderous roar. Yet the moment he understood what was expected of him, Sid moved with an agility that was astonishing for a man his size. With complete disregard for his own safety, he threw himself on the drill. He appeared oblivious to the pounding he got while wrestling to control it, and by the time Dan managed to switch the generator off, was bleeding profusely.

"Okay?" Dan asked, still shouting even though it was now completely quiet.

"Sure," Sid licked at the blood trickling into his mouth from a deep gash across one of his cheeks.

Dan turned to Gallagher. "What about you?"

"Fuckin' knee feels like it's broken."

Bolts holding the wall plate had gouged deep furrows down Edmonds' back, and blood was oozing through his ripped shirt, but he helped Gallagher to his feet. When Gallagher put weight on his right leg it was obvious from his quick intake of breath that he was experiencing great pain.

"Bend it," Dan said.

"I can't."

"Try." Dan's voice had a hard edge.

Gallagher slowly bent his leg, and winced as the ligaments in his knee were extended.

"Christ!" he murmured.

"You'll live," Dan said. "Now get your stuff and let's start setting up."

It was clear that every movement Gallagher made caused him considerable pain, but he managed to hobble across to his duffle bag and start unpacking its contents.

Edmonds crossed to where the bit was still protruding from the rock. It was bent like a corkscrew. He tried to pull it out, but the shaft of metal didn't move.

"Better get that out," Gallagher said. "I can't do my job without a place to put the charge."

Dan joined Edmonds at the rock face and tried to help him pull the bit free. But it didn't budge. Dan summoned Sid.

"I want that thing out of there," he said.

Sid gripped the twisted steel rod with both hands. At first nothing happened. Then he bunched his shoulders and tried again. This time the muscles stood out from his arms like thick vines strangling a tree. The sweat poured off him. And the bit began to move as the rock around it crumbled. When it suddenly sprang free Sid turned to Dan, smiling.

"Nice work," Dan said. "Now let's get this job on the road."

Gallagher seemed to forget his injured knee as he readied his equipment. Carefully inserting a charge of dynamite into the hole Edmonds had drilled, he attached a detonator cap with wire hooked directly into it, and stemmed it with hand-fuls of dirt.

"The hole's not deep enough," he said.

"It'll have to do," Dan replied. "The drill's finished."

"Getting the charge far enough in is the whole trick," the powder man persisted.

"Shit!" Dan managed to compress all his anger into the way he uttered the single word.

"Listen," Gallagher said, "My ass's on the line here, too. Okay?"

"All I want from you is a bang big enough to blast a hole through that pile."

"And small enough so it doesn't bring the rest of this goddam tunnel down around our ears," Gallagher said.

They faced each other in silence for a full minute.

"Well?" Dan asked.

"If it kills us all, don't blame me. All right?"

His humor eased the tension, and both men smiled tightly.

"Take cover," Dan shouted.

He followed Edmonds and Sid as they hurried to take cover behind a pile of steel H-beams stacked about 900 feet away. Gallagher carefully uncoiled wire from a spool. When he reached the other men he attached the wire to the black enameled detonator, and flicked a switch. A red light came on.

"Ready?" Dan asked.

The powder man nodded.

"Let's do it!"

6

CEETRA RAMPLING jolted awake. At first she couldn't identify the sound that had interrupted her sleep. Then she heard it again and realized it was the telephone. She looked at the alarm clock at the side of the bed, and was surprised to see it was nearly 11:00 a.m. Instinctively, she looked at the other side of the bed. It was empty. The only indication that Paul Mayhew had been there was a small gift-wrapped box on the pillow.

His absence didn't surprise her. It was part of the pattern of their relationship. A couple of hours here, a night there, sometimes even a whole weekend. But never anything she could count on. And it had gone on for eight years. She wondered if this was the way she would spend the rest of her life. In a luxurious vacuum, comfortably insulated from the normal things which seemed to mean so much to other women. A man she could care enough about to want to spend the rest of her life with him. A home. Children. At twenty-six it suddenly seemed she was doomed to an endless series of pointless encounters like the one she had just had with Paul. It was a realization that left her feeling worthless.

Ignoring the phone, she got out of bed and went into the bathroom. There was a small plastic vial of 10-milligram Valium tablets that Dr. Carlin had prescribed when she first began experiencing bouts of anxiety. She put two in her mouth and washed them down with a swallow of vodka from a half-empty glass she'd left on the edge of the tub when she showered after making love.

Back in the bedroom the telephone was still ringing. She wondered why so many people were trying to call her. It wasn't usual for a Saturday morning. But she was in no mood to talk with anybody, so she took the receiver off the hook. She picked up the gift-wrapped box and opened it. Unwrapping the tissue paper she saw what first appeared to be an antique brooch. But when she took it out of the box and held it under the bedside light, she saw it was a piece of intricately carved ivory. The figures that decorated it were so thoroughly intertwined that it was only after a moment or two that she realized each couple portrayed a different sexual position. The note accompanying it said: "We live and learn. Happy birthday. Paul."

She shook her head. It was so typical of him. Who else would go to the trouble to find such an exquisite piece, only to use it to vitiate any sentiment that might otherwise have been attributed to the act of giving? For a moment she was angry, but then she laughed. Paul was Paul, and she couldn't expect him to be anything different. If she didn't want things to remain the same, she was the one who was going to have to change.

The Valium was beginning to have its effect, but she decided to turn on the news before trying to get back to sleep. The program was already under way.

... In the United States, where campaigning for the upcoming Presidential elections is picking up momentum, and final plans for the Olympic Games are being made in Los Angeles, an event of a more tragic kind has focused the attention ...

Ceetra was about to switch the set off when a picture flashed on the screen that abruptly made her change her mind. It showed a massive steel superstructure with the words RAMPLING INTERNATIONAL emblazoned across one side.

> ... Soon after midnight Central Standard Time, an explosion rocked a tunnel that is being built a hundred and thirty miles northeast of Amarillo, Texas. It is part of the revolutionary Very-High-Speed-Transit system that will link New York and Los Angeles. ...

The announcer's voice continued over a film clip that showed a group of men loading equipment into an elevator at the head of a shaft. The camera zoomed in on the face of the man who appeared to be in charge. He had ruggedly handsome features.

> ... Among the more than eighty victims trapped at a depth of over four thousand feet are J. B. Rampling, founder of the multinational construction firm that bears his name, and his son Bromley. The pictures you are seeing were transmitted by satellite. So far there is no word from the rescue crew. It is being led by Dan Blake, a close personal confidant of J. B. Rampling's, and experts believe there is still a chance he will be able to get through to the men who are trapped. ...

There was another close-up of Dan Blake as he took a last look around before entering the man trip. There was something about his face that triggered a response in Ceetra, but she couldn't pinpoint why.

> ... The importance of this two-hundred-billion-dollar project is such that the President has an open line to the scene of the disaster, and is being kept informed on a minute-by-minute basis. When we have further details of the rescue attempt, we will interrupt regular programming to bring them to you. ...

Ceetra waited to hear more, but the announcer turned to a report on preparations being made in Los Angeles for the Olympic Games, and she switched the set off. The silence that followed was suddenly broken by the doorbell ringing. She crossed to the window and opened the heavy velvet drapes. It was raining outside, but the reporters clustered on the sidewalk outside her front door seemed oblivious to it. Now she realized why the phone had been ringing so persistently. For years gossip columnists had featured her name in their newspapers, and now that she'd become hard news they weren't about to let her slip through their fingers.

Her first instinct was to think of her father. After not seeing him for so many years, it surprised her that she should be so genuinely concerned about his well-being.

Then she thought of her mother. If the reporters got to her, the consequences could be disastrous. She had no way of knowing whether they knew the location of the sanatorium, but she didn't intend to wait around and find out. The telephone receiver was still on the floor where she had placed it when she took it off the hook. It emitted a high-pitched whine. She replaced the receiver, waited a few seconds, then picked it up again and dialed the sanatorium. It answered on the second ring.

"Miss Rampling?" The woman at the other end of the line sounded relieved. "Oh, I'm so glad you called. We've been trying to reach you for some time, but the operator said your phone was out of order. There have been a number of calls requesting interviews with your mother."

"Is Dr. Amsdon there?"

"Yes, but—"

"Put me through."

"I'm afraid he's in—"

"Immediately," Ceetra snapped.

There was a pause, then the sound of a man's voice.

"Dr. Amsdon here."

"This is Ceetra Rampling—"

"Ah, yes, Miss Rampling. We've been having some difficulty getting through to you—"

"I don't want any reporters talking to my mother," she said.

"You don't have to worry," he said stiffly. "I assure you the welfare of our patients comes before anything."

"I'll be there in about two hours."

"But your regular visit isn't until tomorrow, and there isn't anything you can do."

"Two hours."

"Very well. We'll be expecting you. But I really think it would be better if—"

She didn't wait for him to finish, but hung up and dialed another number. This time the phone rang at least a dozen times before a woman finally answered it.

"This is Ceetra, Mrs. Elseworth."

"Hello, dear," the other woman said. "I was out in the garden and it takes so long to get up those stairs."

"Did you see the news?"

"No, I didn't, dear. Was there something special you wanted me to see?"

"Can you be ready in about forty-five minutes?" Ceetra asked.

"For what, dear?"

"I'm going to visit Mother this afternoon."

"But we always go on Sunday."

"Something's come up. It's important. I'll tell you when I see you."

"Well, yes—all right, I suppose I can make arrangements," the other woman said hesitantly.

"I'll be there about two-fifteen," Ceetra said, and hung up.

Ceetra had started to dress when the phone rang again. Assuming it might be Mrs. Elseworth or the sanatorium calling back, she answered it.

"Miss Rampling?"

"Yes."

"This is Bob Spencer at Reuters."

"I'm sorry—"

"Please, Miss Rampling, don't hang up. I've been trying to get through for over an hour."

"I don't have anything—"

"All I need is a quote about your father." The correspondent sounded desperate.

"I haven't seen my father in twenty years," Ceetra said.

"But you know what's happened?"

"I saw the news—"

"What's your reaction?"

"I can't give you—"

"You must feel something," the reporter insisted.

"Of course I do."

"Tell me."

Ceetra hesitated. It was impossible to describe what she felt.

"My father's a great man," she said. "He's responsible for so many—"

"Your gut reaction's what I need," the man interjected.

Ceetra replaced the receiver and unplugged the phone. The man's questions angered her. He had touched a nerve. The fact was she didn't know what she felt. Concern, yes, but beyond that she wasn't sure. The initial numbness was beginning to wear off, and it left an unaccountable void. Rather than sadness, she now felt a terrible emptiness, tinged with a whirl of ambivalent emotions: anxiety, worry, irritation, anger. For reasons she didn't understand, word of the accident had triggered the sense of abandonment that had haunted her since childhood, and she reacted with an unconscious resentment. It was almost as if she subconsciously blamed her father for reentering her life in a way that obligated her to acknowledge that she cared what happened to him.

She finished dressing and phoned the doorman to bring her car to the front door. There was no rear exit to the house in which her apartment was located. The only way out was through the lobby, and that meant facing the reporters gathered on the sidewalk. She dreaded it, but she knew if she was going to get to her mother before the press started hounding her, she was going to have to run the gauntlet.

Steeling herself, she went into the lobby.

"Your chauffeur is bringing the car, ma'am," the doorman said.

"Thank you, Adams."

The doorman looked at the reporters milling around outside the door. "Bloody animals. Excuse the language, Miss. It's just that I've had my hands full with 'em all morning. Wanted to wait in here, if you please! Cleared the lot of 'em out, I did. But there's not much I can do about 'em out there, is there?"

"No," Ceetra said. "I'm sorry to be the cause of so much trouble."

"Don't you worry yourself, Miss. I'm used to handling 'em. Part of the job you might say." He hesitated. "I heard the news—about your father and brother, and, well—I just wanted to say I hope they get out all right."

"That's very kind of you, Adams. I'm sure everything will be fine."

The doorman held an umbrella for Ceetra as she stepped out into the street, but when the reporters suddenly descended on her he was quickly brushed aside. She looked for the car, but there was no sign of it, and she had to wait as questions were hurled at her from all sides.

" . . . Your father's firm has built more nuclear power plants than any of its competitors. Do you approve of such projects? . . . Why did Rampling International cover up the accident that took place at the nuclear power facility it installed in Saudi Arabia? . . . Is it true the CIA has been using your father's company as a front for its covert activities in foreign countries? . . . Are you aware that eight class-action suits have been filed against Rampling International for discrimination against women? . . . What changes will you make when you inherit your father's controlling interest in the firm?"

"My father isn't dead yet," Ceetra snapped. "And neither is my brother."

"How well do you know your father?" The reporter's

voice sounded familiar, and she wondered if it was the same man who had telephoned earlier.

"No comment," she said.

The chauffeur arrived with the Rolls-Royce, and she found refuge in the back seat, but the reporter's question continued to ring in her ears. "How well do you know your father?" Finally the car pulled away from the curb.

"Sorry about the delay, Miss," the driver said. "I was fixing a few things under the bonnet when the doorman told me you wanted the car."

"It's all right, Walters. I'd like you to go by Regent's Park to pick up Mrs. Elseworth. She's expecting us. Maybe you wouldn't mind going inside when we get there. I've had enough of reporters for one day. And if they follow us on the way to the sanatorium I want you to lose them."

"A pleasure, Miss."

She put her head back against the glove-leather seat and tried to relax, but the question persisted: "How well do you know your father?" Despite her resolve not to think, images of the past began seeping into her mind. Slowly at first, like prints in developing solution, vague and half-formed, but quickly taking on substance until the past seemed more real than the present. Too emotionally exhausted to fight these recollections, she closed her eyes and gave herself up to memory.

7

EVEN BEFORE her birth, Ceetra had been a subject of interest to the press. The society editors of both the *Dallas Morning News* and the *Times-Herald* had kept their readers on tenterhooks with almost daily speculation about her arrival. Their appetite was whetted by a number of factors, not the least of which was the fact that Rampling International was a major advertiser. But this was not the only reason. J. B. Rampling was a flamboyant man, the kind of diamond-in-the-rough that people in Dallas liked to read about because it somehow reminded them of what Texas had been like in the wide-open good old days. His wealth and power made him a larger-than-life figure whose swashbuckling way of doing things evoked admiration and, more often than not, a measure of jealousy. So, when it was announced that his wife, Mary Rampling, was expecting a baby, it was only natural that the impending birth would become a media event.

Jake disliked being interviewed, and normally would speak to reporters only about business matters. But he was so excited by the pending arrival of his first child that he talked openly with members of the press, and made no secret of the plans he had in store for the youngster who would become heir to the dynasty he had built. "I never had a goddam thing when I was a kid," he told a reporter who was preparing an article for *Time* magazine. "But it's gonna be a lot different with my son." Not once did he refer to the child as anything other than a boy. It was obviously inconceivable to him that his offspring wouldn't be male.

When the unimaginable happened, and Ceetra was born on April 20th, 1958, at Baylor University Hospital, Jake's reaction surprised even those who thought they knew him. They understood his disappointment, and realized he wasn't the kind of man to hide it. But it was generally assumed he would adjust to the situation and make the best of it.

They couldn't have been more wrong. Jake left the hospital without seeing either his wife or the child, and in the months that followed he behaved as if neither existed. He arranged a succession of business trips that kept him out of the country for months at a time, and during the brief periods he was in Dallas he barely paid any attention to his wife or daughter. It was almost as if he felt his wife had betrayed him, and even her most fervent pleas couldn't soften his attitude.

For a long time she tried to keep up the facade of their marriage. Mary had been raised to believe in the importance of appearances, but when she got no response from her husband, she finally stopped trying. Instead, she invested her energies in various kinds of social work. Anything that would keep her busy, and away from the house.

She left the care of her daughter in the hands of a nanny, Mrs. McDonald, a thin, florid Scottish woman who had worked for a number of other wealthy families in the Dallas area. She came with the highest references, and quickly demonstrated she could live up to them.

Ceetra's earliest conscious memories were of this woman bathing her, taking her for walks, and putting her to bed. But preceding them was a subconscious awareness of almost always being alone. It generated a vague sense of anxiety that remained with her into adulthood. For years she had mentally blocked this period and been completely unable to remember anything that happened to her before the age of five. But her psychiatrist, Dr. Carlin, had regressed her under hypnosis, and she'd been able to recall bits and pieces of her life before accompanying her mother to London.

Almost all of them related in one way or another to her father. Like the day he had arrived home unexpectedly to find her playing with a pile of colored bricks on the floor of his study. He had lifted her up and studied her for a moment. Then he had placed her on his huge desk, and given her a crystal paperweight to play with while he sorted through a wad of reports. Even under hypnosis the memory was fragmented, but two parts of it had lodged themselves indelibly in Ceetra's mind: the indescribable joy she had felt at being in his presence, and the rainbowlike colors the prism she was holding cast on his face as he worked.

Every afternoon for two or three weeks after that she played with her bricks on the study floor, hoping against hope that she would hear his footsteps striding toward her, but he never came. So she took to lying at the top of the stairs where she could watch the front door, yearning to catch a glimpse of him when he came back from the office. But when he wasn't away on a business trip, he returned home so late that she was invariably asleep when he did finally arrive.

She took to weaving elaborate fantasies around her father. In some she was injured in an accident, and he came to her as life was ebbing away, and took her in his arms. In others he was hurt, but as a result of her dedicated loving care, miraculously recovered when all seemed lost. The permutations of circumstances leading to these crises were endless, but they all concluded in the same way: with Ceetra and her father sharing a closeness so intense neither could exist without it.

During these early years Ceetra's mother was present far more often than her father, but the rapport between them wasn't strong. Mary Rampling was an elegant, fragile woman, with a patrician beauty that gave her an aura of inaccessibility. Fair-haired and pale-skinned, she had high cheekbones that emphasized the perfect set of her enormous brown eyes, and such magazines as *Vogue* and *Town & Country* frequently featured her photograph in their pages. Her skills as a hostess made invitations to the parties Jake held at the ranch for business associates highly prized. She was a sparkling conversationalist with the ability to talk on a wide range of subjects, and she had a knack for bringing together people of disparate backgrounds that bordered on genius. But when it came to communicating with her daughter, she was ill at ease and painfully unsure of herself. Her natural habitat was the salons of Neiman-Marcus in Dallas, Saks Fifth Avenue in New York, Bulgari's in Rome, and the shops on Bond Street in London. Three or four times a year she used one of the company jets to go on shopping sprees in various cities around the world, invariably returning laden with boxes containing the latest fashions.

Ceetra's feelings for her were quite different from those she experienced toward her father. The latter was the subject of outright adulation, while the former belonged more in the category of admiration for a woman who always looked as if she'd just stepped out of an advertisement in a glossy magazine. But this attitude underwent an abrupt change when Mary became pregnant again, and Jake suddenly manifested a renewed interest in his wife. It left their daughter with the impression that she'd been abandoned by both.

She reacted with anger and jealousy. In her mind's eye her mother had usurped a place that Ceetra considered rightfully hers. Her resentment was heightened when Mary gave birth to a boy, and Jake showered the baby with the attention Ceetra always craved but never received.

In a perverse way she was glad when her father began divorce proceedings against his wife shortly after her brother's birth. But when it became clear that she was to live with her mother in London while her brother, Bromley, remained with Jake in Dallas, she went into a depression that was to last, on and off, for years.

But rather than quashing her love for her father, separation from him only increased her fantasies. The prime difference was that now, instead of conjuring up scenarios in which she was dependent, she imagined endless ways of proving her worth to him. In order to add substance to these daydreams, she began collecting information about her father with the same dedication other youngsters invested in collecting stamps.

Fortunately, Mrs. Elseworth understood her obsession. The woman, who had become Ceetra's guardian when Mary entered the sanatorium soon after their arrival in London, was a kind, sympathetic person who had longed to have children of her own. Now that she was widowed she directed her maternal instincts toward Ceetra, giving her the love the child had hungered for ever since she was born. Mrs. Elseworth was aware from the day she first met Ceetra that the girl desperately needed to identify with her father, and she encouraged the youngster to unearth all the information she could possibly find which related to Jake Rampling.

First she purchased a huge album which Ceetra spent hours carefully inscribing with her father's name. She filled the letters in with different colored crayons, and decorated the sides of the front page with an intricate pattern of squiggles. Then they visited every library in London which might offer information about Jake Rampling. They made a game of it. Whenever they found anything new they rewarded themselves with ice cream cones or tea at a Lyon's Corner House.

The older woman felt that it was better for the child to probe for answers than to keep questions about her father festering inside her. She felt certain that after Ceetra's initial enthusiasm passed, she would let the search slide and invest her energies in other interests. But this was not what happened. Ceetra retained her obsession with seeking out all facts she could find, and if anything it only increased with each passing year.

She became a familiar sight at the ancient domed building of the British Library, which was then still attached to the Museum. The librarians were intrigued by the pigtailed girl who pestered them for back copies of such magazines as *Fortune, Business Week, Forbes, Time* and *Newsweek* and various trade publications relating to the construction industry. By the time she was eleven years old she had gleaned every possible source, including libraries at the London School of Economics, the *Times,* and the U.S. Embassy. The latter was particularly productive, thanks largely to help Ceetra received from a vice consul whose home was in Dallas. He had grown up hearing stories about the legendary Jake Rampling, and was able to fill in some of the gaps that remained in the child's intensive research.

It was from him that she first learned about the way her father gained custody of Bromley. In order to ensure that his son would remain with him, Jake had proffered evidence to the court that Mary was mentally unstable, and had backed up his contention by showing the results of an examination by Dr. Earl Robinson, the company physician who was also the family doctor. The judge had ordered her to undergo observation at an exclusive private clinic, where she was interviewed by three different psychiatrists. They testified that she was so unstable that she could not care for two children, but the judge had specified that if Ceetra was put in the care of a legal guardian he would allow her to remain in the custody of her mother. It was ruled that Bromley would be raised by his father.

Discovering that her mother had been judged mentally unstable didn't come as any surprise to Ceetra. By the time she found out, she had grown accustomed to visiting her mother at the sanatorium in Sussex. But it was news to learn that her mother had shown no obvious symptoms of instability prior to being examined by Dr. Robinson, and it left her wondering how, in such a short space of time, she could have suffered a complete mental collapse.

There were other blank spaces, and Ceetra reread the contents of her album again and again in search of clues. But if there was a certain air of mystery about Jake Rampling, there was one aspect of his character he made no attempt to hide: he was a man who couldn't tolerate losing. There were numerous stories in print about the lengths to which he would go in order to win, and when Ceetra read them she sensed they were true. Her own experience with her father had shown him to be utterly ruthless, and yet, for reasons she didn't understand, she still found herself irresistibly drawn to him.

"I'll go in and see if Mrs. Elseworth is ready," the chauffeur said.

His words snapped Ceetra out of her reverie, and she saw they had stopped in front of the house in Regent's Park where she had spent so many happy years as a child. It had been converted into apartments about five years ago, and no longer had the gracious look she remembered. The entrance was littered with refuse, and graffiti had been spray-painted on the outside door.

"Thank you, Walters," she said.

She watched as the driver went inside the building. When he didn't emerge for over ten minutes, she felt her body growing tense. The feeling was similar to that she had experienced in the top floor room of her fashion studio: rapid pulse, sweating, heart palpitations. It seemed as if she were steeling herself for something to happen, but she didn't know what, and it generated an anxiousness tinged with dread.

 **8**   IT WAS LESS THAN fifteen minutes before Mrs. Elseworth walked down the steps, aided by the chauffeur with a hand under her arm, but it seemed an eternity to Ceetra.

"You said you'd be ready," she said, an edge of impatience in her voice.

"I *am* sorry." Mrs. Elseworth looked at Ceetra with a puzzled expression. "Are you all right, dear?"

Ceetra waited until the car was in traffic before answering. The older woman looked tired. She had aged badly in recent months. It showed in the gauntness of her cheeks, and the way her flesh seemed to hang loosely from her bones. Suddenly, Ceetra felt ashamed at the sharp tone she'd taken with her. Mrs. Elseworth was the one person in her life she'd been able to count on, and had always loved without reservation.

"I'm sorry." She touched Mrs. Elseworth's hand. "It's just that—well, I'm on edge, I suppose."

"You've always been tense. I remember when you were eight or nine years old—"

"There's been an accident." Ceetra felt it was easier to say it right out, rather than work up to the announcement. "Rampling International is building a tunnel near Amarillo, Texas," Ceetra continued. "There's been an explosion. My father and brother have been trapped underground."

"Your father trapped?"
"And Bromley."
"I can't believe it."
"Neither could I when I first heard about it on the news. But it's true." She looked at the small electric clock set next to a radio in a console at the back of the passenger seat. It was nearly 2:00 p.m. "The rescue crew went down at dawn. They're six hours behind us, so there's still no word."

Mrs. Elseworth settled back and closed her eyes. Ceetra looked out at the tranquil green countryside. It was alive with spring blossoms. She wondered what it could be like to be trapped almost a mile underground. Just the thought made her shudder. Perhaps Bromley was made of sterner stuff.

She knew almost nothing about her brother. From the few pictures she'd seen he appeared to be a handsome, sensitive person with fine, almost delicate features that didn't closely resemble those of either his mother or father. She had written to him two or three different times, usually around Christmas, but he had never replied. He only seemed interested in communicating with his mother. He sent her letters as often as three times a week. Ceetra was puzzled by his need to correspond so frequently with a women he couldn't possibly have remembered, and had asked Dr. Carlin for an explanation. The psychiatrist had suggested Bromley may have felt so oppressed by living in his father's shadow that he'd invented a parent substitute around whom he could weave whatever fantasies he wished, knowing that the only contact he was ever likely to have with her would be by mail.

Ceetra had never mentioned this to her mother. To her Bromley was a perfect son. She lived for his letters; they had become the core of her existence. In some strange way they gave her a sustenance she needed, one which her daughter had failed to provide. Exactly what it was eluded Ceetra, and often she felt hurt at having so dutifully cared for her mother with so little acknowledgement. But it was too late to expect any change now. Mary's state of mind was too fragile to cope with any emotional stress. Ceetra wondered how

82

she was going to break the news of the accident to her. There was no way of knowing how she would react. Ceetra knew all she could do was wait for the right opening, and put it to her the most gentle way possible.

It was almost 3:30 p.m. when the Rolls-Royce turned into the sweeping driveway leading to the beautifully preserved Georgian manor that had been converted into a sanatorium. Ceetra's mother had been a patient there for almost twenty years. Dr. Amsdon was waiting at the front door to meet her.

"Why don't you wait in the car until I've had a chance to break the news," Ceetra said, addressing herself to Mrs. Elseworth, who had awakened from her brief nap when the car turned onto the gravel surface of the driveway.

"Are you sure you want to go alone? It's going to be quite a shock, and you know how your mother gets when she's upset."

"I think it'll be easier if there's just the two of us."

"All right, dear. You know best. I'll stay here until you come for me."

The driver held the door open. "Shall I park round back, Miss?"

"That would be better," Ceetra said. "Maybe you can find a cup of tea in the kitchen."

Dr. Amsdon came forward and took her arm. He was a thin, balding man with bleak grey eyes, and a smile that seemed too practiced. "I'm so glad you could come," he said, guiding her up the worn, shallow steps that led to the double-doored entrance. "It's so much better for a patient to have family around at times like these."

"Does she know yet?" Ceetra asked.

The doctor shook his head. "There really wasn't any point in saying anything until you got here."

"Have there been any reporters?"

"Yes, quite a few. But we're used to handling them. Quite a few of our patients are rather well known people, you know."

His tone was slightly defensive, and Ceetra sensed he resented her presence.

"How is she?"

"About the same."

"Did she get any letters?"

"There was a batch a few days ago. I think it was Wednesday."

They were inside the cavernous, marble-floored lobby, and their footsteps echoed as they walked.

"I've been trying to think of the best way to tell her," Ceetra said.

"I'll do it, if you'd rather."

"Thank you. But I think it's better if it comes from me."

"Perhaps—" He hesitated. "I've been wondering if we're not being a little bit premature. After all, I gather there's still no word as to the fate of the trapped men. It's possible we're alarming her unnecessarily."

"There have been bulletins on both television and radio," Ceetra said, surprised by his reluctance to confront the issue. "It's only a matter of time before one of the other patients says something to her about it."

"Yes," he murmured. "I suppose you're right."

Ceetra had never liked the man. His manner was more that of a maître d' than a distinguished psychiatrist.

"Where can I find her?" she asked.

"She's on the balcony. I told her you were coming today instead of tomorrow, so she's expecting you."

Ceetra went through the open French doors onto the terrace. It had stopped raining and the sun was beginning to burn through the clouds.

Her mother was sitting at a table under a large blue umbrella. Ceetra observed her for a few moments before going over to her. She was still a strikingly attractive woman. Petite, fragile-looking as the finest porcelain, hair reflecting the sun like spun gold. What a beauty she must have been in her youth.

Ceetra walked briskly toward her. Before she reached the table, her mother heard the sound of footsteps and looked up. For an instant she appeared startled, but then recognition came into her eyes and a bright smile lit her face.

"Guess what," she said, even before her daughter could sit down.

"No clues?"

Her mother waved a sheaf of flimsy air-mail envelopes. "You won the pools!"

"No, silly. You know I don't bet on things."

It was a game they played every time Ceetra visited her mother, and she went along with it because it pleased her.

"I give up," Ceetra said.

"Four letters. All in the same mail. Can you imagine anything nicer than that?"

Ceetra shook her head. She wished her mother would say how glad she was that she'd come. But it never happened that way. After so many years, she took her daughter's presence for granted, and always greeted her with the latest news from Bromley. It hurt, but Ceetra still hadn't found a way of saying so.

"What does he say?" she asked.

"Oh, all kinds of things."

The ritual was always the same. After greeting her with the announcement of news from Bromley, she would deliberately withhold it, as if by so doing she made the contents of the letters a personal secret. Ceetra knew what was expected of her.

"Tell me." She managed to infuse just the right note of little-girl pleading. "Please—"

"Well—" Her mother's wrinkled brow indicated deep indecision. "All right, but I'm only going to read you certain parts."

As Ceetra waited for the other woman to put on her glasses, she watched two swans paddling slowly across the lily pond. Long-necked and pure white, they moved with utter grace in the water, but when they emerged to waddle toward a gardener who fed them, they looked awkward and out of place.

"He writes so beautifully." Her mother sorted through the letters like a child savoring its treasures. "And he draws, too. Did you know your brother's a fine artist?"

Ceetra shook her head. Each visit her mother prefaced their conversation about Bromley by announcing that he was an artist, and every time her daughter feigned the surprise that was expected of her.

"Oh, yes," her mother continued. "And he writes the most wonderful poetry. It's been published, too."

A slender book of verse had arrived by mail the previous Christmas. Her mother kept it by her bed and read it every night before going to sleep. Ceetra had been quite impressed by her brother's achievement until she discovered that the publisher's imprint was that of a printer in San Francisco who specialized in putting out private editions at an exorbitant cost. And after showing the poetry to a friend who taught English at Cambridge, she was informed that almost all of it was derived from the works of various well-known poets.

"Well," her mother said, adjusting her glasses. "It seems he has a friend who has helped him a lot with his sketching—somebody called David Seymour. He's an engineer who works for your father's firm. Apparently they share a lot of common interests." She paused, then added reflectively: "I don't think I've ever known him to write this warmly about anybody before."

She looked at Ceetra as if expecting a reaction, but when her daughter remained silent, turned her attention back to the letter.

"He says: ' . . . I can't tell you what a relief it is to finally find somebody who really understands me, after so many years of having Dan Blake breathing down my neck. You'll remember me telling you about him. He's Father's personal assistant, and is a lot like him. He's been sort of teaching me the business. I wouldn't mind, except I don't have anything in common with him, and always feel so suffocated when he's around. . . .' "

She stopped reading and looked at Ceetra. There was an odd, glazed look to her eyes. "That's exactly how I felt around your father. I couldn't breathe—"

Suddenly she put her head back and drew in a series of labored breaths, as if fighting for air. Spasms shook her body, and her fingers clawed at the single string of pearls around her neck with such force that the thread broke. Pearls spilled out over the broad flagstones of the terrace. Ceetra quickly got up and wrapped her arms around her shoulders. But her mother no longer seemed to recognize her, and looked at her with the terrified eyes of a trapped animal. When she started to struggle two attendants saw what was happening and hurriedly took over. They pinioned her arms to her side and held her firmly until Dr. Amsdon arrived carrying a small leather bag. He took out a syringe.

"Steady," he murmured as he wiped her upper arm with a swab of moist cotton and slid the needle into her flesh. "Just try and keep still. This will make you feel a lot better."

"What is it?" Ceetra asked.

"Thorazine," the doctor replied. "It works very quickly."

"I don't know what happened. She was reading to me from one of Bromley's letters, and suddenly—"

"It could have been anything." He shrugged. "Sometimes even subconscious memories are enough to trigger an episode."

Ceetra watched as her mother's body went limp. The attendants stood back as Ceetra cradled her head in her arms. Her mother's eyes were open. The fear in them had given way to a blank, uncomprehending expression. Her lids flickered and it appeared she was slipping into unconsciousness, but at the last moment her lips moved. The words weren't audible.

"What is it, Mom?" she asked.

Her mother's lips moved again. This time Ceetra lowered her head until her ear was against her mother's mouth.

"Dangerous," she breathed. "Very dangerous . . . "

"Who's dangerous, Mom?"

She felt the stir of hot breath on her ear, but no words came. Moments later the Thorazine took effect and her head fell forward.

"We'll get her to her room," Dr. Amsdon said.

"I'll come."

"There really isn't much you can do. She'll sleep for a few hours. When she wakes up it's quite possible she won't remember a thing that's happened."

Ceetra watched as the attendants lifted her mother in their arms and carried her into the main building. The letters she'd been holding before she went into spasm were scattered on the stone paving. Ceetra picked them up, and held them for a moment. She tried to equate what her brother had written about Dan Blake with the image she'd seen of him on television as he prepared to lead the rescue crew underground. She had no way of knowing if her mother's warning had been about him or her father.

Dr. Amsdon emerged from the open French doors. "I'll have somebody pick up the pearls. Perhaps you'd like me to arrange to have them restrung. There's a small shop in the village that does good work."

"My mother would like that. They're one of the few things left that she brought from America."

"You look pale," the doctor said.

"I'm all right. It's just—well, a shock I suppose."

"Why don't you walk in the garden for a few minutes. It's so beautiful at this time of year."

"Yes. Thank you. I think I will," Ceetra replied.

She went slowly down the steps from the terrace to the lawn, pausing a moment to look back at the door through which they had taken her mother. She wondered what terrible memories had triggered the attack. The question gnawed at her as she walked toward a small chapel situated a short distance from the main house. It was barely big enough to hold twenty or thirty people, but there was a tranquility about its stained-glass interior that made her feel at peace.

She wasn't religious. Not in any formal sense. But there were times when she liked to sit in a church and let herself be enveloped by its ambience. The chapel was empty. She sat in an oak pew that was so old there were grooves in the wood, worn into it by people who had sat there over the centuries. Obeying a sudden impulse, she knelt and rested her head against the backs of her hands. The only prayer she remembered was a simple blessing they had used before meals at Farleigh House School. But she murmured it anyway. And when she stood she felt refreshed. The anxiety that had weighted her down all day had been lifted.

When she returned to the car Mrs. Elseworth switched off the radio. Her eyes were red and she was wiping her nose with a wet tissue.

"What is it?" Ceetra asked.

"Oh, God—" Sobs racked the older woman's body. Ceetra put an arm around her shoulders and tried to comfort her, but without success.

"There was word on the news, Miss." Walters got out from behind the wheel and helped Ceetra put Mrs. Elseworth in the back seat. "It was about the tunnel disaster. The rescue crew got through, but it seems there was a flash fire." He looked at Ceetra somberly. "I'm sorry, Miss, but they say there were no survivors."

 **9**

PEOPLE WHO KNEW Mule Barnes as a country boy would have been surprised by the change he underwent whenever he visited New York. His corn pone image stayed in Texas and, like a chrysalis, he emerged completely transformed. In place of the baggy, ill-fitting suits that were almost a trademark in Dallas, he wore expensively tailored outfits. He traveled in a chauffeur-driven Cadillac limousine, stayed at his luxurious penthouse on Fifth Avenue overlooking Central Park, and had memberships in the best clubs, as well as a private table at the Four Seasons and a suite of offices on Park Avenue that were small but sumptuously furnished.

Even now, as he sat in the Palm Court lounge of the Plaza Hotel, waiting for Bonnie and watching the Saturday evening traffic of people pass through the ornate Fifth Avenue lobby, he was sipping champagne and smoking a Havana cigar.

He saw Bonnie as she emerged from the rotating doors. She was wearing a fur coat and her hair looked windblown. It made her appear younger than the first time he had met her, when he had gone to Washington seeking Ed Morley's services as a lobbyist to ensure that Rampling International would be awarded the most lucrative section of the VHST tunnel. She was the kind of woman he liked: striking without being beautiful, and possessed of an earthiness that appealed to his jaded appetites. From the first he had sensed that she had enough sexual experience to provide what he needed, and their initial encounter had proved him right.

"Hi, Mule, been waiting long?" she asked.

"Hell, no," he replied. "Just got here a few minutes ago."

"You look good."

"I feel real fine." He motioned to the other chair. "Now why don't you park yourself over there and let me order you some of this good stuff I'm drinking."

She hesitated. "Ed says you're meeting him at midnight."

"That's right."

"Well, if we're going to—"

"You figure we'd better get to it, huh?" He laughed and beckoned the waiter. "Reckon you're right at that."

"More champagne, sir?" The waiter had the bottle poised.

"No. Just the check," Barnes said. "And tell the doorman to have my car ready, will you?"

"Is it far?" Bonnie asked.

"Just a little ways up Fifth Avenue."

"Do we need the car?"

"Let me tell you something, little lady—never walk when you can ride."

She laughed and took his arm as he led the way to the limousine which was waiting outside the main entrance.

"Oh, I forgot something." Bonnie disappeared through the revolving doors and was back moments later carrying a large leather bag. "It was at the check stand," she said.

The ride took less than five minutes, but it was still enough time for Barnes to slide his hand under her skirt and discover she wasn't wearing any underwear.

"Jesus," he murmured, beginning to work his finger inside her. "You really know how to drive a guy crazy."

Before she could answer, the car stopped and the driver opened the door.

"Will you need me again, sir?" he asked.

"Yeah, stick around," Barnes said. "I'll be going out around midnight."

The driver nodded and helped Bonnie out of the car. If he'd seen what just happened his impassive face showed no sign of it. Bonnie thanked him and followed Barnes through the ornately furnished lobby of a converted brownstone, to a small private elevator that whisked them directly to the penthouse. They emerged in a room that was furnished with exquisite taste. But the dominating feature of the apartment was the view. Enormous picture windows permitted an unobstructed panorama of Central Park and the galaxy of light from buildings flanking it. The recessed lighting was diffuse enough not to detract from the dramatic sweep of Manhattan's skyline.

"How about that drink?" he asked.

"No thanks," she replied.

"Well, I'm gonna fix myself a martini."

Bonnie opened her oversized purse and took out a small plastic package containing cocaine. "Give your liver a rest, and your nose a real treat."

"And I thought you were just a nice southern girl!"

"I get nicer," Bonnie said, passing him a tiny silver spoon heaped with the glistening white powder.

He placed it under his nostril and sniffed hugely.

"Baby Blue got twenty years for doing this," he said, watching as she refilled the spoon and handed it back to him.

"Who's Baby Blue?"

"I guess I'm dating myself. It's just that down where I come from they do things a little differently."

"You like it, though, huh?"

"Texas?"

"Doing things a little differently."

"Damn right!" He got up and crossed to where she was sitting. Resting one hand on her breast, he started squeezing the nipple, while the other slid up the inside of her thigh.

"What makes you think I'm ready to give it to you?"

"Your cunt's doing the talking, baby. And it's wet." He

knelt in front of her, pushed her dress up around her waist, and buried his head in her crotch. But after a few seconds she pushed him away.

"You need lessons, honey."

"Whad'ya mean, I need lessons?" He was looking up at her with cold, hard eyes. "I eat pussy as well as any guy."

"But not the way a woman does it."

"What the hell's the difference?"

"Talking's a waste of time. There's only one way you're going to understand." She took his hand and led him into the bedroom. "Get on that bed and wait while I make myself ready. You want to know what it feels like to be a woman," she said. "I'm going to show you."

He stripped off his clothes and watched as she slowly began to undress. Her skin had the sheen of alabaster, white and fine-textured. Her breasts were small but firm, and the nipples stood out dark and hard.

"Move it, for chris'sake," he said. "We haven't got all night."

"We'll do it when I'm good and ready." There was a deliberate contemptuousness to her voice. "You're just a goddam whore and I'm going to treat you that way."

She opened her leather bag and took out a pair of handcuffs which she snapped around his wrists. The pressure of them made him wince, but she knew he enjoyed the pain. When she started whipping him with the leather belt she'd worn round her coat, he moaned, and his fleshy body began to quiver.

"What are you?" She gave the question a guttural edge.

"A whore," he murmured.

"That's right."

Suddenly, he lay back and closed his eyes. She could sense the change in him. The moment he ejaculated he underwent a transformation that was so abrupt it had frightened her the first time she saw it. He clenched his fists and slammed them against the side of the bed. It was as if the anguish he was suffering internally was greater than any of the pain she had inflicted. But just as quickly as it began, it stopped.

"Turn the water on," he said, heading for the bathroom.

She did as he asked, and when the tub was full she took a washcloth and started bathing him. He didn't lift a finger to help, but lay there like a child, allowing her to do all the work. Then he stood up while she dried him off and sprinkled talcum powder liberally on his genitals and between the cheeks of his ass. The first time they were together he had asked her to diaper him with a towel, but this time he just strode into the bedroom and began getting dressed.

"You sure Ed's going to be there?" he asked.

"Around midnight," she replied.

He studied himself carefully in the mirror.

"Think I should shave?"

"You look fine."

"And I feel pretty good." He reached for his wallet and took out three one-hundred-dollar bills.

"That's not necessary," she said.

"I know. When Ed wants something from a guy he knows how to grease the skids. But a girl can always use a little something extra."

"I get a good salary."

"Call it a bonus. You do good work."

She hesitated a moment and took the money. If making her feel like a whore was important to him, so be it. Her instructions were to keep him happy.

"He's at the Trattoria Roma," she said.

"I know." He had put on a superbly tailored grey suit, and was adjusting a silk handkerchief in his breast pocket. "Can I drop you anywhere?"

"I'll take a cab to the airport."

"You're going back to Washington tonight?"

She nodded.

"He works you too hard."

She didn't answer. She hadn't wanted to come to New

95

York to take care of Barnes. The lawyer disgusted her. But her years in Washington had bred an instinct for survival, and she valued her job too much to do anything that might jeopardize it.

"Give me a call next time you're in town," she said.

"Count on it."

It didn't worry Barnes to leave her in his apartment. She wasn't an ordinary hooker. He knew Bonnie had class. But the moment he closed the door of the elevator he put her out of his mind completely. He never thought about his sexual encounters once they were over; it was almost as if they had happened to somebody else.

"Evening, sir," the doorman said as he crossed the lobby. "Your driver's waiting. I was going to call up, but he said you were expecting him."

"Thank you, George," Barnes replied. "Looks like a real fine night."

"Yes, sir." He held open the door. "Good to see you again."

The lawyer gave instructions to his driver and looked out of the window as the car moved smoothly along Fifth Avenue. He loved Manhattan, particularly in the spring, and at night it had a special quality. Everything seemed to glitter. But it took a great deal of money to enjoy it in style, and now that Jake was dead he knew he was going to have to play his cards pretty close to the vest if he was to have a chance to assure his future.

"The Trattoria Roma, sir," the chauffeur announced.

It wasn't an elegant-looking restaurant from the outside, but Barnes had discovered on previous visits that it served some of the best Italian food in Manhattan, and he craved some good pasta.

When he pushed his way through the door, Luigi, the owner, hurried forward to greet him.

"So good to see you," the plump, bald man said, pumping

his hand. "You look even better than the last time I saw you. Must be a new woman in your life."

"Something like that," Barnes answered. "Did Ed Morley get here yet?"

"He's in the booth at the back."

"Did he order?"

"He said he'd wait for you."

"Is the kitchen still open?"

"For you I will fix whatever you want with my own hands."

"I'm in the mood for pasta."

"How about some fettuccine, with melon and prosciutto to start, and a nice salad."

"I'll leave it up to you."

"And wine?"

"Bring me a bottle of that Montrachet you keep hidden behind the bar."

"French wine with Italian food?"

"It's an old tradition in Texas."

Luigi spread his hands in mock exasperation and disappeared into the kitchen. Barnes walked slowly toward the back of the restaurant, making a deliberate effort not to think about what he was going to say. It was a technique he had learned during his early years as a trial lawyer. Once he had filed the facts in his mind, he functioned better if he didn't formulate a specific plan of attack. It allowed him to sense situations, or changing moods, and to react accordingly.

"How in hell are you, for chris'sake?" He slapped Morley on the back.

"Hungry," Morley said. "I've been waiting nearly an hour."

"I was tied up." He laughed at his private joke. "I tell you, that Bonnie's pure gold."

"Take good care of you, did she?"

"The best."

"So now let's eat."

"Luigi's laboring over a hot stove this very minute."

"I'd like some scampi."

"He's fixing prosciutto. You like ham?"

"It's not against my religion."

"And fettuccine?"

Morley shrugged. "Is it good?"

"Great."

Their conversation remained superficial until a waiter brought a plate of antipasto and poured the wine. Only when Barnes raised his glass in a toast did they touch on the subject that had brought them together.

"To Jake," the attorney said. "God rest him."

"And Bromley," the other man added.

They looked at each other with unblinking steadiness. It was a moment of testing, and only after each had silently assessed the other did they touch glasses.

"When did you hear?" Morley asked.

"Seymour called. He wanted me to light a fire under the people at headquarters who were responsible for getting a rescue crew up to the camp from Dallas."

"I hear they were hours late getting there."

"There were some delays," Barnes said blandly.

"Due to you?"

"I did my best."

"To help or hinder?"

"That depends on your point of view."

Luigi brought the food, which he served from a small burner on a cart. Only after they had tasted it, and assured him it was the best they'd eaten, did he leave, allowing them to resume their conversation.

"Why don't we cut out the bullshit, and get down to the short strokes?" Morley said.

"Fine with me," Barnes replied. "Where would you like me to begin?"

"What did you have in mind when you called me last night?"

"I figured you'd know."

"I'd like you to spell it out," Morley said.

Barnes took a long swallow of his wine. "It occurred to me that if Jake and his son didn't survive the accident the controlling interest in the company was going to be up for grabs."

"Not necessarily. He has a daughter."

"Ceetra?"

"Yes. And the way I understand the law, if she's the only surviving blood relative, his estate goes to her."

"Not if specific provisions in his will forbid it."

"Do they?"

The attorney hesitated. "He didn't want her to get anything. There's a clause which establishes that in the event of Bromley's death Jake's entire estate is to go to a whole bunch of charities. Mostly medical and educational."

"Charity? That's not like the Jake I knew."

"With his son gone it was his only crack left at immortality."

"I don't see where we even come into it, then. Seems pretty clear-cut."

"Only *if* the will goes to probate."

"Why shouldn't it?"

"First it has to be found."

Suddenly Morley understood why Barnes had called. This was his trump card.

"Go on," he said.

"If a man dies intestate his estate is automatically inherited by his immediate next of kin."

"Which brings us back to Ceetra."

"Exactly."

"And you figure you can get her to sell?" Morley made it sound like the notion had just occurred to him when, in fact, it was the one thing on which his plan hinged.

"Depends," the other man said cannily.

"On what's in it for you?"

"That's right."

"If she does sell the board's going to vote to go public. You know they've wanted it for years. The only thing that's stood in their way is Jake. They'll make a fortune. You will, too."

"I don't own that much stock."

"You'd still make a pile."

"But I'd make more if I had a nice piece of Jake's share."

"And how do you plan on getting it?"

"By performing three invaluable services," the lawyer said. "First I destroy the will. Then I persuade Ceetra to sell, and I give you first crack at coming up with the capital that'll be needed to pay for Jake's share."

"That's a favor?"

"I figured that after the way you were screwed out of your original holdings in Rampling International, you'd welcome the chance to get back into the driver's seat."

"You're the one who pulled the rug out, remember?"

"Just doing my job. Nothing personal."

"It'd take a goddam fortune to buy out Jake's stock."

"That's why I called you," Barnes said. "You have a reputation for knowing people with real money."

Morley felt pleased. He had anticipated Barnes perfectly. Now all he had to do was make careful moves. Nothing that would show he already had the financing.

"Where do you come in?" he asked.

"I get half of everything you make off the deal."

"That could be millions."

"I have expensive tastes."

The lobbyist was silent for a full minute.

"Okay," he said finally. "I'll deliver if you do."

"It's a deal." Barnes reached out his hand, and the other man shook it.

"There's just one problem," Morley said. "What happens if Ceetra decides not to sell?"

"She's in deep trouble," the lawyer answered quietly.

 **10**

THE 747 JETLINER lurched as it hit an air pocket, and there was a metallic grinding noise as the pilot lowered the flaps in preparation for landing. Ceetra swallowed hard. She felt the breakfast she'd eaten about an hour earlier rise sickeningly in her stomach, and looked around for a stewardess. But they were already strapped in their seats.

It had been a nightmare journey. She hated flying and was extremely nervous by the time she reached Heathrow Airport. There had been a crowd of reporters at Heathrow, and they'd pestered her with questions until she found sanctuary in the first-class passengers' lounge and four large vodka tonics. They'd given her the courage she needed to endure the terrors of takeoff, and kept her spirits up for the first two or three hours of the trip, but when their effects began to wear off, she once again experienced the anxiety she always felt at being in any kind of confined space.

She tried to allay her panic by focusing her thoughts on the events of the past few days. So much of what had happened since she'd learned of her father's death seemed like a kaleidoscopic whirl. Reporters had dogged her every movement. A whole series of articles appeared in a wide range of newspapers, all with eye-catching headlines: PLAYGIRL WINS JACKPOT ... MILLION DOLLAR BABY— MAYBE! ... POOR LITTLE RICH GIRL.

They capitalized on her party-girl image and fashion world background to fabricate larger-than-life profiles of a beautiful, willful, outspoken, irreverent woman who, although already rich, had suddenly become heiress to one of the world's great fortunes. Nothing was sacred: snapshots taken by other girls at Farleigh House School; photographs shot when she first started out as a fashion designer and was still modeling her own clothes; even a picture taken by a paparazzo with a zoom lens while she was sunbathing nude at a secluded beach near Punta Carena. All were grist for the media mill.

Only one article contained any real substance. It appeared in the *Guardian,* and consisted of an in-depth profile of her father. It detailed his rise from humble origins, and the brilliant but ruthless means he had employed to build Rampling International into the largest firm of its kind in the world. There was mention of Jake's split with his ex-partner, Ed Morley, and the part Mule Barnes had played in finding legal loopholes that enabled her father to ease the other man out. It touched on the bitter battle Jake had fought to retain custody of Bromley, with the veiled implication that having his wife certified "mentally unstable" was just a ploy he had used in order to win. The incident was used as an example of his ruthlessness, and was accompanied by a number of other illustrations of the lengths to which he would go to ensure he got his own way. These included the allegations by high U.S. government officials that he had used bribery in half a dozen foreign countries where Rampling International had won multimillion-dollar contracts. There was also speculation that he may have allowed the Central Intelligence Agency to use the firm as a front for its covert operations abroad, in return for the kind of favored treatment that had resulted in the company's being awarded a contract for the VHST project.

It was the kind of article no newspaper would have dared to publish if Jake had still been alive. The libel laws in England were too strict to risk his bringing suit. But now Jake was dead they had thrown caution to the winds, aware that

they wouldn't be sued for damaging the reputation of somebody who was no longer living.

In mid-week Ceetra had visited her mother at the
sanatorium. Dr. Amsdon had broken the news about the
accident to her the previous day, and she'd gone into shock.
Ceetra was surprised to find her mother quite calm and
seemingly in control of herself. She even showed glimpses of
a brittle gaiety. Only after the first ten or fifteen minutes did
Ceetra begin to realize her mother was existing in some private niche in time. It was an eerie, frightening experience for
Ceetra, like talking to a ghost. Her mother was perfectly
articulate, but what she said in no way related to the present,
and Ceetra had finally realized it was hopeless to try to com-
municate with her.

She had gone to the sanatorium directly after receiving a
call from Mule Barnes, her father's attorney, asking her to go
to Dallas for a special board meeting at which Jake's will was
to be read. He had told her that it was important for her to be
present, as decisions would have to be made relating to the
continued payment of her mother's medical expenses. Until
now Jake had paid them out of his own pocket, but Barnes
told her the situation had changed and other arrangements
would have to be made. Ceetra had hoped to talk the matter
over with her mother before making a decision, but when it
became obvious she was in no condition to understand,
Ceetra determined her own course of action.

Her motivation in making the trip to Texas wasn't really a
material one. If the board decided against continuing payment of her mother's bills, she was more than able to assume
the responsibility herself. Nor did she suppose her father
had left her anything in his will. He had made his feelings
toward her crystal-clear during the last twenty years. Rather,
it was curiosity. She wanted to find out firsthand about the
father and brother she had never known. Until now one had
existed only in the pages of her scrapbook, and the other in
the letters her mother received. This was the best opportunity she would ever have. She knew if she passed it up she

would spend the rest of her life never really knowing what either of them was like. And to do that would be to deny herself an essential part of her own identity.

Andrea had encouraged her to go, agreeing that it was something Ceetra had to do. "I can manage very well on my own while you're away," she said. Then, impulsively, she had wrapped her arms around Ceetra and murmured: "God, I'm going to miss you. Please hurry back."

Now, as the plane sank through cloud cover at about 5,000 feet, Ceetra wished that she had stayed in England. She looked down at the Dallas/Fort Worth Airport. Despite her discomfort she couldn't help but feel a tremor of excitement, and it mounted as the plane touched down and taxied toward a terminal.

She was the last passenger to leave. As the plane emptied, she remained in her seat, belt still fastened, overwhelmed by a powerful feeling of déjà vu. It triggered so much apprehension she couldn't bring herself to move. Finally, when the stewardess brought her coat, she willed herself to get up, but the feeling lingered as she got off the plane and walked slowly up the ramp. She knew she had lived this moment before, and it had been one that made her feel very threatened.

Barnes had told her he would meet her at the airport. She had no idea what the lawyer looked like, but he'd said he would recognize her from her pictures, and so she stood in the pastel-hued lounge area looking around with an outward show of self-assuredness she didn't feel.

The terminal was vast. Its cavernous interior reminded her in some ways of a church, but it lacked an aura of sanctity, and the decor was strictly ultramodern. Precast concrete, steel and acres of tinted glass. Computerized people movers shuttled passengers from the terminal to their cars with an efficiency that astonished her. She had been in a lot of airports, but never seen anything quite like this one.

"Miss Rampling?"

She turned to see a tall, solidly built man wearing a cambric shirt, faded jeans and scuffed boots coming toward her, holding a battered stetson in one hand. There was something vaguely familiar about his strong, handsome features, but she couldn't place him immediately.

"Mule Barnes couldn't meet you." His flecked green eyes studied her coolly. "He asked me to come in his stead. The name's Dan Blake."

Suddenly she realized where she'd seen him before. It was on the first television news bulletin. He was the man who had led a rescue crew down the main shaft. And she remembered the name, too; it was in the letter her mother had read from Bromley.

"How do you do." She offered her hand, and noticed the slight hesitation before he took it. "I have some luggage. Do you know where it would be?"

He led the way to an escalator that took them down to another level of the terminal. It was carpeted and decorated in the same pastel shades as the rest of the building. Luggage was flowing from conveyor belts onto a slightly angled revolving platform from which passengers were plucking their own bags.

"See them?" Dan asked.

She pointed to two beautifully crafted Vuitton suitcases.

"That all?"

"There should be a small valise." She sensed his impatience as they waited for the other bag. When it didn't arrive, he put the two cases he'd already taken off the revolving platform on the floor next to where she was standing.

"Wait here," he said brusquely. "I'll go and check on the other piece."

She watched as he disappeared. His abruptness puzzled her. But before she had time to think about it, a dozen reporters descended on her. Apparently they had expected her to arrive at another terminal, and their frustration showed in the way they jostled each other. The questions they hurled at her were almost identical to the ones she'd been plagued with ever since the accident happened: " . . . How do you feel about your father being killed? . . . Were you close to your brother? . . . Will you inherit a controlling interest in Rampling International? . . . "

Before she could answer, Dan reappeared carrying the lost valise. He scooped up the other two bags, and strode to a waiting car.

"Get in," he said, holding the passenger door open.

"You're a handy person to have around," Ceetra said.

Dan didn't answer. He'd put on a pair of aviator-style sunglasses, and it was impossible for her to see his eyes. But she could sense his hostility.

"Weren't you one of the men who tried to rescue my father?" she asked.

He nodded, but kept his eyes on the road.

"What happened?" she persisted.

"We were too late," he said.

He didn't elaborate, but turned the car into an area of the airport where private planes were parked. Stopping in front of a hangar marked with the intersecting circle emblem of Rampling International, he got out from behind the wheel and crossed to where a mechanic was checking the engine cowling on a Bell helicopter.

"There are some bags in the trunk," Dan told him. "Load them in back, will you?"

The man nodded and hurried toward the car. As Ceetra got out he eyed her legs appreciatively.

"Nice trip, ma'am?"

"Fine. Thank you." Ceetra walked to where Dan was already strapping himself into the pilot's seat. "Where are we going?" she asked.

"The ranch."

"Is it far?"

"About twenty minutes."

She was tempted to ask why they needed a helicopter to go such a short distance, but decided against it and climbed in beside him. Moments later he started the rotor, and the aircraft lifted off the ground.

"I'd still like to know about the rescue attempt," she said, shouting to make herself heard over the roar of the engine.

He shrugged. "They were trapped behind a cave-in below four thousand feet. We blasted a hole through but, like I said, we were too late."

Ceetra was silent for a moment. Then she asked, "What did you find?"

Dan glanced at her, then turned his attention back to the instrument panel. "It wasn't pretty," he said.

His reticence infuriated her. She felt like a child who was being dismissed. No wonder Bromley disliked him. Under different circumstances she would have found a way to penetrate his defensiveness, but the strain of sustaining a conversation over the clatter of the whirling rotor was more than she could face. And the yawing motion of the helicopter was beginning to make her feel sick again.

She looked down at the scene passing below them. They were flying over downtown Dallas. From an altitude of a little over two thousand feet it looked like a collection of monoliths that had been set up to commemorate some great deed. The sun had burned through the overcast, and it glistened from the towering columns of glass and steel. She recognized some of the buildings from articles she had read in magazines about Dallas: First National Bank, Republic Bank Tower, the First International Building. The thing that struck her most forcibly was their sameness. Only the Reunion Tower, with its tubular concrete stem and ball-shaped top, was unique, and it reminded her of a toffee apple on a stick.

"You all right?" Dan shouted.

"Yes, why?"

"You look lousy."

"Thanks."

"I didn't mean it that way."

"Really?" Despite the roar, she managed to infuse the word with heavy irony.

"Guess I rubbed you the wrong way back there, huh?"

"Yes. As a matter of fact I think you were damned rude."

He glanced at her again. There was a trace of a smile on his face. "I read someplace that you're outspoken."

"And strong-willed?"

He nodded.

"You don't know the half of it," she said.

"I'm beginning to believe it," he replied.

"So how about telling me what I want to know."

He was silent for a moment, and when he spoke he didn't look at her. "There was a flash fire. We'd had a safety inspector below the day before, and he found a number of small violations. Not enough to red-tag the operation, but sufficient for quite a few changes to be made."

"Red-tag?"

"It indicates a hazard which should be corrected but that work can still continue," Dan explained. "If he'd figured the situation was serious enough to warrant shutting down the project he'd have given it a yellow tag."

"You mean men were allowed to continue working even though the inspector knew the conditions were hazardous?"

"He didn't figure it was a life-threatening problem."

"Seems he was wrong," Ceetra said.

"Methane gas has a way of collecting in pockets of rock," Dan said. "Test meters don't show any sign of it until a breakthrough is made. Then it's too late."

"Was it the explosion that killed them?" she asked.

Dan shook his head. "The fire."

"And the bodies—?" Her voice trailed away.

"I've talked enough."

"Let me decide that," she snapped.

"The heat fused them together. They weren't bodies. Just a tarry black mess. We didn't bring 'em out, but the guys who did had to wear gas masks. There wasn't enough left to tell who was who."

Ceetra sensed that he was deliberately trying to hurt her.

"Surely they could have used dental charts, X rays . . ."

110

"For what?" he asked angrily. "We knew who was down there."

"Relatives might have wanted to bury the remains of their—"

"We couldn't even pry them apart," he said. "They were buried in a mass grave."

Ceetra felt sick. She grabbed a paper bag from a recess in the door of the helicopter, and vomited into it.

"Here." Dan handed her a large handkerchief.

"I've got one of my own." She felt in her coat pocket, but couldn't find it.

"Go on, take it," he insisted.

She reluctantly obeyed. "I'll let you have it back."

"When it's washed?"

She knew he was trying to ease the tension between them, but made no attempt to help him.

"I wouldn't have told you," he said.

"I asked."

"That's right."

They remained silent until the helicopter circled the ranch and began its descent. The ranch was situated east of Dallas, near a town called Sunnyvale, and from the air there was nothing particularly impressive in its appearance. Her mother had always referred to it simply as "the ranch," and because she couldn't remember it, Ceetra had created a composite in her mind of the way she supposed it was, an image that closely resembled the ranch in the oil painting on the wall of her London apartment. But what she saw now bore no relationship to that prototype. It was just a complex of sprawling adobe buildings scattered over ten or twelve acres. They seemed to have been put up as needs dictated, and were linked together by short covered walkways.

The helicopter touched down in a swirl of dust a short distance from the largest of the buildings. When the air cleared Ceetra saw a tall man walking toward the craft. He had pale, washed-out eyes and fleshy jowls, and moved with a lugubrious shuffle. He opened the door before the rotor stopped turning.

"Howdy! I'm Leroy Barnes," he announced in a booming voice. "Mule to my friends. Welcome home, little lady."

When he helped her out, she noticed his fingernails were manicured and lightly lacquered. They contrasted oddly with his ill-fitting blue suit and string tie held by a silver clasp shaped like a pair of buffalo horns.

"My lands!" he exclaimed, holding her at arm's length. "But you've certainly grown into a fine-looking woman." He studied her through squinted eyes. "Last time I saw you, why, you were just a tiny little thing."

Ceetra smiled. She found Barnes overwhelming and didn't quite know how to respond.

"Have a fair trip, did you?"

"Well, as a matter of fact—"

"Nothing like travel to broaden the mind," he declared, cutting her reply short. "Particularly for young people like yourself."

This time she just nodded.

"I'm right sorry about not meeting you at the airport," he continued. "A whole slew of things came up right at the last minute. But I just know that Dan here took right good care of you, eh?"

"Right good," she replied, unconsciously mimicking what seemed to her like an exaggerated Texas drawl.

"Well, that's real fine. Now why don't you come on in and set a spell?"

Ceetra looked at Dan, who was unloading her luggage.

"Thanks for the ride," she said.

He tipped his hat. "Any time."

She followed Barnes as he led the way inside, talking continuously in his folksy manner. Her instinct warned that he was deliberately exuding fatherly charm for a reason. What she didn't know was why.

"You must be worn to a frazzle," he commiserated. "What with the time change and all."

"I am feeling a bit of jet lag," she admitted.

"Why don't you take a little nap?" He looked at his watch. "The funeral service doesn't begin till three o'clock. You could get in a couple of hours."

"I'm too tense to sleep."

"Sure you are." His voice took on a sympathetic note. "I want you to know I'm real sorry about your daddy and young Bromley. What happened was awful. Just terrible. I imagine you'll be glad when this whole thing's over."

Ceetra didn't answer.

"You'll be going back to London directly after the board meeting next Thursday, I imagine?"

"Board meeting?"

"That's when I'll be reading your daddy's will."

"I see." She paused. "I'd like to see where he died before I leave."

"The tunnel?"

"Yes."

His facade seemed to slip a little and she glimpsed the taut concern underlying his folksiness.

"That camp's no place for a little girl—"

"I'm twenty-six years old, Mr. Barnes," she said coolly. "And I make my own decisions."

"Of course you do." He slipped back into his role of genial host. "No offense intended. Well—if you don't want to sleep, maybe you'd like me to show you around the ranch."

"I'd rather see it alone," she said. "It's been twenty years. There are a lot of memories to catch up on."

"Go right ahead. Make yourself at home. If there's anything you need just ring the nearest bell and a servant will help you."

"Thank you."

"I've got some business to finish up," he said. "But I'll be back to pick you up for the funeral around two-thirty."

Ceetra watched him talk quietly to an elderly Mexican woman who was busily arranging various cold dishes on a series of massive oak tables that had been lined up next to each other. The woman glanced at her and nodded.

"Maria's fixing a few things for the reception," he said. "If you're hungry she says for you to help yourself."

"I don't feel much like anything right now," she replied.

"Well, it's there if you want it."

She waited until he left and then decided to do some exploring.

As she wandered through the house, she was affected by the atmosphere of the place. The silence was absolute. Her footsteps were absorbed by wall-to-wall carpeting that was so thick it was like walking on moss. But the most distinctive characteristic of the place was its smell: a muskiness she had previously always associated with churches. It triggered a reaction in her subconscious, and provided the link to the past she'd been seeking. Fragments of long-suppressed memory slowly filtered into her mind. They were all visceral: anxiety as she walked down a long, dark corridor; a surge of joy at glimpsing dappled sunlight on a rug woven in rich hues; a claustrophobic fear of losing herself in the complex of rooms.

There were photographs everywhere, though none of her. Most showed Jake and Bromley together in various settings: at rodeos, hunting, fishing, skiing, sailing. The pictures recorded every phase of Bromley's growing up, from earliest childhood to a shot taken of him at the controls of a single-engined Cessna in his late teens.

One whole room, which appeared to have been her father's study, was devoted to the trophies Bromley had won at sports. They ranged from bronc riding to skeet shooting, and included a small bronze statue of a horse forever frozen in mid-air as it sailed over a hurdle. The walls were decorated with the heads of stuffed animals—moose, deer, bears—and under each was a small brass plaque recording the date and place of the kill.

She stood in the center of the richly paneled room and felt the presence of her father all around her. It was almost tangible: the stale smell of cigar smoke, a large glass display case containing half a dozen shotguns with ornately engraved barrels, a model in miniature of a huge oil refinery that was protected from dust under a Plexiglas covering. The place looked as if it had remained untouched since the last time he was in it. The ashtray hadn't been emptied. Some of the drawers in the desk were half-open. Papers were strewn about everywhere, as if caught by the wind and scattered like leaves.

For a long time she remained motionless, letting the ambience envelop her. It was the closest she had come to her father in over twenty years, and she relished the moment. She crossed to the desk and sat in the chair behind it. The leather was torn and cracked in places. She ran her fingers over the areas that had been smoothed by wear, knowing she was touching the same places he had touched.

Sorting through the documents spread on the desk top she saw his signature and traced over it with the tip of her little finger. They were mostly blueprints or cost projections and so highly technical she could barely begin to understand them. Suddenly, it occurred to her that although her father had only received a minimum of formal education, and had never attended college, he must have possessed a vast reservoir of knowledge about everything relating to his business.

Finally, she got up and started for the door. On the way she passed a huge fireplace. It was big enough to take three or four six-foot logs, but now the grate was filled with the ashes of burned papers. The flames hadn't completely destroyed them, and there was enough left for her to see that the documents were similar to those she had examined on the desk. One bore the heading: VHST—FAULT LINE STUDIES. Another: REPAYMENT SCHEDULE ON LOANS FOR—The rest was charred and unreadable. Curious, she ran the toe of her shoe through the ashes, but found only one other piece of paper that was at all legible. It carried the stamp of the Amarillo Police Department, and appeared to be a standard arrest report. But the flames had seared it so thoroughly that the contents were undecipherable.

She left the study, and after making her way down a long, narrow corridor, emerged into an enclosed courtyard. It contained a number of small lemon trees. The air was heavy with their sweet fragrance. They also offered shade from the heat of the glaring overhead sun. She squatted on the grass next to a shallow pond that was filled with water lilies. A variety of fish, ranging in color from gold to the deepest hue of red, swam slowly under the broad floating leaves. She walked across the beautifully manicured grass to look through a large sliding-glass door on the opposite side of the enclosure. The room beyond was too dark for her to discern any details, but when she leaned against the glass it moved, and she realized the door was unlocked. She slid it open and went inside.

It was a moment or two before her eyes adjusted from the glare outside to the gloom of the interior. While she waited she became aware of a strong odor in the room. It was similar to the scent of the blossoms on the lemon tree in the courtyard, but greatly magnified—so much so that the air was sickening to breathe. Then she saw why. Vases containing cuttings of the lemon blossoms had been placed all around the room, and it was obvious that the water in them hadn't been changed for some time. Closer inspection of the vases revealed that the blossoms had been arranged with considerable skill, and it was apparent that whoever placed them had a strong artistic sense.

She flipped a light switch and the room was suddenly illuminated by a soft pinkish glow from bulbs cleverly hidden behind slatted wooden panels. It created an effect that was at once restful and unreal. Mirrors paneled the whole of one wall. The image she saw was diffuse and tinted. The light switch also activated a tape machine that was hooked up to an elaborate system of high-fidelity speakers, and the mellow strains of Sibelius's *Finlandia* flooded the room.

Intrigued by her discovery, she studied the place more

closely. The bookshelves contained volumes on ecology, the American Indian, Zen philosophy, and art. There was a particularly large collection of beautifully illustrated books on the ballet. Alongside them was a large folder containing skillfully drawn charcoal sketches of nude figures—all of them male.

But it was two other finds that made her realize she was in her brother's room. The first was an album of photographs filled with pictures of her mother. Bromley had pasted cutouts of himself alongside her in an attempt to make it appear the two of them had actually been together when the snapshots were taken. The second was a half-finished letter that was still in the typewriter. It was addressed to "My Precious Mother" and contained sentiments that would have been more appropriate between lovers than a son writing to a parent. The final words were: "I don't know what to do. This time I'm really afraid . . ." The sentence was incomplete.

She turned at the sound of the glass door being slid even further open, and saw a white-haired man looking at her with rheumy eyes. He had baby-smooth, pinkish skin that was unlined, but when he spoke there was a faint tremor of age in his voice.

"What are you doing in here?" he asked.

"Just looking. I thought—"

"Who are you?"

"Ceetra Rampling."

"I'll be damned. Ceetra, eh? You couldn't possibly remember me."

"No, I'm sorry."

"Of course not." He moved out of the glare of the sun and offered her his hand. "Silly of me to ask. You were far too young when I last saw you. I'm Dr. Robinson—Earl Robinson—I brought you into this world. Delivered both you and Bromley."

Ceetra suddenly became conscious she was still holding the album of photographs.

"I was just looking at these," she said.

The old man glanced at the album and shook his head. "The boy missed his mother, all right. More than he ever let on, I guess."

"What was he like?"

"Very quiet, introspective—liked to spend a lot of time by himself. Not too many people got close to him."

"Except my father?"

"He thought so, but—well, I often wondered how well he really knew Bromley."

"What do you mean?"

"Jake was a strong-willed man. When he got a notion in his mind nothing on God's earth was going to change it."

"And he had a 'notion' about Bromley?"

"From the day he was born."

"What was it?'

"He wanted the boy to be the spittin' image of himself."

"Was he?"

"He tried. Lord how he tried."

"But he failed?"

"Not entirely. He more than measured up in a lot of ways. It's just that . . ." The doctor paused. "Well, he had another side to him."

"That's what I thought." Ceetra motioned her head toward the charcoal sketches, and the typewriter containing the half-finished letter. "All this is so different from the impression I got of him from the pictures and trophies in my father's study."

Dr. Robinson looked at his watch. He seemed nervous and ill-at-ease. "I've got to go," he said.

"Couldn't we talk a few minutes more?" Ceetra pleaded. "It's been over twenty years, and there's so much I still don't understand."

The doctor shook his head. "I'm sorry."

He turned and walked quickly across the tree-shaded courtyard. Ceetra hurried after him. But before she could question him further, he entered a small guest house situated near the entrance to the ranch.

She followed and saw two open caskets lying across sawhorses in the middle of the room. An overweight, ruddy-faced man was in the process of closing the lids. He looked up as she entered.

"Get her outta here," he snapped. "This ain't no place for a woman."

But Ceetra had already seen that both coffins were empty.

"What the hell's going on here?" Mule Barnes strode into the room.

"She followed me," Dr. Robinson said weakly.

"Leave us be," the other man said curtly.

Dr. Robinson did as he was told.

"And you get the lid on those things right quick," he added, addressing himself to the man standing next to the coffins.

"But they're empty," Ceetra said.

"Now don't you fret." Barnes put an arm protectively around her shoulder, and led her out into the bright afternoon sun. A long black Cadillac limousine was parked in the driveway, and he helped her into the spacious rear seat. "I'll explain all about what you saw in there."

"I wish you would," she said, disengaging his arm.

"The fire was so intense there was no way to identify the victims," he said. "Your daddy and brother were buried along with the others in a mass grave up near the tunnel site."

"Dan told me." She noticed a quick movement of his eyes. "But I didn't realize he meant—everybody."

"The funeral is just a mark of respect on the part of folks who knew your daddy. People find comfort in a bit of ritual in trying times. Particularly families. Quite a few couldn't get up north for the ceremony there, so they'll be at the funeral today. It's their way of paying respects." He paused. "The coffins are just a symbol, if you get what I mean."

Ceetra didn't question him any further. She had begun to feel like a somnambulant moving through a bad dream.

John Sherlock

The funeral service was held at the First Baptist Church at Ervay and San Jacinto Streets in Dallas. The nearly 4,000 guests included senators, congressmen, three members of the President's cabinet, and numerous high-level officials from half a dozen foreign countries. They listened as the hundred-member choir, in white robes and red sashes, sang hymns designed to catch their hearts and turn them toward the faith.

The burial took place at Sparkman—Hillcrest Cemetery, to which guests were driven in a serpentine cortege of gleaming black limousines. The cloudless sky of only an hour before had turned ominously dark, and the air was heavy with the dank smell of earth that presages rain. Guests stood around the open grave site striving to appear unconcerned by the threatened downpour. Lawyers, doctors, oil men, bankers, they were the men who powered Texas. A few were old, their hair gone white. The others were greying, with thickening bodies encased in good wool suits. They were close-shaven and time had broken their squarish faces into many separate planes. They stood a little apart from each other, in the manner of men of power and achievement, as if their presence extended physically beyond them in an aura which demanded respect and distance.

One of the guests was so different from the others that Ceetra felt curious about him. He first caught her eye during the service at the church. Although he was neatly dressed in a dark grey suit, white shirt and narrow blue tie, there was a blandness to his outfit that suggested to her trained eye that the clothes had been newly bought off the rack in a department store catering to low-income customers. And his features were different. While the other guests looked chiseled and well-barbered, his face had a softness and darkness of coloring that implied a Mediterranean heritage.

Now, as she stood alongside the open grave, she glanced at him out of the corner of her eye, and suddenly realized he was watching her. At the same moment it started to rain. The shower quickly turned to a steady downpour. Barnes got an umbrella from one of the chauffeurs and held it over her solicitously. But when he had to move away to play his part in the ritual of burial by throwing a handful of soggy earth on each of the empty coffins, he handed the umbrella to Dan.

He was no longer wearing the faded jeans and scuffed boots he'd had on when he met her at the airport, but was dressed in a well-cut gabardine suit, tie and highly polished shoes. He didn't speak, but when she slipped in the mud as they were leaving the gravesite, he firmly gripped her arm. They passed the man who had been watching her. He was hunched over trying to fit a plastic rain cover over his hat. He looked up and nodded at Dan.

"Who is he?" Ceetra asked.

"An investigator for OSHA," Dan replied.

"OSHA?"

"Occupational Safety and Health Administration."

"Is he the man who issued the warnings you told me about?"

"No. He was a local man. Works out of Lubbock. Al Hunter's looking into the accident for the OSHA people in Washington."

"What's he doing here?"

"George Gains, the man he works for, started out with your father. Gains quit when he got emphysema. Took a desk job."

Barnes had joined them, and she noticed him take a quick glance at Al Hunter, who was still struggling with the rain cover on his hat, even though he was already drenched to the skin.

"Who the hell invited him?" he asked.

"Gains couldn't get here," Dan replied. "He called me and asked if it was okay for Hunter to pay his respects for him."

"And you said yes?"

"Gains and Jake go back a long way together."

"You should have checked with me first," the other man said testily.

Ceetra was surprised at Barnes's brusqueness, but if it bothered Dan he showed no sign of it. After holding the door of the limousine open for her, he tipped his stetson and disappeared into the crowd that was now hurrying to get out of the rain. Rather than attempt conversation with Barnes, she put her head back against the seat and closed her eyes. The driver had turned on the heater. The warmth inside the car, combined with the soft hiss of the tires on the wet freeway, was enough to lull her to the brink of unconsciousness.

But she didn't sleep. She remained in that twilight area where the body rests, but the mind continues to work. Bits and pieces of thought filtered in and out of her mind: The conversation with Dan Blake ... first impressions of Mule Barnes ... her father's study ... Bromley's room ... the photographs he'd tried to splice together ... the half-finished letter ... Dr. Robinson's unwillingness to provide any answers ... the empty coffins.

"We're there." The voice seemed to come from far away, but when she opened her eyes, she saw Barnes leaning over her. "It's good you got a rest. Another couple of hours and this whole thing'll be over."

They proved to be the longest two hours of Ceetra's life. The ranch was crowded with guests who were eager to meet her and took advantage of the reception to make themselves known. A few claimed to have been childhood friends, but she didn't remember any of them, a fact that two or three found difficult to accept. Others were obviously trying to ingratiate themselves for reasons best known to themselves. Perhaps, she thought, it was because they believed what they read in the *Dallas Morning News* and other newspapers about her being heir apparent to Jake's fortune. She couldn't help thinking how put out they were going to be when they discovered nothing could be further from the case.

Only two of the dozens of people to whom Barnes introduced her really came into focus. One was Ed Morley, the man the article in the *Guardian* had described in such detail as her father's former partner. She was surprised to see him at the reception and her expression must have shown it, because when he spoke to her it was almost by way of apology.

"Your father and I didn't always see eye to eye," he said. "But he was a great man. I just want you to know how deeply sorry I am about what happened to him and Bromley."

"Good of you to come." She saw the coldness in his eyes and quickly moved on to greet other guests before Morley could engage her in further conversation.

The other person who made a strong impression was David Seymour. And for a very different reason. His grief was so obviously genuine she would have picked up on it even if they hadn't spoken.

"I'm so glad to meet you," she said. "My brother talked very warmly about you in the letters he wrote to my mother."

"We were quite close," Seymour said.

She noticed the break in his voice and gently touched his hand.

"I know he appreciated your friendship," she said.

Before she could say anything further, Barnes took her arm and guided her through the crowd of people who were milling around in hopes of meeting her. It was beginning to get dark when the guests finally began to leave. By that time she was fatigued to the point of numbness and barely able to stand.

"Miss Rampling!"

The voice came from behind her. When she turned a glass of champagne spilled down the front of her dress. It was cold enough to snap her out of the lethargy into which she had begun to sink. The person responsible for the accident stood a few feet away looking at his empty glass: it was the man who had watched her at the funeral.

"Sorry," he murmured. "But you caught me with a left hook."

He took a linen napkin and began blotting the champagne from the halter of her soaked dress.

"Please—I'll do it," she said sharply.

He handed her the napkin. "You don't get much experience in social graces where I come from."

His Brooklyn accent was so pronounced even Ceetra recognized it.

"I'm all right, really," she insisted.

"My boss, George Gains, was a friend of your father's," he said.

"Yes, I know. Dan Blake told me."

"So you know who I am?"

"An investigator for some agency in Washington, I think he said."

"OSHA."

"That's right."

"Then maybe you wouldn't mind answering a few questions for me," he said.

Barnes hurried to Ceetra's side.

"What's happening here?" he asked.

"Mr. Hunter has launched his investigation of me with champagne," she replied.

"Investigation?"

"He wants to ask me some questions."

"The hell he does."

"Purely routine," Hunter assured him.

"Anybody with an ounce of breeding would know this is neither the time nor the place for—"

"Etiquette was never my strong suit," Hunter said. "I majored in engineering."

"I think it's time you left," Barnes said firmly.

"Maybe you're right." Hunter looked at Ceetra. "If I offended you, please accept my apologies. And if you send me the bill for getting the dress cleaned I'd be glad to pay it."

"Forget it," she said.

"I'll check Emily Post, and next time I see you—"

"There won't be a next time," Barnes said. "Miss Rampling is returning to London very soon."

"That right?"

Ceetra felt both men looking at her with an intensity that transcended casual interest.

"I'm not sure," she replied after a long hesitation. "A lot depends on what happens in the next few days."

 *11*

DAN PAUSED outside the trailer. The camp looked strangely life-less. The heavy-duty equipment that would ordinarily be in use was now parked in neat lines on a dirt area to one side of the main shaft, and the only sign of activity was a dozen workers being lowered in the man trip to relieve the crew that was clearing debris at the 4,700-foot level. Because of the confined space, and the fact that the fan lines and ventilating fans still hadn't been fully restored, it was impossible to put more than eighteen or twenty men on a shift at one time. It had been eleven days since the accident, but cleanup operations were still moving at a snail's pace. Until they were fully completed the rest of the project was at a complete standstill.

As Dan strode through the swirling dust, he heard noise from the union meeting taking place in the recreation hall. As he got nearer the single-story wooden building he was able to distinguish voices above the rhythmic thud of feet being stamped on the floor, and when he opened the swing doors the tumult engulfed him.

The air was so thick with cigarette smoke that everything appeared filtered through a blue veil. It was a moment or two before he got his bearings. He recognized shop stewards from a number of unions: Underground Laborers, Operating Engineers, Teamsters, United Mine Workers, International Brotherhood of Electrical Workers. But the focus of attention was Harry Gallagher. He stood behind an upended packing crate that served as a makeshift lectern, and was trying to make himself heard above the roar of the audience.

"I maintain it's—" The rest of his words were drowned out by the uproar, and he waited for his listeners to quiet down.

The recreation hall had been designed to hold a hundred people, but as Dan looked around he estimated that at least sixty to eighty extra people had managed to squeeze in. They squatted on the floor, stood jammed shoulder to shoulder against the walls, and even sat on the laminated beams which supported the roof. They were angry. It showed in their faces, and in the intensity with which they argued among themselves. The air was filled with shouted epithets and minor scuffles broke out at two or three places in the hall. Almost fifteen minutes passed before Gallagher even tried making himself heard again.

"It's time we faced facts," he announced, still shouting to make himself heard above the hubbub. "A job like this is no place for on-the-job trainees."

A thin man with a bushy beard and clean-shaved head cupped his hands and bellowed: "Bullshit!"

Gallagher ignored the heckling. "We've already seen what it can lead to—"

"Why don't you say what's really bothering you?" the bearded man yelled. "The truth is you don't want us in the union."

"That's right," Gallagher replied.

"You're afraid us newcomers'll take your lousy jobs."

"It's our lives we're afraid of losing!"

A group of miners seated near the stage clapped and whistled shrilly.

"Why don't you drop dead?" somebody shouted from the back of the hall.

"Eighty poor bastards already have," Gallagher snapped angrily. "And all because they had to depend on people like you who are still wet behind the ears!"

Another uproar erupted.

"Listen—" A short, squat man with pug features stood on a chair a short distance from the stage waving his hands in an effort to attract attention.

"Siddown!" a chorus of voices yelled.

"Give him a chance," Gallagher said. "What's on your mind?"

"It's just that—well—" Now that he was suddenly the focus of interest the man hesitated nervously.

"Spit it out!" somebody shouted.

The man on the chair cleared his throat. "I got a wife and three kids—"

Rhythmic clapping greeted his statement.

"Let him get it off his chest," Gallagher said.

"Almost a year. That's how long I been out of work." Anger gave the squat man the confidence he'd lacked. "This trainee program is my chance to get a new start, and still earn enough money to keep my family off welfare—"

He paused, as if expecting a new round of heckling, but it didn't come. The genuineness of his emotion had somehow communicated itself to his listeners.

"All I'm asking is for you to give us a break," he continued. "Every one of you guys was a beginner somewhere along the way. Right?"

The room had suddenly turned quiet. There was an uneasy stir as men self-consciously shifted in their seats.

"Fine," Gallagher said, finally breaking the taut silence. "But while you're learning, it's our balls that are in the wringer!"

A murmur of agreement rippled round the room. But there was less charge in the air now, and Dan's instincts told him the flash point had passed. This was confirmed moments later when the crowd started to disperse. Gallagher was among the last to leave. He had difficulty climbing down from the stage, and walked with a pronounced limp as he made his way toward the back of the now almost empty hall.

"You had 'em going real good for a while," Dan said.

The other man shook his head. He was sweating and there were dark rings under his eyes. "I don't know. Shit, nothing's simple anymore."

"Never was. How's the knee?"

"Like somebody hammered a nail through it."

"See a doctor?"

"Nah. Whadda they know?" Gallagher stood wrapped deep in his own thoughts for a minute. "Dumb bastard had a point, huh?"

Dan shrugged. "I guess."

"Crazy fuckin' business. Why the fuck did I ever let them con me into being a shop steward?"

Dan didn't attempt an answer. He knew the other man had devoted most of his working years to the union. It was the focus of his whole life. But as Dan watched Gallagher limp out through the swing doors he sensed he was preoccupied by worries that went beyond the ones he had heard him express this evening. In recent months he had become increasingly withdrawn, and often spent hours alone in his trailer. Dan had tried to discover what was bothering him, but without success. He either clammed up or changed the subject.

Half the lights suddenly went out. The hall appeared empty. He started to leave, but stopped when he heard footsteps. They came from the far end of the room that was now shrouded in darkness. Seconds later he saw Ceetra Rampling emerge from the shadows.

He had thought about her a number of times since he last saw her at the funeral. When he had met her at the airport she'd seemed to be exactly what he expected: arrogant, self-willed, spoiled. Yet during the short helicopter flight to the ranch he'd found himself admiring her spirit. The way she pushed for details of how Jake died showed she wasn't squeamish when it came to facing facts. It had left him with the strong impression she had more of her father in her than he'd anticipated.

"What brought you up here?" he asked.

"The company plane," she replied.

"I mean—"

"Would you believe I wanted to return this?" She proffered the handkerchief he had given her when she was sick in the helicopter. It was washed and neatly ironed.

"Not for a minute," he said.

"Didn't think so." She folded the handkerchief and slid it in the pocket of his parka.

"So why did you come?" he persisted.

"To see where my father died."

Dan suddenly felt oafish, and tried to hide it by mumbling. "It's just that I was surprised you were at the meeting."

"A man at the landing strip said I'd find you here," she replied.

There was a strained silence.

"Staying overnight?" he asked finally.

She nodded. "Mr. Seymour's arranged a room for me at the project guest house. I'm taking the plane back to Dallas first thing in the morning."

"There's not much to see. The only people allowed down the main shaft are the crews clearing the debris. The tunnel won't be in operation until Friday at the earliest."

"I just wanted to get the feel of the place."

"The meeting should have given you a pretty fair idea about what's going on."

"A lot of it didn't make much sense."

"It's simple enough," he said. "They're mad as hell."

"About the accident?"

"That only sparked it. Trouble's been brewing a long time."

"Union problems?"

"That's the way Gallagher made it sound, but the real causes go a lot deeper."

As they talked the other half of the lights went out. Dan took Ceetra's arm and led her outside. The sun had sunk toward the horizon, and its glare was softened by the ever-present clouds of churning dust. Signs of life had returned to camp. A game of baseball was underway on the diamond; two teams were engaged in a rowdy game of touch football; a metallic clink sounded from a spot near the cookhouse where men were tossing horseshoes.

Nearer to where the two of them stood, an operator was putting his bulldozer through a series of complex maneuvers in preparation for the heavy-equipment rodeo that had been rescheduled because of the accident for early the following week. The movements of the huge, yellow-painted machine were precise and fluid, its enormous bulk somehow lightened by the skill with which the driver handled it.

"You're in luck," Dan said. "Dave Ebins is about the best there is when it comes to handling a 'dozer."

Ceetra sensed his respect and tried to fathom its cause. To her the caterpillar tractor looked like a lumbering yellow behemoth.

"What's he doing?" she asked, shouting to make herself heard over the engine's roar.

"Practicing. Not that he needs to, really. We've worked together on projects all over the world. I remember one time on the Alaska Pipeline—" He paused and smiled to himself. "Damnedest thing I ever saw."

"What happened?"

"It was late spring," he said. "We had to get some heavy winches up a three-thousand-foot pass in the Brooks Range. Normally, we'd have used a chopper, but the snow was melting and the downdraft from the rotor could have started an avalanche. Ebins volunteered to take a bulldozer up. Everybody figured he was crazy. If the snow shifted, they knew there was no way to stop the 'dozer rolling. But that didn't bother Ebins. Hell, he went up the side of that pass like he was on a goddam Sunday drive. His fuel lines froze, but he pissed on 'em and kept going. When the sweat from his forehead ran over his goggles and froze, he had to take them off. The sun was shining and glare was real bad. About a hundred yards from the top he started going snow-blind. He

132

had a two-way radio and I talked him up the rest of the way." Dan shook his head. "Saved us a three-week delay."

Ceetra didn't know how to react. For all she knew, he might have been talking about something that had happened on the moon. And for the first time she began to realize just how vast the chasm was that separated the world she knew from the one in which her father existed. Camps like these were his and Dan's natural habitat, but she felt like a stranger here. Mule Barnes had warned her against coming and she'd taken umbrage. Now she wondered if he hadn't been looking out for her best interests.

"You were with my father a long time, weren't you?" she said.

"Nearly fifteen years."

"I barely remember him. What was he like?"

"Jake?" Dan stuck his hands deep in the pockets of his quilted parka and stared at his scuffed boots. "He had dirt under his fingernails."

"Dirt?" she sounded puzzled.

"The stuff the reporters liked to write about—the ranch, the fancy new headquarters in Dallas, the fleet of company planes, the yacht—it was all just a lot of window dressing. He liked to be where the work was being done. Right in the thick of it, getting his hands dirty."

"Is that why he was so successful?"

"I guess that was part of the reason," he said. "A lot of guys who make it big lose touch with the thing that made them winners in the first place. But not Jake. He always kept a finger on the pulse of what was going on. Knew every damn thing there was to know about all of Rampling's projects."

"But that was only part of the reason?"

"Yeah." Dan squinted his eyes as he looked into the sun. "Well, he loved to win, too. Didn't figure the game was worth playing unless he ended up with all the chips. Not that money meant a damn thing to him. Hell, half the time I'd have to remind him he'd been wearing the same clothes for a week." He shook his head. "Nah, winning was everything to Jake. And he didn't give much of a goddam how he did it."

As he talked they had walked to the outer fringes of the camp. Although the sun was still above the horizon, the floodlights ringing the perimeter had come on. They gave off a cold, harsh illumination that made everything seem oddly lifeless.

"Where's the mass grave you told me about?" she asked.

"Over near Amarillo."

The wind suddenly turned chill and she shivered.

"Here." Dan took off his parka and draped it over her shoulders. "It always gets this way toward night."

"Thanks," she said.

His gesture surprised her. From the moment of their first meeting at the airport he had been distant and she'd sensed he disapproved of her. His only concession had been giving her his handkerchief when she got sick in the helicopter. Now she wondered if she'd judged him too hastily.

"I'd better get you back to the guest house," he said.

It had begun to get dark. Night seemed to emphasize the vastness of the Panhandle, and left Ceetra feeling acutely alone. Instinctively, she took Dan's arm and pressed herself closer to him as they walked in silence back toward camp.

"Did my father ever talk about me?" she asked as they neared the now-empty baseball diamond.

"Some," Dan said.

"What did he say?"

"Just general things. You know—" The words hung there, and she knew he was trying to spare her feelings.

"I used to send him Christmas cards," she said. "But he never responded."

"He wasn't much when it came to sentiment."

"Was he that way with Bromley, too?"

"I guess—"

"Did you like him?"

"Jake?"

"Bromley."

He hesitated. "He was a nice enough kid. It's just that I had a tough time understanding him."

"Did he get along with my father?"

"He tried. But they were made of different stuff."

"What—"

"Why all the questions?" he asked, suddenly irritable.

"I was five years old when I last saw him," Ceetra replied. "Twenty years of wondering about somebody—a parent— well, it leaves quite a void."

They walked on in silence. A shimmering veil of billowing dust made the lights from the camp dance like fireflies. The sound of laughter from workers waiting outside the cafeteria rose and fell, whipped by the wind. The night air had turned raw. There was a bitter-cold edge to it that cut through to the bone. Ceetra felt the strength of Dan's arm, and the warmth of his body. It gave her the comfort she needed at that moment, and when they came to the path that led to the project guest house she didn't want to leave him.

"Will you show me some more of the camp?" she asked.

"It's no place for a woman."

"You're the second person to tell me that."

"Oh?"

"Mule Barnes said the same thing."

"He was right."

"Maybe, but it doesn't sound any better coming from you than it did from him."

Dan glanced at her, surprised by her sudden pique, but didn't say anything.

"It's just that I have to leave in the morning," she added, more softly. "They're going to read my father's will at a board meeting on Friday."

"I know. I'll be there."

"Are you a stockholder?"

"Lowest on the totem pole," he said. "Jake once gave me a few shares as a bonus."

135

"You're higher than me," Ceetra said. "I'll just be there as a spectator. Then it's back to London. So this is my only real chance to see the camp."

"I don't know—"

"All right." She dropped his arm. "I'll go on my own."

She had taken a couple of paces when he grabbed her elbow. "No you don't. It can get rough in there."

Dan led the way toward the main part of the camp. He had relinquished his hold on her arm, and didn't take it again. Walking two or three paces ahead, he managed to create the impression he wanted to get the tour over with as quickly as possible. In some strange way he seemed threatened by the moment of closeness they had shared. Ceetra flashed on a long-forgotten fragment of memory: her father picking her up and holding her, then abruptly putting her down when her mother arrived to take her to the airport for the trip to London. She had experienced the same confusion and hurt she was feeling now.

"What's the hurry?" she asked.

"I've got things to do," he replied brusquely.

She deliberately slowed her pace. When he saw she was lagging behind he shortened his steps.

"I'd like to take a look inside the bunkhouses," she said.

"I wouldn't, if I were you."

"You're not me."

Before he could stop her she started up the steps leading to the nearest bunkhouse. They were built in tiers, four stories high, and overlooked the main shaft. The corridor she entered was narrow and dimly lit. It smelled strongly of disinfectant. The sound of country-western music blasted from public address speakers set high on the wall. A door opened and a man poked his head out. His eyes widened with surprise when he saw her.

"You ain't gonna believe what I'm lookin' at," he said.

Seconds later three more heads peered over his shoulder.

"Wowee!" one of them yelled. "Come right to Daddy, sugar."

"Don't pay him no heed," another shouted. "I got what you're lookin' for, baby!"

Other doors along the corridor slammed open, and men poured into the hallway. Many of them were only wearing jockey shorts. One was naked. Their whistles were earsplitting in the narrow confines of the passageway.

Ignoring the ruckus, she looked inside the nearest room. It contained four iron cots. Two had been shoved together to form a makeshift table for shooting craps. The others were littered with freshly laundered clothes somebody had been in the midst of folding when the disturbance started.

"Satisfied?"

She turned and saw Dan standing behind her.

"They act like I'm the first woman they've seen in months," she said.

He took her arm. This time his grip was painfully firm as he propelled her back down the steps.

"For a lot of 'em you are." He tried to sound stern, but she knew he was trying to control a grin. "The nearest town's Amarillo, and that's about a hundred and thirty miles away. Quite a few of the guys stay in camp to save money. They figure the quicker they make a stake, the sooner they get back to their families."

"Sounds like a prison."

He shrugged. "They're free to quit any time."

"It isn't natural for men to be without women that long."

"Oh, there are plenty of whorehouses in Amarillo. A place called Vanita Beth's gets most of the business. My problem's seeing the men get back to camp after they've been cleaned out. We're always several workers short on shifts after a weekend."

As they got deeper into camp it wasn't necessary for Ceetra to enter bunkhouses in order to see how the workers lived. Despite the chill night air they sat around in small groups around the doorways of various storage buildings, and outside the general store, like neighbors on the stoops of tenements, gossiping and tossing nickels.

137

Yet it was impossible to ignore the hostility that existed between experienced miners and more recently arrived trainees. It had split the camp into two distinct factions, and everywhere she looked there was visible evidence of the tension. She sensed that even the slightest pretext would trigger violence. As Dan guided her through camp she found herself waiting for the friction that would provide the spark. She found it at the heavy-duty repair shop.

A group of welders were working on the long boom of a huge crane. Their goggles were pushed back on their heads, and she saw from the wavering yellowish-orange flame from their torches that they were just heating the metal rather than cutting it. She recognized two of the men as belonging to the group that had given Gallagher the loudest vocal support at the meeting in the recreation hall. But there was a furtiveness to their movements that puzzled her. As they worked backwards along the 200-foot boom they kept glancing up at the open door of the repair shop, where two of their members were keeping watch on a group of trainees waiting to take over where the other men left off.

"What's happening?" she asked.

"Wait here," Dan said. "You'll see."

They remained in the shadows, watching as the scene in front of them unfolded. The men were starkly outlined by the harsh, blue-white glare of the mercury-vapor floodlights. Ceetra was reminded of tableaus she had seen during childhood visits to chateaus along the Loire Valley in France. The eerie illumination made the men's grease-stained clothes look like costumes. The welders finished heating the highest struts of the boom, and signaled the driver. He started the engine and slowly edged the massive crane inside the corrugated steel building where heavy-duty equipment was repaired.

From where they stood it was impossible to see what was happening inside the building. After two or three minutes Dan motioned Ceetra forward. As they stepped through the door she saw the short, squat man with the pug-featured face who had spoken out against Gallagher at the meeting. He had swung himself onto the boom and was starting to climb it. An array of tools dangling from his belt clinked on the metal as he moved steadily toward a strut in the lifting mechanism that was hanging loose.

The welders who had preheated the boom stood just outside the door, watching as the man clambered higher and higher. It was clear from the way they whispered and nudged each other that they were waiting for something to happen. But their expectant murmuring abruptly stopped as Sid suddenly emerged from behind a pile of coiled steel cable. He glanced at Dan, then mounted the crane and waved the broom he was holding.

"Hold it!" he shouted. "I gotta clean this thing off."

"It's okay," the man on the boom replied. "I can manage without—"

"No, sir. I got my orders."

"Well, stick 'em. This one time—"

Before the other man could finish his sentence, Sid grabbed his leg and pulled him back down to the platform on which he was standing in front of the control cab. Then, with an agility that belied his enormous size, he started up the boom. There was a deliberateness about his every action that added drama to each move he made. It was almost as if he knew he was giving a performance, and didn't want to disappoint his audience. When he neared the section the welders had preheated, he slowed but still kept going.

"He'll get burned," Ceetra said.

Dan didn't answer. His eyes were fixed on Sid.

"Stop him—"

Her words were drowned by Sid's bellow as his hands touched the searingly hot metal. He grabbed for other struts, but each one he reached for was equally hot, and he swung from one metal support to another like a monkey. The welders began to laugh. The sound betrayed their presence, and the men inside the repair shop immediately tensed. They knew the heated boom had been meant for one of them.

Then they looked up where Sid was still swinging around trying to find a handhold, and began to chuckle.

Suddenly Sid let go of the boom, his giant limbs flailing in mid-air. His fall was broken as he plunged into a large trough of sludge that had been drained from the oil sumps of numerous pieces of heavy-duty equipment that had been repaired during the previous week. He emerged covered with thick, foul-smelling slime, but smiling broadly. All the men roared their approval.

Stunned by the crude brutality of what she had witnessed, Ceetra turned on Dan angrily.

"You knew that was going to happen."

He nodded.

"Why in God's name didn't you do something?"

"If I had, the other guy would've been hurt, and there'd have been trouble."

"But Sid's your friend. You said you'd been together a long time."

"We have. I taught him his job."

"Job?" The sickly smell of burned flesh had wafted to where they stood. "That wasn't work. He did it to please you."

"You don't understand," Dan interjected coolly. "You came up here with your head full of fantasies about the world your father lived in. Well, now you know the way it really is—crude, dirty, brutal. But Jake loved it. And so do I."

"Are you quite finished?"

"Yes. Now why don't you go back to being a party girl, and let me get on with my work?"

"You may be an expert at handling men," Ceetra snapped, "but you've still got a lot to learn about women."

12

DAVID SEYMOUR was glad when the company's Lear jet touched down at Dallas/Fort Worth Airport. Though the journey from camp had been short, the tension between Ceetra Rampling and Dan Blake had made it seem an eternity. Despite the narrow confines of the cabin, the two had managed to sustain a separation that defied all his efforts to bridge it by conversation, and finally he had given up trying.

Seymour had been present when Ceetra returned from her tour of the camp the previous evening, and gauged from the brusqueness with which she responded to his pleasantries that she was deeply upset. But she hadn't offered an explanation, and he knew better than to press for one. He simply reminded her that she was expected in Dallas for the board meeting on Friday morning, and told her the plane she'd expected to take in the morning had developed a mechanical problem which would delay its departure until early in the evening.

A limousine was waiting to meet Ceetra at the airport and she offered Seymour a lift into Dallas. She pointedly failed to extend the invitation to Dan. The project engineer had declined, explaining he had an appointment in Fort Worth. Dan ignored the slight and hired a rental car. If he was affected by Ceetra's behavior he gave no indication of it, an attitude Seymour sensed made her even angrier.

It was dusk as the taxi carrying Seymour neared Fort Worth. The towering glass facade of the triangular-shaped National Bank building reflected the lights of the city, and traffic heading into the downtown area was much lighter than usual.

"Let me off at the Convention Center, will you?"

"At twelfth or fourteenth?" the driver asked.

"Anywhere near the Water Garden is fine."

He put his head back and closed his eyes. The pressures of the past week and a half suddenly had caught up with him, and he felt drained. First the accident, then the funeral, and most recently, signs of strain among the idled men which threatened to erupt into violence. They had all brought tensions that had stretched his nerves to near breaking point.

"Here okay?" the driver asked.

Seymour opened his eyes and saw the graceful outline of the Tarrant County Convention Center silhouetted against the night sky.

"Fine." He handed the driver a twenty-dollar bill.

"Jesus, haven't you got anything smaller?" the other man asked.

"It's okay," Seymour said. "Keep the change."

"Hey, that's real big of you." The driver folded the bill carefully and put it in his wallet. "Thanks, mister."

Seymour nodded and got out of the cab. He walked briskly across 14th Street toward the Santa Fe Railroad terminal. The night air smelled of gasoline fumes. He guessed they came from the nearby Greyhound bus depot. Somewhere in the darkness there was a clank of metal-on-metal as freight cars were jockeyed into place. He paused at a railing overlooking the Sante Fe tracks. Floodlights cast a white sheen where a section of rails was being replaced. His throat was parched and there was an acid taste under his tongue— both indications that he needed a drink. But he remained motionless for three or four minutes, wrapped in his own thoughts. Uppermost were memories of Bromley, but recalling them was still too painful, and when an ambulance careened past, its wailing siren jolted him out of his introspection, and he continued up Jones Street.

The Blue Dawn Club was situated in a building that had formerly been a fire station, and much of its old character had been retained when it was converted into a bar. But in the last year it had changed owners again, and undergone a radical transformation that wasn't apparent until a customer pushed his way through the old-style swing doors. A wooden ramp now occupied what had previously been an area used for tables, and booths had been built around it in such a way that customers could look out without being observed. Anonymity was further assured by lighting that was so dim it was difficult for customers not accustomed to the place to find their way from the door to the massive oak bar that occupied the entire length of one wall.

The club now featured male strippers. The idea had originated in Los Angeles in the late seventies, and had proved so popular that similar clubs had sprung up all around the country. Their owners capitalized on the discovery that women got as much titillation from displays of nudity as men did. And it was evident that the scores of females watching the performance this evening were thoroughly enjoying themselves.

Seymour ordered a drink and watched as a young man barely out of his teens strutted his stuff on the wooden runway. He had long blond hair and his features were good, except for his lips, which were too thick and petulant. But the women liked his supple, well-muscled body, and shrieked their approval. The young man responded by slowly unzipping the tight-fitting jumpsuit he was wearing. It was made of a brocaded material interwoven with gold threads. When he moved, the lamé glistened in the spotlight. He stopped in front of the booth where Seymour was sitting alone and thrust his hips forward. Their eyes met and held. The young man continued to rotate his body sensuously for almost a full minute before finally moving on to where a group of women in their late twenties were waving to get his attention. They had folded five-dollar bills over the low metal railing that edged the runway, and the stripper knew what was expected of him.

Stepping out of his jumpsuit, he carefully placed it on the floor of the runway, and squatted in front of it with his knees spread wide. Except for scanty bikini pants made of the same gold lamé as his jumpsuit, he was nude. His well-oiled skin reflected the spotlight in a way that further defined the contours of his body, making him look like a Greek statue. He could see himself in a mirror set over the bar, and his blatant narcissism heightened the effect of what he was doing. As the disco beat from the jukebox quickened he swayed to the rhythm, moving his legs so that his bikini pants were stretched aside just enough for the women to catch glimpses of his genitals. They seemed mesmerized. A few shouted obscenities; others cheered wildly.

Seymour drained what was left of his second double Scotch. When he turned to signal the waiter he saw a man leaning against the entrance to the booth. His features were familiar, but Seymour's brain was too numbed by alcohol to immediately establish an identity. Then he remembered where he'd seen the man before. He was the OSHA investigator who had flown in from Washington and had been with the crews that went in to remove the bodies.

"Hi!" The man shook his head. "Some place, huh? The guys at camp had told me about it, but—well, I had to see it for myself."

Seymour didn't say anything. He had the uneasy feeling their meeting wasn't the coincidence the investigator wanted it to appear to be.

"Mind if I sit down?" the other man asked.

Before Seymour could respond, Hunter—yes, that was his name—had stepped inside the booth and drawn a chair up to the table.

"Scotch, right?" he said.

Seymour nodded.

Hunter signaled the waiter. "Double Scotch and a vodka on the rocks with a twist."

He spoke with a thick Brooklyn accent and displayed an easy friendliness that only increased Seymour's wariness. So far Hunter had been very close-mouthed about the results of his investigation. He had talked with Seymour briefly a couple of times, but only in the vaguest generalities. His only specific request had been for permission to spend time in camp interviewing workers.

"How's the investigation going?" Seymour asked.

Hunter shrugged. "Much slower than I'd figured."

"I'd hoped to see a preliminary report by now."

"When it's ready you'll be among the first to see it." He sipped his drink. "Three bucks a shot for this piss! Somebody should investigate their prices."

"It's not drinks that make this place so popular," Seymour said.

"So I see." Hunter glanced toward the far end of the runway where the male stripper was still titillating the women.

"Any clues?"

"A few." The investigator seemed more preoccupied with the reaction of the women. "I don't believe this place. It's crazy."

"Don't they have clubs like this in Brooklyn?"

"The section I come from, Bedford-Stuyvesant, a guy could get killed showing himself off like that."

"It takes all kinds." Seymour drained his glass. "Well, I've got to be going. There's a board meeting in the morning."

"So that's what brought Ceetra Rampling and Dan Blake back to Dallas."

Seymour started to get up, but his legs felt unsteady, and he lowered himself back into his seat and lit a cigarette.

"We'll all be there," he said, enunciating the words carefully to avoid slurring them.

"All?"

"Everybody with stock in the company."

"So Barnes is finally going to read the will, eh?"

"That's what I've been led to understand," he said.

"How do you think it'll turn out?"

"Your guess is as good as mine."

"But you knew J. B.—Jake, as you call him."

"Not really. I worked for him a lot of years, but that doesn't mean I knew him. Not well. Dan Blake's about the only man who really knew what made him tick."

"When did you last see Jake?"

"The night of the accident."

"What time?"

"He went below in the middle of swing shift—must have been around eight or nine o'clock."

"Did you notice anything unusual about him?"

"He seemed tense, on edge. But he'd been that way for weeks. He was under a lot of pressure. I guess it was getting to him."

"What kind of pressure?"

"It's no secret he spread himself pretty thin to come up with the guarantees of completion on this project."

"And the job was behind schedule earlier on, wasn't it?"

Seymour tensed. Jake had blamed him for not handling the workers with enough firmness. Was Hunter needling him? "We've had labor problems right from the start," he replied guardedly.

"How did this pressure affect his behavior?"

"Like I said, he was edgy."

"Bad-tempered, nervous—how did his edginess show?"

"He was obsessed with the notion that somebody was trying to ruin him. Don't ask me why, I don't know. But he was suspicious about everything. That's why he was underground when the accident happened. I'd reported the violations the safety inspector from Lubbock had come up with, and Jake insisted on flying up to check them out for himself."

"Had you made the changes the safety inspector required?"

"Most of them. Continuous testing equipment had been installed at the tunnel face, and we'd put in new continuous pumps. As to the excavation hole he wanted us to drill in the face, well, we already had an existing hole about seventy feet long that we'd put in for prewatering purposes. I requested that we be allowed to monitor that hole instead of drilling a new one."

"And the inspector approved it?"

"Yes, provided we'd stop drilling if any measurable amounts of gas were encountered."

"What about the oxygen-breathing apparatus?"

"We had twelve units in camp. I ordered additional ones from Dallas, but they were still on the way when—" His voice faltered.

"What were you using to test for gas?"

"I've been through all this with you before—"

"I'd like to hear it again."

"An MSA explosive meter."

"And how many men did you have doing the testing?"

"One man doing constant monitoring."

"Why did you only have one?"

"One was considered adequate."

"By whom?"

"By me for one."

"By who for two? What I'm trying to find is who made the decision as well as you."

"I know what you're doing, Mr. Hunter."

"Good. Then you won't mind answering my question."

"I participated in that decision."

"Who else participated?"

"Dan Blake."

"And he was the one responsible for implementing the changes the safety inspector required?"

"As project manager it was ultimately my responsibility."

"But Blake spent the day underground making sure they were installed?"

"Yes. A very long day. About fourteen hours."

Hunter sat silently for a moment, seemingly lost in thought. The stripper had finished his performance, and the crowd had thinned. It was after midnight. Seymour felt sober enough now to leave, but before he could get up Hunter resumed his questioning.

"I gather you were very friendly with Jake's son," he said.

"And I think we've gone quite far enough with this interrogation," he replied.

"Interrogation?" The other man laughed. "Is that what it sounds like?"

"That's what it is."

"It wasn't meant that way. I just wanted to talk with you man-to-man. Off-the-record, if you like. There are a number of things bothering me, and I thought you might be able to help by filling in some blank spots."

"The situation seems quite clear to me," Seymour said. "They hit a pocket of gas. It could have been methane or any other flammable gas. There was an explosion—"

"It would have required ignition."

"There were at least a hundred pieces of non-explosionproof electrical equipment down there, and that's not counting the lights. Any one of them could have ignited the gas."

"But you weren't tunneling through shale or the type of rock that characteristically harbors gas."

"At that depth it's hard to anticipate what you'll encounter."

"And gas couldn't explode without oxygen."

"That could have come from the blowers in the fan lines."

"You seem to have all the answers."

"That's not hard with the kind of questions you're asking."

"You think they're naive?"

"Let's say simplistic."

"There's a reason." Hunter swallowed his drink. "I've been into every crevice in that tunnel with the most sophisticated testing equipment available. I've probed the muck,

148

checked the seams and done everything but ram it up the miners' asses. There is no gas down there. No methane, nor any other flammable gas—period."

"It may have been an isolated pocket."

"All right, let me try this one on you," Hunter continued. "We found the gas reading logs and they showed nothing. Whoever you assigned the task of checking the meter either wasn't doing his job, or didn't get an indication that there was any gas present."

"Things must have been pretty chaotic down there. He may not have had time to record his readings."

"We'll never know. He was cremated along with the rest of them. Or at least we think so."

"Why doubt it? There were no survivors."

"The coroner isn't so sure. He checked what was left of the bodies before they were buried. Preliminary findings indicate one corpse fewer than the number of men we believe were underground."

"The only way of knowing how many were down there is from the brass board, and that's not infallible."

"You're right, it isn't. But there's one final thing that bothers me. The gas testing meter still hasn't been found."

"It was probably blown to bits."

"Maybe. But the logs were still intact. And even if the meter had been blown to bits you'd still think we'd have been able to find some splinters of it."

This time Seymour didn't attempt an answer. These disclosures were news to him. He wondered why Hunter had picked a setting like the Blue Dawn Club to reveal it.

"Maybe it'll turn up," he said finally.

"It's possible," the other man replied. "But the way things stand now there are a lot of pieces that don't fit, and that worries me."

 *13*

MULE BARNES cradled the phone between his shoulder and ear, leaving both hands free to light a large Havana cigar he took from a humidor on a small table to one side of his desk. He didn't normally smoke before lunch, but this morning was special, and called for something out of the ordinary to mark it as such.

"I'm sorry, sir," the secretary at the other end of the line said. "Mr. Morley is still on a long-distance call. Shall I ask him to call you back?"

"I'll hold," Barnes replied.

Ordinarily he would never have waited. It was bad strategy to give anybody the impression they were important enough for that. Particularly a man like Ed Morley. But this was one of the rare times he was willing to make an exception.

He exhaled a cloud of smoke. It hung like a blue veil in the morning sunlight that filtered into his office through the broadly spaced louvers over the windows.

"Mule?"

Barnes deliberately waited a few moments before answering.

"Who the hell else do you know who'd be calling you from Dallas this time of morning?"

"Out of character for you, too, isn't it?" the other man chuckled.

"That depends."

"On what?"

"Just how much I'm likely to profit from making such an effort."

"There's plenty in this thing for both of us," Morley assured him.

"Well, I'm ready here," the lawyer said. "How about things at your end?"

"I've lined up a syndicate."

"Mind telling me who's in it?"

"Not over the phone. But they're willing to come up with whatever it takes."

"Just so long as it's enough, and they're ready to move fast."

"They are," Morley said. "When's the board meeting?"

Barnes looked at the old pendulum clock set in a corner near the window. It was nearly 10:00 a.m.

"About an hour from now."

"What about the will?"

"Leave it to me."

"And the girl—Jake's daughter. I met her at the funeral. She seemed like a pretty self-assured woman to me. I got the feeling she didn't like me too much."

"She won't give us any problems."

"You'd better be right," Morley said. "These guys I've lined up for the money are real heavyweights. They play rough."

"Trust me," Barnes said.

"Do I have a choice?"

"No."

"That makes me nervous as hell."

The attorney was smiling when he hung up. His whole life had been a series of complex games, most of which he'd won, and in this one he held the trump card. It lay on the desk in front of him: a thick document bearing the heading THE LAST WILL AND TESTAMENT OF JAMES BOWEN RAMPLING.

He lifted it and weighed it in his hand. It was heavy. There must have been thirty or forty pages, all of them filled with detailed instructions as to how the founder of Rampling International wished his estate to be disposed of after his death. The length of the document was attributable to Jake's obsession with ensuring there would be no loopholes that might prevent his son from inheriting control of the firm. Barnes had worked on it from the beginning, and had gone over it so many times with Jake that he almost knew its contents by heart.

It wasn't quite the way he had described it to Morley at their meeting in New York. In fact, Jake had set up an irrevocable trust in 1974, when Bromley was eleven years old. Under its terms, Jake had transferred all his holdings to his young son in the form of a gift. The object was to avoid the exorbitant death duties that would otherwise have been assessed on Jake's estate when he died.

But about a week before the accident, Jake had undergone a sudden and totally inexplicable change of mind. Barnes had received a phone call well after midnight asking him to go to the ranch, where he found Jake in an emotional state that bordered on hysteria. For months he had been showing signs that he was suffering from extreme mental stress. Apparently, the pressures of trying to keep the VHST project on schedule had taken their toll. They manifested themselves in delusions of persecution and an irrational distrust of everybody around him. He suspected even his closest associates, and Barnes had had difficulty in making him understand that he couldn't do what Jake wanted, which was to cut Bromley out of his will entirely. Once established, the trust was irrevocable. Nothing short of the boy's death could enable Jake to get back control of his own assets. In effect, Barnes explained, Jake had given everything he owned to his son years ago, and there was nothing he could do under law to change the situation.

At first Jake had refused to accept the explanation, and it had taken the attorney several hours to convince him.

Now, as Barnes looked at the sheaf of papers on his desk, he no longer cared what had made Jake attempt to change his will. He had the trump card he needed. Barnes had led Morley to believe their scheme hinged on his being able to destroy the will. In fact, now that both Jake and Bromley were dead, the irrevocable trust automatically became void, and as Jake's only surviving blood relative, Ceetra inherited everything.

The old grandfather clock chimed the half hour. He flicked on the intercom and informed his secretary he was ready to leave.

"The car's waiting, sir," she replied.

"Tell the driver I'll be out in a couple of minutes, will you? And if I'm not back by noon do your best to juggle my appointments."

"Yes, sir."

He hesitated before putting the will in his briefcase. For some unaccountable reason he experienced a pang of anxiety, but couldn't determine why. He settled into the back of his Mercedes limousine for the short ride to Rampling International's headquarters near the junction of the Stemmons and Lyndon Johnson Freeways in north Dallas. The unease was still with him when the car finally slowed to a stop in front of the impressive ten-story building.

The guards in the main lobby went through their check-in procedures with a doggedness that Barnes found maddening. They knew perfectly well who he was, and yet each time he entered the premises he was required to go through the same ritual of identifying himself, being checked against a computerized list, and finally receiving a plastic identification tag he was required to wear throughout his stay in the building. There were no exceptions to the rule. Even Jake had been obliged to go through it every time he entered or left. Because the company worked on many government contracts, it had to meet security standards imposed by Washington.

"You're cleared to go in, Mr. Barnes," the guard announced. "Have a nice day."

The lawyer hated the expression, but this was one time he didn't mind hearing it.

"Thank you," he said. "I intend to have an exceptional day."

Barnes used his identification tag to open the door of the elevator that led to the executive offices. It was magnetically coded, and only a special few had tags that would activate the lift mechanism. He knew that he was being watched constantly by concealed closed-circuit television cameras, and microphones that picked up and recorded all sounds in the hallways.

He emerged on the ninth floor. The difference between the executive offices and the decor of the rest of the building never ceased to affect him. While the latter was the epitome of contemporary design, the former was in complete contrast. The motif was traditional eighteenth-century, with oak paneling, hardwood floors and antique furnishings. It was like stepping backward in time. A sweeping staircase joined the two floors, and over it hung a massive crystal chandelier. He had been told the reason for the old-fashioned look was that heads of state from the Middle East preferred it, but to him it had a self-conscious formality that made it seem more like a museum or an exclusive funeral parlor than the nerve center of one of the most progressive firms in the world.

The receptionist, a middle-aged woman with a prim manner but an easy smile, looked up from where she was seated behind a Louis XV desk.

"Good morning, Mr. Barnes," she said brightly.

"Everybody here?" he asked.

"I think so," she replied. "Most of them are waiting in the conference room."

Barnes looked at the ornate gilt clock artfully recessed into the wall above the desk. It was exactly 11:00 a.m.

"I'll be just a few minutes," he said.

He pushed open the door to the men's toilet. Years ago he had learned the value of staging an entrance. He had won some of his most profitable cases by unpredictable in-court timing that was cleverly designed to throw the opposing attorneys off balance. He took off his wristwatch and set it on the edge of the sink while he washed his hands. Then he wiped them with the deliberation of a surgeon preparing to operate. He studied himself in the mirror over the sink. Journalists always described his hair as "thinning," but in fact he was almost bald. The only thing that prevented him from being completely so was a wisp of hair that had stubbornly withstood the ravages of time. He arranged it carefully over his forehead, but it did little to hide the fact that the years had taken their toll. There were pouches under his eyes, and jowls hung like the cheek meat of a hog under his chin. In another four years he would be sixty, but he already looked more than that. He sighed, picked up his briefcase and walked back into the reception area.

"Can I get you anything?" The receptionist glanced nervously at the clock.

"Some coffee would be real fine."

"There's some in the board room. I just took it in."

She started to get up, but he rested his hand on her shoulder before she could rise.

"Don't you worry about it," he said. "I'll take care of myself."

He strode into the room where the others were waiting. It was paneled in dark oak, and the lighting was recessed into the ceiling in such a way that it cast a minimum of illumination on the men seated around a massive oval conference table. There were no windows, and the air conditioning had been put at an unusually low setting. Once again Barnes was reminded of a funeral parlor.

He paused at the door and looked around the room. The men seated around the table were mostly company vice presidents. He made a mental checklist: Tom Heslop, vice chairman of the board, silver-haired, disarmingly affable, but possessed of a ruthlessness that had made him a driving force behind the firm's rapid expansion; Norm Gross, rough-featured, stubby-fingered, raspy-voiced vice president of finance; Phil Greene, a kindly, soft-spoken man who had been with Jake almost from the beginning and now was the engineer in charge of overseas project development. Among the others present he recognized the heads of various departments: Power, Petroleum and Chemicals, Systems, Mining and Metallurgy, and the Civil Works Division. Dan Blake and David Seymour were also there. The men were deep in conversation and it was a moment or two before anybody was aware Barnes had arrived. It was Seymour who finally looked up and saw Barnes. He nodded, and as the attorney took his place at the head of the table the hubbub slowly gave way to an expectant silence.

Barnes milked the moment by mutely acknowledging the presence of each man seated at the table. It was a technique he had used many times with juries, and always found effective. Level eye-to-eye contact, the slightest inclination of the head. That's all it took to establish that he was in command. He saw that two of the chairs were empty, and realized Ceetra wasn't present.

"Does Miss Rampling know we're ready?" he asked.

Before anybody could reply, the door at the far end of the room opened, and Ceetra strode into the room. She was wearing a light print dress that was fine-textured enough for the curve of her breasts to be faintly visible. It was also obvious that she wasn't wearing a brassiere. The outfit was so blatantly inappropriate for the occasion that Barnes got the impression she was deliberately trying to shock those present. If so, it was apparent she had succeeded. Every eye in the room remained fixed on her as she walked round the table to an empty chair.

Aware that Ceetra's entrance had broken the tension he'd so carefully contrived to create, Barnes resorted to another technique. Clearing his throat as if about to speak, he waited until the people gathered around the table had returned their attention to him. But instead of saying anything, he crossed to the antique walnut sideboard where the coffee pot stood, half filled one of the delicate, willow-patterned cups, poured in some cream, and stirred it. By the time he returned to his seat he could feel the tautness in the room.

"I wish I could say it's a pleasure to be here today," he said, speaking in a voice that was so low his listeners at the far end of the huge table automatically leaned forward in their chairs in order to hear him better. "But it isn't. It is a very unhappy occasion for us all."

A murmur of agreement stirred round the room.

"My association with Jake Rampling covered a good many years, and I think I can say without contradiction that I knew him as well as, or better than, any man alive."

He paused and looked directly at Ceetra.

"He wasn't always the successful man most of you knew him to be. When I first met him he was operating out of a converted warehouse over near the railroad terminal on South Houston, and having a tough time laying his hands on enough money to meet his payroll. I arranged his first big loan, and I can tell you in those days it wasn't easy to find anybody who was willing to back him. Things got so tight he couldn't afford to pay me. That's how I ended up owning stock in the company."

Two or three men at the table chuckled.

"Even after the firm expanded to a point where it was doing more dollar volume abroad than Bechtel, Fluor, or Brown & Root, Jake left the business of drawing up contracts to me. He hated paperwork. Or that's what he liked people to believe. But I want you to know that once I'd outlined a deal he went over it like a monkey looking for fleas. He'd make believe he didn't understand arrangements we made with the International Monetary Fund or the Asian Development Bank, or how our access to capital gave the company a unique bargaining edge with Third World countries—but he knew all right. And why not? He hired a former secretary of the treasury to explain it to him!"

This time the laughter was less guarded. But when Barnes glanced at Ceetra he saw her features were set in the same purposeful expression that had been there when she entered the room.

"All I'm trying to say," he continued, "is that Jake Rampling was an exceptional man. He made his mark on the world, and it is up to each one of us here to continue where he so tragically left off. Without him to lead the way it will be a supreme challenge. The complexities of international commerce in today's rapidly changing world are beyond the scope of all but the comparative few who have spent a lifetime in it. One wrong step could prove disastrous. I for one intend to dedicate myself to ensuring this never happens, and I know I can count on your support in the difficult months to come."

When he stopped speaking there was absolute silence in the room. For a moment Barnes feared he'd overplayed his hand, but a steady smatter of applause dispersed his anxiety, and he realized he had gauged his audience accurately. Jake's death had left them badly shaken. All of them held stock in the company, and stood to lose heavily if the firm floundered. He had deliberately milked these fears by implying that only he could provide the leadership necessary to an orderly transition.

Only Ceetra failed to react. Her expression remained unchanged, and he began to wonder if she was simply bored. If so, he thought, she was about to be jolted out of her apathy.

"This is Jake's will," he announced, reaching inside his briefcase and holding the bulky document up for them all to see. "I could stand here and read every word of it to you, but it would be a waste of time."

There was a quick murmur of surprise.

"I've had copies made and they will be distributed on your way out." His manner suddenly turned brisk. "But I can give you the bottom line now. Ten years ago Jake created an irrevocable trust. Under it he transferred the ownership of his stock in the company, and everything else he possessed, to his son. He did this on the recommendation of his accountants and myself. The object, of course, was to avoid death duties. I had been warned this loophole would soon be closed, and we decided to take advantage of the law while there was still time."

He looked directly at Ceetra.

"I'm sure you know your father wanted Bromley to succeed him. It was his greatest wish. But now—well, technically your father had nothing to leave, and your brother died without making a will. Under existing intestacy laws, that makes you, his only living relative, the heir to everything—"

Exclamations of disbelief drowned out the rest of his sentence. Everybody in the room had assumed that now that Jake was gone, the board would vote to go public, and the stock each of them held would increase in value astronomically. The sudden discovery that their fortunes were now inextricably linked to Ceetra Rampling left them stunned.

"That's not quite accurate," Ceetra said quietly when the noise had abated sufficiently for her to make herself heard. "My mother is still alive. Isn't she considered a living relative?"

"No," Barnes replied. "She may be living, but her kinship to your father was only through marriage, and she waived all future claims on your father's estate at the time of the divorce."

"Voluntarily?"

The attorney bridled. "It was part of the settlement."

"One you arranged."

"I really don't think—"

"You also had my mother certified."

"That was the opinion of Dr. Robinson and two court-appointed psychiatrists."

"If she was mentally unstable," Ceetra persisted, "it would seem she was in no condition to make any legally valid decisions."

"This is hardly the place for us to discuss anything but the matters at hand," Barnes replied brusquely. "I'm sure all this has come as quite a surprise, but if you'll leave everything in my hands I can arrange to liquidate the stock you have inherited, and have you on your way home in a week at the most."

"Home?"

"To London," the lawyer said.

"Ah, I see." Ceetra nodded. "But you're overlooking something. I was born right here in Dallas. As far as I'm concerned this is home. And there's something else you should know. I've had enough experience running my own business to have learned never to make snap decisions. I'll have to think the whole thing over very carefully. It would be rash of me to make any move before I'm fully acquainted with all the facts, wouldn't it?"

Barnes didn't answer. She smiled at him with exaggerated sweetness as she left the room.

 ## 14

IT WAS NEARLY 8:30 p.m., almost
nine hours since her confrontation
with Barnes at the board meeting,
and in many ways the time since then had seemed like an
eternity.

Feeling desolate and alone she decided to go back and
visit her father's office on the tenth floor of Rampling International. She was curious to see where he had worked.
Maybe it would provide another clue to his personality.

"You'll need your I.D. tag," the security guard said.

"Do we have to go through all that again?" she asked
angrily. "I'm Ceetra Rampling."

"I know," he said. "But we've got rules, and they apply to
everybody. No exceptions."

"Of course," she said. The man was right. He was only
following orders. It wasn't his fault she was on edge.

As the elevator silently whisked her up to the tenth floor,
she tried to remember how she had felt when she arrived for
the reading of the will earlier that morning. Anxious, nervous, apprehensive. Yet there was a stronger, more domi-
nant emotion: a slow-festering resentment of the feeling that
she didn't belong here, a feeling that everyone seemed to
encourage. Dan Blake had been the first to make it evident
when he'd met her at the airport. Her visit to the camp had
been an attempt to show him he was wrong to prejudge her,

but it had backfired when she'd protested his callous treatment of Sid.

Mule Barnes patronized her, which she found even more infuriating than Dan's hostility. Resentment was what had caused her to pull the rug out from under the attorney at the board meeting. It wasn't a premeditated action. The last thing she expected was any part of her father's fortune. Why should she? Jake had done everything in his power to deny her birthright simply because of her sex.

Now, as she crossed the priceless Persian rugs that decorated the pegged hardwood floor of the reception area on the tenth floor, she wondered again why Barnes hadn't told her about the inheritance when he telephoned her in London, instead of resorting to the excuse that her presence was required in order to determine who was to continue paying her mother's medical expenses.

This and numerous other anxieties had continued to churn in her mind all day as she tried to come to grips with the enormity of what had happened. Her first reaction when she walked out of the board meeting had been to call her mother. But instead of connecting her directly to Mary, the operator at the sanatorium had put her call through to Dr. Amsdon.

"I've been hoping you'd call, Miss Rampling," the psychiatrist said. "Your mother hasn't been too well these past few days."

"What's the matter?" Ceetra asked.

"Nothing serious. Just a minor setback."

"I'd rather you didn't mince words, Doctor."

"All right. As you know she experienced a rather abrupt regression when I gave her the news about your brother's death—"

"She seemed to be getting over it."

"Yes, we all thought so." The doctor paused. "But after your call at the beginning of the week she suffered a relapse. Apparently her subconscious rejects the reality of Bromley's death. Despite every effort on my part, she persists in believing he is still alive. I'm sure it will pass. Her therapist is working on it. But—well, until she's a little better, perhaps it would be best if I simply tell her you called. Was there anything particular you wanted her to know?"

Ceetra hesitated before answering. "No," she said finally. "Just that I love her."

Entering the office adjoining the conference room, she stood for a moment and looked around at the place that had been her father's office. Spacious and paneled, it contained his aura. There was a large color photograph above the gigantic U-shaped desk. It showed Jake with his arm draped over the shoulders of Dan Blake. They were standing in front of the headquarters building which was still only half-finished when the picture was taken. Switching on a floor lamp, she twisted the shade so the light shone directly on the picture. Outwardly her father appeared the epitome of a successful Texan: a handsome, weathered face; thick steel-colored hair that was cut short and swept back from his forehead; strong, blunt features and a wide smile. But his eyes were as cold as granite.

Dan appeared much younger in the photograph. She tried to pinpoint why. He was just as striking then as now, but there was a subtle difference. She wondered if it had to do with the tension he'd been under as a result of the accident. It was evident from the coolness with which the men responded to him at the union meeting that they still blamed him for delaying the rescue attempt. But if he was suffering he certainly wasn't ready to admit it. And after the way he'd behaved toward her at camp she found it difficult to feel sorry for him.

It was because of Dan that she had worn the flimsy dress to the board meeting. She wanted to show how unimportant she considered him and the business he took so seriously. Now she regretted her decision. Far from being shocked, Dan had only seemed amused. On reflection she realized it had been a childish gesture, and his reaction had been the only appropriate one. Despite everything, she had to admit she respected a lot of things about him. He was outspoken and rude, but there was none of Barnes's artifice in him. He seemed to possess the self-assurance she lacked, and for a moment she wished he were here to share some of it with her.

Taking a last look at the photograph over the desk, she switched out the lights and walked back to the elevator.

The building was strangely quiet. It was Friday evening and most employees had left early in order to get a head start on the weekend. Only a skeleton crew remained: draftsmen working against deadlines on blueprints that had to be flown to Washington in time for a subcommittee hearing on the VHST project that started on Monday; a few secretaries who were standing by to Xerox the originals; a handful of supervisors; and the ever-present security guards.

Before getting into the elevator she looked over the balustrade. The ten-story chasm yawning below triggered a sudden attack of vertigo that made her senses whirl. It was similar to the attacks of claustrophobia she had experienced for as long as she could remember, and left her feeling nauseated and unsteady.

The extent of her disorientation became apparent when the doors of the elevator slid open and, instead of the lobby, she found herself in a large basement area. Suddenly a security guard bolted out of a small room with his hand on the butt of his holstered revolver.

"Okay, stay right where you are!" the guard snapped.

"I just pushed—"

"This area's restricted. Where's your I.D. tag?"

Ceetra started to open her purse.

"Hold it!" The guard motioned her forward with his free hand. "Throw the bag over here."

She did as he ordered, and watched as he emptied the contents of her purse on the cement floor. Crouching down, he sorted through the jumbled pile of makeup, wallet, and tissues. Finally, he found the plastic identification tag.

"I tried to tell you—"

"Would you mind stepping over to the desk, Miss?" His tone was more considerate and she complied. He studied her I.D. tag, then picked up a phone and dialed a number.

"What's going on out here?"

The voice came from a door further down the corridor.

"This woman wasn't wearing her I.D. tag, Mr. Seymour."

"Don't you know who she is?"

"No, sir. Just checking to find out."

"Never mind. I'll vouch for her."

The man had moved forward and was near enough for Ceetra to see his face. She recognized the project manager who had arranged for her to stay at the guest house on camp. He looked tired and pale.

"I got the wrong floor," Ceetra said.

"Don't let him worry you. They hire these guys because they're big, not smart." Seymour gave her a weary smile. "Well, now that you're down here why don't you come and take a look at what the firm you own is doing to change the course of life in these United States."

"I don't know that I'm ready to—"

"Nonsense," Seymour said. "It took your brother years to learn the business. If you're going to take his place you'd better grab every opportunity you're offered. My guess is they may be few and far between."

Ceetra suddenly remembered the letter Bromley had written to their mother saying how much his friendship with Seymour meant to him.

"All right. Why not?" she said.

Seymour led the way into a vast chamber, most of which was in darkness. The only corner that was well lit contained a large drafting table. There was also an automatic coffee-maker, and he poured two cups from a freshly brewed pot.

"Did you spend a lot of time teaching my brother?" she asked.

He glanced at her quickly, almost defensively, then handed her the coffee.

"Quite a bit," he said.

167

"The coffee's good."

"You've got Bromley's tact."

"Really. I mean it."

"More sugar?"

She shook her head. "Did he need a lot of tact?"

"It was a primary requirement in dealing with Jake."

"Was my father that bad?"

"Worse."

"Everybody I talk to seems to have a different impression of him."

"He was a multifaceted person."

"But I gather most of those facets weren't particularly likeable."

"Not true," Seymour said. "You saw all those people at his funeral."

"But how many were friends?"

"All, in their own way."

"I mean real friends."

"Probably more than you think. He had a lot of charm, particularly when he wanted something. And he could be a very generous man—"

"When he wanted something?"

"Which was most of the time."

Ceetra laughed. The longer she talked with Seymour, the more she began to understand why Bromley had liked him. He was bright and funny and wasn't afraid of opening himself up. This was a characteristic she'd rarely found in men.

"That accounts for all those sanctimonious faces I saw in the congregation at the First Baptist Church," she said.

"A lot of them were there to make sure he was dead."

"They would have been disappointed to know the coffins were empty."

His expression suddenly changed. She'd thought he knew about the empty coffins. Now she wasn't sure.

"He could be utterly ruthless."

"I know."

"Yes, I suppose you do. Better than most."

"A lot of people feel it's a necessary element of success."

"Do you?"

"I don't know."

"You'd better find out if you intend to take over the reins of this company."

"I may not," she said.

"Then why didn't you accept Barnes's offer?"

"Because he assumed I would."

"I admire the principle," he said. "But you could be playing a far more dangerous game than you know."

"Dangerous?"

"There's a great deal more at stake here than you seem to understand."

He crossed to a large console and manipulated a series of dials. First, ceiling lights came on in the dark recesses of the chamber. They revealed a sight that Ceetra found impossible to absorb at a single glance. Spread throughout the gigantic, subterranean room was a perfect scale model. It looked very much like the intricate model train layouts she'd seen as a child in the window of Hamley's, a toy shop in Regent Street. But in this instance the display featured a cross section of the United States between New York and Los Angeles. It was bordered on the north by latitude 36 degrees and on the south by latitude 32 degrees. The topographical relief was done in such a way that it showed the relative positions of mountains, valleys, rivers, lakes and major cities.

"It's unbelievable," she said.

He pressed another button and half the topographical map was lowered to reveal a cross section of the earth's strata beneath the surface. At a depth of over a mile two tubes linked New York and Los Angeles.

"The end product of your father's dream," Seymour said.

"What is it?" she asked.

"A tunnel linking both coasts."

He touched another control and the display suddenly sprang to life. Blunt, non-aerodynamic gondolas moved through the tubes. Starting at one-minute intervals in oppo-

169

site directions, they passed each other at a point about a hundred miles east of Amarillo. Fine wires representing utility lines gave off a neon glow in another section of the tunnel. Models representing freight containers moved steadily back and forth between New York and Los Angeles, frequently shifting to branch lines that spread to other parts of the country. Pneumatic tubes, stenciled with the word "mail," glowed ghostly blue in the surrounding darkness.

"I'm impressed," Ceetra said. "Now how about telling me what it all means."

"About twelve years ago a scientist at the Rand Corporation in Santa Monica, Robert Salter, devised a concept for a pollution-free transportation system that could operate at speeds in excess of those of passenger aircraft," Seymour explained. "The general principle was relatively simple: electromagnetically levitated and propelled gondolas operating in a near-vacuum. He called it the Very-High-Speed-Transit system. His scenario for this VHST operation not only called for it to be used as a fast and convenient transit method, but also suggested the tunnel could be used for utility transmission and auxiliary freight-carrying operations."

"What amazing foresight."

The engineer nodded. "He began with the assumption that future transportation approaches would be extensions of present ones, including subways for local mass transit and automobiles for intra- and intercity travel."

"He couldn't have anticipated that gasoline would go up to its present price?" Ceetra said.

"Actually, I think that might have been uppermost in his mind," Seymour replied. "Back in 1972 almost ninety percent of the travel between cities was by automobile. He knew an alternative had to be found. His concept called for the improvement of existing mass transit systems to include 'people movers' in the downtown areas of most major cities, and a system whereby passengers would step off a subway, or a 'people mover' from auto parking facilities, and get directly on a VHST gondola at the same terminal."

"How does this VHST thing work?"

"The gondola rides on and is driven by electromagnetic waves in the same way a surfboard rides the ocean's waves. Have you ever tried surfing?"

"It's not high on the list of available sports in London," she said.

"But you know the principle of how a wave drives a board?"

"Basically, yes."

"Good." Seymour spoke with the patience he might have used with a child. "In the VHST system electromagnetic waves are generated by pulsed or oscillating currents in electrical conductors that form the roadbed structure in the evacuated tube. Opposing magnetic fields in the vehicles are generated by means of a loop of superconducting cable carrying on the order of a million amperes of current."

"Wait a minute," Ceetra said. "You're beginning to lose me. I don't even know how a car engine works."

Seymour ran his hand through his hair. "All right, I'll keep it as simple as possible," he said. "The essence of the idea is to dig a tunnel that will contain several large tubes for the east-west travel of trains that float on magnetic fields, moving at speeds of ten thousand miles an hour."

"Ten thousand!"

"Maybe more."

"That's better than the Concorde."

"Faster than any aircraft."

"How is that possible?"

"For the same reason that spacecraft are able to reach speeds high enough to take them on voyages into outer space," the engineer said. "Because there's no air friction in a vacuum."

"You mean the inside of the tubes will be like space?"

"Pretty close. The gondolas will leave New York and Los Angeles terminals at one-minute intervals. On the main line there will be intermediate stops at Amarillo and Chicago. Feeder lines will intersect the main tube at both locations.

171

There will also be subsidiary lines coming into the two main terminals from such cities as San Francisco, Boston and Washington."

Ceetra was silent for a moment. The enormity of the project made it hard to grasp. She had read a little about it in the newspapers and heard it mentioned by the B.B.C. correspondent during his broadcast from the camp, but this was the first time she'd had it explained in detail.

"How did the VHST concept come about in the first place?" she asked.

"It was an outgrowth of the space program," Seymour replied. "Scientists realized that hypersonic speeds were possible on earth if we could reproduce the environment of space. The idea of high-speed train travel using electromagnetic suspension wasn't new. It was first put forward around the turn of the century. If memory serves, I think it was actually patented in 1912. So there was nothing particularly new about that. But the notion of underground tubes running across the width of the continent was an innovation. When it was first suggested nobody took it very seriously, but after some preliminary studies had been done it quickly became apparent that the idea had a lot of advantages."

"In addition to speed?"

"Yes."

"Like what?"

"Well, in the first place there's the matter of the conservation of immense amounts of energy," he said. "An airplane that travels faster than the speed of sound uses up a large part of its energy supply just in climbing to an altitude where the speeds for which it was designed are possible. That's true of rockets, too. Much of their energy is spent in getting above the atmosphere. But none of this will apply to VHST gondolas traveling on their electromagnetic roadbeds."

"Why not?"

"Like I've said, the tubes will be emptied of air, almost to the point of a perfect vacuum, so the trains won't need much power to overcome air resistance. They won't even have to be

172

streamlined. In addition to an electromagnetic roadbed, the opposing loops in the floors of the gondolas will be super-cooled with liquid helium to further eliminate resistance."

"How will they stop after attaining such incredible speeds?"

"The same way old-fashioned trolley cars used to," he replied. "Through friction that in itself will generate power."

"I don't remember trolley cars," she said.

"I guess that dates me, doesn't it?" Seymour chuckled. "Well, since trains will be leaving New York and Los Angeles simultaneously every minute, the power generated by cars braking when they come into a terminal will be transferred to the power lines propelling cars going the other way."

"You just lost me again."

"Let me give you a simple example," he said. "There will be halfway points between each stop. Trains will use power getting to that halfway point, and generate power going the other half of the way to the stop. Each will use the power generated by trains going in opposite directions. That's the way trolley cars operated for eighty years—taking power from the overhead lines while accelerating or running along at a steady speed, and putting power back into the lines while braking or coasting."

"It seems like such a simple concept," Ceetra said. "Why hasn't it been attempted before now?"

"Because of the expense," Seymour replied. "Over two hundred billion dollars. It would have been half that years ago when Rand came up with the idea. Even then it was more than anybody was willing to spend. Even the government. And if it weren't for the fact that the government needs a project this size to stimulate the economy, and provide jobs for the unemployed, I doubt if it would have been attempted even now. Short of a war, this tunnel is about the best way to keep people working and money circulating. And even though it's costing so much, estimates project that by charging a fare of seventy-five dollars per person each way, the project will be paid off in less than thirty years."

"It hardly seems possible. Not when they have to pay off two hundred billion dollars."

"Passenger volume between coasts is already heavy," he said. "But it will increase with the added conveniences the VHST offers. Not only will the passenger be able to travel regardless of weather conditions, but the time expended in going from the heart of one city to another will be radically reduced. Nonstop trips with a constant one-g acceleration/deceleration between New York and Los Angeles will take about twenty-one minutes. With this same acceleration and two intermediate stops, the coast-to-coast time will be thirty-seven minutes. For a passenger traveling from San Francisco to Boston, the overall time will be around fifty minutes."

"But two hundred billion dollars," Ceetra repeated.

"If you figure one hundred passenger cars operating on one-minute headways in the central corridor," Seymour explained, "it amounts to almost three hundred thousand passengers crossing the country every day. That adds up to well over one hundred million passengers a year. Or, another way of looking at it is that the rate is equivalent to the cross-country air traffic of a dozen or so jumbo jets per hour. But it goes beyond that, really, because if the VHST offers greatly reduced travel time at such reasonable fares it will undoubtedly create a much larger demand than the present one hundred million passengers a year. And since the operating costs are so low once the system is in place, fares will probably come down as the passenger volume increases."

"It's incredible," Ceetra said.

"It gets more so." Seymour turned and looked at the model which was still operating. "Particularly when you add the fact that it will be handling eight or nine million tons of freight each day. And there are obvious environmental benefits. No sonic booms; no buildup of pollution, particularly in the upper atmosphere; no more problems about where to locate airports to accommodate supersonic aircraft. The tunnel will also be used by pipelines for oil, water, gas, waste disposal, and slurries of materials such as coal and other bulk commodities. Add to that communication links, including channels for lasers and microwave waveguides; electrical power transmission lines; as well as passenger and freight-hauling systems, and you begin to understand the importance of this project. Particularly when you realize that all these facilities will be out of sight and completely protected against sabotage."

"You think that's a factor?"

"Yes. I'm convinced this country is in for a wave of terrorism that will be far worse than anything that's happened anywhere else in the world. It's already happening, and it's going to get a lot worse."

"From whom?"

"Not the terrorist groups that captured the headlines in the seventies," Seymour said. "The real danger is going to be from our own people. This country is on the verge of anarchy. Every major corporation knows it. IBM was drawing up contingency plans to combat it eight or nine years ago. Private police forces already far outnumber those in the public sector."

"I saw what was happening at the camp," Ceetra said. "There seemed to be real animosity between the experienced workers and on-the-job trainees."

"The friction isn't limited to that level." Seymour flipped a switch on the control console, cutting the power that operated the models. "A project of this scope was bound to generate enormous opposition."

"From whom?"

"Oil companies, airlines, utilities, unions—anybody whose profits are threatened by an improved system of coast-to-coast transportation. Until now an organization like the Teamsters had a virtual stranglehold on everything that moved between New York and Los Angeles. That gave them enormous power, and they haven't hestitated to use it. But the moment the VHST goes into operation they're going to lose that monopoly. There have already been a lot of accidents—"

"Sabotage?"

Seymour nodded. "The project is too big for any one firm to handle, so consortiums have been formed, and each of them is responsible for specific segments of the job. It's an arrangement that was encouraged when bids were submitted. The idea was to provide jobs to relieve the unemployment problems in as broad a cross section of the country as possible."

"So the tunnel is being worked from a number of faces," Ceetra said.

"That's right. And at least half of them have had accidents that were traced to sabotage."

"Do you think the explosion that killed my father and brother was sabotage?" she asked.

"I don't know. It's possible." Seymour thought about Hunter's probing questions at the Blue Dawn Club the previous evening. "You met Al Hunter?"

"At the reception after the funeral."

"He's conducting the investigation. It isn't complete yet, but I've got a hunch he knows more than he's telling anybody."

"He's a strange man."

"Don't let him fool you. Hunter's a lot brighter than he looks."

Ceetra sipped her coffee and was silent for a moment. "Maybe I was wrong," she said.

"About what?"

"Not accepting Barnes's offer."

"I suggest you give it very careful consideration," Seymour said. "Any other course of action could prove as hazardous to you as it did to Bromley."

"Are you saying his death wasn't an accident?"

Before he could answer, the telephone rang. He picked up the receiver and listened. His face turned ashen.

"There's an emergency at the tunnel," he said. "I've got to go up there immediately. Why don't you come up with me and we can talk on the plane?"

"As long as you don't expect me to go underground."

"I think you should. It'll give you a firsthand look at what you'll be getting into if you don't sell those shares."

Ceetra hesitated. The thought of going a mile below the earth's surface sent chills down her spine. But she knew Seymour was right. It was something she should experience before making up her mind about Barnes's offer.

"All right," she said. "Let's get it over with as quickly as possible."

15

"WELL, what do you think?"

Dan Blake shone the beam from his flashlight on the large wooden cabinet bolted to the wall about a hundred yards down the tunnel leading to the work-face. The glass panel was broken and the plastic containers inside were empty.

Harry Gallagher shrugged. "No experienced miner would do a thing like that. They know better than to swipe food and blankets they may need in an emergency."

"That's the third we've found broken into since the beginning of the week," Dan said.

"A guy on my shift says there's another down near where those sets are stored."

"It doesn't make one goddam bit of sense. I mean nobody's short of food, and who in hell needs blankets when it's so fucking hot down here all you do is sweat?"

"You asking or just thinking out loud?" the other man asked.

"Take your pick."

"I'll tell you one thing," Gallagher said. "It isn't any of my men."

"What makes you so sure?"

"They've all worked with me before."

"And that puts them above suspicion?"

"They wouldn't be dumb enough to swipe supplies that

could save their lives if they were trapped," he replied. "Hell, if a guy had enough air, he could stay healthy for weeks down here on the amount of stuff that's missing."

"And you think it's the new guys, huh?"

"Who else?"

Dan didn't answer. He knew Gallagher was biased, but he couldn't fault his logic. Experienced miners were all too aware of the dangers of their job to do anything that would lessen their chances of survival. And with the deaths of so many of their fellow workers still fresh in their minds, it was even less likely they would have tampered with the wall boxes that were part of the standard safety equipment.

But he also couldn't overlook another possibility. Friction between the old and new factions had grown to a point where it was quite possible either group could have deliberately looted the food and blankets in order to make it appear the others were to blame. This wasn't the only incident about which he'd received reports since the cave-in debris was cleared and tunneling resumed on a regular three-shift basis. There had been at least a dozen complaints of lunch pails having been stolen.

"You're shifter on this shift, aren't you?" Dan asked.

"Sure am."

"Well, get a carpenter down here to fix this thing. And make arrangements for all four of them to be restocked."

"Okay," Gallagher replied. "But if you want to stop it happening you should see to it those goddam trainees are limited to jobs above ground."

"When I want your advice, I'll ask for it."

There was ice in Dan's voice, and Gallagher knew better than to argue. He'd worked a lot of jobs with Dan and knew what he could be like when his back was up.

"I'll pass the word," he said.

"You do that."

Dan watched Gallagher lumber away toward a low-profile transporter that was loaded with miners waiting to be taken to the work-face. He was a good man, but not a flexible one.

He had come up the hard way. For him the Underground Laborers' Union was an elite club which he believed should only admit members who had earned the right through years of experience to call themselves miners. No wonder he resented being required by law to accept newcomers who were still learning.

It was a difficult situation. Dan understood the argument from both sides. And he hadn't sided with either. All he cared about was keeping the project on schedule. But that was becoming increasingly difficult. There had been numerous outbreaks of violence since the one Sid had managed to defuse by climbing the preheated boom. The most recent outbreak had been between a group of high-riggers and electricians over whose job it was to string some power lines. Instead of going to arbitration, which was the usual way of resolving such a dispute, they had battled it out. The electricians used their equipment-laden belts as weapons, the high-riggers the steel spikes they attached to their boots to help them climb poles. The fight had put four men in the hospital and added friction to an already volatile situation.

Dan had hoped these animosities would lessen when the men resumed work on the tunnel. It was exhausting, mind-numbing work that left most miners so spent at the end of their shift that their only concern was a hot shower, a meal and sleep. But the company had offered bonuses for shifts that tunneled the most rock during each twenty-four-hour period, and the resulting competition had refocused attention on the ineptness of the trainees. He had tried to convince the cost/efficiency experts that their effort to get more work out of the men was resulting in serious labor disputes, but as most of the infighting occurred during off-duty hours, his pleas fell on deaf ears.

Things had been different when Jake was alive. As right-hand man to the president of the company, Dan had had real power. When he made a suggestion, people listened because they knew their jobs were on the line. Jake had trusted him implicitly, and always acted on his recommendations, often with such ruthlessness that even Dan was surprised. It hadn't won him many friends in high places, a fact he was reminded of when Jake was no longer there to back him up. Many of the executives resented him, and made no secret of the fact that they were just biding their time until they could get back at him.

It was fairly evident that his days with Rampling International were numbered. Mule Barnes was obviously doing his utmost to gain control of Jake's stock, and if he succeeded it wouldn't be long before he arranged for the firm to go public. The other members of the board wouldn't oppose him. Why should they? Once the stock went public their shares would skyrocket in value. The only person standing in their way was Ceetra Rampling, and they didn't seem to think she was much of an obstacle.

A week ago Dan would have agreed with them. Now he was no longer so sure. He'd been prepared to dislike her. From everything he had read she appeared to be a spoiled party girl who only cared about having a good time and getting her name in the gossip columns. But after the way she had stood up to Barnes at the board meeting, it was apparent that she possessed more substance than he'd imagined.

"We're ready to test the closure doors."

Dan turned and saw Russell Edmonds standing behind him.

"Another one." Dan nodded toward the broken glass of the cabinet that had contained emergency supplies.

"Harry told me."

"What do you think?"

Edmonds shrugged. "Hard to say."

"Take a guess."

"Could be anybody."

"I'd like your opinion."

"As a miner or an Indian?"

"Which instinct do you trust?"

"Both."

"So?"

"All I can tell you is that something's brewing," the other man said. "I don't know what. But the guys are real angry. It won't take much for the shit to hit the fan."

Dan nodded. "What about those closure doors?"

"They're fixed."

"Okay. Let's check 'em out."

The two men walked back toward the main shaft. It opened into a large, cavernous area that had been the first section to be blasted out. Now it served as a place for the storage and assembly of equipment. Everything used below ground had to be lowered down the main shaft. If it was too big, it was taken apart on the surface and reassembled underground. The area where this was done was big enough to house a football field. It was like a subway terminal, with tunnels joining main and auxiliary lines. Each gallery led to a different work area, all of which converged on the main work-face from different angles and were linked by a network of cross-passages the miners used to avoid having to retrace their steps whenever they shifted from one drilling area to another.

At the end of each access tunnel were huge steel doors, enlarged versions of those found in a bank vault. It was obvious from the shine on them that they had just been installed. Two men were still working on one door, sweating as they labored with crowbars to pry a hinge into place. Sid stood a short distance away, looking on intently but offering no help. His hands were still badly blistered from the burns he had received when he climbed the heated boom, but that hadn't stopped him from turning up for work every day.

"I thought you said they were ready," Dan said.

"Just passing along what they told me," Edmonds replied.

One of the men released his grip on the crowbar and wearily wiped his parched lips with the back of his hand.

"Goddam spring," he muttered. "We're gonna have to get a hydraulic jack to lift it."

"How about some guys helping you?"

"There isn't room on the bar." The man spit. "Fuckin' thing is sheer deadweight."

"How long'll it take you to rig a lift?"

"It's getting it down here that takes time."

Dan looked at Sid. The big man smiled broadly. He shouldered his way past the other two men and grasped one of the steel crowbars.

"The only thing that'll move that hinge is a hydraulic jack," the man who had spoken earlier said.

The crowbar began to bend, but Sid still refused to relinquish his grip.

"Holy shit!" the other man gasped. "That bastard ain't human."

The veins stood out like cordwood on Sid's neck, and blood pulsing to his face had half closed his eyes. He grunted with each short intake of breath, and a fleck of saliva bubbled at the corner of his mouth.

"Sure as hell he's gonna rupture himself," the man who had been working on the door said.

"Not Sid." Dan spoke with quiet assurance. "Anybody else, maybe, but not Sid."

There was sudden screech of metal on metal as the hinge abruptly snapped into place.

"I'll be goddamned—" The man who had been working on the door shook his head in disbelief. "The fuckin' ape did it."

Sid lowered the crowbar and looked at Dan. He was drenched in sweat and the palms of his hands were bleeding. But his eyes glittered.

Dan moved toward a large grey-painted console and flipped some switches. An eerie wail echoed deep inside the tunnels. It rose and fell, getting louder with each passing second. It brought workers running from all directions. They poured from the spokes of the wheel and gathered at the hub. Dan had briefed them earlier about the routine to follow when they heard the siren, but this was the first time

184

he'd actually put them through an emergency drill since the closure doors were installed a few days before.

"All right," he announced loudly as the last few miners straggled into view. "I've already told you how this system works. I'm going to run through it once more so there won't be any misunderstanding."

He pointed to the metal console. "Special sensors have been installed throughout each tunnel," he said. "Any sudden change in pressure will register on instruments down here and on the surface. They're linked to computers that can determine whether there's been an explosion and emergency procedures are required. If a general evacuation of all underground personnel is warranted, the siren you've just heard will automatically sound. It means you have exactly eight minutes to clear the work-faces and assemble here at the main shaft."

"That isn't much time," a bearded miner said. "What happens if we don't make it?"

Dan strode over to the console and pressed a red, mushroom-shaped button. The hulking steel closure doors immediately swung shut, and locked into place.

"The doors can be operated manually from here," he said. "But only during an additional four-minute period. After that—"

"Guys who don't make it are shit out of luck, huh?" the other man said.

"Flash fires move fast," Dan said. "Eight minutes is enough to give most guys a chance—"

"If they run like hell."

"That's the whole idea."

Nervous laughter rippled through the miners. But there was no humor in their eyes. Many of them had been on the crews that removed the charred remains of their coworkers, and the memory of that ghastly task was still fresh in their minds.

"What happens when those doors close?" another miner asked.

"You're a powder man," Dan replied. "What does a fire need to burn?"

"Oxygen."

"Right. And what's the quickest way to exhaust all the oxygen in a confined space."

"An explosion."

"Right again," Dan said. "After twelve minutes charges placed at strategic locations will be automatically detonated."

"The blast'll pulverize anybody left in there." This time it was Gallagher who spoke. "They wouldn't stand a chance."

"Nobody's kidding anybody, Harry. It's a calculated risk. But it's one we've got to take—" Dan's voice trailed away. He knew as well as any of them that eight or even twelve minutes was barely enough time for men working on the most distant work-faces to make it to the base of the main shaft. Particularly if the transporters were out of commission. The whole system was predicated on the logic that it was better to sacrifice a few lives rather than risk a major disaster. The closure doors weren't his idea. Safety engineers at the company's headquarters in Dallas had dreamed them up after the legal department decided it needed something it could point to if OSHA wanted to know what additional precautions had been taken to prevent another accident.

"It's crazy," Gallagher said.

"Maybe," Dan replied. "But my orders are to make sure you guys go through the drill at the beginning of every shift. And that's exactly what I'm gonna do. In the future, anybody who isn't out of those tunnels and here at the main shaft in eight minutes can find another job. Is that clear?"

"We don't have to put up with this shit," Gallagher said.

"Try me," Dan snapped.

"The unions won't stand for it."

"Bring a grievance."

"Don't think I won't," the other man replied heatedly.

"Okay," Dan said, addressing the men. "Let's all get back to work."

The miners hurried away, leaving Dan and Gallagher facing each other.

"Did you mean that," the powder man asked. "About firing the guys?"

"Damn right."

"You're asking for trouble, Dan, and it may be more than you can handle."

"We'll see."

Gallagher started to say something, but checked himself when he heard the man trip rattle to a halt at the bottom of the main shaft. He abruptly walked away. Dan watched him go. When he turned he was surprised to see David Seymour striding toward him, accompanied by Ceetra Rampling.

"Well, I'm here," the other man announced brusquely.

"So I see," Dan replied.

"It better be worth dragging me all the way up from Dallas at this time of night."

"I don't get you."

"The company operator said you'd called to say there was an emergency down here—"

"Not me," Dan said. "I haven't been near a phone since I got back from Dallas this afternoon."

"We heard a siren while we were coming down," Ceetra said.

Dan heard the tremor in her voice. "We were testing the closure doors. Just a routine procedure. Nothing to worry about."

"I don't understand," Seymour said. "Somebody must have called."

"Beats me." Dan looked at Ceetra and saw she was shaking. "You okay?"

"Just nervous," she said. "It's my first time below ground."

"How about some coffee?"

"No thanks," Ceetra said. "I'll just sit here a while until I get my bearings."

Her head was spinning. It had started the moment she stepped into the man trip. Seymour had found some jeans and a work shirt for her, and she'd put them on in his office. A man at the change house had equipped her with a yellow slicker outfit, heavy rubber boots and hard hat. Just preparing for the descent had filled her with apprehension, and it had increased as the man trip lowered her into the depths. She'd experienced all the symptoms that heralded an attack of claustrophobia, and had to will herself not to panic.

Now she sat on the edge of a wooden packing crate and tried to calm herself by taking a series of deep breaths. The air had a sharp, acrid smell, and was heavy with dust. It was also unbearably hot. Sweat drenched the jeans and shirt she was wearing under the yellow slicker.

"Did the closure doors work all right?" Seymour asked.

Dan nodded. "They worked, but the men weren't happy about them. And I think they're right. Twelve minutes isn't long enough—"

"According to the studies our safety people have done there's more than—"

"Fuck the studies," Dan snapped. "I'm talking about men's lives."

"You think they don't know that?"

"I think they don't care."

"They care just as much as—"

"Listen." Dan's voice turned hard. "Don't jerk me around. You know as well as I do why they put those doors in."

"Why did they?" Ceetra asked.

Dan looked at Seymour. "Want to tell her?"

"Seems you know all the answers."

Dan crossed to where Ceetra was sitting on the wooden crate. "Over eighty men died in the blast that killed your father and brother," he said. "They had wives, kids, dependents, and those people don't like this company very much right now. Some have already filed suit for negligence, and there'll be a hell of a lot more before the dust settles."

"Is that right?" Ceetra asked, looking at Seymour.

"Yes."

"Will there be a trial?" Ceetra persisted.

"Unless the company can reach out-of-court settlements."

"Oh, they'll settle all right," Dan said. "This is a federal project. The last thing the company wants is to offend the administration. Particularly in an election year."

"I see," Ceetra said. "But what has all this to do with those—" She hesitated, groping for the right words.

"Closure doors," Dan said.

"Yes. Where do they come into this?"

"There will be special committee hearings in Washington," he replied. "A lot of politicians, particularly the ones who pushed for Rampling International to be awarded the contract for this section of the tunnel, are going to have to cover their asses. The way they'll do it is by pressing to know what measures have been taken to prevent another disaster. Lobbyists like Ed Morley will show them fancy pictures of these doors and a bunch of reports from our safety engineers about an efficient new system the company has installed at enormous expense—"

"But you said the doors work." Ceetra's voice reflected her confusion.

"I also said eight or twelve minutes isn't enough time for miners on scaffolds at the work-face or jumbo drill operators to get out. The way this system's set up now it's a goddam death trap."

"That's ridiculous," Seymour protested.

"I'm right, and you know it."

"This isn't getting us anywhere. The doors are in place and they're going to stay." Seymour turned his attention to Ceetra. "Now, as long as we're down here, why don't I show you around?"

"I think I'll just sit here a while longer," Ceetra said.

"Are you feeling any better?"

"Still queasy."

"I can stay if you'd rather."

"It isn't necessary, really."

"All right. When you feel well enough you'll find me at the work-face."

Ceetra watched as Seymour strode to where a group of miners were already seated on one of the low-profile transporters that ran at regular intervals between the main shaft and wherever work was being done at different places in the tunnel. She sensed he was reluctant to leave her with Dan.

"I'm gonna get some coffee," Dan said.

She didn't answer. Her eyes were fixed on the face of a miner seated on the transporter with his back to Seymour, slightly apart from the others. His head had been down, but as he raised it he seemed to look deliberately in her direction. His cheeks were smeared with muck, but his features seemed familiar. The eyes particularly. She had seen them before, but couldn't recall when or where. The transporter had begun to move before it came to her. They belonged on snapshots she had studied in her father's room at the ranch house in Dallas. They were her brother's eyes.

"Wait—" She got up and started after the transporter, but before she'd taken more than a couple of steps her knees buckled and she fell. The impact of her fall was softened by the thick mud, but was still enough to knock the breath out of her. Her head spun and for a moment she thought she was going to lose consciousness. Then she looked up and saw Dan standing over her. She felt his arms under her shoulders as he lifted her to a sitting position.

"What happened?" he asked.

"I—I thought I saw my brother."

"You what?"

"My brother." Her voice was stronger. "He was on that transporter."

"Put your arms round my neck."

"Really. I saw him."

"Okay, you saw him. Now do as I say."

It was obvious he was humoring her.

"But I'm certain—"

"Don't talk."

He picked her up with ease and carried her back to the packing case. When she raised her hand to wipe the mud from her eyes it trembled so badly she couldn't control it.

"Bromley was with those men," she said shakily.

"I told you—"

"Listen to me, dammit."

"Your brother's dead."

"But I saw him."

"You thought—"

"I know."

Suddenly, her frustration gave way to tears. She didn't want to cry. But she couldn't help herself.

"It's all right," Dan said. "You've been living on your nerves ever since you arrived."

He tore a strip of cloth from a rag that hung near the coffee pot and gently wiped her cheeks.

"You think I imagined it, don't you?" she asked.

He nodded.

"But it was so real," she insisted.

"Did you ever meet your brother?"

She shook her head.

"Then how do you know what he looks like?"

"From pictures," she said. "Dozens of them."

"Where?"

"At the ranch, and ones my mother received from Bromley."

"Were any of them taken recently?"

She hesitated. "I don't know."

Dan didn't press his point. Instead, he found two mugs and filled them with steaming coffee. "Here." He handed one to her. "This'll help."

She sipped the hot, bitter liquid, and realized how silly she must sound. Dan had found the bodies. He knew better than anybody that everyone who was underground at the time of the flash fire had perished.

"It's good," she said.

"Want more?"

"This is fine." She hesitated. "I didn't mean to get hysterical like that."

"Being underground for the first time can be a very frightening experience," he said.

"I've always been terrified of confined spaces."

"Then why did you come?"

"It wasn't my idea."

"Seymour's?"

"Yes." She sipped the coffee. "He figured I'd better see what kind of world I'll be getting into if I decide to hang onto my father's shares."

"Is that what you're going to do?"

"I don't know. It depends."

"On what?"

"I'm not sure I know how to explain it." She hesitated. "You knew my father better than almost anybody," she said.

"Probably. But there were sides to him he never let anyone see. I never could understand the way he disowned you. It must have made you feel—" He paused, groping for the word.

"Angry, hurt, puzzled—like an outsider. I seem to have spent my life on a dark street, in a strange city, looking in windows at other people's lives and wondering what it would feel like to belong."

"And you think you'll find that feeling in your father's business?"

"Why not? My brother did," she replied. "And who knows, in time maybe I could put my own imprint on it."

Dan seemed about to answer, but checked himself and took her empty mug.

"More coffee?" he asked.

She shook her head. "It was good. Thanks."

"You still look pretty shaky. The best thing you can do is to take the next man trip above ground and get a good night's sleep."

"You're probably right. But now that I've come this far, I

might as well go the rest of the way. It may be a long time before I have the nerve to come down again."

"Well, I'm afraid you'll have to do it alone," he said. "We're three men short on this shift. That means I'm gonna have to do a lot of ass-kicking before morning."

"Are they sick?" Ceetra asked.

"No. It's always the same on Friday night. Guys take their paychecks into Amarillo and blow them on girls at bars or in the whorehouses. By the time they're cleaned out it's too late for them to get back. It'd solve a lot of problems if those women moved nearer to camp."

"Why don't they?"

Dan looked at her in surprise. A slow grin spread across his face. "Probably would, but there's no place between here and Amarillo for them to set up shop."

She got up. Her legs were much stronger and her head had stopped spinning.

"I'd better let you get on with your work."

"Sure you're okay?"

"I'm fine. Just point me in the direction of the work-face."

"The transporter should be back in fifteen or twenty minutes."

"I'd rather walk. It's about time I started getting the feel of the business."

"It's slippery as hell in this muck."

"I'll manage," she said. "I'm used to taking care of myself."

Dan motioned toward the gallery down which the transporter had disappeared. "Just follow the conveyor belt," he said. "It's straight—"

The sudden wail of a siren drowned out his words. He swung around and looked at a board suspended on the wall to one side of the main shaft. It contained three lights and the words DRILL, SHOOT, MUCK. The red-painted bulb opposite SHOOT was flickering.

"What's happening?" she asked.

He grabbed her by both arms and pulled her into a nearby alcove. "Open your mouth wide," he yelled.

Instinctively, she obeyed. Seconds later a wall of hot air whooshed past them. It sent the coffee pot flying across the open storage area. Almost simultaneously, she heard a series of low rumbles. They were like ripples of distant thunder which steadily grew louder and then abruptly stopped. The acrid air stung her nostrils. She looked at Dan, who was still holding her.

"It's all right," he assured her. "They're only blasting. I should have warned you."

"How often does it happen?" she asked.

"Only once or twice a shift. After the rock's down they muck it out." He continued to hold her. "Sure you want to go?"

"I guess—"

He nodded and released his grip. "Keep your eye on the blasting boards. You'll see them all down the tunnel. If you hear the siren, find cover and yawn."

"Yawn?"

"It'll relieve the pressure on your eardrums."

It took all the willpower Ceetra possessed to leave the sanctuary of the storage area and start down the long narrow tunnel that led to the work-face. A V-shaped rubber conveyor belt carried freshly mined rock in an endless stream along one side of the passageway. The rollers over which it ran gave off a whirring sound, and the muck writhed in wet, slippery fragments as it slid in a glistening mass to be loaded into massive steel skip buckets that were hauled to the surface under the man trip. High above her huge fan lines were suspended along the naked rock walls. The roar of their blowers was deafening. It was punctuated by the staccato chatter of pneumatic drills, the revving of compressors, and the grinding scrape of front-end loaders.

Miners wearing hard hats and yellow slickers glanced up from their work as she passed. Some smiled, others winked, a few whistled. All were visibly surprised at her presence. She found herself searching their grime-covered faces for Bromley's features, still unwilling to accept that the earlier glimpse had been imagined.

When she finally reached the work-face, it wasn't at all the way she had expected it to be. Instead of miners picking away at the rock in a confined space, which was the way tunneling had been portrayed in the movies she'd seen, there was a huge, cavernous space, larger even than the storage area at the base of the main shaft. And it was filled with heavy-duty equipment. Most was either diesel-powered or hydraulically operated. Front-end loaders scooped up muck and emptied it onto conveyor belts. Bulldozers scraped piles of newly blasted rock into heaps near the loaders. Forklifts scurried back and forth loaded with drill bits.

But the scene was dominated by a massive Garner-Denver drilling jumbo. Mounted on a converted Euclid truck, it consisted of four hydraulically operated booms, each of which was controlled by a separate operator. These men stood on steel-grille platforms and manipulated fifteen-foot tungsten-tipped drills remotely through a bank of levers which protruded from a console that was welded to metal frames. It looked to Ceetra like a giant octopus whose tentacles were all pressed against the rock work-face. Water poured from the holes the bits were gouging in the stone. Each time pressure was increased on the hydraulic booms, there was a hideous screech that echoed from the walls of the chamber at an earsplitting pitch.

"Impressed?"

Ceetra turned and saw David Seymour.

"Very!" She had to shout to make herself heard. "But I haven't the vaguest idea what's happening."

"They've just blasted," Seymour replied, leaning forward so his lips were almost touching her ear.

"I know. The blast was pretty strong down by the main shaft. It must really have been something up this close."

"It gives me a powder headache every time. But the guys who work down here all the time are used to it."

"Looks like they really earn their wages."

"You're right. It's got to be one of the most mind-numbing jobs imaginable. Drill, blast, muck. That's all there is to tunneling. It hasn't really changed very much in the last fifty years."

Ceetra looked at where debris was being dumped onto a conveyor by two low-profile loaders. "What happens to all that stuff when you get it above ground?"

"We've used a lot of it to dam up the arroyos on the northeast side of camp. Flash floods aren't common in this part of Texas, but if we get any sudden heavy rains there's no telling what might happen. We're pretty close to the Canadian River."

"And the rest?"

"There's a mile-long ravine about halfway between here and Amarillo. The environmentalists were against us using it as a dump site. They claimed the muck would ruin the natural ground cover. It cost the company a fortune to do impact studies, but the courts finally gave us the go-ahead. Now we're back on three shifts. We'll have dump trucks hauling muck out there round the clock."

"What are those called?" Ceetra pointed to the octopuslike rigs.

"Drill jumbos."

"How do the operators know they're pushing the tunnel through in the right direction?"

"When I started in this business they used to use a surveyor's transit," Seymour replied. "But that's all changed. Now they rely on laser beams linked to a computer. The manufacturer claims it's so accurate they could hit a dime through three miles of solid rock."

"Amazing. How on earth do they get all this stuff down here?"

"Every bit of it had to be lowered down the main shaft. The bigger pieces were dismantled and reassembled at the work-face. It's mostly an on-rubber job."

"On-rubber?"

"Just an expression," Seymour said. "Some projects are better suited to mining cars on rails for transporting the muck. But on this job we decided to go with conveyor belts and rubber-tired vehicles. It required more ventilation to get rid of the diesel fumes, but the flexibility it adds made it worth it."

Tired of trying to make herself heard over the cacophony surrounding her, Ceetra watched as a group of miners rolled a gigantic section of concrete pipe into position near the drill jumbo. Its size dwarfed them. Yet, with the help of a front-end loader, they made handling it seem easy. The smooth precision of their movements fascinated her. There wasn't a single wasted motion. Each man knew exactly what was expected of him. In its own way, what they were doing was as choreographed as the most intricate ballet.

As she stepped forward for a better look there was a blinding flash. It came from behind her. When she swung round, she saw an electric cable snaking toward her. It was spewing showers of bluish-white sparks as it jerked crazily from side to side, moving with a rapidity that made it impossible to guess which way the tension it was under would make it jump next. It was less than a few feet away from her when she instinctively leaped to the left. It missed her by inches.

Seymour wasn't as lucky. He saw it coming, but lacked Ceetra's reflexes, and was still in mid-stride when the cable hit him. She watched in horror as the protruding strands of wire, stripped of their insulation, gouged deep furrows across his forehead and down the side of his right cheek. The current jolted through his body, jerking him about in a series of grotesque contortions that made it appear he was wrestling with the loose cable. Then his skin started to smoke.

Ceetra looked around frantically for help, but the miners standing nearby seemed transfixed by the sight and made no move to assist him. When she turned back to look at Seymour she understood the look of horror in their eyes. He wasn't wearing rubber boots. There hadn't been any his size in the change house, and because he believed there was an emergency below he had decided against waiting until a pair could be found that would fit him. And he was standing in a shallow pool of water. It served as a conductor for the current that was surging through his body. To make matters worse, in attempting to maintain his balance when the cable first hit him, he had grabbed the metal blade of a nearby bulldozer, and his hand had become caught in the steel struts.

As Ceetra watched his eyeballs bulged and split. Viscous fluid spurted from the sockets. Then his face turned scarlet and puffed up. Jagged cracks appeared in his skin. Smoke appeared at his nostrils and ears. His hair melted in a thin, tarry mess that dribbled down the sides of his skull like thick molasses.

She tried to turn away, but couldn't. And her eyes refused to close. The stench of burning flesh enveloped her: sweet, pungent, sickening. Her senses began to slip away, but not quickly enough for her to be spared the sight of the skin on the back of Seymour's hand peeling back in charred curls. The bone was showing by the time she found sanctuary in unconsciousness.

 *16*

"CEETRA!"

She heard her name, faint and very far away.

"Open your eyes."

The words registered, but her lethargy was such that she made no effort to obey.

"Come on, you can do it."

Her feelings were similar to those she had experienced the first time she tried opium: tranquil, aware but not involved, existing behind a soft grey veil of her own well-being. She heard the words repeated again and again, but their urgency was lost on her.

"She's coming round."

Her peacefulness gave way to a sudden, unaccountable anxiety. It was like the moment before fully awakening, when there is still a choice between reentering sleep and facing the rigors of another day. She knew the moment she opened her eyes her place of refuge would be lost. But a force beyond reason parted her lids.

"Good. That's the way. Now, how are you feeling?"

She saw a face. Its features were blurred. The mouth moved, but the words seemed oddly out of sync. It was a minute or two before she was able to recognize the man leaning over her. She remembered him from their brief meeting in Bromley's room the day she arrived in Dallas. He was a doctor. She couldn't remember his name.

"I—" There was a terrible dryness in her throat.

"Get her something to drink."

She felt moisture against her lips, and gratefully swallowed what tasted like grapefruit juice.

"I'm Dr. Robinson. Remember me?"

She nodded.

"Dan Blake called me in Dallas. He told me what happened. I thought you might appreciate a friendly face."

Ceetra angled her head slightly and saw two other men standing at the side of her bed. They were both younger, and she guessed from their white coats that they were doctors. Behind them was middle-aged nurse, arranging a frame of glass vials on a steel tray.

"You're in High Plains Baptist Hospital in Amarillo," Dr. Robinson said.

"How long have I been here?"

The old man glanced at his watch. "About thirty-six hours. You suffered a severe shock. The best cure is sleep. We've kept you under sedation, but there's nothing to worry about. A few minor abrasions, some nasty cuts, but that's all."

The two young doctors looked at each other, nodded and left the room. They were followed moments later by the nurse. Dr. Robinson pressed a lever at the side of her bed and she felt herself being raised into a sitting position.

"The last thing I remember—"

Suddenly, like a sea mist abruptly lifting, the haze that had clouded her memory dissolved, and she saw Seymour's face as the electric current from the broken cable coursed through him. Eyes bulging, skin peeling, nostrils smoking. She recalled it all and began to tremble.

"Now then," Dr. Robinson said, leaning forward to hold her shoulders. "That's quite enough."

She smelled liquor on his breath and saw his eyes were bloodshot.

"That's better. Just try to relax." He pulled a chair to the side of the bed and sat down. "I want you to know you're a very lucky young lady."

"Lucky?" Her voice was still hoarse.

"If Dan Blake hadn't realized you were in shock—well, it could have been a lot more serious."

"Dan?" She tried to remember what part he had played.

"He did all the right things. Made sure you hadn't swallowed your tongue, kept you warm, got you above ground and here to the hospital in a hurry. No wonder your father thought so highly of him."

Now Ceetra wanted to talk. It was a way of not remembering.

"I understand they were very close," she said.

"Jake treated him like a son."

"Bromley must have resented that."

Liquor had obviously loosened the doctor's tongue. "I'm not sure he cared," he said. "I think he was kind of glad to have a buffer between himself and his father."

"I remember your telling me you delivered him."

"It wasn't an easy birth. Didn't think he'd live. Started coming out with the umbilical cord wrapped around his neck. He'd have choked to death if I hadn't managed to push him back in far enough to get the damned thing untangled. Don't mind telling you that was a night I won't forget in a hurry. And your father was right there looking over my shoulder all the time, swearing he'd kill me if anything went wrong."

"You delivered me, too, didn't you?"

"That's right."

"Was my father there when I was born?"

The old man shook his head.

"Jake was a strange man. Knew him most of his life, and still didn't understand him. There were times when I honestly wondered if—"

"What?"

"He was the most driven human being I've ever come across," the doctor reflected. "When he set his mind on doing a thing, that was it. The devil himself couldn't have stopped him. He was always like that. Came to me with a badly fractured leg not long after he came out of the service. I told him he'd have to take it easy with his leg busted up like that, but I might as well have been talking to a wall. He didn't heed a word I said. Went right out and continued working eighteen and twenty hours a day, on crutches."

"Was that when you became company physician?"

"Lands, no." He chuckled. "Your father was hocked to the neck. Couldn't afford a pot to piss in, let alone a full-time doctor. Wasn't until he had a fair-sized company that he put me on retainer. Somewhere in the mid-fifties, I guess it was. A while before you were born, anyway."

"Was Ed Morley his partner then?"

"That's right. I'm surprised you know about him."

"He was at the funeral."

"I saw him. And I must say I was surprised, what with the way him and your daddy felt about one another. There was no love lost, I'll tell you."

"What happened to split them up?"

Dr. Robinson thought for a moment before answering. "It's a long story. No point in rehashing stuff that happened way back then."

She didn't press. Her instincts warned it might make him cautious. This was the opportunity she'd been hoping for ever since she returned to Texas. A chance to find out what lay behind doors that had been locked to her all her life. She didn't want to do anything to jeopardize the situation.

"It happened around the time Bromley was born, didn't it?" she said, making the observation sound casual.

"More or less," Dr. Robinson admitted.

"Was my mother happy about being pregnant?"

"It was a difficult time for her."

"In what way?"

"She was always a high-strung woman. Knowing Jake wanted a boy so badly can't have helped any. It was a crime the way he treated her when she had you."

"I gather it was worse after she had Bromley."

"That's right. He fair took over the poor boy's life. He had such hopes for him."

"Did my brother disappoint him?"

"You saw his room."

"I thought maybe—"

"He just wasn't made of the same fibre as Jake. And the more the boy fell short, the more his father turned to Dan Blake as a kind of substitute son. It was pathetic to see it happening."

"Did Dan want that role?"

"I don't think so, but there wasn't much he could do to stop it. I know he took Bromley's side a lot of times, but it only made the boy feel less wanted. I watched him withdraw. He began to create a fantasy world for himself."

"Those cutouts of my mother—"

"He worshiped her."

"But they never really knew each other."

"Don't you see, that made her perfect," the old man said. "He could imagine her any way he wanted."

"Her whole world revolved around his letters."

"Doesn't sound like she's changed one little bit."

"Was she—fanciful when you knew her?"

"Lived in her own world."

"Is that why you had her committed?"

"She was examined by two court-appointed psychia-trists—"

"But you recommended the examination."

Dr. Robinson averted his eyes.

"Did you believe she was insane?" Ceetra asked quietly.

"The answer to that is something that's haunted me for a lot of years," the old man replied.

"You mean she wasn't?"

"I just don't know. She behaved so oddly after they'd had her in that clinic a couple of days. And I was under all kinds of pressure—"

"From my father?"

The doctor nodded.

For the first time since they'd begun to talk, Ceetra realized the old man wanted to purge himself.

"Do you think insanity can be inherited?" she asked.

"There are a lot of theories. Why?"

"I thought I saw Bromley."

"Saw him. When?"

"While I was underground. Among a group of workers."

Dr. Robinson seemed about to answer when there was a sound at the door. He turned to see Mule Barnes.

"Go ahead, Earl," the other man said. "I'd like to hear your professional opinion."

The doctor underwent an abrupt change. His garrulousness vanished, and he became guarded. "We were just talking, Mule," he murmured.

"That right? Well, maybe I can answer the young lady's question." Barnes came toward the bed. "The first time a person goes underground they're likely to get real nervous. Isn't that what happened to you?"

Ceetra nodded.

"Sure you did," the lawyer continued smoothly. "And I don't blame you one little bit. Like I told you the day you arrived, camps and tunnels are no place for a woman. Right, Earl?"

"I guess—"

"Lord, it's a frightening experience," Barnes continued, cutting the doctor short. "And folks who are scared begin to imagine things. First time I ever went down that shaft I was so goddam petrified I could hardly move. What's it called when a person's in that kind of state, Earl?"

"Hysterical paralysis," the older man replied.

"Hysterical paralysis." Barnes rolled the words round his mouth. "That would account for a whole lot of things, wouldn't it?"

"I saw my brother," Ceetra said firmly.

"Did you talk to him?"

"No."

"Who was with you when it happened?"

"Dan Blake."

"Did he see Bromley?"

"He wasn't looking—"

"Well, then." He looked at the doctor. "Sounds to me like this little lady needs some more rest. Why don't you give her something to quiet her down?"

Dr. Robinson took a plastic container from his pocket. "Valium," he said. "Have you taken it before?"

Ceetra nodded.

"Good, then you know what to expect." He shook two tablets into the palm of his hand. "I want you to take both of these now, and if you're still not relaxed in an hour try another."

He handed her the pills and a small paper cup half filled with water. Ceetra swallowed them and lay back against the pillow.

"That's fine," Barnes said. "Now if you don't mind, Earl, I'd appreciate a few moments alone with your patient."

"Yes, of course." The doctor's manner was completely subdued. "I'll look in on you in a little while. Try not to tire yourself."

The attorney waited until Dr. Robinson closed the door.

"Poor old Earl," he said, infusing just the right touch of confidentiality into his voice. "Sometimes he worries me. Doesn't look well at all. Getting on in years. Happens to us all sooner or later, I guess."

Ceetra remained silent. She had disliked Barnes from the moment she first met him, and every contact she'd had with him since only verified her first impression.

"Been bending your ear with a lot of stories about the past, has he?"

"I asked some questions," Ceetra replied coolly. "He answered the ones he could."

Barnes nodded. "Wouldn't put much stock in what he told you, though. Between you and me, Earl's quite a drinker. Likes to nip from that flask he carries around in his hip pocket. Thinks nobody's on to him, but—well, doesn't do any harm, I suppose."

"I like him," she said.

"Sure you do. Everybody likes old Earl. It's just that there aren't too many would trust him with surgery, if you take my meaning."

He chuckled at his own joke, but when he saw Ceetra wasn't smiling, he manner turned serious.

"About that little misunderstanding we had at the board meeting," he said, exaggerated concern wrinkling his brow. "I want you to know how much I respect your feeling the way you do about your momma. The world'd be a lot better place if there were more kids who looked out for their parents—"

"Why did you lie to me?" Ceetra interjected.

"I don't take your meaning."

"When you called me in London you told me I should be present at the reading of my father's will because the continued payments of my mother's support were involved."

"That was no lie." Barnes managed to sound offended. "Jake always paid Mary's bills out of his own pocket. It was set up that way in the divorce. Now that he's dead some other arrangement will have to be made."

"That could have been done without my being there," Ceetra said.

"All right, I'll level with you. I wanted you there because I knew what was in the will."

"Then why did you make up that story about my mother's support?"

"Would you have come if I hadn't?"

"I would if you'd told me about the will."

"I couldn't do that," he said. "It's against the law to leak that kind of information prematurely."

Ceetra didn't answer. What Barnes said was logical, yet an inner voice still warned her against trusting him. She tried to reason why, but the pills Dr. Robinson had given her were beginning to take effect, and her brain was too dulled to reach any conclusion.

"You all right?" he asked.

"Just tired."

"You're lucky it wasn't worse. Lord knows what you were doing down there, anyway."

"I wanted to see what my father's world was like."

"You should have asked me," he said. "I could have told you that running this firm is like juggling two dozen balls and keeping them all in the air while you're playing "Yellow Rose of Texas" on a xylophone. Problems you can't imagine. And I'm gonna need your help."

"How?"

"By giving me power of attorney to make the best deal I can for you on your daddy's stock."

"I told you I wanted to think about it," she murmured. She had to struggle to keep her eyes open.

"Okay. I guess that's your privilege." He sounded irritated. "But while you're doing that thinking there's something else you might want to consider. That cable didn't break, it was cut. Somebody did it deliberately."

"You mean they wanted to kill David Seymour?"

"Or you."

She tried to focus on his words, but it was no use. The moment she closed her eyes, she drifted into sleep.

When Ceetra opened her eyes the room was filled with a soft golden light. The late afternoon sun shone in narrow shafts through the slats of the half closed Levolor blinds.

"Are you feeling any better?"

Ceetra looked toward the door and saw the nurse peering in.

"How long have I been asleep?" she asked.

"Almost five hours." The nurse came in and closed the blinds. "And you had a visitor."

"Who?"

"Dan Blake." The nurse switched on a light over the bed. "He waited nearly an hour."

"You should have wakened me."

"Dr. Robinson left strict orders you weren't to be disturbed."

"Did he say he'd come back?"

"Said he'll try and make it during this evening's visiting hours."

"When do they start?"

"Six o'clock."

Ceetra glanced at the wall clock. It was nearly five. She felt a prickle of excitement.

"God, I feel such a mess."

"Why don't you wash your hair? That always gives me a lift."

"I don't have a dryer."

"You can use mine. It's in my locker. I'll go and get it."

When she was alone Ceetra swung her legs over the edge of the bed and tried to stand up. But her legs were weaker than she thought and she collapsed back onto the bed. After two or three minutes' rest she made a second attempt. This time she managed to wobble to a small bathroom adjoining the private room. Running the water until it was hot, she stepped into the shower. The needle-thin jets were powerful and she could feel her blood flow increasing as she let the water stream against her. She squeezed some shampoo from a plastic bottle, massaged her scalp until it tingled, and felt her lethargy give way to a sense of eager anticipation.

"Now don't start overdoing things," the nurse warned when Ceetra stepped back into the room. "Doctor said you've had quite a time of it, and should take it real slow for a while."

"It's about time I—" Ceetra stopped abruptly. She had leaned over to pick up a towel that had slipped to the floor, and her head suddenly began to spin. If the other woman hadn't seen what was happening and grabbed her arm she would have fallen.

"What did I tell you?" the nurse clucked reprovingly. "I'm not sure you're ready to have any visitors."

"I'm fine. Really. I just stayed under that hot shower too long." The nurse helped her to the bed.

"I'd better get the doctor," she said.

"I told you I'm all right," Ceetra insisted.

"This fella you're expecting must be special."

"He is."

The nurse smiled knowingly. "Okay. But you take it easy. I'll dry your hair for you."

Ceetra didn't argue. She felt weaker than she was ready to admit, and without the nurse's help she doubted if she would have had the strength to get ready.

It was almost six o'clock by the time the nurse finished drying her hair and teasing it into shape with a hot iron curler she had brought with the dryer.

"Well, that's the best I can do," she announced, standing back and examining her handiwork through squinted eyes. "What do you think?"

As Ceetra looked at herself in the mirror she experienced a sinking sensation. Her hair was fluffed in a bouffant style that made it look like a bird had nested in it.

"It's—different," she said.

"Saw it in one of those glossy magazines in the visitor's lounge," the nurse said proudly. "It suits you just fine."

It was almost an hour before Dan arrived.

"Sorry I'm late." He looked tired and badly in need of a shave. "I stopped in to chat with Dr. Robinson and couldn't get away. That man loves to talk."

"He's an admirer of yours. Tells me you did all the right things after I passed out."

"It was just simple first aid."

"That's not what he told me."

There was an awkward silence. Dan seemed embarrassed by her gratitude. He looked at where a cigarette was smoldering in an ashtray. "I hate smoking," he said. "Mind if I put it out?" He crushed the stub against the bottom of the ashtray.

"The nurse left it," Ceetra said. "I don't smoke."

She uttered the denial instinctively.

He looked at her with a faintly puzzled expression.

"You look different somehow."

"It's my hair."

"Mmmm."

"Well, don't leave me in suspense."

"It looks good enough to eat."

"Like cotton candy?"

"Exactly."

Ceetra laughed. "The nurse fixed it. She figured it suits my personality. What do you think?"

"It doesn't match the impression I've got."

"That's a relief."

He chuckled and the tension slowly dissolved.

"There's something I wanted to ask you."

"Yes?"

"You said it was Seymour's idea for you to visit the tunnel."

"That's right."

"Did you ask if you could, or was it his idea?"

"Why?"

"It's important," Dan said.

Ceetra was silent for a moment. Thinking about the project engineer brought back memories that were still too fresh to have lost their horror.

"He said there was some kind of emergency," she replied finally. "He thought it might be a good idea if I saw what went on underground before I make up my mind about what to do with my father's shares."

"Were you there when he got the telephone call—about the emergency?"

She nodded. "I was standing right next to him."

"Close enough to hear what was said?"

"Only his end of the conversation."

Dan was silent. He kept turning the brim of his stetson between his fingers.

"Why all the questions?" she asked.

"Al Hunter checked on that broken cable."

"Hunter?"

"The investigator from Federal OSHA. He tried to question you at the reception after the funeral."

"I remember. He ruined my dress."

"He might not be strong on social graces," Dan said, "but he's considered one of the best accident investigators in the business. He says there's no question that the cable was deliberately cut."

"Barnes told me. He was here earlier today."

"What did he say?"

"He thought I might have been the intended victim," she said quietly.

"Did you believe him?"

"I don't know—"

"There could be all kinds of other reasons," Dan said.

"I'd like to hear them."

"There have been quite a few instances of sabotage on other sections of the tunnel."

"That's what Seymour said."

"And you know there's an ongoing conflict between experienced miners and on-the-job trainees. It's possible either faction could have severed that cable to stir up trouble."

"Then why would Barnes be so sure somebody wanted to kill me?" she asked.

Before Dan could answer, the door opened and the nurse bustled into the room.

"I'm afraid you'll have to leave," she announced, addressing herself to Dan.

"Just a few more minutes," Ceetra pleaded.

"Sorry," the nurse replied firmly. "Visiting hours ended half an hour ago. The head nurse on this shift's a stickler for rules. If she found your friend here I'd be out of a job in no time."

"It's all right," Dan assured her. "I'll come by tomorrow afternoon. Maybe I can take the patient for a drive."

"I'll be waiting," Ceetra said.

"Better check with Dr. Robinson before you start making plans," the nurse cautioned. "He may not feel you're strong enough."

"I'll be ready, approval or not."

Dan grinned.

"There's more of Jake in you than I figured," he said.

When she was alone Ceetra put her head back against the pillows and gazed at the ceiling. Seeing Dan again had confirmed her earlier feelings. She was beginning to care for him. And in a way that was very different from anything she had experienced with men like Paul Mayhew. He emanated a strength she needed. She closed her eyes and tried to imagine herself in his arms. It evoked a warm, secure feeling.

"And how's my favorite patient?"

Dr. Robinson had come into the room without her hearing him. His cheeks were even more flushed than the last time she saw him.

"I hope Dan Blake's visit didn't tire you too much."

"No," she replied. "Quite the contrary. He just left."

"I know. I saw him on the way out," the doctor said. "He wanted to know if it would be all right to take you for a drive tomorrow."

"I'd like to go."

Dr. Robinson lifted her wrist and felt her pulse.

"I told him not to keep you out more than an hour," he said. "You're still very weak. I don't want you overdoing things."

"I won't," she assured him. "I promise."

He patted her hand. She sensed he was on the verge of saying something, but checked himself at the last minute. When he walked toward the door she noticed he weaved slightly, and wondered how he had managed to keep his job as head company physician for so long when he had such an obvious drinking problem. That was something she would have to look into if she decided to take control of the company.

The thought surprised her. It was the first time since the

board meeting that she'd given any serious consideration to the idea. When Barnes assumed she would sell, she had demurred out of sheer stubbornness. The thought of actually taking over the reins of Rampling International hadn't really entered her mind. The responsibilities that went with operating a firm that size were more than she wanted to shoulder. Running her own business in London was enough of a burden, and she had Andrea Cooper to share that load. Here she would be completely alone—unless Dan helped her.

The thought stayed with her, and when she slept he played a central role in her dreams. The scenarios differed, but each shared the common denominator of helplessness. She was being chased and her legs wouldn't move; attacked, and her cries for help went unheeded. But all the time she was aware of Dan's presence, and knew that he would rescue her at the very last moment.

Time and again she awoke to find herself drenched in sweat. Finally, the only way she was able to get any rest was by taking two of the 10-milligram tablets Dr. Robinson had left in a plastic vial at the side of the bed.

It was almost noon when she awoke. Even then she only emerged from a drugged sleep when the nurse dropped a metal tray holding her breakfast.

"Hope you like 'em scrambled," the other woman said.

"Do I have a choice?" Ceetra asked.

"You could order lunch."

Ceetra looked at the clock.

"My God, you should have wakened me."

"The doctor told me to let you sleep."

"Dan will be here and I won't be ready." She got out of bed and put on her robe. "Where are my clothes?"

The nurse finished cleaning up and opened a closet. It contained the outfit Ceetra had been wearing under the yellow slicker when she went down the tunnel. She remembered the mess she'd been in when she fell in the mud, and was surprised to see the jeans and work shirt had been freshly laundered.

"Did you have them washed?" she asked.

"Honey, if I hadn't the smell would have been enough to keep you on your back permanently."

"Thanks," Ceetra said.

"All part of the service," the other woman replied.

"What about shoes?" she asked.

"You were wearing rubber boots when they brought you in. Maybe you can buy a pair while you're out driving around. There's a real nice shopping mall near First Federal Savings on South Polk in downtown Amarillo."

"What about now? I can't walk out of here in rubber boots."

"Might start a whole new craze." The nurse looked at Ceetra's feet. "You're about my size. I'll see if I can find something."

The nurse took the tray and went in search of the shoes, leaving Ceetra examining herself in the mirror over the wash basin in the bathroom. There were dark circles under her eyes, and she looked washed out. But she decided both could be remedied by the skillful application of a little makeup. The major problem was still her hair. After a night spent tossing and turning, it looked less like cotton candy, and more like a squashed basket.

The only solution was another shampoo. This time she blew it dry herself, letting it fall naturally around her shoulders. When it was finished she stood back from the mirror and appraised herself again. She seemed thinner than she had been when she left London. The slight hollow in her cheeks added emphasis to her cheekbones. But, she realized, the change went beyond the loss of a few pounds. In some indefinable way she had matured. Not in her physical appearance so much as the presence she projected. In some odd way her return to Texas had precipitated an inner transformation.

Before she could give thought to what might have caused it, the nurse bustled back into the room carrying a pair of brown loafers.

"Mine were all work shoes, and white isn't going to look good with those jeans," she announced. "But I found these. They belonged to a patient. Poor soul passed on a week or so ago. Why don't you try them on?"

Filling a dead person's shoes seemed prescient in the light of Seymour's death, but Ceetra tried them on. They were an inch too long.

"How are they?" the other woman asked.

"Perfect."

The nurse nodded approval. Then her eyes moved to Ceetra's hair.

"My lands," she exclaimed. "What happened to the lovely hairdo I fixed for you?"

"It got wet while I was showering," Ceetra said, deciding a half-truth was better than hurting the woman's feelings.

"But you looked so precious."

"Maybe you'll fix it again for me before I'm discharged?"

Mollified, the nurse took Ceetra's jeans and work shirt out of the closet and laid them on the bed. Then she hurried away to answer a page on the public address system.

It was absurd, Ceetra thought, but she was behaving like an adolescent getting ready to go out on her first date. Nervous, slightly tense, even a little apprehensive. It was a sensation she couldn't ever remember experiencing. There had been so many men. But they belonged in the past. Dan was a new beginning.

Visiting hours began at 2:00 p.m., but she was ready half an hour early. When there was no sign of Dan by 2:30, she left her room and went to sit in the lobby of the hospital. It was filled with visitors talking with patients who were ambulatory. She found a seat near the gift shop that afforded her a clear view of the main entrance. She craved a cigarette, but willed herself not to have one. Now that she had discovered Dan disliked smoking so much, she had decided to quit. In an effort to distract herself, she purchased a copy of the *Amarillo Globe-Times*. She found herself glancing toward the tinted glass doors. She wanted to spot him before he took the elevator up to her room. She turned her attention to the newspaper, but found it impossible to concentrate, and finally she gave up trying. Each time there was an announcement on the public address system she listened intently for her name, but it never came. Time dragged by. Finally, chimes sounded and a voice announced that visiting hours were over.

As the lobby began to clear, she crossed to the reception desk to ask if any messages had been left for her. There were none. She was overcome by a numbing sense of abandonment. But it quickly passed and was replaced by seething anger at having allowed herself to believe Dan Blake was different from the other men in her life.

She had convinced herself that the bond which kept her tied to Paul Mayhew had finally been severed. That at last she had found somebody who could be trusted. A man she could feel proud about loving. Now she resented having opened herself up to him. She had been a damned fool.

17

AL HUNTER was worried.

He sat alone at the back of the recreation hall, trying to make some
sense of the fragments of information he had gathered since
he arrived at the project the day after the accident that killed
J. B. Rampling and his son. A flash fire where there was no
indication of methane or any other flammable gas; the lost
MSA meter; charred logs that showed entries which gave no
indication of trouble underground; a body still unaccounted
for; food and blankets taken from vandalized emergency
storage cabinets; stolen lunch pails. And now a deliberately
severed cable that had killed David Seymour.

It was his job to find a common denominator in these
seemingly unrelated incidents, but so far none of what he
had discovered made any sense. Once again he reviewed in
his mind the disappointing conversation he'd had with
Seymour at the Blue Dawn Club. He had hoped to find out
more about the man's relationship with Bromley, but the
project engineer had made it perfectly clear that was a subject he wasn't about to discuss. When he left the bar Hunter
had the distinct impression the other man was deliberately
hiding something.

He looked at the stage where a group of miners were
assembling to rehearse a show they intended to present at the
end of the month. Getting to his feet, Hunter quietly opened

the door, and let himself out. It was mid-afternoon, but there was no sign of the sun, and a chill wind blew across camp from the nearby Canadian River. It was brisk enough to send clouds of dust billowing across the tops of the earthen dams that had been erected out of the debris from the tunnel at the confluence of a series of deep arroyos. He wondered why the camp had been built on low ground where it was vulnerable to flooding. Probably because the present location allowed easier access to the storage areas at the head of the main shaft.

It was an inconsistency that had caught his eye the first day he visited the camp, and he'd made a mental note to ask Dan Blake about it. If the river ever overflowed, only the dams would prevent the camp from being inundated and closed down permanently.

The sudden roar of a diesel engine shattered his reverie and focused his attention on a dirt clearing in front of the mess hall. Thirty or forty men were clustered around a huge Caterpillar tractor. When he got closer he saw that its operator was Dave Ebins. Harry Gallagher was in the front row of the spectators, but it wasn't until Hunter shouldered his way through the crowd that he could make out what they were watching.

The object of their attention was a thin, hollow-cheeked man in his late twenties. An egg was lodged in his mouth, and his eyes were fixed in terror on the heavy steel blade that Ebins was slowly lowering toward his face.

"What the hell's going on here?" He had to shout to make himself heard over the roar of the engine.

When the other miners recognized him, they instinctively pulled away, as if they suspected him of carrying a highly infectious disease. Only Gallagher didn't move.

"Just checking him out," the other man replied.

"Who is he, for Christ's sake?"

"Came here claiming to be a heavy-duty mechanic. We're letting him prove it."

Ebins handled the controls with a deftness that made the

descent of the blade a single fluid movement. It was only halfway down, but the man on the ground was petrified.

"Get him out of there," Hunter snapped.

Gallagher shook his head. "Not until we see if he fixed the hydraulics on this baby the way he should have. Been workin' on the damn thing all morning. If he's half the mechanic he says he is he doesn't have a thing to worry about."

"Bullshit." Hunter strode forward and hauled the man on the ground out from under the blade.

"Stay out of this," Gallagher warned.

"No way."

Hunter saw Gallagher's looping left coming and ducked. But it was followed by an uppercut that caught him flush on the jaw and sent him sprawling. He was dazed, but he got up and assumed a boxer's stance.

"Kick the shit out of him, Harry," somebody in the crowd shouted.

"That what you want?" Gallagher asked.

"Take your best shot," Hunter replied.

Gallagher was older than his opponent, but taller and much stronger. More importantly, he'd fought more brawls than he cared to remember, and was confident he could handle anybody in a fight. But it didn't take long for him to realize that Hunter was far from the milquetoast he appeared to be. He moved fast, and had a flicking straight left that was almost impossible to penetrate. Each time Gallagher tried to get past it he got hit in the face. The blows weren't hard, but they stung and kept him off balance. A slashing right from Hunter started his nose bleeding. Moments later a series of combinations landed on his left eye, opening an ugly cut across his brow. He tried to fight back, but Hunter never stayed still long enough for him to get in a solid shot. The blood from the cut blurred his vision, and when his eye began to swell shut he knew it was all over.

"You're better than I figured." He was breathing heavily and could taste the blood from his nose.

"Enough?" Hunter asked.

"You must be kidding—"

The words were barely out of his mouth when Hunter slammed a crashing left hook to his temple. It was followed by a right jab to his belly that sent him crumpling to his knees.

"More?" Hunter barely seemed out of breath.

It was more than a minute before Gallagher replied.

"You made your point," he mumbled, spitting blood. "Where the hell d'ya learn to fight like that?"

"Golden Gloves."

"Shit." Gallagher shook his head.

"You okay?"

"I'll live."

Hunter offered his hand and helped Gallagher to his feet.

"What about him?"

The man who had been lying under the bulldozer blade was standing now. He looked at Gallagher hopefully.

"Still hasn't proved he fixed those hydraulics," the powder man replied stubbornly.

Hunter took the egg out of the thin man's hand, put it in his mouth and lay under the blade. Dave Ebins looked at Gallagher, and then back at the man sprawled on the ground in front of the Caterpillar tractor. He seemed unsure what to do until Hunter motioned with his hand. It was the cue the operator had been waiting for. The men crowded around for a better look as Ebins smoothly lowered the heavy steel blade until it lightly touched the egg and cracked the shell.

The yolk ran down Hunter's chin in a thin yellow trickle. Some of it dribbled into his mouth. But he didn't move. His eyes remained fixed on the blade as Ebins slowly lifted it up. The experience had terrified him more than the men watching could possibly have imagined. It was only through a supreme effort that he forced himself to sit up.

"Convinced?" he asked with a nonchalance he didn't feel.

"I guess." Gallagher looked at the waiting mechanic. "Looks like you're okay."

Gallagher offered his hand, and Hunter took it. Lying under the blade hadn't been a display of bravado so much as a gesture aimed at winning the acceptance of men whose cooperation he needed. He sensed he had finally made the breakthrough.

"I could use a drink," he said.

"That makes two of us," Gallagher replied.

Hunter looked up at where Dave Ebins was sitting at the controls of the bulldozer.

"You do good work."

The operator nodded. "Any time you want an egg cracked, let me know."

Gallagher led the way back to his trailer and took a bottle of bourbon out of his metal footlocker.

"You'll find a glass on the shelf over the icebox," he said. "Help yourself. I'm gonna wash up."

He took a towel and some soap, leaving the other man alone in the trailer. Hunter poured some bourbon into a glass. As the drink spread its warmth through his body, he felt his muscles relax and the tension begin ebbing away. At ease with himself for the first time all day, he sat on the bed examining his surroundings. The trailer was sparsely furnished: a couple of chairs, some built-in cabinets, and shelves on which lay half a dozen copies of *Penthouse* magazine. The only evidence that even hinted at Gallagher's private life was a framed photograph showing him holding the halter of a pony on which was seated a young girl. She appeared to be about twelve years old and was very pretty. She was smiling, but there was a strangely vacant expression in her eyes. Hunter was holding the picture when the door opened and Gallagher came in. When he saw what Hunter was doing, he took the picture out of his hands and replaced it on the shelf.

"Your daughter?" Hunter asked.

Gallagher nodded. "How's your drink?"

"I didn't know you were married."

"There are a lot of things you don't know," the other man said coldly.

"I could sure use some answers."

"Not about my daughter."

"Okay. It's none of my business."

"Damn right." Gallagher raised the bottle and clinked it against the other man's glass. "You learn fast."

"Only by asking the right questions."

"Try me."

"You were near that cable when it was severed."

"Severed?"

"That's what I said."

"You mean some dumb bastard cut it?"

"Deliberately."

"No shit." Gallagher shook his head. "And you wonder why I'm so hard on those fuckup trainees."

"What makes you think it was one of them?" Hunter asked.

"Who else would be that stupid?"

"Could have been one of your guys who wanted them to look bad."

"No way," Gallagher replied firmly. "They've worked underground too long to risk another flash fire."

"What about Sid? He was close enough to have done it."

"He may act crazy, but he's too damn smart to do a thing like that."

Hunter was silent. "What about Edmonds?" he asked finally.

"Russ?" The other man thought a moment. "He has his problems, but—"

"What kind of problems?"

"You know he's an Indian?"

"I've seen his records."

"This whole area used to be an Arapaho burial ground. It goes way back. They still believe it's sacred."

"But he's been away from his people since he was a kid."

"He never really made the break. I guess he wasn't really accepted by whites. Kinda left him in the middle somewhere. Anyway, he visits his family over in Oklahoma every month, regular as clockwork. Takes them stuff. I guess he feels guilty or something."

"About what?"

"Who knows." Gallagher shrugged. "Maybe because he sold out his heritage. Or because he makes a damned good living from shoving a tunnel through ground his people consider sacred. I've known him a long time. Best damned hard rock driller I ever saw. But I can't say I ever understood him. Not really. Indians are—well, they think different. You know?"

"Might he have cut that cable?"

"Nah. Why should he, for chris'sake? I mean what's in it for him?"

"That leaves Dan Blake. Or you."

"I don't get it."

"There were only four men who were close enough to that cable when it was severed to have done it: Sid, Edmonds, Blake and yourself."

"Why would I do something like that?"

"It's no secret you had a beef going with Seymour."

"He didn't like unions."

"He thought you were a troublemaker, and had put in a formal request that you be transferred to another project. In fact, I hear you hated his guts."

Gallagher stood up. "I've had enough of this shit. I offered you a drink. Well, you've had it. Now I'd appreciate it if you'd get the fuck outta my trailer."

"Easy, okay?" Hunter said. "I'm not accusing anybody. Just trying to get at the facts."

"Facts?" There was a cold fury to Gallagher's voice. "I'll give you facts. Some bastard broke into the powder storage shed last night. Whoever it was swiped a couple of hundred yards of electric lead, a detonator and enough dynamite to blow this whole fucking camp to hell. Now if you want to do something really useful, why don't you find out who did it and let me know. I'd just as soon not be around when that shit goes off."

18

CEETRA Rampling felt more alone than she could ever remember. The only sound in the basement room of the company headquarters building was a soft whisper from the air-conditioning vents. The sheet-metal ducts reminded her of the fan lines in the tunnel, and she flashed on the image of David Seymour skewered by the cable and jerking around hideously as the current coursed through his body. The sight of his eyes bulging until they split was still fresh in her mind. Even the stench was etched in her memory. It was nearly two weeks since it happened, but time had done little to erase the horror of the recollection.

She pressed a button on the control console. The ceiling lights came on in the dark recesses of the huge, vaultlike room that housed the elaborate scale model of the VHST project. She was as awed by it as she had been the first time Seymour showed it to her. But now there was another emotion: a gnawing, deep-rooted fear.

She had felt it ever since Mule Barnes suggested she might have been the intended victim. Even Dan Blake's attempts to reassure her hadn't lessened her apprehension. She had hoped he would tell her more when he took her for a drive the following afternoon, but he hadn't shown up, and she hadn't seen or heard from him since.

She was still angry as she recalled that day he stood her

up. Instead of going back to her room, she had left the hospital and asked the driver of a cab parked in front of the hospital to take her for a drive. She didn't know where she wanted to go, but asked him to head out of town so she could see some of the countryside beyond the city limits.

They were on Interstate 40 when she saw a sign bearing the words "Vanita's Place," and remembered what Dan had told her about the problem of workers going into town on weekends and being cleaned out at whorehouses. Suddenly curious, she told the driver to turn off the main highway and head up the dusty, unsurfaced road that led to what appeared to be some kind of military base. The driver looked at her in the rear-view mirror with a mixture of surprise and amusement, but remained silent as he eased the cab over the deep ruts which constant use had carved into the earth.

The place had an aura of desolation about it. Rows of Quonset huts with wooden slats nailed across their windows; a parade ground patterned with cracks through which weeds had sprouted; piles of rusting steel Marston mats.

"Used to be an Air Force training base," the driver said. "It was built back in 1942, but they trained pilots for Korea and Vietnam here, too. It's been empty a long time. After the military pulled out there was talk of pulling it down, but when old Pop Walters made the government an offer they sold the whole damned thing to him just the way you see it. Pop figured he'd make back his investment selling off the surplus equipment, and then subdivide the land, but he up and died before he ever got around to doing much about it. Left the whole kit 'n caboodle to his missus."

A neon light covered one whole side of the largest structure, spelling out in garish purple letters: Vanita's Place. The parking lot was full of cars and pickup trucks. A jukebox blared out a Willie Nelson rendition of "Redheaded Stranger."

"Sure this is where you want to go?" the driver asked as he pulled to a stop in front of the neon-lit building.

She hesitated, then nodded. The driver got out of the cab

226

and accompanied her up the shallow wooden steps fronting the main entrance.

The interior was decorated like a huge surplus store. Walls were decorated with M-1 rifles, machine pistols, flame-throwers, bayonets, revolvers, grenades, and a wide selection of different caliber ammunition. Interspersed among them were photographs of aircraft: everything from a Sopwith Camel to F-14s. A parachute formed a canopy over the dance floor, which was crowded with couples swaying to the music, and other customers were seated at tables constructed from packing cases which had formerly contained parts for airplane engines. Brass shell cases served as ashtrays.

A bar occupied one whole wall and was presided over by a tall, rawboned woman wearing olive-drab fatigues. She studied Ceetra through narrowed eyes, and it was only when the cab driver explained she was a tourist who wanted to catch a glimpse of some local color that she opened up. Smiling broadly, she poured Ceetra a drink, straight vodka over ice, and began a friendly conversation that she continued until Ceetra left and returned to the hospital.

That was five days ago. It seemed much longer. She had had ample opportunity to reflect on her meeting with Vanita Beth. Somehow it epitomized the radical change in her life since she had left London, and forced her to try to equate what had happened in the past weeks with what she'd anticipated before she came to Texas.

It had brought her to the conclusion that her underlying reason for returning home had been to find a spiritual renewal. But that's not what had happened. If anything, the experience had only heightened the feelings of worthlessness that had haunted her since childhood. For as long as she could remember she had idealized her father and the world he seemed to represent. She had woven endless fantasies about how it would be when she returned from her enforced expatriation. But they bore no relationship to the reality of

227

recent events. It seemed Jake's only legacy to her was further rejection. When he was alive he had abandoned her because she was a girl, and even in death would have denied her her birthright if he could.

Mule Barnes was the only person who had shown any concern for her. During her last few days in the hospital he had come to see her several times. His manner had become more relaxed and friendly, and he never failed to bring flowers or small gifts to please her. Despite inner warnings that his kindness was only a facade, she began to believe that her earlier suspicion of him was unfounded. True, he had personality traits that irritated her, but she attributed them to habits he had developed during the lifelong practice of law, and increasingly made allowances for them. His concern for the well-being of the firm seemed genuine. And the more he explained the problems her father's death had precipitated, the more clearly she understood the necessity for making a quick decision about the disposition of her unexpected inheritance. Finally, she had promised that she would make her intentions known at a board meeting she asked him to schedule for the day after she was released from the hospital.

Now, as she sat alone in the basement of Rampling International's headquarters building, she knew the moment she had been dreading was finally at hand. It was 10:15 a.m. In exactly forty-five minutes she must appear before the board and make her decision known. During the dark hours before dawn she had repeatedly weighed the pros and cons, but each time she reached a conclusion it was immediately voided by additional anxieties. Only when the first rays of the sun cut across her bed did she finally settle on an answer. It was more the product of emotional fatigue than reason. She was just too exhausted, too drained, to shoulder the responsibilities her father had carried for so many years. All she wanted was to go back to London and be left alone.

She touched a button and watched as a section of the

topographical model automatically dropped away to reveal the VHST tubes. At the flick of another control the display came to life. Blunt-shaped gondolas moved through the tubes, starting at one-minute intervals in opposite directions. Fine threads of glass representing utility lines glowed dimly in the darkened room.

David Seymour had deliberately used the simplest terms in describing how the VHST system worked, but she still hadn't understood most of what he said. How, she wondered, could she even have considered taking over the reins of the company when she couldn't begin to comprehend the most rudimentary aspects of its most important project?

She turned out the lights and left the basement room. When she emerged from the elevator on the tenth floor, the woman behind the desk looked up. The regular receptionist had been replaced by an attractive middle-aged woman Ceetra didn't recognize.

"You're new here, aren't you?" she asked.

"Hardly," the other woman replied with a bright, hard smile. "I was your father's secretary for over ten years. Miss Wilson."

The name didn't register, but Ceetra was careful not to show it.

"I'm sorry," she said. "I didn't know."

"This job is only temporary. Until they find something suitable for me."

"Of course."

"I hear you were in the hospital?"

"Got out yesterday," Ceetra said.

"You look well."

"I feel fine."

The woman glanced at her watch. "You're a few minutes early. Mr. Barnes scheduled the board meeting for eleven o'clock."

"Is he here yet?"

"He's on his way. Can I get you some coffee?"

"Yes, that would be nice." Ceetra started toward the office adjoining the board room. "Perhaps you wouldn't mind bringing it in here."

"But that's your father's office—" She checked herself.

Ceetra looked at the other woman coolly, but didn't speak. The hostility Miss Wilson had managed to hide behind her forced good humor had slipped out, and both of them knew it.

"I'm sorry. It's just that—well, after so many years of working so closely—"

"Let me know when the others arrive."

Ceetra's voice was hard-edged. Miss Wilson's remark had touched a raw nerve. She closed the door of the office and leaned against the heavy oak paneling. Her pulse was racing. Breathing came hard. She crossed to the window intending to open it but saw the glass was sealed. She sat down in the leather chair behind the huge mahogany desk and waited for the anxiety attack to pass. In an effort to take her mind off it, she focused her attention on the contents of the room. On her previous visit she had only got a general impression. Now she studied the room more carefully. The walls were decorated with color photographs of projects Rampling International had constructed in numerous foreign countries: Venezuela, Mexico, Canada, China, Korea, Malaysia, Indonesia, Libya, Nigeria, the Ivory Coast, Australia. Examples of everything from the world's largest plant for processing coal into fuel liquids and gases in South Africa to a massive nuclear-powered generator in Saudi Arabia.

On easels to one side of the desk were large graphs showing performance profiles of the company in the years 1979–84. She lit a cigarette and tried to decipher them. They appeared to show that new orders had increased from 6.93 billion to 11.2 billion dollars, while earnings had almost doubled.

She noted again the large color photograph of Jake and Dan. But the item that riveted her attention above all was a photograph in a silver frame on the desk. It showed her father standing on the deck of a huge motor yacht. His arm was draped around Bromley and both were smiling broadly. She picked it up and studied it more closely, searching for something in their expressions that might give her a clue to the real nature of their relationship. But there was nothing. They appeared the epitome of a perfectly happy father and son.

"It was taken aboard the *Nova* about a year ago."

The voice startled her. She looked up and saw Dan Blake standing in the open door.

"I didn't hear you knock," she said coldly.

"I've been coming into this office without knocking for almost fifteen years. Your father—"

"What he allowed and I expect aren't the same."

"I see."

There was an awkward silence that ended when Miss Wilson bustled into the room carrying a tray containing a silver thermos of coffee.

"I brought two cups," she announced briskly.

"Are the board members here yet?" Ceetra asked.

"Mr. Barnes telephoned to say he'll be about fifteen minutes late," the woman replied. "I've told the others and they want to wait for him. Is that all right?"

"I suppose it will have to be."

"Cream and sugar?" the secretary asked.

"Just cream."

"And I know you like yours black, Mr. Blake."

She smiled at him warmly. Ceetra took a long pull on her cigarette and waited for the ritual to end.

"I didn't know you smoked," Dan said after Miss Wilson left the room.

"I'm like you," Ceetra replied. "Full of surprises."

"What's that supposed to mean?"

"I waited for you at the hospital. You were going to take me for a drive. Remember?"

"I'm sorry about that," he said. "There was an emergency. I had to leave for Saudi Arabia that night."

"You could have let me know."

"I phoned from the airport, but they told me you were asleep and couldn't be disturbed."

"Why didn't you leave a message?"

"I did."

"With whom?"

"I asked Mule Barnes to give you a note."

Ceetra didn't answer. Suddenly she wanted to cry. He must have sensed her reaction, because when she turned away to hide the tears, he put his hand on her arm and squeezed it gently.

"I feel like a fool," she murmured.

"He didn't deliver it?"

She shook her head.

"Did he come to see you?"

"Several times."

"And he didn't say anything?"

"Not about you."

Dan was silent for a moment. "What did he talk about?"

"How hard it is to juggle two dozen balls while playing the xylophone."

He looked surprised and then chuckled.

"That's Mule all right. Don't you see what he's trying to do?"

"He says he wants to keep the bankers happy. Make sure they don't call in their notes."

"There's some truth to that," Dan said. "But he's a hell of a lot more interested in looking out for Mule Barnes."

"He also pointed out a dozen other reasons why I should give him power of attorney to sell my father's shares so I can pack up and go home."

"Is that what you're going to do?"

"I thought so, but now I'm not sure."

"You'd better decide fast. Time's running out."

"When you visited me in the hospital—" Her voice trailed away.

"Yes?"

"You never told me what Barnes was trying to achieve by telling me I might have been the intended victim when Seymour was killed."

"All you have to do is look at these figures." Dan motioned to the graphs standing on the easels. "With earnings like that, do you realize how valuable the shares of Rampling International would be if the firm ever went public?"

"But they're privately owned."

"Only because that's the way your father insisted on keeping it. He didn't want to share the control of his company with anybody. The rest of the board didn't like it. They knew the stock they owned would increase ten or twenty times its present value if it could be traded publicly."

"What's stopping them from doing it now that he's dead?" she asked.

"You hold the controlling interest. Their hands are tied until you decide what you're going to do with the stock you inherited."

"And you think Barnes was trying to frighten me into selling?"

"Why not?" Dan said. "He stands to gain along with the rest of them. The only thing that puzzles me is why he's making such a determined effort when he owns less stock than anybody on the board except myself."

The door opened and Miss Wilson poked her head into the office.

"Mr. Barnes has arrived," she announced. "And the others are ready to start whenever it's convenient for you, Miss Rampling."

"Tell them I'll be there in a minute." When the woman withdrew, she turned to Dan. "I'm terrified. Tell me what to do."

"I can't," he replied. "It's a decision you're going to have to make all by yourself."

"I'm not sure I can."

"I am."

"What makes you so certain?"

"You're Jake Rampling's daughter." He touched her cheek lightly. "I'll tell them you're on your way in."

"Will I see you afterwards?"

"I'm leaving for Saudi Arabia this afternoon," he said. "The problem I mentioned still hasn't been solved."

For a long moment neither of them spoke. "Go on in," she said finally. "I'll be ready in a few minutes."

When he left it was as though a support had suddenly been removed, leaving her acutely aware of her own frailty. On an impulse she closed her eyes and silently prayed.

"Miss Rampling." She opened her eyes and saw Miss Wilson at the door. "Everybody's waiting."

Ceetra nodded and took a small makeup case out of her purse. She glanced at herself in the tiny mirror. Tears had smudged her mascara, but it was easily repaired. And a dab of powder took away the shine from her nose. She smoothed the skirt of her beautifully cut two-piece suit. It was one she had designed herself; a far cry from the sheer see-through dress she had worn to the first board meeting. As she followed Miss Wilson out of the office, she found some comfort in knowing that, whatever her inner trepidations, at least she looked like a woman who was capable of making serious decisions.

When she entered the board room murmured greetings stirred among the men gathered around the gigantic oval table: "How are you feeling? . . . Terrible about the accident . . . You look fine . . . Good to see you back." But she detected no real warmth in their voices, and there were indications that their geniality hid a tension they were striving to conceal.

The only person to appear genuinely relaxed was Mule Barnes, and he lost no time in asserting himself.

"All right, let's quiet down. I'm calling this meeting to order," he announced loudly. "I suggest we dispense with formalities and get right down to the reason we're all here."

He glanced round the table, mutely challenging the other board members to offer an objection, but none of them spoke. It appeared they were accustomed to having Barnes take over, and Ceetra found herself wondering if it had been this way when her father was alive.

"The issue is quite simple," he said, addressing himself to Ceetra. "We need your decision as to the disposition of your father's shares."

She acknowledged him with a slight nod, but deliberately waited a beat before answering.

"Before I speak my piece," she said, "I'd like to hear from each of you gentlemen separately."

"That's not necessary," Barnes said. "I know I represent everybody's feelings when—"

"Yours are the only opinions I have heard," Ceetra interjected calmly. "Now I'd appreciate a word or two from the other members of the board."

The men glanced at each other nervously.

"Why don't we start with you, Mr. Greene?" Ceetra said, looking at the tall, square-jawed man who had replaced David Seymour as chief manager of the VHST project.

"It won't be easy for a woman," he said quietly. "Construction is traditionally a man's world. But that won't always be the case. Personally, I'd have the greatest admiration for any lady with the guts to take that first step."

"Thank you." Ceetra looked at Barnes and saw from the set of his jaw that he didn't like what he'd heard. "Now how about a word from our vice president of finance?"

Norman Gross was a thickset man who looked as if he'd have been more at home with a drill than an adding machine.

"We all know J. B. took a hell of a gamble on the VHST project," he said. "Truth is the company had to hock itself to the eyeballs to come up with the completion guarantees. I've got to tell you the banks aren't going to be happy with an inexperienced woman running the show. It doesn't take much to make them nervous, and your taking over could do that—and more."

The next man to speak was George Powell, vice president

of petroleum and chemicals. He took a sip of water and cleared his throat before beginning.

"Two of our largest projects—the gas-gathering program in South Africa and the turboexpander plant in Nigeria—both moved out of the engineering stage and into field construction during—"

"For Christ's sake, George," Barnes interjected sharply. "We don't want an operations report. Just a simple answer to Miss Rampling's question."

"What was that?" the other man asked.

"She wants to know if you think she can run the firm."

"It's a highly complex business," Powell said. "I believe it would be difficult for anybody, however experienced."

Brian Megran, the vice president of metals and metallurgy, made his statement brief.

"The biggest job we've got going is a copper mine and concentrator in China. The people we deal with are mostly engineers or bureaucrats. Neither type is used to listening to women voice their ideas."

"You're going to have the same problem in Saudi Arabia," Bill Daniels added. The vice president of the power division seemed eager to express himself. "Those people over there aren't going to do business with a woman. It's as simple as that. Females in that country have about as much social stature as domestic pets. Maybe less."

One by one the other members of the board voiced their feelings. Some were more diplomatic than others, but most shared the view that it would be a severe blow to the firm's well-being if Ceetra were to take over its active leadership.

One exception was Tom Heslop, vice chairman of the board, and a longtime associate of Jake's who was now nearing retirement age. "Whoever runs this operation is going to have problems," he said. "Jake operated out of his hip pocket a lot of the time. Hell, it'll take us months to pick up the loose ends he left when he died. What I'm saying is that a woman could do it as well as any man. Depends how much she's willing to apply herself to learning the business."

When he finished speaking a taut silence settled on the room. It continued for a full minute before Barnes finally got to his feet.

"Norm Gross put his finger on the real problem," he said. "When Jake bid on the VHST project he took the biggest gamble of his life. The consortium of banks he borrowed from were willing to take a risk because of his reputation for getting jobs done on schedule. But they still wanted guarantees. All he could offer for loans that size was the company's share of the various joint ventures it's involved in around the world. If the banks call those loans—"

He left the sentence unfinished.

"Is that what they've done?" Ceetra asked.

"Not yet," Barnes replied. "They're waiting to see which way you go."

"If I sell?"

"They'll be happy as cows in deep clover."

"And if I don't?"

"Put yourself in their position," the attorney said. "All they see is a woman trying to fill her daddy's shoes who doesn't know a megawatt from a metric ton."

Barnes opened his briefcase and placed a sheaf of papers on the table in front of where Ceetra sat.

"What happens if I sign these like you want me to?" she asked.

"You immediately become the only woman in the world worth close to a billion dollars," he said.

"And the firm will become publicly owned?"

A flicker of discomfort showed in Barnes's eyes. "It's possible," he admitted.

"Is that what my father wanted?"

"The situation was very different when he was alive—"

"Cut the bullshit, Mule." Dan Blake spoke for the first time since the board meeting began. "It's a simple enough question."

Barnes was white with anger, but managed to keep his voice steady. "Jake wanted to keep the company privately

237

owned," he said. "But he could afford that luxury. Now things have changed."

"In what way?" Dan asked.

"I just finished spelling it out."

"All I heard was you trying to scare the hell out of her."

"I gave her the facts."

"The way you wanted her to hear them."

"The way they are," Barnes countered.

"Have any of the banks threatened to foreclose?"

"No, but they will."

"How do you know?"

"It's fair to assume—"

"Has a single banker told you they won't go with a woman as president of Rampling International?"

"They don't have to. It's common knowledge—"

"That's a crock of shit and you know it," Dan said. "I admit there's a strong chance the banks won't like it, but they're going to think twice before pulling the rug out. If we go belly up they stand to lose a goddam fortune, and that means a lot of very unhappy stockholders."

"What the hell do you know—"

"All I have to." Dan looked at the other board members. "I knew Jake Rampling a lot better than any of you. He was a difficult man. No doubt about that. But he was also a visionary who parlayed a dream into the biggest construction company in the world. He never ducked a challenge or was afraid to take risks. Particularly if he figured winning was worthwhile. That's why he hocked everything to bid on the VHST project. It's the most ambitious tunnel ever attempted, and he wanted his company to be part of it."

He glanced at Barnes as if expecting him to say something, but the attorney kept his eyes fixed on the table.

"You all know Jake wanted Bromley to succeed him," he continued, less heatedly this time. "Now that that isn't possible I think we owe it to his memory to let his daughter show us what she can do."

When he sat down there was another tense pause. The

other board members looked at Barnes as if searching for a clue as to how they should react. He had picked up a pencil and was absently tapping it against the rim of a glass half full of water.

"That's quite a speech, Dan," he said finally, still tapping the pencil. "Now I reckon it's time I set you straight on a few—"

"I think you've already made your sentiments perfectly clear," Ceetra said, cutting him short.

"I'm not through yet."

"You are so far as influencing me is concerned," she replied coldly.

Barnes didn't answer, but he stopped tapping his pencil against the glass.

"Thank you," she said pointedly, "I appreciate your opinions," she continued, turning her attention to the rest of the board. "But I've made my decision. I intend to hold on to my father's shares. And before I ask if any of you intend to oppose my election as president of Rampling International I would like to remind you of a clause that is in each of your contracts. It specifies that in the event of death or termination, each shareholder agrees to sell his stock back to the company at a price to be determined by whoever holds the majority interest. Now, shall we put it to a vote?"

Nobody uttered a word.

"I must assume by your silence that nobody opposes my election?"

Again there was silence.

"Good. Well, now that we all understand each other I suggest it's in everybody's best interest to start pulling together," she continued. "As a first step I intend to take a firsthand look at a number of key projects the firm is presently involved in overseas. Toward that end I will be leaving for London with Dan Blake this afternoon."

She looked at Dan. His face was expressionless. After the way he had stood up for her his lack of reaction puzzled her.

"From Europe," she said, "we will continue around the

world via the Middle East, Singapore, and Australia. I would appreciate your keeping my decision to assume the presidency a secret until I return and can make a formal announcement at a press conference. Does anybody else have anything to say before we end this meeting?" she asked.

Barnes spoke without looking up. "You're backing yourself into a very dangerous corner," he warned.

"You could be right. But then I'm beginning to realize that I've been in one ever since my father died," Ceetra replied quietly.

 *19*

DAN BLAKE felt his body being pressed back in his seat as the Grumman Gulfstream III lifted off the runway at Dallas/Fort Worth Airport and surged into the cloudless afternoon sky. He had flown in the company jet many times, yet still hadn't accustomed himself to the sudden increase in body weight that was caused by the gravitational stress of climbing at a rate of 4,000 feet a minute.

"You all right?" Ceetra asked.

"Sure, why?"

"You're so pale."

"Would you believe I flew a helicopter in Vietnam for over a year, and I still get airsick?"

"You don't know how good that makes me feel," she smiled. "I thought I was going to be the only one puking on this trip."

She pressed a button in the arm of her chair, and a steward wearing a well-cut chocolate-brown uniform emerged from the galley in the tail section of the luxuriously appointed twelve-passenger aircraft.

"Yes, ma'am?"

"Have we any Fernet Branca aboard?" she asked.

"I believe there is a bottle."

"Would you bring me some with a glass of plain soda water on ice?"

"A pleasure, Miss. Would you like some cigarettes? We have quite a selection of different brands."

Ceetra glanced at Dan. She craved nicotine, but shook her head.

"Quit?" he asked.

"I'm trying."

A trace of a smile crossed his face but he didn't make any further comment. The steward reappeared moments later carrying a bottle containing a liquid the color of black molasses.

"Do you want it in the soda?" he asked.

"Straight is fine." She took the glass and sipped the contents. "Ugh! It tastes like syrup of figs and burned paint. But it really stops you feeling sick."

She passed the glass to Dan and he emptied it at a single swallow.

"Jeeesus—" He grimaced.

Ceetra laughed. "Drink the soda. It'll take the edge off."

Dan followed her instructions and immediately began to feel better.

"It works," he said. "Where did you learn that trick?"

"On a yacht in the Bay of Biscay. We got caught in a storm. God, those waves were the size of houses. One of the guests was a doctor. He fed me Fernet Branca and dry crackers for two days. I was about four pounds lighter when we finally got into La Rochelle."

"A tough way to diet," he said. "Thanks, anyway."

"It's me who ought to be thanking you."

"For what?"

"Standing up for me that way at the board meeting."

Dan looked embarrassed. "I wasn't the only one. Tom Heslop sided with you, and Phil Greene."

"I like him."

"Phil?"

She nodded.

"We go back a long way together," Dan said. "Shared a trailer with him for almost a year on the Alaska Pipeline. I guess you know he's taken over Dave Seymour's job as project manager on the tunnel?"

"I didn't," Ceetra replied.

"He's a good man. It's comforting to know somebody like that is in charge. Keeping the project on schedule is vital."

"What happens if it gets behind?"

"We pay penalties. Hundreds of thousands a day. That's why the delay caused by the cave-in was so serious. Another work stoppage like that could bankrupt the company."

Ceetra was quiet for a moment looking out of the large oval window.

"Why did you speak up for me?" she asked, suddenly turning back to him.

Dan shrugged. "It seemed like the right thing to do."

Once again she sensed his discomfort and didn't pursue the subject.

"What time do we reach New York?" she asked.

He glanced at a console displaying a digital readout. It showed altitude, air speed, time of departure and estimated time of arrival.

"We've got another three hours at least. But my body's still operating on Middle East time. I think I'll take a nap."

But when he closed his eyes he found it impossible to sleep. His brain was racing too fast. Why, his inner voice kept asking, had he supported Ceetra so vocally at the board meeting? It was completely out of character.

"Will Mr. Blake be eating anything?"

Dan heard the steward's voice but kept his eyes closed.

"I don't think so," Ceetra replied. "Sleep will do him more good than food."

"What about you, Miss?" The steward sounded almost plaintive. "I've fixed a very nice salmon mousse and there's plenty of caviar."

"It sounds wonderful," Ceetra said. "I'll have a small helping of each."

"And some Dom Perignon?"

"Why not? It is rather a special day."

Dan continued to maintain the appearance of being asleep. But the more he tried to rid himself of the question his inner voice had posed, the more it continued to nag at him. Why had he stood up for her? Maybe it was because he detected a certain vulnerability that made him begin to believe that her sophistication was a facade she had developed to protect herself from further hurt. He'd found himself responding to it. Yet each time she reached out, he pulled back. He wanted the contact, but found it somehow threatening.

He had structured his life in such a way that solitude was an intrinsic part of his existence. His mother had died giving birth to him, and his only experience of women was what he had gained in whorehouses around Odessa and Midland, in west Texas, where he had worked as a roughneck on various oil drilling operations until he was drafted at eighteen. It had been the same thing in Vietnam: girls were always available in Saigon, often for the price of a pack of cigarettes.

It was dark when the Grumman Gulfstream finally touched down on the runway at Kennedy Airport. Ceetra had hoped to do some shopping before the stores closed, but had forgotten the time difference between Dallas and New York.

"Where are we staying?" she asked as they got into the limousine that was waiting to meet them when the company jet taxied to a stop in an area of the airport that was reserved for executive planes.

"The firm's yacht is berthed in the Hudson River," Dan replied. "They bring it up from Florida every year around this time. Your father liked to spend a couple of weeks each summer aboard the *Nova* cruising the coast off Maine. I thought you might like to see it."

"I'd love to," Ceetra answered excitedly. "Are they expecting us?"

"I asked Bill Weeks, the director of public relations, to make the arrangements. He said he'd put through a call to the captain."

"When do we leave for London?"

"First thing tomorrow."

"I can get some clothes over there. Free, too. Did you know I own a fashion design business?"

"Jake told me."

"Did he approve?"

"Why wouldn't he?"

"Habit," she answered. "He automatically disapproved of everything to do with me."

"You're wrong," Dan said. "He mentioned your success in business two or three times."

"That many?" Ceetra made no attempt to hide the irony in her voice. "And how did he feel about it?"

"I think he was—quite surprised," Dan replied hesitantly.

"That a daughter of his should succeed?"

"It's a pity you never got to know each other. I think you would have found you had a lot in common."

Ceetra fixed her eyes on the passing traffic. "I wonder," she said, more to herself than to Dan.

She remained silent, wrapped in her own thoughts, until the limousine stopped at a berth near the foot of 43rd Street. Getting out onto the wharf she gazed up at the *Nova*'s graceful hull. "It's huge. I didn't know they made yachts this big anymore," she said.

"They don't," Dan answered. "She's the only one left in this country with an overall length exceeding two hundred feet."

He took her arm and led her up the gangway to where the captain was waiting to welcome them aboard. A thin, taciturn man in a white uniform, he wore a nervous half-smile.

"I only got word that you were coming about an hour ago," he said. "I explained to Bill Weeks that we're operating with a skeleton crew. He said that as you are only staying overnight, perhaps you wouldn't mind the inconvenience."

"All I care about is a place to sleep and something to eat," Ceetra said. "I'm starving."

"I'm afraid the chef went ashore in Miami." The captain's smile had dissolved. "As we didn't have any guests aboard I thought it would be a convenient time for him to take his annual vacation. Perhaps you'd like me to arrange reservations for you somewhere ashore?"

"Not on your life," Ceetra said. "It isn't every day a girl gets to dine aboard one of the world's largest yachts. I'm a pretty poor cook, but if you'll show me the kitchen—"

"Galley," Dan said.

"Galley, kitchen—who cares? How do I get downstairs?"

"Below."

She looked at Dan. "I know you're a pilot, but where did you get to be such an expert on boats?"

"Ships."

"Jesus—"

"I spent a lot of summers aboard with your father," Dan explained with a smile. "He had a little booklet printed that was put in all the cabins. It described the facilities, rules, meal times. Things like that. He liked guests to know what was expected of them. It even included a list of nautical terms. I spent a lot of time in my cabin being seasick. That booklet was the only thing I had to read. Memorized the whole damned thing. Anything you want to know about the binnacle, forecastle, reefer—"

"Reefer?" She giggled. "You mean grass?"

"Not aboard this ship," he replied with mock severity. "Your father hated drugs of any kind."

"All right, astound me. What's a reefer?" she asked.

"A frozen food locker."

"That's exactly where I'd like you to take me. Right now. I haven't eaten a thing since breakfast."

"Salmon mousse, caviar, a little Dom Perignon—"

"I thought you were asleep."

"Just resting with my eyes closed."

He led her down a companionway to the cabin deck. The galley was located on the starboard side of the ship, opposite the laundry. It was occupied by an elderly steward wearing a white jacket that had what appeared to be a ketchup stain across one lapel. He obviously wasn't expecting them and appeared startled.

"I was just fixing my supper," he said. "We've had to fend for ourselves since the chef went ashore. Can I get you anything, Miss?"

"How about a plate of cold cuts and some cheese?"

"I know there's some ham, and there may be a side of beef in the food locker—"

"The reefer," Ceetra said.

"That's right, ma'am."

Dan laughed, but the steward looked puzzled. "I'll go and have a look," he said.

"And some salad if you can find any," Ceetra added.

"Shall I serve it in the dining room?" the steward asked.

She looked at Dan. "Let's have a picnic."

"At this time of night?"

"Haven't you ever tried it?"

He shook his head.

"There's a first time for everything. Where's a good place?"

"Your father liked to eat out on the sun deck," the steward said.

"Great. We'll have the moon and the lights of Manhattan," Ceetra said. "Now, if you'll show me to my cabin I'll freshen up before we eat."

"Don't bother, I'll show her the way," Dan told the older man. "You go ahead and fix the food."

Dan conducted her to the main deck and ushered her into a room that was spacious enough to contain easily a king-sized bed, half a dozen easy chairs, sofas and a beautiful antique Empire period writing desk.

"This was your father's stateroom," he said. "But it's also been used by so many heads of state of Middle East countries that the crew calls it 'The Harem.' "

"I should feel right at home," she replied.

He grinned, but she sensed her comment had somehow embarrassed him. "I'll meet you on the sun deck," he said.

"About fifteen mintues. Okay?"

He nodded and closed the door. Ceetra remained motionless. There was something about Dan that still puzzled her: an almost puritanical streak that totally contradicted his apparent worldliness. It was almost as if he instinctively put women in two groups: bad and good. The former could be handled and enjoyed, but the latter were objects to be put on a pedestal and admired from a distance. She knew the only way to make headway with Dan was for her to make the first move. Only then, she believed, would she be able to make him understand that he was wrong to try to categorize women.

She needed something to calm her nerves, so she started opening drawers. Her search revealed a liquor cabinet, and she poured herself a stiff drink of vodka.

Her bags had already been placed on metal racks at the foot of the bed. They contained the few things she had brought with her from London. Because she hadn't planned more than a week's stay in Dallas she had only packed a few dresses, and she still hadn't found time to buy anything new.

Now, as she sorted through the contents of her suitcases, she wished she had made a more determined effort. The two-piece suit she'd worn at the board meeting, and still had on, was too formal, while her skirt/sweater combination was too casual. She needed something revealing enough for Dan to understand the message she was trying to convey.

She finished her drink and poured herself another one. Finally, she settled on the light print dress she had worn to the meeting at which Barnes had read the will. It was sheer, and the material had a sensuous texture that added measurably to the effect she was intent on creating.

After showering she sprayed her body lightly with Joy perfume and slipped on a pair of bikini pants. She left her breasts bare. They were her best feature: firm and perfectly shaped.

When she was ready she finished her second vodka and looked at herself in a full-length mirror behind the state-room door. Satisfied that she'd done everything possible to stack the odds in her favor, she went up the companion-way and stepped out onto the sun deck.

"Hi. Hope I haven't kept you waiting too long." It was much chillier than it had been when they arrived an hour earlier, and the moist dampness of the river knifed through her flimsy dress, making her shiver.

"You look wonderful," Dan said. "But that dress is awful thin for out here. Why don't I get you a warm coat?"

"No," she replied quickly. "I'll be fine. Really."

The steward was over by the rail opening a bottle of wine. He had spread a checkered tablecloth on the deck and set cushions on either side. A silver candelabrum supported a cluster of candles that shed a soft, flickering light over plates of cold cuts, slices of three different kinds of cheeses, butter, French bread, salad and a huge bowl of fruit. Everything was exactly the way she had wanted it. If she couldn't seduce Dan under these conditions it was obvious she was never going to do it.

"Everything all right, ma'am?" the steward asked.

"Perfect. You've done a wonderful job. What's your name?"

"Wilkins, ma'am. Stanley Wilkins."

"How long have you worked aboard?"

"Going on eight years now."

"You sound English."

"I am, Miss." The steward smiled broadly, revealing un-even, tobacco-stained teeth. "Born in Southampton. Used to work the trans-Atlantic liners. Those were great days. When they stopped operating I got a job with your father. He was partial to British people."

"I didn't know. When was the last time you saw him?"

John Sherlock

"A month, maybe six weeks ago. He came down to Miami to do some fishing." His voice took on a solemn tone. "It was quite a shock to hear what happened to him and the boy. The crew were very fond of Bromley. He came aboard for a few weeks every summer, even when his father wasn't with him—" The old man checked himself, as if suddenly realizing he had overstepped himself. "I'd like to offer you my condolences, ma'am."

"Thank you, Wilkins."

"May I pour you some wine, ma'am?"

"Yes." She held up her glass and the steward half-filled it with Tattinger.

"I don't know when I last drank champagne," she said.

"I'll tell you," Dan said. "About thirty minutes after we took off from Dallas/Fort Worth."

She laughed. "I forgot. You were just resting with your eyes closed."

The steward poured Dan some champagne and then served them both helpings of cold cuts and cheese. "If you need anything," he said, "just ring."

He pointed to a small silver bell standing near the candelabrum. Ceetra recognized it as an exquisite example of early Georgian craftsmanship, and found herself thinking about the beautiful antiques in her London apartment. She wondered if Mrs. Elseworth had received the cable she'd sent from Dallas. She'd said she would be arriving in London and asked her to check the apartment to make sure it would be ready for her use.

"Thank you, Wilkins," she said. "I'm sure we have everything we're going to need."

The old man carefully folded the napkin he'd used to uncork the champagne, draped it over his arm, and slowly made his way toward some steps that led back down to the cabin deck.

"You made quite an impression," Dan observed. "I haven't seen him open up like that since he joined the ship."

250

"I always feel sorry for old people who have to go on working."

"Don't feel too sad about Wilkins. He's got a nice soft berth here. The only worry he's got is whether or not the company will keep the *Nova* now that Jake's gone."

Ceetra sipped her champagne. Combined with the vodka, the alcohol was beginning to make itself felt. She was slightly light-headed.

"What do you think we should do?"

Her words were faintly slurred, and it was apparent from the way Dan looked at her that he didn't approve.

"It's your decision," he said. "Frankly, I never cared much for boats—"

"Ships."

"Whatever—they weren't around where I grew up."

"You never talk about your background."

He shrugged. "There's not much to tell."

"Was your father in the construction business?"

"My old man ran a small grocery store on San Antonio's west side. A twenty-by-twenty tarpaper shack. When that went broke he worked as a migrant picker. Died when I was fifteen."

"What about your mother?"

"She died giving birth to me."

"So you were on your own?"

He nodded.

"What did you do?"

"Jumped a freight heading north. Worked as a rough-neck on oil rigs around Odessa and Midland. Kept moving. East Texas. You name it."

"You said you were in Vietnam."

"That's right."

"I saw a movie about it—*Apocalypse Now*. Was it really that insane?"

"Worse."

He took a long swallow of champagne. She leaned over to refill his glass. It was a deliberate gesture, intended to reveal

251

a glimpse of her breasts. But she lost her balance and only quick action on his part prevented her toppling into the food. She tried to cover her gaffe by laughing, but the sound had a shrill edge that made it seem forced.

"You're not much of a talker," she said.

"I guess not."

"Don't you trust people?"

"Not until they've proved themselves."

"Have I proved myself?"

He got up and strode across the deck. She waited for him to return, but he remained at the railing, his eyes fixed on a point somewhere over the glittering lights of Manhattan. There was a rigidity to his stance that implied rejection. Her first reaction was anger, but that quickly gave way to an unaccountable anxiety. Getting up, she crossed to where he was standing and wrapped her arms around his waist from behind. She could feel his tension. Putting her mouth against his shirt at a point midway between his shoulder blades, she breathed out hard.

"I'm sorry," she whispered. "I didn't mean to—"

He suddenly swung around, his eyes filled with an expression that frightened her. When he reached out and clamped his hands on her arms she instinctively backed away, but he held her firmly against him and pressed his mouth against hers.

"Don't—" She tried to pull herself free, but he was too strong for her.

"Who are you trying to kid?" he demanded hoarsely. "You want it as much as I do."

"Not like this—"

He studied her face for a long moment and then kissed her again. When she didn't respond he relaxed his grip, and she twisted away and ran across the deck. At the head of the companionway, she paused for breath and glanced over her shoulder, half expecting to see him coming after her. But he hadn't moved from the railing. He had resumed the same hunched stance she had so resented only moments ago.

She was trembling when she reached her father's stateroom. Her breath came in great sobs. She locked the door and went into the bathroom where she leaned over the basin and splashed cold water on her face. Then she returned to the cabin and lay on the bed listening to the sound of Dan's footsteps as he paced back and forth on the deck overhead. Now that it was over she wished she had handled the situation differently. She had panicked, reacted like a frightened schoolgirl. Suddenly she felt ashamed. Dan was right. She had behaved like a whore. Worse. A drunken whore.

Tears welled in her eyes. She had thought Dan was a new beginning, but it was an illusion. And she couldn't blame him. It was her fault. Now she was back where she started. Tomorrow, when they arrived in London, she would have come full circle. And for what?

In many ways her life in London was preferable to anything she had experienced since leaving it. At least she understood the fashion business, was good at it, and nobody there was trying to kill her. For a moment she thought of calling Mule Barnes and telling him she had changed her mind, that it had been a terrible mistake to think she could fill her father's shoes. But then her eyes fixed on a portrait on the opposite bulkhead. It showed Jake and Bromley posed against a background of a massive nuclear power plant the company had built in Saudi Arabia. Suddenly she knew there was no going back. She had been given the opportunity she'd waited for all her life: the chance to prove her father wrong in assuming that just because she was a woman she was incapable of shouldering the responsibility of running Rampling International. But she also knew that she didn't stand a chance without Dan's help.

The footsteps on the deck overhead changed their rhythmic pattern and she heard him coming down the companionway toward her cabin. Quickly getting up, she blotted her eyes with a tissue, and hastily applied a few dabs of powder to her nose. It took less than a minute, but by the time she had completed her task Dan had passed her door. His footsteps began to die away as he continued down the stairway.

Assuming he was heading for the salon at the rear of the ship, she hurried across the stateroom and opened a sliding glass door that fronted onto a narrow walkway which ran the full length of the ship. Her plan was to step out the moment she heard him approaching. As she waited in the shadows she frantically searched her mind for the right words to use, an explanation that would justify her childish behavior, but nothing came to mind. She'd just be honest with him and hope he understood.

When he didn't appear after two or three minutes, waiting became intolerable and, abandoning all attempt at pretense, she went out onto the deck. But there was no sign of him. Only the hollow echo of his footsteps as he descended the gangway. And by the time she crossed to a point at the side of the ship from which she could see the wharf, he had disappeared into the darkness.

 **20**

IT WAS RAINING when the Gulfstream touched down at London's Heathrow Airport, and although it was still only late afternoon the sky was so full of dark clouds that it seemed much later.

Ceetra felt thoroughly disoriented. They had picked up five hours since leaving New York, but her body clock was still operating on Dallas time. It left her feeling tense, a condition that hadn't been improved by the strain of flying three thousand miles across the Atlantic with a man who remained coldly withdrawn throughout the entire journey.

Admittedly, it was an awkward situation. She still felt extremely guilty about what had happened aboard the *Nova* the previous evening, and had made two or three attempts to bridge the chasm. But each time she tried to broach the subject he responded so coldly that finally she had abandoned any further efforts and passed the remaining hours of flight in bouts of fitful sleep.

The tension between them continued after the plane landed and they underwent the ritual of customs and immigration. Fortunately, Walters was waiting to take them from the airport into the city.

Mrs. Elseworth told me you were coming, Miss," he said. "And I called the London office of your father's firm to find out what time you'd be arriving. I must say it's good to see you back, Miss."

Ceetra noticed his left hand was bandaged, and he experienced considerable difficulty loading their luggage into the trunk of the Rolls-Royce.

"What happened to your hand?" she asked when they were on the A-4 road into London.

"My youngster, Miss," Walters replied. "Left his roller skates on the steps in front of my house, and I went arse over tea kettle. If you'll excuse the expression."

"Is it all right for you to drive?"

"Oh, yes. Quite safe, ma'am. The doctor said I sprained a couple of fingers. That's all."

Ceetra settled back in the deep leather seat and turned her attention to the passing scene. What had been so familiar a few weeks ago now assumed a uniqueness that made her feel like a stranger. Traffic on the left side of the road, double-decker buses, black chunky-looking taxis; they seemed like relics of a time she had almost forgotten. It barely seemed possible to have severed the bonds of almost a lifetime in less than a month, and yet she felt less at home in London than she could ever remember.

"Excuse me, Miss?" Walters glanced over his shoulder. "I understand the gentleman will be staying at Claridge's?"

She looked at Dan.

"I called from New York," he said.

"Your firm told me they were able to confirm your reservation, sir," the chauffeur said. "Will you be needing me tomorrow?"

Dan turned toward Ceetra. "Still want me to show you that fiberglass manufacturing complex we're putting up near Eastbourne?"

She hesitated. It was one of the subjects she had tried to talk about on the flight from New York, but he had limited his answers mainly to monosyllables. She hadn't found a chance to explain that her interest in the project was linked to the fact that, by making a detour of less than a couple of miles, she would also be able to visit her mother at the sanatorium.

"Yes," she replied. "I think it's important for me to take a look at every major project the company's involved in."

They had stopped in front of the staid brick hotel on Brook Street.

"I'll be ready about ten o'clock," Dan informed the driver. "Okay?"

"Yes, sir. Ten o'clock it is."

Dan looked at Ceetra. "Will you be staying at your apartment?"

She nodded.

"See you in the morning, then."

He instructed the doorman which bags to take out of the trunk, and followed him through the art deco swing doors into the elegant lobby.

"Straight home, Miss?" Walters asked.

"The quicker the better," Ceetra replied. "I'm so tired I could go to sleep right here."

It took him less than five minutes to reach her apartment on Hill Street. When she put her key in the lock of the front door she was surprised to find it unlatched. Plucking up courage, she nervously pushed the door open and stepped inside. The sound of footsteps in the kitchen made her spine tingle.

"Is that you, Mrs. Elseworth?" she called.

There was no answer, but remembering the woman's hearing had begun to fail, she tried again.

"Mrs. Elseworth!"

The footsteps abruptly stopped.

"Who's there?"

Ceetra relaxed as she recognized the voice. Mrs. Elseworth was standing near the sink holding a carving knife, and she looked terrified.

"It's just me," Ceetra assured her.

"Lord, you frightened me."

"I'm sorry. I thought you'd be expecting me. You must have got my cable."

"It arrived yesterday, dear. I've been here all day making

257

sure everything would be just the way you like it." She came forward and put her hands on Ceetra's arms. "You look—well, different somehow. How are you?"

"Fine," Ceetra replied. "Just tired. It's been a long trip."

The older woman studied her a moment longer and then wrapped her in a warm embrace.

"It's so good to see you, love. How was Dallas?"

"Not at all the way I imagined."

"Well," she said, "you're home now and that's what matters, isn't it?"

"Not for long, I'm afraid."

Mrs. Elseworth looked puzzled. "You're not going away again?"

Ceetra nodded. "In a day or two."

"But why, for goodness sake?"

Ceetra hesitated. She had specifically asked everybody at the board meeting to keep her decision a secret until after she got back, but there didn't seem any harm in confiding in Mrs. Elseworth.

"You might as well know," she said. "I'll be in the papers soon anyway. I've taken over the presidency of Rampling International."

"I don't understand."

"It's a long story. My father divested himself of his assets some years ago, gave them to Bromley to avoid paying death duties; but as my brother didn't survive him I automatically inherited everything."

The other woman looked stunned. Then she began to laugh.

"I'm sorry," she said. "But I can't help it. After the way he treated you it's so ironic. God, how I wish your mother was well enough to understand."

"How is she?"

"Not good, I'm afraid, dear."

"I called Dr. Amsdon two or three times from Texas and he said she was doing as well as can be expected."

"That man." Mrs. Elseworth shook her head. "I never liked him. Too smooth by half."

"Is he hiding something?" Ceetra asked.

"I'm afraid your mother's a lot worse, love," she said quietly. "She never really got over the relapse she suffered when she heard about Bromley's death. Will you see her before you leave?"

"I'm going down tomorrow."

"I wouldn't expect too much. She may not even recognize you. Last time I went she didn't know who I was." Her voice broke and she began to cry. But she quickly regained her composure. "Tears aren't going to make things right, are they? It's silly of me, but I've been watching her slipping away—" Once again, tears spilled down her cheeks.

Ceetra put her arms around her shoulders.

"My mother's very lucky to have a friend like you," she said. "I only wish I'd been able to get as close to her."

"Oh, she loves you, dear. In her own way."

"But never as much as Bromley."

"But she barely knew him."

"Maybe that's why."

They sat for a long time without speaking. Finally, Mrs. Elseworth got to her feet.

"I'd better be going," she said, wiping her eyes. "The cat hasn't been fed all day. He must think I've deserted him."

"Please stay."

"No, dear. It's kind of you to ask, but I really do have to get back."

"I'll call a taxi."

Ceetra put her hand through the other woman's arm and walked with her to the corner of Hill Street.

"Sure you'll be okay?"

"I'll be fine." The other woman kissed Ceetra. "Take care of yourself, love."

"I'll call you tomorrow."

It had stopped raining and the streets glistened under the

streetlights. A soft wind had come up, bringing the scent of freshly cut grass from Hyde Park. The breeze triggered memories of the night she had walked the camp with Dan, and suddenly she didn't want to be alone. Perhaps Andrea Cooper was still awake.

She tried calling Andrea's home number, but there was no answer, so she decided to telephone the studio. It was late, but fashion wasn't a nine-to-five business, and it was possible Andrea could still be working. She answered on the fifth ring.

"Darling!" She sounded slightly drunk. "When on earth did you arrive?"

"Just got in a few hours ago," Ceetra said. "I know it's late, but I won't be here long and I thought we could talk—"

"Come on up, for God's sake," the other woman said. "We're having a party. Celebrating the autumn line."

"I'll be there in about half an hour."

"Hurry, darling. I can't wait to see you."

It was almost midnight by the time Ceetra arrived at the studio on Cheyne Walk in Chelsea. She paused before entering the elegant Georgian mansion, and looked at the brass plate at the side of the door. It was engraved with the words "Rampling-Cooper, Ltd." She remembered how proud she had been when that sign had first been put up. While she had been away somebody had scratched the metal with a series of Arabic symbols, and the words "nuke killer." Before she could give it much thought the door swung open and Andrea threw her arms around Ceetra's neck.

"My God, you look absolutely fabulous, darling. It must be all those wide-open spaces. Come on in and let me get you a drink."

She grabbed Ceetra's arm and led her up the broad, winding staircase to where the party was taking place on the second floor.

"Everybody!" Andrea commanded attention with the authority of a drill sergeant. "Look who's here."

The room was filled with people, and they swarmed around her shouting greetings and kissing her.

"You look great . . . wonderful . . . marvelous . . . missed you so terribly . . . "

Andrea rescued her from the crowd of well-wishers and pushed a drink into her hand.

"Now I want to hear everything. Absolutely everything. Are those Texans all really as beautiful as that perfectly divine man in the Marlboro ads?"

Instinctively Ceetra thought about Dan. "Would you believe I didn't see a single cowboy?"

"But, darling, you obviously missed the whole point of the place. I mean nobody, absolutely nobody goes to Texas except to make it with a cowboy."

"You're looking at the exception."

Andrea studied her closely. "You've changed," she said. "I can't put my finger on it, but something's definitely not the same."

Suddenly, Andrea's scrutiny made her self-conscious. She didn't know why. But one thing was clear: if she told her partner about her decision to take over Rampling International it would be common knowledge all over London by morning. She would have to find another reason to explain her wanting to get rid of her share of the fashion business.

"Nobody's the same after spending any amount of time in Texas," she laughed.

"I'm serious, darling," The other woman continued to examine her. "Are you in love?"

"Why on earth—?"

"Yes, that's it. My God, I don't believe it."

"Don't be—"

"Everybody," Andrea announced in her booming voice. "Our little Ceetra has met somebody—"

"Stop it, for Christ's sake—"

"And she's in love."

Ceetra realized her partner was drunker than she thought.

But it was too late to stop the flood of renewed attention. Once again everybody pressed around her, shouting questions and probing for details. She tried to appear amused, but found the situation oppressive, and pried herself free the moment she was able. She sought sanctuary in a small kitchen off the main room, but the moment she entered she realized she had made the wrong choice.

"How are you, Ceetra?" Paul Mayhew was standing near the refrigerator with a drink in his hand.

"Fine, Paul." She tried to sound nonchalant. "And you?"

"Great." He smiled. "Long time, huh?"

"Less than a month."

"Seems longer."

"Want a drink?" he asked.

"I have one."

"Where?"

Ceetra realized she had left her glass in the other room.

"It's in there—"

"What was it?"

"White wine."

He opened the refrigerator and took out a bottle that had already been opened.

"Soave Bolla. Your favorite."

He poured some in a glass and handed it to her. Then he raised his own in a toast. "Old times?"

"Things have changed."

"So I hear. What's this about you being in love?"

"Oh, Christ—"

Andrea appeared at the door of the kitchen holding two glasses.

"Ooops! Am I interrupting something?"

"No." Ceetra put her wine down on the draining board and edged past Paul.

"We were remembering old times," he said.

"Differently," Ceetra added.

"Why don't I show you how the autumn collection turned out," Andrea said.

"As quickly as possible," Ceetra replied.

Andrea looked at Paul. "Any time you're ready to leave, don't hesitate," she said.

She turned and led the way down to the main workroom on the ground floor where the autumn collection was being displayed.

"Bastard," she said. "He came with a group of buyers and I couldn't keep him out."

"It doesn't matter. He's past tense as far as I'm concerned."

"You mean it this time?"

"Never more sure in my life."

"I'm going to hold you to it."

"You won't have to," Ceetra said. "I won't be around."

"I don't understand."

"I'm leaving in a couple of days. For good."

"But what about the business?"

"Looks like you've done fine while I was away."

"Only because you'd already done the designs."

"You can hire designers. There are lots of young talented people who would jump at the chance to work for a major house."

"What the hell's got into you?"

Ceetra hesitated. "I just don't want to be in the business any more."

"You know I can't afford to buy you out."

"You don't have to," Ceetra said. "I'm giving it to you."

"Why?"

Again she paused, unwilling to reveal the truth. "I'm an American," she said. "I never really felt I belonged here. Now that my father's dead—well, there's nothing to stop me from going back to my roots."

"What about your mother?"

"She's very ill. The prognosis isn't good."

Andrea was silent. Then her chin began to quiver. "God, I'm going to miss you."

"Hey, come on," Ceetra said. "This is meant to be a celebration, remember? These outfits look great. I'm going to try a few on."

The two women gathered an armful of clothes and Ceetra selected half a dozen outfits for herself. She also picked out a beautifully cut camel's hair coat for her mother, which Andrea carefully gift-wrapped.

"There's too much to carry," Andrea said. "Why don't I have somebody drop it off at your apartment first thing in the morning?"

"Good idea," Ceetra agreed. "But I'll take my mother's gift with me."

"You're not leaving now?"

The spurt of nervous energy Ceetra had felt earlier in the evening had given way to fatigue.

"I think I will." She picked up the box containing her mother's coat. "The jet lag's beginning to hit me."

Andrea kissed Ceetra on the cheek. "I'm going to miss you terribly," she murmured.

"I'll be in and out of London all the time—" Ceetra checked herself before she said too much. "We'll keep in touch."

"I'll never change this." Andrea touched the Rampling-Cooper, Ltd. logo on the box Ceetra was holding. "It'll always be both of us as far as the rest of the world's concerned."

"Thanks." Ceetra was close to tears.

"Call me before you leave," Andrea said.

"I will. Promise."

Andrea opened the door and held it until Ceetra was on the sidewalk. There was a taxi parked against the opposite curb.

"You're in luck," Andrea called. "They're as rare as—" There was a crash and the sound of broken glass from the second floor. "Lord. I'd better go up and sort things out. Take care of yourself, darling."

Ceetra watched as the other woman closed the door. She experienced a sudden sense of loss and remembered how Andrea had held her the night she lost her virginity. It all seemed so long ago. She crossed to where the taxi was parked.

"Sorry, Miss," the driver said. "I've already got a fare."

"It's all right." Paul Mayhew leaned forward in the back seat. "This is the person I've been waiting for."

"I think you've got the wrong—"

"Don't be silly. It's way past the time when the buses stop running, and I doubt if you'll find another cab this side of Marble Arch."

"I'll take my chances," Ceetra said.

The driver took out a thermos and poured himself some steaming hot tea. "Let me know what you decide," he said. "Not that I care much either way. The meter's been running for close to fifteen minutes now. It ain't going to slow down any."

"You heard the man," Mayhew said. "Your arguing is making him rich—on my money."

For a moment she considered walking, but it was a long way and the box she was carrying was getting heavier by the minute.

"I don't want to get into another argument," she said.

"Promise," Mayhew said solemnly.

"And you'll take me straight home?"

"Scout's honor."

Ceetra climbed into the back seat.

"Where to?" the driver asked.

"Hill Street," she replied. "Around the corner from the Dorchester. I'll tell you when to stop."

"Right you are." He emptied the remaining tea back into his thermos and screwed on the plastic cap. "The thing I admire about you Yanks is the way you make split-second decisions."

Mayhew laughed. "You really asked for that one."

"It's the first time anybody called me a Yank."

"Because you always sounded so British."

"And now?"

"A definite twang."

"I haven't been away that long."

"Seems ages to me." He put his hand over hers, but she quickly withdrew it.

"Don't Paul. You promised. Remember?"

"I'm sorry," he said. "It's just that I've missed you. A lot."

He waited for Ceetra to answer, but she averted her eyes and looked out at the shops along King's Road.

"I'm talking to you," Paul snapped.

"It'd be easier if we didn't."

"What the hell's got into you?"

"Please, Paul. I'm in no mood for—"

"You're in no mood?"

"I'm worn out. It's been a long day."

"It's been a long month for me. Didn't even know where you were until I read about your going to America in the papers. Not even a call to say goodbye. After all we've been through together I think I deserved that courtesy."

"Courtesy?" She shook her head. "When did that ever play a part in our relationship?"

"You're right. Maybe I have taken you for granted in the past. But a lot of things have changed since you've been away."

The taxi had turned off Park Lane and was slowly making its way down Hill Street.

"Tell me when you want me to stop," the driver called over his shoulder.

"Right here," Ceetra said.

She had hoped Paul would stay in the cab, but he paid the fare and walked with her to the door of her apartment.

"I told you, Paul—"

"I have to talk to you."

"It's no use."

She unlocked the door. When she opened it he shouldered his way past her into the living room.

"I'm leaving my wife." He made the announcement sound like a proclamation. Even he must have realized it, because he smiled. "God, that sounded like it should have been accompanied by a blast from the royal trumpeters. I feel like a bloody fool prostrating myself like this. But I don't mind wearing a hair shirt—"

"It doesn't suit you."

She struck a nerve. His attempts to ingratiate himself suddenly vanished.

"Boots and a stetson. Is that what you prefer nowadays? This new chap of yours—"

"Paul, stop it."

"Is he dark and handsome or more the Clint Eastwood type?"

"Please."

"Either way I'll bet he rides tall in the saddle. Oh, yes. That's a prerequisite of yours. All your men have to be able to fuck the daylights out of you, don't they?"

"I wish you'd leave."

Suddenly he hit her. The blow knocked her back on the sofa. Before she could move he caught her and forced his knee between her legs. She felt his left hand clawing her panties down.

"You want fucking? I'll show you what fucking's all about."

He moved his knee and ripped her pants off. Then he grabbed her blouse and tore it from her. The sight of her breasts made him pause. It was almost as if he were examining them for signs of bruises or other marks that would indicate some other man had sucked them.

"For Christ's sake—"

Her words snapped him out of his momentary inaction, and he was too strong for her. Finally, realizing further resistance was hopeless, she gave up.

"That's better," he breathed. "Now you're coming to your senses."

He took off his trousers and forced her legs apart. Her submission seemed to excite him. He grasped her breasts, and soon ejaculated. She winced as he dug his nails into her skin. Then slowly his fingers relaxed, and he lay back panting.

267

She got off the sofa and went into the bathroom, where she douched and put on a robe. She felt curiously at peace. Paul's raping her was the catharsis she'd needed; the final purgation of whatever lingering feelings she might have had for him. She was cleansed and, in a strange way, spiritually renewed.

He had put his trousers back on by the time she returned to the living room, and was pouring himself a drink.

"I was right, wasn't I?" he said.

"About what?"

"You needing that."

"More than you'll ever know," she replied.

"That's my girl." He raised his glass. "Here's to the two of us, and the future."

"There isn't going to be any, Paul. This is the last time we will ever see each other."

"You've said that before."

"This time I mean it."

He finished his drink and went to the door. "I was lying about my wife," he said.

"You needn't have bothered."

"I'll call you."

"I won't be here."

"You will," he replied. "For just as long as I want you."

"Don't count on it."

"Oh, but I will," he said. "It's taken me eight years to learn your flaws. They are one of the few things left in life that I can absolutely rely on."

21

CEETRA SLEPT SOUNDLY. It was as if a great burden had been removed from her, and even the snide observations Paul had made when he left failed to disturb her. She was still asleep when Walters arrived with the car, and only his persistent ringing finally awakened her.

She dressed quickly and didn't bother with breakfast. When she handed Walters the box containing the coat she had picked out for her mother, she noticed him wince as he opened the trunk of the Rolls with his bandaged hand.

"Are you sure you're all right?" she asked.

"Well, it is a bit sore this morning, Miss," he admitted. "The missus thinks it may be infected."

"Have you seen a doctor?"

"Not yet. I've been too busy these last few days."

His answer puzzled Ceetra. While she was away the only duties Walters had had was taking care of the car.

"What have you been up to?" she asked.

"That's what I wanted to talk to you about, Miss." He sounded tense. "I didn't want to bring it up in front of Mr. Blake, so thought I'd wait until this morning."

"What is it, Walters?"

"Me and a mate—we was in the army together during World War Two—well, we're both getting along in years, and we've been thinking about opening a small shop. A tobacconist's that sells newspapers and magazines. That kind of thing. Nothing elaborate, mind you. Just enough to supplement our pensions."

"It sounds wonderful," Ceetra said. "Why haven't you done it?"

"Oh, a lot of reasons," the driver said. "I have a good job working for you. Then there's the problem of raising enough money to get started—"

"How much do you need?"

"We reckon about twenty thousand pounds each ought to see us through. He's already got his half, and I'm pretty close."

"I'd be glad to put up the balance," Ceetra said.

"That's very kind of you, Miss, but I couldn't—"

"You could look on it as severance pay."

"Severance, Miss?"

"Yes. I'm going to be staying in America. It's something I planned to discuss with you before I left. Since it's come up you might as well know now. And I'd like to show my appreciation for everything you've done over the years by helping you get that shop."

"The only way I could accept it would be as a loan," he said.

"All right. If that makes you feel better. I'll tell my bankers to get in touch with you. So that's settled."

"I don't know how to thank you—"

"Take care of that hand," Ceetra told him. "How old's your boy now?"

"Going on sixteen, Miss."

"Well, give him a paper route. That'll keep him too busy to leave his skates on the step."

Dan was waiting when they stopped in front of Claridge's.

"You're late," he said as he climbed into the Rolls.

"Sorry."

"And you look terrible."

"Thanks. You really know how to make a woman feel great first thing in the morning."

"Did you have breakfast?"

"Not yet."

"We can stop somewhere along the way."

"I wondered—"

"What?"

"My mother isn't well. I'd like to visit her. It isn't far out of the way. Do you mind?"

"You're the boss," he said.

It wasn't exactly the answer she'd hoped for, but it didn't surprise her. Dan was obviously still angry about what had happened in New York. She decided to make one last try at remedying the situation.

"I owe you an apology," she said.

He looked at her but didn't speak.

"My behavior aboard the *Nova* was—very childish."

"I guess I asked for it."

"Let's just say we both make a mistake."

"That's fine with me."

"Good."

For a long time they were both silent. The city had given way to a patchwork of lush green fields. The sky was still overcast, but holes had begun to appear in the clouds and rays of morning sun penetrated the greyness. There was little traffic on the road, and Walters was making good time. When they stopped, Ceetra got out and watched as Walters took the heavy box from the trunk. It was obvious from his pained expression that handling the package was hurting his injured hand.

"Let me help," she said.

"I'll take it," Dan announced.

Dan's gesture surprised Ceetra, but before she had time to comment on it, Dr. Amsdon hurried down the steps to greet her.

"I got your cable," he said. "It's good you were able to get here. Your mother's—well, I'm afraid she's slipping away fast."

"Why didn't you let me know?"

"I tried," the psychiatrist said. "But you'd already left New York. As you were on your way I didn't see much point in upsetting you more than was necessary."

As he talked he led the way into the sanatorium. He must have assumed Dan was a relative, because he didn't question his presence.

Ceetra had prepared herself for the worst, and was surprised to find her mother sitting up in bed with a brightly colored wool shawl draped around her shoulders. If anything, she appeared in better health than the last time Ceetra saw her. The only visible indication of anything seriously wrong was an occasional brief spasm.

"Don't stay too long," Dr. Amsdon warned. "Your mother's very tired."

"Nonsense," the woman in bed snapped. "I feel better than I have in weeks. Now you go about your business and leave me to talk to my daughter."

"I'll check back in a little while," he said. "If you need anything just ring the bell."

When the door closed Mary Rampling fixed her gaze on Dan.

"Mother," Ceetra said. "I'd like you to meet Dan Blake."

Dan shifted his feet uncomfortably and put the gift-wrapped box on a table at the end of the bed.

"Nice to meet you, ma'am. I hope I'm not intruding," he said.

"Blake. Dan Blake." The woman in bed kept repeating the name until tumblers in her mind finally clicked into place. "I remember. You're the man Bromley wrote about in his letters. He said you were a protégé of my husband's."

"I was Jake's personal assistant."

"And he assigned you to keep an eye on my son." Her tone was sharp and accusatory.

"Mother!" Ceetra's face was flushed.

"It's all right," Dan said. "It's true. I did act as a kind of surrogate parent to Bromley. Jake felt because I was nearer the boy's age I—well, he had difficulty communicating with his son."

"My husband had difficulty communicating with everybody," Mary Rampling said.

"I got along with him pretty well," Dan said.

"But not with Bromley, apparently."

"I tried."

"Without much success, I gather."

"Mother, please!" Ceetra turned to Dan. "You have no right—"

"You're wrong," Dan interjected quietly. "She has every right."

"Tell me about my son," she said.

"He was a fine young man," Dan said without the slightest hesitation.

"Did he ever talk about me?"

"Often. He loved you very much."

She looked at Ceetra. Her eyes were fixed on Dan, and there was an expression in them that made her realize her daughter cared deeply about this man.

"I've been lucky with my children," she said.

Ceetra leaned over the bed and gently kissed her mother's cheek. Her skin felt dry and unusually hot.

"Are you sure you're all right?" she asked.

"Just a bit tired."

"We'd better let you get some rest."

"Give me your hand," the older woman said, looking at Dan.

She took it and placed it over Ceetra's.

"Be kind to each other," she murmured. "There's so much cruelty in the world."

Before either could answer, the door opened and Dr. Amsdon came into the room.

"I think that's long enough for the first visit," he said.

Ceetra looked at her mother and saw her eyes were

273

closed. But as they were filing out of the door, she heard her voice.

"I had another letter from Bromley," she said weakly. "It came just the other day. I'll read it to you next—"

Her voice trailed away.

"Will she be all right?" Ceetra asked when they were out-side the room.

"I wish I could be more encouraging," the doctor replied. "But the truth is your mother's a very sick woman. Her mind wanders in and out of the present. A lot of the time she doesn't recognize people."

"She was much sharper than I expected."

"That's because I gave her an injection before you came. A stimulant. But when it wears off—" He shrugged. "There comes a point where even the best medical care isn't enough."

Ceetra managed to control her emotions until they were back in the car, then she put her head on Dan's shoulder and started sobbing.

"Go ahead," he said. "Let it all out."

Walters waited somber-faced behind the wheel. "Will you be going on to Eastbourne, sir?" he asked quietly.

"No," Dan replied. "I don't think so. In fact, I'd ap-preciate it if you'd get us back to London as quickly as pos-sible."

It was early evening by the time Walters stopped the Rolls-Royce in front of Ceetra's apartment on Hill Street. Rain had begun falling as they passed through the neatly ordered streets of Croydon, and by the time they reached the city it had turned from a fine drizzle to a torrential downpour.

"We'll have to make a run for it," Dan said, helping her out of the car.

The distance between the curb and her apartment was less than a hundred feet, but by the time they reached the shelter of the porch over the front door they were both drenched.

"Do you want me to wait, sir?" Walters called.

Ceetra looked at Dan's dripping clothes. "Why don't you come in and dry out," she said.

Dan turned to the chauffeur. "I'll be fine," he shouted. "But we have to be out at the airport by ten-thirty at the latest in the morning."

Walters touched the peak of his cap, and guided the Rolls smoothly into the light early-evening traffic.

Ceetra unlocked the door and led the way into the living room. She drew the heavy velvet drapes and put a match to the fire.

"How about a drink?" she asked.

"A bourbon would be great."

"I'm not sure I have any."

"How about brandy?"

"I know I've got that."

"Anything to get the dampness out of my bones."

"You get used to it when you live over here." She took the stopper out of a ship's decanter and poured some cognac into a balloon glass made of hand-cut Waterford crystal. "This should do the trick. It's over a hundred years old."

"About the age I feel."

She laughed. "If you give me your clothes I'll put them next to the hot water heater. You can change in the bathroom down the hall. You'll find a robe on the back of the door."

Five minutes later he entered the kitchen carrying his damp suit and shirt. She wondered if he would ask why she had a man's robe in her bathroom, but he made no comment.

"What about you?" he asked.

"I'll take a shower in a few minutes," she said. "I just want to get things started in here first."

Dan saw she had taken food from the refrigerator and a pan was already heating on the stove.

"We could go out for dinner if you'd rather."

"And get soaked to the skin again?" She shook her head. "Anyway, I want to finish up some of this food Mrs.

275

Elseworth brought. No point in keeping it if we're leaving tomorrow. Like omelettes?"

"Love 'em."

"Good. They're about the only thing I know how to make, and even with them there's a certain risk."

"Why don't I do it while you take a shower?"

"You cook?"

"I think I can manage an omelette."

"Okay," she said. "I put some butter in the pan so watch out it doesn't burn. If you can't find anything you need, just yell."

She left Dan in the kitchen and went into her bedroom. The rain was still coming down hard. She could hear it pattering against the windows. She liked the sound; it evoked memories of nights at Farleigh School when she would lie snug and warm in bed as a storm raged in the darkness over the English Channel. It was like being in a cocoon, safe and secure, while all around the world roared in anger.

This is what her apartment had been to her all these years: a haven from the storms, a sanctuary in which she could hide when the going got too rough for her. As she showered she wondered why she felt such an urge to leave it, particularly when she already knew the discomfort, even the terrors of the new world she was entering. Perhaps, she thought, it was partly because the years had taught her that a cocoon, no matter how luxurious, could also be a prison.

She dried herself off. When she returned to the bedroom she heard Dan clattering around in the kitchen. This time she decided she wouldn't give him any cause to accuse her of behaving like a whore. She put on a plain linen shirt and jeans. No perfume. Not even any makeup. And she tied her hair back with a plain red ribbon.

In the living room she saw he'd spread a tablecloth on the floor in front of the fireplace, and arranged a number of cushions around it. Apart from the burning logs, the only illumination came from half a dozen candles in an exquisite Louis XV candelabrum which normally stood on the bon-

netiere near the window. The wineglasses and silver shimmered in the soft light. It reminded her of the picnic the
elderly steward had prepared for them on the sun deck of
the *Nova.*

"Looks familiar," she said.

Dan glanced up from where he was using a spatula to
transfer a large omelette from a pan to the plate in front of
him. "I thought we might pick up where we left off," he said.

"A second chance?"

"Maybe we both learned something first time around."

She squatted on a cushion and used her fingers to taste the
omelette he had served.

"Mmmm. Delicious. What's in it?"

"Cheese, asparagus tips, tomatoes, mushrooms—a bit of
everything I found in the refrigerator."

"Where on earth did you learn to cook like this?"

"On a lot of oil rigs around west and east Texas."

"You worked as a cook?"

He laughed. "No, I was a roughneck. But the food was
usually so lousy I took to fixing my own. Border-style Mexican is my specialty."

"I've never tried it."

"I'll fix some for you when we get back."

"When will that be?"

"A week, maybe ten days. Depends on how long I have to
stay around Ju'aymah."

"Where's that?"

"It's an eastern province of Saudi Arabia."

"Is that where you were while I was in the hospital?"

"That's right."

"You said there was an emergency of some kind."

"That's pretty well resolved now."

"What kind of a project is it?"

"A nuclear power plant."

"Has the construction phase started yet?"

He hesitated. "We completed it about a year ago."

"Then why are we still involved with it?"

"There were a few problems." She sensed his evasiveness. "You don't have to go. I could meet you in Singapore."

"Now I'm really curious. What is it you don't want me to see?"

"It's just that you're not likely to enjoy the way they treat women over there."

"It can't be that different."

"It is."

"Then I'd better begin getting used to it," she said. "I gather we do a lot of business in that part of the world."

He finished his brandy and refilled his glass. When he stood up his robe parted enough for her to see he was naked under it. He swallowed the drink in a single gulp.

"My clothes should be dry by now."

She followed him into the kitchen.

"Am I beginning to sound like an executive?" she asked.

"A bit."

"I didn't mean to—not now, anyway."

"It's something *I'd* better get used to."

"Aren't you going to finish your omelette?"

"I'm not sure I should stay. After what happened aboard the *Nova* maybe—"

"Please stay," she said.

He turned to face her.

"Sure?"

She nodded. "New York—well, it just didn't happen the right way."

He picked her up in his arms and carried her into the bedroom. After putting her on the bed, he knelt down and gently kissed her on the mouth. She felt herself tremble. She drew back and looked at him for a moment, then kissed him on the lips, her mouth partly open, a slow, soft kiss which went on and on until her head began to spin.

They drew apart. She stood up and took off her clothes. He remained seated on the edge of the bed. When she was naked he reached both hands behind her buttocks and pulled her against him. His breath was hot as he pressed his mouth against her pubic hair, and she felt the slight pressure of his tongue probing into her.

"God," she murmured. "You feel so good."

His fingers trailed over her breasts. She flinched slightly as they touched the scratches Paul had made.

"Am I hurting you?"

"I never felt better in my whole life," she said.

His fingers moved down the back of her thighs. When they returned to her buttocks it was to part the cheeks in a way that allowed the side of one hand to rest in the crease. The tip of his little finger was over her anus. For a moment she thought he was going to enter her that way, but he only exerted enough pressure to make the sphincter muscle relax.

"Lie down," he whispered.

She obeyed, and watched as he got up to take off his robe. She saw his erection. It was huge. As he came toward her it swayed from side to side. He cupped her face in his hands and leaned over to kiss her. She took hold of his penis and put it against her cheek. She could feel the blood vessels standing out under the skin, and lightly ran her tongue over them until she reached the tip. She kissed it. He lay down next to her on the bed and ran his hands over the contours of her body. His fingers explored the underside of her breasts, then slowly worked their way down until they were between her legs. She took his penis and guided it into her. She was already wet, and it slid into her vagina with an ease that surprised her. It was so immense she had thought it would hurt, but there was no pain. Only the most exquisite pleasure. Spreading her legs wide, she arched her back until he was all the way inside her. Then she slowly moved back. The friction of his shaft against her clitoris sent quivers through her whole body and she moaned. He picked up the rhythm and drove in and out in strong, steady strokes. She kept her eyes open, watching his face. There was enough light from the other room for her to see the sweat glistening on his brow.

"Now," he commanded.

She shuddered. Her orgasm was so intense it went on and on until she thought she was going to faint. Suddenly she passed the peak and slumped back against the pillow with a deep sigh.

Still hot and trembling, she put her head on his chest. His breathing was rapid and she could hear his heart beating. She felt his penis. It was still hard. Sliding down, she kissed it and took it in her mouth. Then, wordlessly, she made him lie back as she straddled him. This time the pace was slower. Each seemed to savor the other more completely than before. There was no more urgency; just a gentle, mounting rhythm that went on and on until it seemed she was slowly merging herself into him. As his sperm spurted into her, she arched her body in another orgasm of her own. Then she settled against his chest and closed her eyes, content in the knowledge that they were still joined together.

 **22**

FROM THE AIR Riyadh looked like a smaller version of an American city that had been capriciously set down in the midst of a vast desert. Unlike other major capitals of the world, which owed their existence to the proximity of ports or the confluence of major rivers, Riyadh appeared to have no logical reason for being, other than the dubious distinction of being located at the geographical heart of Saudi Arabia.

Ceetra turned away from the window of the Gulfstream III and focused her attention on Dan, who was deeply engrossed in studying blueprints.

"It isn't at all the way I imagined it," she said.

"What were you expecting?"

"Oh, I don't know. Something a little more romantic, I guess."

"You should have seen it when I first came here with your father. It wasn't much more than a desert village."

"I think I would have liked it better that way."

"Fasten your safety belts, please," the pilot announced over the plane's loudspeaker system. "We will be landing at Riyadh in about three minutes."

When the plane taxied to a stop and the steward opened the door in the fuselage, heat flooded into the cabin. It was overwhelming. As Ceetra stepped outside she felt as if she'd suddenly walked in front of a blast furnace. When they emerged from customs, a glistening white Mercedes was waiting to take them into the city.

The car belonged to Mr. Hisham Shawaf, whom Dan introduced as the head of the company with which Rampling International joint-ventured in all its projects in Saudi Arabia. He was tall, with great presence, and Ceetra sensed an almost mystical aura about him. He moved well, yet his pale, almost transluscent skin seemed to reflect pain and weariness. She guessed he was in his late forties, but his slumped shoulders seemed bent by the burden of far more years.

"I am very honored to meet you," he said to Ceetra in a voice so small that it whispered deprecation. "The news of your father's death was most distressing. Please accept my deepest condolences."

"Thank you."

"I have arranged accommodation at the Intercontinental Hotel," Mr. Shawaf said. "And my wife has planned a very simple dinner for you and a few of our friends this evening. I hope you won't be too tired."

"Of course not," Ceetra replied, as he ushered her into the merciful coolness of the air-conditioned car.

Mr. Shawaf then turned his attention to Dan and launched into a discussion of various business dealings, making no attempt to include Ceetra. It was almost as if she had ceased to exist. After years of being ignored by her father, Mr. Shawaf's attitude touched nerves that were still very raw. In an effort to control her anger, she fixed her attention on the city they were rapidly approaching.

Riyadh presented striking evidence of the boom Saudi Arabia was experiencing. Dozens of new office buildings were in various stages of construction, as were scores of villas that fronted onto newly paved streets. Traffic jams were frequent, and at one busy intersection near the Ministry of Petroleum and Mineral Resources, she saw an overpass that was packed solid with unmoving cars. The shops carried a wide selection of Parisian fashions, Swiss watches and German cars, all at staggering prices. But what most impressed her was the number of banks. It seemed there was at least one from every major nation in the world, and for the first time she began to realize that what had appeared from the air to be a small town of minor importance was, in fact, the hub of one of the wealthiest countries in the world.

"I will send the car for you at seven o'clock," Mr. Shawaf announced as the Mercedes rolled to a stop in front of the ultramodern portals of the Intercontinental Hotel. "My wife is very much looking forward to meeting you, Miss Rampling."

Ceetra smiled stiffly, but the moment she entered the cavernous marble lobby her expression changed.

"What's eating you?" Dan asked.

"I don't like being ignored," she said.

"I warned you about the way they treat women over here."

"You could have made an effort to include me in the conversation."

"It wouldn't have done any good. Women aren't even allowed to drive in Saudi Arabia. They sure as hell aren't going to begin discussing business with one."

Ceetra didn't answer.

Two rooms had been reserved for them on the top floor. When Ceetra reached hers she went into it quickly and closed the door. Only after she'd undressed and gotten under a cool shower did her anger begin to dissolve, but it left a residue of apprehension. She realized the dilemma that faced her now was one she would be confronted with wherever she went: men who occupied decision-making positions in business, especially men in the male-dominated construction industry, were not accustomed to asking the opinion of a woman. Although the situation was exaggerated in Riyadh, the problem wasn't limited to Saudi Arabia. It would still be there when she returned to the United States, and she was going to have to come to grips with it if she was going to function effectively in her new role as president of Rampling International.

She lay down on the bed and closed her eyes. Suddenly she heard a knocking sound. Wrapping a large bath towel around her, she went to the door and opened it, but nobody was there. Then she realized the knocking was coming from another door set in the wall nearer the window. When she unlocked it Dan stepped into the room. He was naked except for a pair of bikini shorts.

"Still mad at me?"

"Furious."

"I know just the remedy." He scooped her up in his arms and carried her to the bed. Pulling the towel away from her he leaned over to kiss her nipples.

"Don't," she said.

He ignored her and moved his tongue down to her belly.

"Please, Dan—"

His hand slid between her legs.

"For Christ's sake—" She twisted away, picked up the towel and wrapped it around her.

"What the hell's the matter with you?"

"This isn't going to solve anything."

"Maybe," he said. "But it can't hurt."

He lowered his head again. Her flesh quivered as he continued to run his tongue down the inside of her thigh, but she experienced a perverse unwillingness to let herself be taken.

"I mean it," she said, rolling over on her stomach. "I've got a lot of thinking to do, and you aren't helping."

He looked at her with a grin, but saw she was serious. His eyes turned hard and his face took on an expression identical to that which had frightened her the night they picnicked aboard the *Nova*. He got up and crossed to the door linking the two rooms.

"Have it your way," he said. "If you change your mind you know where to find me."

She regretted her reaction the moment he closed the door, but pride prevented her from going to him. It wasn't that she didn't want Dan; simply that she didn't relish being treated as an object simply because she was a woman. She went to her briefcase and took out the Cartier flask Dan had insisted on buying her, since they were entering a Moslem country where alcohol is forbidden. She filled a tumbler half full of Vodka and sat back on the bed trying to calm her nerves.

Dan was already waiting when she finished dressing and went down to the lobby. He didn't speak throughout the short journey to Mr. Shawaf's villa on the outskirts of the city. And immediately after their arrival, he allowed their host to guide him to a small library where he quickly immersed himself in conversation with a group of other male guests.

"You must be Miss Rampling."

Ceetra turned to see a beautiful, dark-haired woman wearing an Yves Saint Laurent gown.

"I am Wahida Shawaf." She extended an exquisitely shaped hand that glistened with diamonds. "Welcome to our house. You must excuse my husband for not introducing us."

"It seems he's more interested in business," Ceetra said. "I can see how a woman gets to feel like a second-class citizen around here."

The woman laughed. "This must be your first visit to Riyadh."

She took Ceetra's arm and led her around the room, introducing her to half a dozen other women who turned out to be the wives of men gathered in the library. They all wore expensive dresses and jewelry, and proved to be easy conversationalists in English.

Soon the men appeared from the other room and they all sat down to dinner.

Dan sat on the opposite side of the table from Ceetra, but paid little attention to her. She had no way of knowing

whether his attitude was a carry-over from their earlier conflict or simply behavior dictated by the other men, who continued to talk among themselves and ignore their wives.
Whatever the reason, it irritated her so thoroughly that she
found herself making comments that became increasingly
more outrageous as the evening progressed.

She also began to realize that she was feeling the effects
of the Vodka she'd had in her hotel room. Perhaps she had
had a bit too much, for by the time dinner was served she was
tipsy. But she didn't care. During one of the frequent lulls in
conversation she lit a cigarette and blew a cloud of smoke
across the table. It drifted directly into Dan's face, and she
saw him grimace, but beyond that he didn't acknowledge her
deliberately defiant gesture.

"Is the hotel crowded?" Mrs. Shawaf asked, attempting to
lessen the tension that Ceetra had generated, particularly
among the men, who were visibly disturbed by her lack of
decorum.

"The lobby looked like a meeting of the U.N. General
Assembly," she said. "With the Japanese making up the
largest delegation."

"Ah, the Japanese," Mr. Shawaf sighed in his whisperlike
voice. "They come in hordes, stay a while, take a lot of photographs, and then vanish. One wonders what they do, why
they are here?"

"Maybe they're planning an invasion," Ceetra said wryly.

Her host looked confused. He didn't know whether the
remark was intended as a joke, or if he should take it seriously.

"No nation would be that naive," he said.

"I wouldn't be so sure." Ceetra realized she had him on a
string and decided to play with him. "A lot of Americans are
tired of being made to pay through the nose for oil. Quite a
few think the problem could be solved by sending in a
quick-action strike force to take over the fields."

"Miss Rampling is playing devil's advocate," Dan said.
"You must excuse her."

"When apologies are called for, I'll make them," Ceetra said brusquely.

The silence that followed was fraught with tension. The men at the table had never heard a woman express herself so defiantly in public.

"Why don't we all move into the other room?" Mrs. Shawaf said with a brightness she obviously didn't feel.

When the others got up, Ceetra remained seated at the table, pulling on her cigarette.

"Are you all right?" Mrs. Shawaf asked.

"Just angry, and a little upset. I'm sorry if I ruined your party."

"I haven't enjoyed an evening as much in ages," the other woman replied. "It was a pleasure to listen to a woman who isn't afraid to say what she thinks."

"I doubt if your husband feels the same way."

"It's time he learned."

Ceetra stood up and the two women went into the other room. The awkward pause in the conversation when she entered indicated to Ceetra that the others had been talking about her. Mr. Shawaf, ever conscious of his social duties, brought a chair for her.

"How long are you staying?" he asked politely.

"That depends on how long it takes to see the nuclear power plant at Ju'aymah," she replied.

"I'm afraid there's been a small change in plans," he said. "The minister of the interior thinks it inadvisable for you to make such an inspection at this time."

"I don't understand."

"What my husband's trying to say," Mrs. Shawaf explained, "is that the presence of a woman at a project of that kind would cause too much of a stir."

"Wahida, please—" Her husband's reprimand was uttered with uncharacteristic volume.

"Is that true?" Ceetra asked.

"The minister simply feels it would be in everybody's best interest if you remained here in Riyadh."

"And if I insist on going?"

"It could seriously jeopardize the good will it took your father years to establish with key government officials."

There was a tense silence as everybody in the room waited for her response, and an almost audible sigh of relief when she pleaded fatigue and asked to be excused in order to return to the hotel.

"Would you like me to go with you?" Mrs. Shawaf asked.

"Thank you," Ceetra replied. "But I'll be fine. Really."

She looked at Dan.

"I'm staying," he said. "Mr. Shawaf and I have business to discuss."

She nodded and walked to the door, closely followed by Mrs. Shawaf.

"Why don't you spend the day with me tomorrow?" she said. "I work at the company clinic here in Riyadh."

"As a volunteer?"

"I'm a doctor. A pediatrician by training, but I also practice general medicine." She saw Ceetra's look of surprise and laughed. "It doesn't fit the image at all, does it? You'll find this country is full of contradictions. Will nine o'clock be too early for you?"

"That will be perfect. I'll be ready."

"Good," her hostess said. "It will give us a chance to talk."

She led the way outside and issued instructions to the waiting chauffeur.

Ceetra was glad to reach the cool sanctuary of her room at the hotel. The evening hadn't gone well and it was her fault. She had behaved like a child, and could have seriously jeopardized the firm's relations with its Saudi partner. It made her realize that if she was going to be effective as president of the company, she must learn to overcome the fact that people would treat her differently because she was a woman. What she needed to master was a technique of asserting herself in such a way that it would automatically command respect. But how? No answers came, and she soon sought refuge in sleep.

She awoke to find herself drenched with sweat. It was 2:45 a.m. She looked at the door linking her room with Dan's and wondered if he had come in yet. Getting up, she crossed to the door and turned the handle. The drapes in the adjoining room were open, and light from a neon sign outside the window shed enough light for her to see the bed was empty. His pajamas remained neatly spread over the pillow where the maid had left them.

She stood motionless at the door for almost a full minute. His absence made her feel anxious, insecure, like a child who wakes in the night to find the house empty. It also triggered thoughts about Paris and Rome. In both cities he had gotten up when he thought she was asleep, dressed and quietly slipped out of the room, only to return just as silently an hour or two later to slip back into bed with her. When she asked where he'd been he was evasive, mentioning something about liking to take a walk when he couldn't sleep, and she hadn't pressed him. This time she suspected he was still with Mr. Shawaf and wondered what time he would get back.

Taking a Valium, she lay back down on the bed and tried not to think of him. Finally fatigue got the better of her, and she drifted back to sleep.

The shrill ring of the telephone woke her. She was still groggy when she picked up the receiver.

"I'm downstairs in the lobby." She recognized Mrs. Shawaf's voice. "Had you forgotten our date?"

"No, of course not," Ceetra replied. "I'll be down in ten or fifteen minutes."

It was 9:30 when Ceetra stepped out of the elevator. She saw Mrs. Shawaf near the reception desk and was surprised to see she was wearing a very simple white dress. Her hair was pulled tightly back in a chignon.

The chauffeur was outside in the Mercedes, and less than half an hour later had transported them to one of the poorest sections of Riyadh. He stopped the car outside a white two-story building that had large patches of plaster peeling from its walls.

"Is this it?" Ceetra asked, surprise showing in her voice.

"Welcome to the Rampling International—Shawaf, S.A. company clinic," the other woman said. "It might not look like much, but it's all we've got."

She briskly led the way inside and was greeted by a young, dark-eyed woman wearing a nurse's uniform.

"Good morning, Farida. When have you scheduled my first patient?"

"Eleven o'clock."

"That's fine. I've got a lot of paperwork to catch up on."

She entered a small, sparsely furnished room that was spotlessly clean but scarcely big enough to contain anything more than the barest necessities: a desk, two chairs, a glass-fronted cabinet for medicines.

"It doesn't look like the firm is too generous with funds," Ceetra commented.

"At least we have a clinic," the other woman said. "That's more than most other companies."

She started sorting through a stack of letters, most of which carried American stamps.

"Skilled manpower is scarce over here," she continued. "Most of the top jobs are filled either by friends of my husband, or people your father's company brings over from the States. When they get ill they are cared for by doctors at the construction site or, if it's something serious, at the King Faisal Hospital. We only get the workers they bring in from poorer lands to do the heavy manual work: Pakistanis, Indians, Baluchis, Omanis and Yemenis."

"The expendables."

"You could put it that way," the other woman said. "But even 'coolies' or unskilled laborers earn over forty dirhams a day. That's about ten dollars. A lot more than they could make in their own countries."

"Aren't there times when you begin to feel a bit like a 'coolie' yourself?" Ceetra asked.

"Because I'm a woman?"

Ceetra nodded. "The way you're treated—well, doesn't it

bother you to have your social identity take precedence over being a doctor?"

"You musn't judge things by what happened last night," Dr. Shawaf said. "We wives aren't nearly as submissive in private as we might appear to be in public. When I was at the King Abd al Aziz University eight years ago there were only thirty female students, and the only specialties they were allowed to adopt were pediatrics, gynecology and obstetrics. There was even a stigma attached to being a nurse who treated male patients. But times have changed a lot since then."

"Not enough to convince your husband I should be allowed to visit the nuclear power project."

"He was raised in a very traditional family," the other woman explained. "All the Sudeiris are like that."

"Sudeiris?"

"Crown Prince Fahd is from the Sudeiris family. My husband owes his position to the fact that he has access to the royal family. He has to be very careful about the way he behaves. That is why he didn't want you to go with Dan Blake to Ju'aymah."

"When did they leave?"

"Early this morning. Dan stayed at the house and managed to get a few hours' sleep, but he still looked tired. They should be back this evening."

The door opened and the nurse came into the room carrying a small tray containing a glass flask of coffee and two cups.

"The patient I scheduled for eleven o'clock has arrived," she said.

"I'll wait outside."

Dr. Shawaf poured some coffee into a cup and handed it to her. "Take this with you. I should be through here about noon. We can have some lunch then." She turned to the nurse. "Show Miss Rampling how to get to the garden, would you please?"

"Yes, Doctor."

The nurse led Ceetra out of the office, down a long corridor and out into the garden. It was really a small cobbled courtyard that had a tiny square of parched grass at its center, and a few lemon trees dotted at random around the enclosed area. But because it was well shaded on all sides by the roof of the clinic, it was relatively cool. Putting her coffee cup on a metal table under a large umbrella decorated with the Martini & Rossi logo, she took off her shoes and lowered herself into a canvas deck chair.

"Can I get you some more coffee?" the nurse asked.

"No. Thank you," Ceetra said. "And don't let me keep you away from your duties. I'll just sit here and rest until Dr. Shawaf finishes with her patients."

When she was alone she closed her eyes. The heat combined with the heavy scent of the lemon trees was pleasantly relaxing. Her thoughts drifted to Dan. The heat aroused her. Now she wished she had behaved differently when he tried to make love to her the previous evening. She needed him. Now more than ever. Images of the moments they had spent together in Paris and Rome filtered into her mind, and with them came a contentment that manifested itself in a relaxed torpor. Soon she drifted off to sleep.

"Ceetra." She opened her eyes and saw Dr. Shawaf looking down at her.

"Are you hungry?" Dr. Shawaf asked.

"Not really. It's too hot."

"Well, I'm going to make my rounds. Would you like to come with me?"

"Very much," Ceetra said.

Dr. Shawaf led the way down a corridor. It was quite dark and impossible to see inside the small cubicles. Their occupants remained completely hidden.

"Are these patients in isolation?" she asked.

"They're terminal cases," Dr. Shawaf said.

"All of them?"

The doctor nodded. "They're all unskilled laborers who worked at the nuclear power plant in Ju'aymah. There was an explosion there about a year ago. These men were closest to the scene of the accident."

She flicked on a light and went to one of the small rooms. Ceetra followed, but when she saw what the bed contained she immediately wished she hadn't. The face of the man under the sheet was barely human. There was a gaping hole where his nose had been, and his upper lip was a huge, festering sore. The lid of one eye was missing. It gave him a ghoulish appearance that was at once frightening and pathetic. His exposed eyeball followed as she moved around the bed and he tried to smile, but the effort only twisted what was left of his features into a hideous leer.

Dr. Shawaf seemed unaffected by the sight. She gently pulled back the sheet to reveal scars covering the rest of the victim's body. He had undergone so many grafts that his skin looked like a clumsily put together quilt.

"Does he understand English?" Ceetra asked.

Dr. Shawaf shook her head. "Even if he could he wouldn't be able to hear you. His eardrums were perforated by the blast."

"Is there any hope?"

"None," the other woman said. "The burns are bad enough. He's in terrible pain. But it's the radiation he was exposed to that's killing him. The others, too. Perhaps if they'd been treated at the King Faisal Specialist Hospital and Research Center, where there are better facilities—"

"Why weren't they?"

"It was far too risky," Dr. Shawaf replied.

"Risky? I don't understand."

"Both your father and my husband knew that if word got out that there had been a failure in a nuclear power plant the firm had built—well, it would have meant all the other units the company had installed in various countries around the world would have to be shut down and carefully checked. It would have cost a fortune, and the bad publicity—"

"Are you telling me they were able to cover up the accident?"

"Thanks to quick action by Dan Blake."

"One man could do that?"

"It wasn't hard," the other woman explained. "Not in a country like this where everything is ultimately controlled by a handful of people. They weren't eager to let the rest of the world know what had happened. Their own interests were at stake. And Ju'aymah is so isolated that it was unlikely anybody would find out."

Ceetra suddenly remembered the way Dan had hedged when she asked him the reason for his abrupt departure for Saudi Arabia while she was recuperating in High Plains Baptist Hospital.

"Has there been other, more recent trouble at Ju'aymah?" she asked.

"There was another accident," she said quietly.

"About a week ago?"

"Yes. Not an explosion this time. Something to do with a leak in one of the pipes leading to the main core. I don't understand the way those things work, but my husband said it's quite serious. We have five men who were exposed to radiation in another ward."

"Will they survive?" Ceetra asked.

"I doubt it."

"And it is being covered up, too?"

"That's why Dan is here," Dr. Shawaf admitted. "It's his job to supervise repairs and make sure none of this leaks to the press. I thought you knew."

There was a knock at the door and the nurse came into the room.

"You are needed in ward two, Doctor," she said. "It's an emergency."

"I'd better go back to the hotel and get out from under your feet," Ceetra said.

"My chauffeur will take you. And call me if you don't feel like being alone this evening. I should be home after seven o'clock."

"When do you think Dan will get back?"

"Not too late," the other woman said. "It isn't a long flight from Ju'aymah. I would guess somewhere around nine or ten o'clock."

On the trip back to the hotel all Ceetra could think about was the terribly injured worker she had seen. The knowledge that he and others might have been saved if it hadn't been for the cover-up kept gnawing at her, and when the shock of what she had seen finally began to wear off it was replaced by cold anger.

In her room she lay on the bed trying to make some sense of what Dr. Shawaf had told her, but nothing she could think of justified such a callous disregard of human life. Finally, around midnight, she heard the door in the next room open and close. There was a pause of about five minutes, and then the sound of running water. Forcing herself to wait another quarter of an hour, she got up and went to the door linking their two rooms. It was still unlocked. She pushed it open and saw Dan coming out of the bathroom. He had a towel draped around his waist and his hair was still wet.

"I thought you'd be asleep," he said.

"I've been waiting for you to get back."

"After your performance last night I would have thought you could use an early night," he said, his voice heavy with irony. "How was your day?"

"Enlightening," she said.

"In what way?"

"I spent it at the company clinic with Dr. Shawaf."

"She's a bright woman."

"I learned a lot," Ceetra said. "And almost all of it was appalling."

His eyes narrowed.

"Why didn't you tell me about the accident at Ju'aymah?"

"So that's it." He started drying his hair with a towel. "What other earthshaking discoveries did you make?"

"I saw one of the men who was injured."

"Mrs. Shawaf showed you?"

Ceetra nodded. "*Dr.* Shawaf," she corrected him.

295

"I guess she's not as smart as I thought."

"Why was it covered up?"

"Isn't it obvious?"

"Dr. Shawaf says it's because the company didn't want to risk extended shutdowns and losing contracts on other nuclear power installations."

"That's the bottom line." Dan's voice had a hard edge. "I could give you half a dozen other reasons, but I doubt if they'd change the way you apparently feel."

"Was it my father's idea?"

"His and Mr. Shawaf's."

"And you carried out their orders?"

"It's my job."

"Doesn't it matter that people were terribly injured—that a lot of them will die?"

"The explosion was an accident," Dan said flatly. "Telling the world about it wouldn't have helped those men."

"Dr. Shawaf says a lot of them might have survived if they'd been treated at the King Faisal Hospital—"

"That woman talks too damned much."

"But what she says is true, isn't it?" Ceetra persisted. "They were kept in the company clinic because it meant they would be out of the public eye."

"Of course," Dan snapped. "Grow up, for Christ's sake. Each one of these installations represents over two billion dollars to the company. What the hell do you expect us to do, hold a press conference every time something goes wrong?"

"That's exactly what I'm planning to do," she said quietly.

He stopped toweling his hair. "You're what?"

"You know I've scheduled a press conference for when I get back to Dallas."

"To announce you're taking over presidency of the company—"

"I also intend to spell out what my overall policy will be," she said. "And the top of the list will be no more nuclear power projects until we have completely rechecked existing designs for possible flaws."

"You're crazy."

"Maybe," she said. "But that's exactly what I am going to do."

He walked toward her and put both hands on her shoulders. "You're tired," he said. "Why don't you get some sleep, and we'll talk the whole thing over on the flight to Singapore."

"My mind's made up, Dan."

He studied her face for a long moment. "I'm warning you," he said finally. "What Barnes told you about the banks being nervous is true. The company is mortgaged to the hilt. The people who loaned us all that money for completion guarantees aren't going to be wildly enthusiastic about your taking over management of the firm, but they may be willing to give you a chance to prove yourself if—I repeat, if—you don't rock the boat."

"And if I do?"

"They'll call in those loans so fast it'll make your head spin. A lot of very powerful people are going to get jumpy. All of them have a hell of a lot at stake. There's already been one attempt on your life. If you go ahead with this insane scheme of yours, I guarantee the next won't be long in coming."

23

MULE BARNES was sweating. The cause of his anxiety was twofold: Ceetra was forty-five minutes late for the press conference, and even when she arrived, he wasn't at all sure what she was going to say.

Bill Weeks, the flabby, bald-headed man who was the firm's vice president of public relations, had asked for a copy of her statement for prior distribution to the reporters covering the event, but she had declined and offered no reason for her refusal.

Now the press corps was growing restless. Many of them had deadlines to meet and didn't appreciate being kept waiting. Reporters from the *Dallas Morning News,* the *Herald Press,* Associated Press and local bureau representatives from various national publications, including *Time* and *Newsweek,* milled around the auditorium complaining to each other about the delay.

"Hey, Bill," one of the reporters shouted. "Let's get this show on the road. If I don't get my copy in pretty damn quick you can forget about it making the early edition."

"Stay cool," Weeks replied. "It's a woman's prerogative to be late."

He hurried across to where Barnes was standing.

"Where is she, for chris'sake?"

"She'll be here."

"She'd better be, and quick, or my ass is in the—"

His sentence trailed away as Ceetra suddenly walked on stage and stood behind a small lectern that supported a forest of microphones. Relieved, Bill Weeks hurried to her side and exchanged a few quick words as the television camera crews clicked on their lights.

"Ladies and gentlemen," he announced, "it is my distinct pleasure to introduce the new president of Rampling International, Miss Ceetra Rampling."

Barnes was impressed by her obvious self-confidence since she returned from her round-the-world trip the previous day. It showed in her bearing: the easy smile, relaxed stance, and tolerant willingness to pose for photographs before beginning her address.

Her newfound confidence worried him. He'd been under constant pressure from Ed Morley ever since she announced her intention of taking over her father's controlling interest in the company. Morley wanted him to deliver on the promises he had made to ensure that Jake's shares would be available for purchase, and he made no bones about the fact that he was being squeezed by the group who were set to make the takeover bid.

Barnes had done his utmost to reassure the other man, but he was no longer convinced the task was going to be as simple as he had anticipated. Even though Ceetra hadn't seen her father since she was five years old, it was becoming increasingly evident that his blood flowed in her veins.

He watched her closely, trying to gauge her the way he had learned to assess a potential juror, looking for clues that would indicate how she could be expected to react under the pressures of her newly assumed responsibilities. She was an enigma. It was impossible for him to tell whether she fully understood the importance of her performance at the press conference. Her every word and move would be dissected by men with vested interests in the company, and their reaction to her could have a profound effect on the future of the firm. And the most vitally interested of all the viewers would be the bankers who had underwritten the loans. If they were impressed it was possible they might extend the due dates on their loans. Or they could call them in and put Rampling International in financial straits from which it might never recover.

He decided his only course of action was to wait and see. His guess was that sooner or later she would stumble. The job of filling Jake's shoes was too great for any man, let alone an inexperienced young woman. One wrong move is all it would take. And when it happened he would know exactly how to turn her failure to his advantage.

"I'm sorry to keep you all waiting," she announced. "The truth is I had a terrible time getting past the guard at the main gate. He wouldn't believe I worked here."

The laughter that followed immediately dispelled any tension that had been caused by her tardiness. Her statement had just the right touch of self-deprecation. Barnes even found himself smiling. He knew it was exactly the kind of thing Jake would have said under similar circumstances, and again he was reminded that Ceetra had inherited more from her father than his name and estate.

"I asked you all to come here today so I could formally announce that I am assuming the presidency of Rampling International," she continued when the laughter subsided. "But as Bill Weeks has already stolen my thunder by making that fact known to you in his introduction, I think the simplest thing would be for me to try to answer whatever questions you might have."

A chorus of voices immediately rose up, and reporters jostled each other as they vied for her attention.

"Okay," Bill Weeks announced over the public address speaker. "You'll all get a chance. Let's start with people who have deadlines to meet. Joe, you were complaining the loudest. Why don't we start with you?"

The reporter who had needled Weeks about Ceetra's late arrival stood up.

"Will the company go public?" he asked.

"Not in the foreseeable future," Ceetra replied.

"Are you planning any major changes in top-level management?"

"I will be reviewing every aspect of the company in the upcoming weeks," she said. "When I have a better idea of what's going on I'll decide what shifts in personnel there are going to be—if any."

A woman with the CBS television news crew took over the questioning.

"There have been rumors that the explosion which killed your father might not have been an accident. Can you comment on this?"

"Not at this time. The accident is still under investigation, and until an official report has been made I'm not at liberty to say anything."

"There have been similar rumors about David Seymour's death," the woman persisted.

"Again, I can't comment on that until all the facts are in."

"Was either accident due to sabotage?"

Bill Weeks stepped to the microphone. "I think Miss Rampling has made it quite clear that—"

"It's all right," Ceetra said. "I understand these people have a job to do, and I'm here to cooperate as fully as possible. That just happens to be one subject I'm not in a position to talk about at this time."

"Are you having labor problems on the VHST tunnel project?" the reporter from the *Dallas Morning News* asked.

For the first time Ceetra hesitated before answering. "It's true that we've fallen a little behind schedule in the past month," she admitted. "Largely due to the cleanup operations that were necessary after the cave-in. But we're running a highballing operation now, three shifts a day, seven days a week, and according to most recent estimates the project will be slightly ahead of schedule by the end of June."

Barnes admired the way she handled the question. In fact, work on the tunnel had slipped largely because Dan Blake hadn't been on the job site supervising operations.

While he and Ceetra were away on the world tour there had been at least a dozen eruptions of violence among the miners. The most recent had occurred less than a week ago, and resulted in two men being seriously injured.

"Miss Rampling." A thin man wearing a conservative three-piece suit waved his notebook in an effort to attract attention. Bill Weeks recognized the head of *Time* magazine's Dallas bureau, and pointed him out to Ceetra. She acknowledged him with a nod.

"Is there any truth to the stories that have appeared in various liberal magazines which allege that companies like Bechtel and Rampling International are being used as covers for CIA operations in countries where major construction projects are presently underway?"

A tense silence settled on the room. Bill Weeks looked at Barnes as if for guidance, but when he didn't receive any, he stepped to the microphone.

"That kind of question isn't—"

"So far as I know," Ceetra interjected, "there has been no such cooperation."

"There have also been unconfirmed rumors," the wire service reporter persisted, "that a serious accident occurred about a year ago at a nuclear power plant which your company constructed at Ju'aymah in Saudi Arabia. Is there any truth to these stories?"

"None whatsoever," she answered without a moment's hesitation. "I have just returned from Riyadh and can assure you the facility at Ju'aymah is running perfectly smoothly."

Her coolness astounded Barnes. He knew she was lying, but her demeanor was so utterly convincing that he was sure he was the only person in the room who was aware she wasn't telling the truth. His admiration was such that he began to wonder whether he hadn't backed the wrong horse in going along with Ed Morley's scheme to make a takeover bid for control of the firm. It was beginning to appear that the company was in better hands than he'd first imagined.

He didn't stay for the rest of the press conference. The

wire service reporter's questions had been a high point, and when his probing produced no results, the proceedings quickly began to draw to a close. Striding out of the auditorium, he took the elevator to the tenth floor of the corporate headquarters and waited for Ceetra to return to the office that had previously been her father's.

"You were magnificent," he said as she lowered herself into the padded leather chair behind the huge desk. "I haven't seen a performance like that since Jake appeared in front of a Senate subcommittee hearing to answer charges that the firm had paid millions of dollars in bribes to Nigeria's Lieutenant Obasanjo in return for giving us a contract to build a refinery."

"Was he cleared?" she asked.

"Damn right."

"And did he pay the bribes?"

"Of course." Barnes sounded puzzled. "How else do you think we got all those overseas projects?"

Ceetra didn't answer. She felt sick. The ease with which she had lied disgusted her. There were all kinds of justifications, and she'd ultimately allowed herself to be swayed by the logic that it was better to try to change things from within the firm, rather than to risk destroying it for the sake of a principle. But it didn't make her feel any better right now. The memory of that horribly injured worker at the company clinic in Riyadh was still too fresh in her mind to enable her to feel anything but guilt.

"Are you feeling okay?" Barnes asked.

"Does it matter?"

"You should be goddam proud of the way you handled yourself," he said.

"I knew you'd be impressed."

The heavy irony in her voice went unnoticed by the attorney.

"So will the bankers. I want you to know they've been biting their nails. But no more. I'll get in touch with them today and set up a meeting—"

"That won't be necessary," she said.

"They'll want to—"

"There's something you still don't seem to understand," she interjected, cutting him short.

"What's that?" he asked.

"That from here on in I make my own decisions."

He bridled. "Your father relied on my—"

"I am not my father. Nor do I expect to depend on you for anything other than the services normally expected of a general counsel to the board of directors."

"I don't understand," he said.

"And I don't intend to explain. Except perhaps to say that so far your reliability appears highly questionable."

His eyes narrowed. "What does that mean exactly?"

"I gather Dan Blake gave you a note to deliver to me when he was suddenly called away when I was in the hospital—"

"He told you that?"

She nodded.

"It's a goddam lie," he blustered.

"Your word against his."

"Mine would stand up in any court of law."

"This isn't a court, and you aren't on trial," Ceetra said quietly. "But if we are going to continue working together, I think it's important that you know exactly where I stand."

"All I've done is try and help."

"If trying to scare the daylights out of me by suggesting that somebody is trying to kill me is your idea of help—"

"What I said was true."

"There's absolutely no evidence—"

"If you wait for that it's liable to be too late."

"I'll take my chances."

"You may have to," Barnes said. "Because I've got a hunch that whoever tried to get you by severing that cable isn't going to give up. They'll try again. Mark my words."

He turned and left the office. Ceetra managed to retain her composure until the door closed behind him, but the

305

moment she was alone she sank back into the leather chair. Suddenly the facade she'd managed to maintain in front of Barnes and the reporters dissolved, and was replaced by an overwhelming sense of apprehension. The attorney's warning wasn't the cause of it. She recognized that he was desperately trying to maintain a hold over her by whatever means he thought would be effective. The anxiety she now felt had started the moment she arrived back in Dallas.

Even though she still hadn't made a formal announcement, somehow word had leaked out that she was assuming the presidency of the company, and people at the firm's headquarters treated her differently. She was no longer a guest to be humored with good-natured tolerance. Rather she was the head of the world's largest construction company, and men who had spent their whole lives in the business now looked to her for answers involving the expenditure of millions of dollars, and the well-being of thousands of employees.

It was a huge responsibility. She was expected to digest reports from projects all over the world: refineries, turboexpander plants, pipelines, crude-stabilization units, herbicide and chemical plants, pulp mills, even an entire city the company was building in Abu Dhabi.

She was required to make on-the-spot decisions that would affect the future of the firm for years to come. There were plenty of experts to advise her, but when it came down to it, hers had to be the final word. For the first time in her life she began to realize the enormity of the dynasty her father had created, and to understand the incredible pressures he must have been under in ensuring its smooth day-to-day operation. It evoked a grudging admiration. Until now she had taken for granted the privileges that went with the Rampling name and never once stopped to consider the phenomenal amount of work that must have gone into accruing the wealth with which she'd been surrounded for as long as she could remember.

The buzzer on the intercom sounded. When she flicked

the switch Miss Wilson's voice came through: "There's a long distance call for you on line two, Miss Rampling. It's from England."

Ceetra pressed the lighted button on the telephone console and picked up the receiver.

"Hello." The line was full of static and there was a slightly out-of-sync quality to the voice at the other end of the line. "Miss Rampling?"

"Yes."

"Dr. Amsdon here. I'm afraid I have bad news for you."

She knew before he said it: her mother was dead.

"When did it happen?" she asked.

"Early this morning. She'd been in a coma for almost a week. The end was quite peaceful. I doubt if she felt anything."

There was a long pause, as if the man at the other end of the line were waiting for her to say something. When she remained silent, he said: "I don't know what plans you want to make for the funeral—"

"I'll leave that in your hands," Ceetra said.

"Will you be coming over?" Dr. Amsdon asked.

"I'm afraid that won't be possible."

"I see." There was another pause. "Well, I'll make all the arrangements."

She tried to focus on what he was saying, but the words didn't register, and when he finally hung up it was a full minute before she replaced the receiver. It wasn't shock. She'd been expecting her mother to die. Rather it was astonishment at her own callousness in deciding so quickly not to return for the funeral. There were dozens of reasons why she couldn't go, all quite valid, but the truth was she simply didn't want to go. That part of her life was over now, and she wanted to be rid of it completely. No emotional attachments. Her future was here now, and she had no intention of jeopardizing it by going away at a time as crucial as now.

The buzzer on the intercom sounded again.

"Mr. Greene is here. Shall I send him in?"

"Yes, please," Ceetra replied.

Moments later the door opened and Phil Greene strode into the room. He had been the first to speak up for her when she had polled the board members about her taking over the company. She knew he had replaced David Seymour as project manager on the VHST project, and had sent for him to try to discover firsthand why the tunnel had slipped so far behind schedule while she and Dan were away.

"Sit down," she said, motioning him to a chair. "I imagine you can guess why I asked you to come."

Greene shifted his weight uncomfortably.

"I guess you've read the reports," he said.

Ceetra lifted a folder containing a sheaf of reports she'd stayed up half the night to read.

"I thought you could fill me in," she said.

"It's all there," the engineer said. "Problems between the experienced miners and men who are new on the job have resulted in a lot of slowdowns."

"Is that why the shifts are working shorthanded?"

"Partly."

"What's the rest of the reason?"

"Can I speak bluntly?"

"Of course," she said. "That's why I sent for you."

"Isolation is a big factor," he said.

"Isolation?"

"The camp is a long way from the nearest town. Men go into Amarillo looking for women. When they find one they get drunk, and more often than not don't get back to the project until the next day."

Ceetra remembered Dan mentioning this problem during her first visit to the camp.

"How can we cut down that kind of absenteeism?" she asked.

"Short of opening a whorehouse on camp, I don't see any way," he replied.

She talked to him for another hour, but his suggestion regarding the whorehouse was the one that stayed uppermost in her mind. It made so much sense. More importantly, he had unwittingly provided exactly the opportunity Ceetra had been looking for: the chance to prove herself capable of taking the initiative and solving problems without guidance from anybody.

After Phil Greene left, she pressed the button on the intercom. When Miss Wilson answered, she said: "I'd like you to make arrangements for the company plane to fly me to Amarillo this afternoon."

"What about your other appointments?"

"Cancel them," Ceetra said. "This is important."

It was nearly 6:00 p.m. when the Gulfstream III touched down at Amarillo Air Terminal. The June heat was made worse by a dry wind that leached moisture from her skin and made her hair impossible to manage because of the static electricity. She smelled the pungent odor of cattle-churned earth from a huge feeding facility, and saw dust devils squirrel across the high desert as she drove the Hertz car she had rented along Interstate 40.

Half an hour later she turned up the short, dusty road toward the abandoned military base Vanita Beth had converted into a whorehouse. She parked the car and sat for a while, thinking about Dan.

She had not seen him since they returned to Dallas. He had immediately gone to the camp. They had received word of labor troubles while in Singapore, and throughout the balance of the trip he had worried about getting back. She had only talked to him on the phone once, and he'd sounded brusque. She sensed that in some strange way he blamed her for finding a chink in his emotional armor, and was undergoing a kind of penance by spending inordinate hours supervising the progress of work underground.

A horn blared as a beat-up panel truck slid to a stop in a cloud of dust. Four men wearing hard hats climbed out and ambled into the bar. She saw the Rampling intersecting circle emblem on the door of the vehicle and realized they were

309

from the camp. What if they recognized her? She quickly dismissed the thought as absurd. It was highly unlikely they either knew or cared that she had assumed control of the company.

Getting out from behind the steering wheel she mounted the shallow steps and went inside. The jukebox was going full blast, a Michael Murphy tune from his early Austin period, and the small dance floor was jammed with couples swaying to the music. Vanita Beth saw her come in and hurried out from behind the bar.

"Well I'll be." The big, rawboned woman wrapped Ceetra in a hug that was so hard it momentarily pressed the breath out of her. "If this isn't the damndest thing. We was just watchin' you on the television news. Why didn't you tell me your daddy was J. B. Rampling? Hell, my old man worked for J.B. ten, maybe fifteen years ago. And now they're sayin' you've taken over the whole goddam operation."

Ceetra glanced at the color television set over the bar. There was too much noise from the jukebox for her to hear the newscaster, but she recognized herself standing at the lectern behind a forest of microphones.

"Hey, guys, look who's come to visit us," Vanita Beth hollered. "It's J.B.'s daughter."

"No, please—"

Ceetra's protest was drowned by a chorus of greetings shouted by the men at the bar.

"Damn." One of the miners slapped his leg. "Never thought I'd ever be workin' for no woman."

Another man pushed his hard hat back on his head and squinted at her through a cloud of smoke he exhaled.

"Mind if I ask a question, ma'am?" he asked.

"Not at all," Ceetra said.

"Where in hell do you come off tellin' them reporters that Rampling International isn't fronting for the CIA?" he asked. "Hell, I was in the company in Chile. We put in a hydroelectric facility. Shit, the CIA damn near ran the operation. The project was out in the boonies, and the CIA guys used it as a place to train counterrevolutionaries. They brought in a whole slew of automatic weapons hidden in sections of concrete pipe—"

"Lay off, Charlie," Vanita Beth warned.

"He's right," another miner said. "And I was on that nuclear generator project out in Saudi Arabia. There was an accident all right. And a lot of them coolies were hurt real bad. It was covered up good, but I know it happened."

"Let's get out of here," the big woman said.

She led the way to a small back room across the far side of the dance floor. The glass panel in the door was cracked, and cardboard boxes piled against the walls were covered with dust. It smelled strongly of mold and decay.

"Don't pay them no heed," she said. "They don't know their ass from a hole in the ground about anything except digging tunnels. Now what's on your mind, honey?"

She plumped herself down in a chair that had steel coils sprouting through the torn plastic cover, and looked at Ceetra.

"I don't really know how to put this."

"Come on, spit it out. You can talk to me."

"I want to set up a whorehouse," Ceetra blurted.

"You what?"

"I need a place like the one you've got here, only much closer to camp."

"For the miners?"

Ceetra nodded. "I need your help," she explained. "Most shifts at the tunnel are working shorthanded because the men aren't getting back to camp. It's created a real problem."

Vanita Beth laughed raucously and shook her head. "I gotta hand it to you, honey," she said. "It's one hell of an idea. But it ain't gonna be as easy as you seem to think."

"Why not?"

"Listen, I been out where they're diggin' that tunnel. Apart from the camp there ain't nothin' there. Where the hell're my girls gonna work—you plannin' on puttin' 'em in a bunkhouse or somethin'?"

"What's wrong with those?"

Ceetra crossed to the window and pointed to the rows of boarded-up Quonset huts.

"You're kiddin'—"

"They could be fixed up," Ceetra said. "You turned the offices in this building into bedrooms."

The other woman joined her at the window and gazed through the grime-covered glass. She rubbed a circle clean with the palm of her hand.

"How in hell d'ya figure on gettin' 'em from here to the camp?"

"I'll assign trucks," Ceetra replied. "And anything else you need. All you have to do is provide the girls and supervise the operation once it gets going."

The other woman shook her head. "Shit. I don't know," she said pensively. "This dump sure ain't makin' me rich. Maybe a place closer to camp ain't such a bad idea at that—"

"Well?"

"I gotta do a lot more thinkin', honey."

"I've got to know soon."

"Where'll you be?"

"I'll be at the camp for a day or so," Ceetra replied. "After that I'll be back at company headquarters in Dallas."

"I'll call you the minute I get this thing figured out," the other woman assured her. "It's crazy, but maybe it'd work. I just don't know."

Ceetra left by a back door. She didn't want to face the miners at the bar. Lying at the press conference had left her feeling guilty enough without being reminded of it any further. There was no way of explaining to them that if she'd told the truth they would have been out of work in a matter of weeks.

She drove the rented car to camp and spent the night at the project guest house. Although it was nearly 11:00 p.m. when she arrived, she didn't go to bed immediately. Instead, she walked around camp until the swing shift surfaced in the man trip. She hoped to see Dan, but there was no sign of him. Finally, she asked one of the miners if he had seen him and was informed that Dan was conducting a series of spot checks on each shift. He added there was no way of knowing when he would emerge from below-ground.

She considered going down to find him, but finally decided against acting on the impulse for two reasons: the memory of Seymour's death was still too fresh in her mind, and after the conflict between Dan and herself in Riyadh she wasn't at all sure he wanted to see her.

As she lay in bed in the sparsely furnished but spotlessly clean room that had been reserved for her at the guest house, she thought about him. When Dan had made love to her in London she'd assumed it marked the beginning of a bond that would grow stronger. And their days together in Paris and Rome had seemed to confirm her assumption. Their moments together before landing in Riyadh were idyllic, everything she had ever dreamed of in a relationship. He was tender, warm, loving, funny, considerate. But after Riyadh things had changed. Her spurning Dan's advances at the Intercontinental Hotel had been the turning point. God, how she regretted it. But every attempt she'd made to make amends had failed miserably. He had withdrawn into the shell he seemed to have existed in most of his life, and the more she tried to reach him, the more remote he became.

She fell asleep remembering the way he had held her after they made love at her apartment in London: the strength of his arms, the warmth of his body, the steady rhythm of his breathing. It was a recollection which evoked a feeling of contentment and a deep sense of yearning. Perhaps, she thought, he would feel differently about her once she had proved she could fill her father's shoes. Perhaps he would see her through new eyes—

By morning she felt drained. It required a determined effort to drag herself out of bed, shower and dress. She ate breakfast in the mess hall that was filled with miners who had worked the graveyard shift from midnight to 8:00 a.m. They hadn't showered and their features were still streaked with grime from eight hours of drilling, blasting and mucking rock in the tunnel. Instinctively, she searched their faces for Dan, but he wasn't there. The men showed visible signs of resentment at her scrutiny and turned their heads away. As she moved through them they pulled back and a tense silence settled on the mess hall. She guessed that news of what she had said at the press conference had spread around camp. They knew she was the new president of the company. They also felt betrayed. None stated their feelings as openly as the men in Vanita's Place, but there was no mistaking their hostility.

When she took her tray to a table at which a group of men were sitting, they got up and found seats elsewhere. None of them spoke to her directly, but she heard comments muttered behind her back. It was an uncomfortable situation, and Ceetra escaped the moment she had finished her coffee.

The company plane was still being serviced and refueled when she walked across to the dirt strip. One of the gravel deflectors had come loose, and the pilot told her it would be early afternoon before they could take off. She passed the intervening hours in the control center that straddled the main shaft. Phil Greene was one of the few who seemed sympathetic to her, and she was grateful for his presence now.

"There's a call for you," he announced just before noon. "Take it in my office."

When Ceetra picked up the receiver she immediately recognized Vanita Beth's loud, gruff voice.

"I been up half the goddam night tryin' to figure this crazy idea of yours," the other woman said.

"And?"

"It just might work."

"It can't miss," Ceetra said.

"What makes you so sure?"

"Supply and demand."

Vanita's throaty chuckle sounded in the earpiece. "What's the first move?" she asked.

"I'll arrange for trucks and a crew of men to pick up the Quonset huts either later today or first thing in the morning."

"Today's fine with me," Vanita Beth said. "The sooner we're open for business the happier I'll be."

"I'll take care of everything at this end," Ceetra said. "The rest's up to you."

She hung up and walked back into the control center. Phil Greene was hunched over some blueprints, but he looked up when she came in.

"You look like a cat that just swallowed a bird," he said.

"I feel better than that."

"Want to tell me why the sudden change of mood?"

"I've decided to take your advice."

"My advice?"

"About bringing a whorehouse to camp."

"I was just kidding, for chris'sake."

"I know," Ceetra said. "But the longer I thought about it, the more it made sense."

"You'll never get away with it. There are laws against that kind of—"

"Not if it's run as a bar, on company-owned property."

"The people at headquarters aren't going to like it."

"They've got a choice," she said. "They can like it or quit. I make the decisions around here now."

"I guess." Greene didn't sound convinced.

"I want you to arrange transportation to pick up some Quonset huts. Find a place where they can be put up close to camp. I'll give your secretary the details. I want a crew of men working on the job on a three-shift basis. And after it opens I want daily reports on the effect it's having on absenteeism."

"Have you talked with Dan about all this?" Greene asked.

"I don't need his approval."

"Maybe. But I can tell you he isn't going to like it one damned bit."

Ceetra thought about Phil Greene's warning as she flew

back to Dallas later that afternoon. It was true Dan wouldn't appreciate her acting independently, particularly when such on-site decisions were his domain, but it was something he was just going to have to accept. How else was she going to prove herself? And if absenteeism was effectively reduced, she didn't see how he could object. If anything, it would open his eyes to the fact that, even though she was a woman, she still had what it took to follow in her father's footsteps.

The next two weeks put Ceetra's newfound confidence to the test. Each day she met with the heads of different departments for briefings that were aimed at acquainting her with every aspect of the business. But the more aware she became of the complexities of the operation, the less secure she felt. The task she had undertaken was awesome. There were many times when she felt like walking out and taking the first plane back to London. Only the patient understanding of Tom Heslop kept her from taking such radical action, and as the days wore on she came to rely on him more and more.

The vice chairman of the board had worked for her father for almost twenty years and seemed to take an almost paternal interest in Ceetra. From the moment he spoke out in support of her at the board meeting, he did everything in his power to encourage her, and spent hours showing her around the various departments, carefully explaining how each of them worked.

"I always tell people we're in the self-destruct business," he told her. "Most folks spend a lifetime building up one company. Our work consists of forming companies to get a product out, then liquidating and moving on."

She learned that it was by following this policy that her father had built Rampling International into the largest construction company in the world. Although its biggest single job was the VHST tunnel, many other projects came close: a complex of facilities in Saudi Arabia which, when complete, would gather five billion cubic feet of sour gas being flared daily from oil wells and refine it into fuel; a coal-conservation plant for the Republic of South Africa in the Transvaal; a copper mine and processing plant in the People's Republic of China. There were more than two-hundred other jobs of varying sizes on Rampling International's current schedule, including a uranium mine in Yugoslavia, a coal mine in Australia, three gas plants in Siberia, and oil-drilling projects off the coasts of Africa, Greece, Mexico and Malaysia.

According to Tom Heslop, all the clients were in a terrible hurry. This was especially true of projects involving energy. Even the Chinese, once famous for their patience, were pushing hard for their new copper mine, which was high on their list of achievements aimed at making the People's Republic a nation that could stand alongside the other industrial giants of the world.

"How on earth do you keep these huge jobs under control, yet moving fast?" Ceetra asked.

"Major projects are segregated and each is assigned its own team," Heslop told her. "Not only designers and procurement men, but controllers, transportation experts and labor recruiters. When the job is huge, like the VHST project, it is divided among several complete teams which stay with it for the duration and work on nothing else."

As Ceetra's education progressed, she learned that even the shape of the gleaming engineering building expressed the firm's organizational style. Although only four stories high, it contained thirty-six acres of floor space, which was about as much as a conventional sixty-six story skyscraper. The structure had four wings, each of which was divided into distinct lofts for task forces working on one project at a time.

If the job involved the design of an oil refinery, or a nuclear generator, the desks and drawing tables of the design specialists were grouped around a scale model of the project. It was not, Heslop assured her, just a symbol, but a detailed scale representation of the final assembly. It was a concept Jake had introduced in the early seventies as a better way of showing the client his plant under development, while at the same time improving communication among members of the design team.

As the design progressed the model grew more complex. Heslop explained that clients often sent their own staff to Dallas as kibitzers, and while Ceetra was touring the facility she saw teams of French and Algerian engineers, hired by the Algerian government to act as monitors on a 300-million-dollar gas plant for Algeria. Another group of twenty-three Exxon engineers had been assigned to work with Rampling's designers during the concept phase of a refinery that was going to be built in Venezuela.

She learned that the firm's project teams operated worldwide, from Europe to Saudi Arabia and Australia. Over them all stretched a canopy of central administration that served every project. The headquarters in Dallas was a highly computerized nerve center, with connections to every office and to the major job sites as well, by cable and/or satellite. Its memory banks contained a storehouse of every imaginable detail.

She watched as a draftsman working on one of the thousands of electrical diagrams involved in the process work plugged a video terminal into a computerized library of schematics that had been used in other similar projects. Immediately, a diagram was flashed on a display console. He was then able to relay the information on to a supplier, a job site or a division of his project team working halfway across the world.

Little by little Heslop introduced her to every phase of the firm's operations: sales (there were sixty-four salesmen stationed around the world, making calls, talking up the company in twenty-five languages and listening for the rumble of projects in formation); marketing (presentations sometimes cost as much as one percent of the potential contract); even corporate financing (there was a corporate finance squad whose only function was to help clients arrange backing from friendly banking syndicates, or if appropriate, the Export-Import Bank).

No detail was too small to be brought to her attention. Mrs. Abernethy, housekeeper for the executive floors of the headquarters building, showed Ceetra how she operated the kitchens that provided banquets for visiting dignitaries. They were equipped to produce food that would satisfy even the most discerning palate, and the three full-time cooks were required to be experts in preparing the national dishes of dozens of countries. Mrs. Abernethy kept a large leather-bound book that carefully documented the preferences of numerous important clients, and they ranged from hot dogs to Paupiettes de Veau Clementine. There were also notes as to which guests liked what kind of wines. Some of the visitors from the Middle East, whose religion forbade the consumption of alcohol, had let it be known that when they ordered a Coca-Cola they expected to be served a glass of burgundy on ice.

The intense pressure of trying to absorb so much in such a short time began to take its toll. She found it difficult to sleep, her joints ached, she lost all interest in food, and was constantly tired. Once again she discovered from firsthand experience the kind of pressures her father must have been under during the final months of his life. Dr. Robinson gave her frequent shots of B-12, but they only brought temporary relief, and when the effect wore off she felt worse than before. Yet she continued to work fourteen to eighteen hours a day. Because she was rarely hungry, she often went without meals, and this only aggravated her fatigue.

Two weeks after her meeting with Vanita Beth, Phil Greene called Ceetra to say the Quonset huts were up and the bar/whorehouse was in full operation.

"There's been a marked decline in absenteeism already," he said, "and it's only been open a few days. Vanita's having an open house tonight. Why don't you come up and see for yourself what she's got going up here? It's something you've got to see to believe."

"I wish I could," Ceetra said.

"A break would do you good. Jake worked himself into a—" Greene checked himself. "Too much time on the job isn't good for anybody."

"I'll try."

After she hung up Ceetra wondered if Dan would be at the party. During the last two weeks they had talked by phone a number of times. He had limited his conversation strictly to business matters, mostly the progress he was making in getting the project back on schedule. She'd thought he would comment on her plan to establish the whorehouse nearer camp, but when he made no mention of it she stubbornly refused to ask his opinion.

She pressed the button on the intercom. "I've decided to go up to the camp this evening," she told Miss Wilson. "Would you make arrangements for the plane to be ready?"

On the trip up she wondered if she had made the right decision. She desperately wanted to see Dan, but was reluctant to give him the impression she was chasing him. If their relationship was going to be reestablished, they were both going to have to bend.

Phil Greene met her at the camp strip when the plane landed and drove her in his jeep to where the Quonset huts had been erected. The site was less than a mile away. It had once been a ravine, but debris from the tunnel had been dumped into the chasm, and now it was quite level. There was nothing pretty about it, but it was obvious from the line of men waiting to get in that they didn't mind.

"Looks like standing room only," she said.

Greene smiled wryly. "I've got to hand it to you," he said. "I thought your idea was crazy, but it's working. There's less absenteeism now than at any time since the project started."

He led the way inside. The Quonset huts had been joined together in such a way that they formed a series of large rooms. They were furnished in much the same way that Vanita Beth had fixed up her other bar. Wooden crates that had originally contained aircraft parts served as tables. Empty brass shell cases were being used as ashtrays. The walls were decorated with an assortment of surplus weapons, and a parachute formed a canopy over a small dance floor on which couples were energetically gyrating to the earsplitting sound of country-western music blasting from a jukebox.

The air was blue with cigarette smoke and it was unbearably hot. The area around the bar was packed solid and only after Phil Greene had shouldered a path for her was she able to move through to where Vanita Beth was busily pouring drinks.

"Goddam." The other woman saw her and ducked under the bar. "You made it. Well, what do you think?"

"Fantastic," Ceetra replied. "Absolutely incredible."

"You ain't seen nothin' yet, honey." She grabbed Ceetra's hand. "Come on, I'll show you the rest of the layout."

The big woman cut a swath through the couples thronging the dance floor and guided Ceetra through a door at the rear of the building. Outside the air was clear and crisp. Ceetra took several deep breaths, then followed Vanita Beth into another complex of Quonset huts that had been erected on a graded area a short distance away. They were linked together in the same way as the others, but the interior was quite different. Instead of tearing walls out to create a large area, the original partitions had been left, and small cubicles installed.

"Officially, these are living quarters for the staff." The other woman chuckled. "It's a long way to Amarillo. My girls can't be expected to commute. And seein' as they more or less live here during the week, there's no harm in them bringin' their honeys back here for a little lovin', is there?"

"Is that what you tell the police?"

"They don't give a damn so long as they get theirs," Vanita Beth said.

A door opened and a thickset man emerged from one of

the cubicles still zipping his fly. As he squeezed past the two women in the narrow corridor he nodded and grinned.

"Some place you got here, Vanita." He eyed Ceetra from head to toe. "Next time I'll take her."

Moments later a shapely girl with doughy skin and huge dark eyes came out of the same cubicle carrying a purse into which she was stuffing a wad of twenty-dollar bills.

"Doin' okay, huh?" Vanita Beth said.

"Okay?" The girl giggled. "Shit, this is like shootin' fish in a barrel. These guys can't wait to give you their dough."

When Vanita Beth finished showing Ceetra around, they returned to the bar. Vanita Beth poured her a double vodka and then went back to helping the other two bartenders serve customers. Ceetra looked around the crowd for Dan, but there was no sign of him. She was finishing her drink when somebody touched her arm from behind.

"I want you to notice how my manners have improved."

She turned to see Al Hunter standing behind her. She remembered how he had spilled champagne down her dress at the reception after the funeral.

"You still owe me for that cleaning bill," she said.

"Would you settle for a drink?"

"Thanks," she replied. "But I don't want any more."

"Then how about a dance?"

She hesitated.

"To show there are no hard feelings," he said.

"How can I refuse if you put it that way?"

"You can't."

He led her to the dance floor. The last time she saw Hunter he'd been wearing an ill-fitting suit and he'd impressed her as being a timid, soft-bodied man. But now he had on a tight-fitting T-shirt that emphasized the width of his well-muscled shoulders, and she realized her first assessment had been an illusion.

"How's the investigation going?" she asked as he put his arm around her waist and started moving to the music.

"Pretty well wrapped up," he replied.

"What have you found out?"

"Wish I could tell you." He winked. "Top secret until I talk with my boss."

"When will that be?"

"I leave for Washington tomorrow."

The crush of dancers prevented them from doing much but standing in one place and swaying to the music.

"Have you seen Dan Blake around?" she asked, striving to make the question as casual as possible.

"He's not here, if that's what you mean."

"I was just curious—"

"Is something bothering him?"

"Why do you ask?"

"He spends sixteen, eighteen hours a day underground," Hunter said. "It isn't natural for a guy to live like that."

Ceetra suddenly felt uncomfortable. Her meeting with Hunter hadn't been the coincidence he'd made it appear to be. It had been the same way at the reception after the funeral. What he really wanted was to probe. When the record on the jukebox ended, she used the break to disengage herself.

"I've got to be going," she said.

"So soon?"

"Afraid so. Thanks for the dance."

"My pleasure," he said. "And I'll let you have the results of my investigation just as soon as I'm able. I think you're in for quite a surprise."

He ambled away, leaving her wondering what he had meant.

"Penny for your thoughts."

She looked around and saw Phil Greene leaning against the bar.

"Isn't that what they say in England?" he asked.

"They used to," she replied. "Before the inflation rate got out of hand."

"Want to get out of here?"

She nodded, and followed the engineer as he led the way out to his jeep.

"It was a mistake to come here, wasn't it, Phil?"

"Depends what you were hoping to find."

He started the engine and backed up. The night had turned raw, and she was glad she'd worn a fleece-lined leather jacket. She watched her companion as he looked over his shoulder and sensed he knew her real reason for being at the party.

"Is it that obvious?" she asked.

He nodded. "To me it is."

"You haven't even seen us together."

"I don't need to. You seem to forget I've known Dan for years."

"Has he said anything?"

Greene shook his head. "That's not his style. But when you've shared a trailer with a guy through an Alaskan winter you get to know a lot about him."

"Enough to know when something's bothering him?"

"Dan's a born loner," the engineer said. "Relationships don't come easy to a man like that."

"Why not?"

"He's just not equipped to handle them."

"Is anybody?"

"Maybe not. I don't know. But Dan's something else."

"In what way?"

"He's spent his whole life learning to live alone. The idea of sharing himself with another human being is threatening as hell."

Ceetra didn't answer. What she'd heard made a lot of pieces that had been jumbled in her mind suddenly fit.

"Is that why he's been staying away from me?" she asked.

"Listen," the engineer said. "I don't want to get in the middle of this. Dan's a good friend. For what it's worth, my guess is he's trying to come to grips with what he feels the only way he knows how."

"By being alone?"

"Looks that way to me."

They had stopped outside the project guest house.

"Where is he now?" she asked.

"Went below with the swing shift."

She looked at her watch. It was 11:45 p.m.

"Can I take the jeep?" she asked.

Greene glanced at the sky. Clouds had obscured the moon and there was a dank smell of earth in the wind. "It's gonna rain," he said. "You'd better take my Plymouth."

He pointed to a dust-covered vehicle in a parking stall and handed her the keys.

"But if you're planning on talking with him, leave me out of it. Okay? He'd be mad as hell if he thought I'd been sticking my nose into his business."

She nodded and crossed to the other car. Starting the engine, she eased out the clutch. It wasn't far to the main shaft, but by the time she reached it a fine mist had begun to fall. She parked near the project control center, but stayed in the car and left the engine running so there would be some heat. Taking a cigarette out of her purse, she rummaged through it looking for her lighter. It wasn't there, and she remembered leaving it on her desk in Dallas. Pushing in the lighter on the dash, she waited until it popped out and then touched the glowing red tip to the cigarette. Inhaling deeply, she put her head back against the seat and let the smoke slowly filter out through her nostrils. The windshield wipers slapped back and forth with a hypnotic regularity. The sound induced a feeling of deep relaxation. For almost two weeks she had lived on her nerves: not only because of the pressures of trying to learn the business, but because she didn't know where she stood with Dan. Now, after talking with Phil Greene, things were clearer. It was obvious she was going to have to swallow her pride and take the first step if the deadlock between herself and Dan were ever to be broken.

The shrill wail of the siren marking the end of the swing

shift jolted her out of her reverie. She looked past the windshield wipers to where a group of miners were streaming out of the man trip. In the glare of the floodlights that garlanded the steel superstructure over the main shaft like decorations on a giant Christmas tree, their faces looked like those of long-dead corpses: hollow eye sockets, deep shadows. She studied the features of the men as they passed the car. They looked bone-weary. Most of those who glanced at her showed no sign of recognition. Finally, the flow slowed to a trickle, and there was still no sign of Dan. As the last of the miners approached she rolled down the window and asked, "Have you seen Dan Blake?"

"Yes, ma'am," the man said. "That guy never quits. He's still down there."

Ceetra waited a few moments and then got out of the car and hurried across to the man trip. It was already full of miners waiting to be lowered underground to work the graveyard shift. The foreman, a thickset man with a drooping moustache, looked surprised when he saw her.

"This here's a restricted area," he said.

"I'm Ceetra Rampling—"

"Doesn't make no difference who you are, ma'am."

She stepped aboard.

"Now just you hold on—"

Before the foreman could protest further, the steel gate slammed shut, and the man trip began its descent. As the fall quickened she experienced the same apprehension that had threatened to overwhelm her the last time she went underground. By the time the man trip slowed to a stop and the miners began to file out, she was bathed in sweat. But she willed herself to go on, and followed the men as they boarded the low-profile transporter that was waiting to take them to the work-face.

The vehicle had begun to move when a voice shouted, "Hold it." The driver immediately braked to a stop and Ceetra saw Dan striding toward her.

"What the hell's she doing down here?"

He fired the question at the foreman, ignoring Ceetra completely.

"I told her, Dan, but she wouldn't—"

"It's not his fault," she interjected.

"Get off there," he snapped.

Ceetra obeyed.

"Now you guys get to work."

The transporter took off down the gallery leading to the work-face.

"I'm beginning to feel like a trespasser," she said.

"You are," he said.

"Aren't you forgetting something?"

"If I am—"

"I own this firm."

"So you keep reminding me."

"And I'll go anywhere I damned well please."

"Not dressed like that you won't. Safety regulations call for all personnel to wear hard hats and steel-toed rubber boots. As long as I'm in charge those rules will be obeyed."

There were deep shadows under his eyes, and his skin had a waxy look from too many hours spent underground. Suddenly she realized his sharpness was less an expression of anger than a manifestation of fatigue. She watched as he went inside a small plywood office. When he emerged Sid was with him. The big man carried a pair of steel-toed rubber boots, a yellow slicker and a hard hat.

"Put these on," Dan said.

She did as she was told.

"Have you got any cigarettes in that purse?"

"Yes. Why?"

"There's no smoking allowed down here."

"I'm perfectly able to—"

"Give your purse to Sid. He'll keep an eye on it until you're ready to leave."

She handed the large leather purse to the big man, and he hung it on a nail just inside the door of the makeshift office.

"I talked to Phil Greene," she said. "He tells me you've been spending all your time down here."

"This is where the problems are."

"I thought everything was pretty much back on schedule."

"That's not what's worrying me."

"I kept tabs on all the daily work sheets—"

"You've been busy in a lot of areas from what I hear."

"What do you mean by that?"

"I don't have to spell it out."

"I assume you're referring to the bar—"

"What else?"

"It's reduced absenteeism—"

"And made this firm the laughingstock of the industry."

"I thought—"

"But you didn't ask," he said icily.

"I don't have to," she replied.

"I've got better things to do than stand here arguing with you," Dan said.

The transporter had returned. Ceetra swung on her heels and boarded it.

"Want to go to the work-face, Miss?" the operator asked hesitantly.

"Yes," Ceetra snapped.

Ten minutes later she was still trying to get a grip on her emotions as she stood in the huge central chamber watching the drill jumbo boring into the rock heading. She felt anger and a driving determination to prove herself. She didn't care what it took to show Dan he was mistaken to assume she couldn't cope. It was the same attitude her father had demonstrated toward her for as long as she could remember, and she'd hated him for it.

She took the next transporter back to the main shaft. There was no sign of Dan. Sid was loading cylinders aboard the man trip. He immediately stopped what he was doing and went into the plywood office. He returned with her purse and handed it to her. She thanked him and he grinned at her. When she entered the man trip he held the steel gate open and then let it fall with a clang. He activated the controls. The last thing she saw were his eyes looking up at her as the man trip began its ascent.

Halfway up the shaft she heard a hissing sound. It appeared to be coming from one of the cylinders. Some letters were stenciled on the metal near a valve, but before she could get a close enough look to see what they said, the lights in the man trip suddenly went out. All her old fears immediately surfaced. When the man trip abruptly stopped, she began to shake. The hissing seemed louder now there was no movement, and she sniffed the air in a desperate effort to identify the escaping gas. But the atmosphere was so fetid it was impossible to isolate any one odor. She opened her purse and felt around for her lighter. Then she remembered she had left it on the desk in her father's office. Panic gripped her. It was like a clammy hand clutching at her guts. She willed herself not to lose control, but when the man trip suddenly dropped she screamed.

The cage fell for what seemed like minutes, but was in fact only seconds. Then it came to an abrupt halt. The impact wasn't that of hitting something solid, but rather as if the cable had been stretched to its limit. It yo-yoed up and down, throwing her up against the headers and then slamming her back to the floor. The cylinders were hurled around the confined space. By some miracle none of them hit her with more than a glancing blow. But the hissing continued as she lay in the pitch dark screaming hysterically.

Then the lights came on and the man trip started upwards again. It reached the surface without further incident. The steel door opened automatically and she stumbled out. A security guard standing near the main shaft saw her tottering toward him and grabbed her under the arms.

"What the hell—"

"The man trip," Ceetra gasped. "Something's wrong. Gas leaking—"

Her words trailed away as the guard lowered her to the

wet ground and ran toward the cage. The cylinders were scattered across the floor. He examined each one carefully.

"Just oxygen, ma'am," he announced. "The welders use it. Nothing to worry about. Not unless you lit a match, that is."

"A match?" Ceetra's voice was barely audible.

"Any kind of open flame," the guard said.

"A lighter?" Ceetra whispered.

"That would have done it all right."

"What?"

"Blown you to hell'n back, that's what, ma'am. Pure oxygen."

 **24**   IT WAS RAINING HARD when Al Hunter entered the modern concrete and steel building that housed the headquarters of the Occupational Safety and Health Administration in Washington, D.C. As he stepped from the elevator on the third floor the secretary outside George Gains's office looked up from a letter she was typing.

"You look like a drowned rat."

"Still know how to make a guy feel good, huh, Peggy?"

"I thought you were down in Texas soaking up sun," she said.

"Sun?" He shrugged out of his jacket and shook the rain off it. "It's coming down there a lot worse than it is here."

"The old man's expecting you."

"How is he?"

She shrugged. "You know how it is with emphysema. Some days he's fine. Others he can hardly breathe. Smoggy days are the worst. Everybody tells him he should quit, but he won't listen. Stubborn as all get out."

Hunter knew what she meant. George Gains was a sick man. And he was slowly getting worse. He'd spent his early years digging coal in the mines around Kentucky, and the dust had slowly eaten away at his lungs. Now they were little more than a cobweb tangle of withered tissues. But he had a wife and three kids in college to support. The department had made several attempts to ease him out, but he'd stubbornly resisted, and because he continued to do his job well, and was one of the most experienced men in his field, they had finally turned a blind eye to his disability.

"Want to tell him I'm here?" he asked.

"He knows." She turned back to the letter in her typewriter. "His lungs may be shot, but he's got eyes like an eagle. Saw you getting out of the cab. Go on in."

Hunter crossed to a door marked: OSHA INVESTIGATION DIVISION.

"Al?" A voice from inside the office wheezed the word. "What the hell are you standing out there for? Come on in, for chris'sake."

Hunter pushed open the door. It was ten weeks since he'd last seen Gains, but he looked as if he'd aged ten years. His pale, gaunt face seemed to have sunk in on itself, but when he shook hands his grip was firm.

"Hey, George—" Hunter strove to sound cheerful. "You look great."

"Liar," the other man breathed. "I look like hell and you know it."

"Aw, come on—"

"It's these goddam Washington summers. The humidity. Jesus. I wish to hell I'd been down in Texas with you. All that hot sun—"

"The rain was coming down in sheets when I left. They've got flash flood warnings out."

"Ever seen one?"

Hunter shook his head.

"Damndest thing you'll ever see," Gains said. "You're going along minding your own business when this wall of water twelve or fourteen feet high suddenly comes blasting down an arroyo. God help you if you're in the way. I remember—"

The rest of his sentence sputtered away as he began to cough.

"Listen," Hunter said. "We can do this thing tomorrow if you're not up to it."

"I'll be okay." Gains opened a desk drawer and took out a small cylinder of oxygen with a mask attached. He put it over his mouth and nose, and inhaled deeply. The change it induced was startling. When he spoke again his breathing was normal. "They're on my ass to retire every time I turn around. Just looking for an excuse to send me out to pasture. And I'm not about to give 'em the satisfaction. Besides, I've got to testify in front of that committee investigating the problems the VHST project's been having. That's why I sent for you."

"It's all in my reports," Hunter said.

"I read 'em. Yours and that local inspector they sent out of the OSHA office in Lubbock. You meet him?"

"A couple of times."

"Nice guy?"

"Seemed like it."

"His reports read that way. Full of technical stuff, but soft on the real dirt I need. That's what I want from you."

Gains lit a cigarette and took a long pull.

"Those things'll kill you," the other man said.

"What the hell. On my way out anyhow. Might as well enjoy the trip. Now let's get to it."

"Off the record?"

"If that's what it takes."

Hunter hung his damp jacket over the back of a chair and sat down.

"Want it from the beginning?"

"Know any better place to start?"

"The explosion that killed J.B. Rampling and his son was no accident."

"You're sure?"

"Yes," Hunter replied. "I tested every nook and cranny for methane, but couldn't find a trace. Not methane or any other flammable gas. Wrong rock formation. That blast was

333

deliberately triggered. And whoever placed the charges was an expert."

"What else?"

"The cable that killed Dave Seymour was deliberately severed. Again, by somebody who knew how to cut into a power line without burning himself to a crisp."

"Who wanted him dead?"

Hunter shrugged. "Your guess is as good as mine."

"All I know is what I read in your reports," the other man said. "Gas meter missing . . . no indication of any trouble in the gas reading logs . . . at least one body still unaccounted for . . . stolen lunch pails . . . vandalized emergency-provision cabinets . . . violence between experienced miners and on-the-job trainees . . ."

"There's something that isn't in my report."

"What's that?"

"Somebody tried to kill Ceetra Rampling last night," Hunter said.

"How?"

"In the man trip."

"What the hell was she doing in that?"

"She went underground with the graveyard shift."

"Why?"

"Says she wanted to make a spot check."

"Like her old man." Gains took another long pull on his cigarette. "J.B. loved to catch people with their pants down. You never knew when he was going to turn up. Sure as hell kept us on our toes, I'll tell you. She sounds like a chip off the old block. What happened?"

"Somebody monkeyed with the hoist mechanism. And the cage was loaded with oxygen cylinders. The valve had been ripped off one of them. It was leaking bad. Lucky as hell she didn't light a match when the lights went out."

Gains stubbed out his cigarette. "You're reaching, Al," he said. "Those hoists often slip. They have built-in brake devices. And apparently they worked."

"What about the oxygen?"

"Those cylinders get handled pretty rough. It doesn't take much of a blow to break a valve."

"The thread on this one was stripped. That takes real strength."

"Or the right tool."

"Either way it would have had to be deliberate."

"So who do you suspect?"

"Could have been Sid."

"The big guy?"

Hunter nodded.

"Why would he want to take her out?"

"Who knows? He isn't the brightest guy around. Maybe he's jealous. Doesn't like the way Ceetra Rampling's coming on strong with Dan Blake."

"Why should he care?"

"They've been together a long time. Dan's the only family he's got."

Gains was silent for a moment. "What about this Indian?" he asked finally.

"Russell Edmonds?"

"Yeah. You figure he's got an ax to grind?"

This time it was Hunter's turn to pause. "Maybe," he said. "He's a quiet guy. Keeps pretty much to himself. Used to visit his mother over in Oklahoma all the time. She died about a month ago. I gather he was pretty broken up. Not that he showed it. Just withdrew. I tried talking with him about it, but didn't get anywhere. Gallagher says the Arapahos are real upset about the tunnel. Seems the tribe used to bury their dead around where the camp is now."

"What about Gallagher?"

"Tough, outspoken, one of the best powder men in the business."

"And a troublemaker."

"He doesn't want the trainees in the unions until they've proved themselves."

The other man glanced at the neatly typewritten sheets in front of him.

"Seymour wanted him off the project," he said. "Lodged an official complaint with the arbitration board."

"You suggesting that's a reason for Gallagher killing him?"

"Just thinkin' out loud."

"And you said I was reaching."

Once again Gains retreated into his own thoughts.

"You reckon this thing between Ceetra Rampling and Dan Blake is serious?" he asked.

"Hard to say," Hunter replied. "Right now he seems to hate her guts. But who knows what happened on that round-the-world trip."

"Dan's a strange guy. Known him off 'n on for years. Competent as hell. But always in a spot where he had to play second fiddle. First to J.B., then Bromley. Hell, Dan virtually ran the goddam firm during the last couple of months. J.B. seemed to lose interest. The pressure really seemed to have gotten to him."

"What are you getting at?" Hunter asked.

"Ever wonder what it does to a guy, knowing you're carrying the load, but always having to walk in the shadow of somebody else? Dan must have resented it. He spent half his life covering J.B.'s ass. Then he gets lumbered with the job of grooming a snot-nosed kid to take over a spot he had every right to figure he's earned."

"Are you suggesting Dan—?"

"Why not? He's got a stake in this whole thing. Fifteen years of his life. If Ceetra Rampling wants to throw herself at him, why shouldn't he cash in?"

"How?"

"By marrying her."

"That still wouldn't give him control of her stock," Hunter said.

"It would if she dies," Gains replied quietly.

 **25**

THE CAMP SHOW had been scheduled to begin at 7:00 p.m., but it wasn't until almost two hours later that the lights in the recreation hall dimmed and the revue finally began.

The reason for the delay was rain. It had been falling for over two days and showed no signs of letting up, moving in relentless sheets across the watershed of the Canadian River and beyond. Sometimes it slowed for a minute or two before beginning to fall again, often with even greater force than before.

Rain gauges set up around the camp measured a few inches, then were emptied and began to fill again. Range animals felt the ground soften under their feet and began drifting toward higher ground. Water ran from the bottom of every gully and the draws that usually were dry suddenly carried small rivers of water. Now darkness had come again and the rain had turned increasingly ugly as water thundered down on the camp.

It drenched the men dashing between the bunkhouses and the recreation hall. And yet they still came. The show had been in rehearsal for nearly six weeks, and everybody was curious to see how it turned out. They were also bored after being trapped in their rooms between shifts with nothing to do but eat or lie on their cots listening to the deluge as it drummed on the roof. Now they leaned forward eagerly on the rows of wooden benches for a better view of what was taking place on stage.

Dan Blake stood at the back of the hall, slightly apart from the rest of the audience, listening to one of his men up on the stage taking a reasonable crack at Jimmy Buffet's "Margaritaville."

There was a tug at his arm and he turned to see Harry Gallagher.

"Trouble," the other man whispered.

"What's the problem?" Dan asked.

"We just got word from the weather bureau. The Canadian River is flooding about half a mile south of here."

"Shit. We'd better check those dams. If they don't hold the whole goddam camp could go."

He pressed the snap studs on his yellow rain slicker closed and put on his hard hat. The rain was still coming down hard. In the bluish-white light cast by the banks of mercury-vapor lamps around the perimeter of the camp, the lancing water looked like fine shards of glass slicing through the night sky, sharply angled by the wind that was blowing in gusts from the northeast. Mud squelched under their steel-toed rubber boots as the two men hurried to where the first earth dam was situated at the end of an arroyo about half a mile west of the recreation hall.

It was composed of debris taken out of the tunnel: rocks, scree, boulders, earth. Tons of it. All solidly packed into a broad-based earth wall that towered a hundred feet above where they stood. As they mounted the steps that had been cut into the side they had difficulty maintaining their balance. The concrete slabs were slick with muck oozing from the sides of the dam.

"Looks okay." Dan shone his flashlight down the steep-sided gulley, and shouted to make himself heard over the roar of the wind.

"I don't know." Gallagher aimed his powerful dry-cell spotlight at the surface of the water, picking out the dark, swirling turbulence of the floodwater which inched up the smooth sides of the draw as they watched. "It's rising awful goddam fast. Must be twenty or thirty feet deep already."

Dan quickly made his way across the top of the dam to a ridge that led to a confluence of four other arroyos. The dam blocking these gullies was much bigger than the first one. It had taken all the rock blasted during the first six months of tunneling to build it, and cement had been forced under pressure between the fill to ensure the structure would hold.

"Damn." Dan slipped on some muck, slammed against a boulder, and the flashlight jolted from his hand. "Shine your light down there," he shouted.

Gallagher flashed the beam down and immediately saw the water was much higher than it had been in the first arroyo.

"Looks bad," he bellowed. "If this fuckin' rain doesn't let up soon—"

The wind whipped the rest of his sentence away as the beam of his flashlight picked out the shape of a man huddled next to the churning black water.

"Who the hell—?" Dan's words trailed away as the man on the steep siding below slowly turned to face them.

"It's Russ Edmonds," Gallagher said.

"What the hell's he doing down there?"

"Beats the shit—" Gallagher cupped his hands round his mouth and yelled. "Hey, Russ."

Edmonds didn't move, but continued to stare into the beam of light as if transfixed by it.

"What's that he's holding?" Dan asked.

Gallagher moved his flashlight a fraction, picking out a metal box in Edmond's hands.

"Looks like a detonator." Suddenly he remembered the blasting equipment that had been stolen from the powder storage shed. "Jesus Christ, he's gonna blow the goddam thing."

"Russ." Dan shouted the name as loud as he could, but the wind tore it away.

"He's been acting weird ever since his mother died," Gallagher said. "But I never figured him for something this crazy."

Dan started quickly down the slippery rock face toward where the Indian stood. But Edmonds saw him coming, and started clambering in the opposite direction. He moved with an agility that was astonishing considering the conditions. Sure-footed as a mountain goat, he jumped from boulder to boulder, often across chasms five or six feet wide and nearly impossible to measure because of the darkness.

Dan found it hard to keep up. The tread on his boot soles had filled with mud, negating whatever traction they might otherwise have offered, and making it almost impossible for him to keep his balance on the wet, treacherously angled rocks. Twice he fell headlong into piles of razor-edged scree that sliced his flesh and left the palms of his hands bloody. Once he misjudged a leap and slammed into a steel beam that was one of dozens set into the dam to add rigidity to the earthen structure. His left shoulder took the full impact and a shaft of pain jolted down his arm. When he grabbed the piling in an effort to keep his balance, his head jerked forward and his face struck the rusted metal support. The blow dazed him for two or three minutes, and by the time he had shaken off its effects Edmonds was nearing the top of the steep incline.

"Russ, for chris'sake." Gallagher's voice came from above where Dan stood and he saw he was rapidly closing on Edmonds. "What the fuck're ya tryin' to prove, man?"

The Indian shouted a reply but his words were lost in the wind as he started scrambling up the final twenty yards. The top of the dam was illuminated from behind by the glare of floodlights. They created a milky white nimbus against the night sky and the pouring rain that added radiance to the serrated edge of the bare rock. As Edmonds climbed higher, the outline of his body was silhouetted against the shimmering brilliance. The detonator was clearly visible as he shifted it from the crook of one arm to the other.

"He's got that goddam thing wired," Gallagher shouted.

Before Dan could respond, Edmonds took a step forward and lost his balance. He thrashed around as he struggled to regain it, but his flurry of movements loosened the rock on which he was standing. It pulled loose of the surrounding earth and began a slow arcing descent toward the churning dark floodwater far below. Edmonds fell with it, but somehow slid free a split second before the boulder splashed into the rapidly rising torrent. He landed in a cluster of rocks about eight feet above the water. His body doubled over the detonator. There was a three- or four-second pause, then a deep-throated rumble followed by the blinding flash of an explosion.

Dan felt the earth under his feet tremble. It was no more than a tremulous shiver at first. But as the shaking continued it grew more violent. The dam heaved and twisted, straining against itself with a low groaning sound that turned thunderous as the friction of rock against rock became ever more torturous.

He saw Gallagher trying to claw his way up the now-shifting incline and watched transfixed as he repeatedly slid back down toward the churning water below. There was nothing he could do to help him. He opened his mouth to shout encouragement and was surprised by the taste of blood flowing from a deep gash down the side of his cheek.

Suddenly the dam collapsed. A last fiber hidden in its depths parted and the massive earthen wall crumbled. It happened in seconds, but the events that followed seemed to occur with infinite slowness: slabs of rock tilted, earth splattered, gravel splayed out in a cloud that kept expanding, and water spumed through the gap in the dam with a force that crushed everything in its path.

Dan felt himself lifted by an invisible hand. It was an odd, vaguely pleasurable sensation. There was a sense of being completely dissociated from himself as the blast set him gently down in the raging torrent. But the shock of suddenly being immersed in the icy water jolted him out of his torpor.

He saw water smash into rows of forklift trucks and front-end loaders. Repair shops and storage sheds splintered as the flood slammed into them. The recreation hall was lifted completely off its foundations. Men spilled out of the doorways and windows, screaming as they were hurled into the seething stream.

It was pointless to try to fight the terrible force of the current. Instead he hung on to a tire and wheel that had been torn from a dump truck and let himself be carried forward by the churning tide, aware that sooner or later the furious energy driving the flood must exhaust itself. Debris thudded into the tire. Planks of splintered wood, window frames, doors, beams, oil drums and objects too far submerged to be recognizable hurtled past him. Many of them hit his arms, chest, legs and hands, but he managed to maintain his hold. Trailers floated and tumbled around him. He thought he recognized one as his own, but it bobbed away in the darkness before he could be sure.

The bunkhouses were among the last buildings to go. But the onslaught finally ripped them loose from the pilings on which they stood, and sent them crashing into the churning flood. At one point he looked back and saw a giant section of one tumbling along grotesquely, slowly gaining on him. But at the last moment before it caught up he was swept over an underwater obstacle that momentarily caught and held the wreckage, allowing him to escape.

At last, after what seemed an eternity but was in fact less than twenty or thirty minutes, his feet touched ground. He waded to a patch of high ground and sprawled exhausted on his back in the mud. Rain was still falling, but it had settled to a fine drizzle which felt good on his badly lacerated face. He could hear the cries of men floundering in the muck and see heads bobbing in the water where the recreation hall had once stood. By some miracle the floodlights surrounding the camp had stayed on, perhaps because the generator was situated on a small hill some distance away from the water.

But the scene they illuminated resembled a battlefield after a saturation barrage.

Not a single building that had been in the path of the flood was left standing. The bunkhouse was gone, the repair shops were a mass of splinters, trailers lay scattered like blocks left by a child who had tired of them, and the recreation hall was completely demolished. The torrent that had flowed through the dam had cut a broad swath which, now that the water had finally begun to recede, was turning into a debris-strewn wasteland of mud. It gave off a sour odor that was heavy with the stench of ruptured septic tanks and spilled diesel oil.

The wind was still gusting but was no longer near the gale it had been. As Dan got slowly to his feet he wondered if the floodwater had reached the main shaft. Probably not, because it was located on slightly raised ground. Even if it had, the man trip cage would have prevented much of it from flowing underground. He tried to focus his attention on the problems at hand, and determine what action he could take to solve them.

But when he tried to move white-hot pain knifed through his body. Each step sent a new jolt of agony across his left shoulder, down through his rib cage and across his abdomen. He had lost a lot more blood than he thought, and it had left him so weak he could barely drag one foot after the other. Suddenly his knees buckled and he toppled to the ground. He tried to get up but his legs refused to obey. Each new effort proved futile, and finally drained away what little strength he had left. Utterly exhausted, he gave up trying and lay back down in the mud. He could feel himself slipping into a dark void. A voice inside urged him to fight, but for the first time in his life, he had lost the will.

Dawn was streaking the sky in faint hues of rose, blue and green when the helicopter carrying Ceetra Rampling circled over what was left of the camp.

From an altitude of 2,500 feet it looked like a flotsam-strewn tide pool after the tide had gone out. The breach in the dam wall was a jagged gap from which a fan-shaped area of mud glistened wetly in the early morning light. It was an awesome sight. The shambles of splintered buildings, overturned trailers and scattered equipment half-buried in muck bore no resemblance to the well-ordered camp she had visited only a few days previously. The operations control center, situated high off the ground in the steel superstructure over the main shaft, was one of the few buildings to have survived the onslaught untouched.

Her first thought was of Dan. She found herself silently praying that he hadn't been hurt. But as the helicopter fluttered to a landing on a patch of high ground, she saw Phil Greene waiting, and knew from the expression on his face that her hopes were in vain.

"They're still looking for him," the project engineer said, even before she could ask. He was pale. His weariness showed in bloodshot eyes and hollow, unshaven cheeks. "We still don't know what the hell happened. That dam was strong enough to hold back more than twice the amount of water that was backed up behind it."

Ceetra examined the grim scene. Although it was still early, the heat from the sun was sufficient to start drying out the mud. Steam rose over the muck and hovered in a transluscent layer like ground mist. For the first time she could remember there was no wind. The calm lent an eerie silence to the desolation, and heightened the stench from broken sewer lines.

"Where was he when it happened?" she asked.

"I don't know. I was in the project control center. Most of the guys were watching a show in the rec hall. He could have been there or below ground—"

He didn't complete the sentence. His eyes were fixed on where the recreation hall had once stood. All that remained were concrete pilings. Near them rescue workers wearing long rubber boots and yellow slickers were probing the muck

344

with steel rods. They worked methodically, silently, inching through the slime in their grisly search for bodies. The suction caused by the movement of their legs through the foul-smelling goo made slurping sounds that were oddly obscene. As victims were found the men carried the corpses to where half a dozen ambulances were parked on dry ground, and laid them out in neat lines for examination by doctors who had arrived from Amarillo. Those judged to be dead were bundled into zippered black plastic bags and loaded into the waiting vehicles.

Suddenly Ceetra saw Sid. He was recognizable only because his hulking frame so completely set him apart from the other men picking through the wreckage. He was caked from head to toe with mud. His shoulders were stooped and he moved like an automaton. Abruptly he knelt down near a tire and wheel that had been torn from a dump truck.

"What's he—" Her sentence trailed away as the big man slowly stood up with a limp body in his arms.

"Oh, God—" she murmured.

Phil Greene took one look and ran to where a group of ambulance attendants were dispensing medication to injured men from the tailgate of their vehicle. She saw him talk animatedly to them and point in the direction of Sid, who was walking toward where she stood, carrying Dan.

"Please—let him be all right."

Sid heard her words and paused long enough to fix her with his eyes. She glanced at Dan's face. It was so thickly smeared with mud it was impossible to tell whether he was dead or alive.

"Okay, buddy," one of the ambulance attendants, who had arrived at a run, said breathlessly. "We'll take him."

Sid appeared oblivious to him.

"He'll be fine with us." The other ambulance attendant touched the big man's arm, but quickly pulled back when Sid angrily shook himself free.

"What the hell—?"

The huge man warily studied the two men holding a

stretcher. He was like a she-bear who sensed one of its cubs being threatened. There was the same coiled-spring tension, the same readiness to lash out. The whole set of his body was a warning against pushing him too far, and both men instinctively stepped back.

"It's all right, Sid," Ceetra said. "These men will look after him."

He glared at her but didn't respond. His dirt-smeared face wore an expression that was a blend of perplexity and fear. It was Phil Greene who broke the tension.

"Nobody's going to harm him," he assured Sid quietly. "All they're going to do is take him to the hospital. You can go with him if you want. Now let these men show you where to take him."

The ambulance attendant stepped forward and took Dan's wrist. His eyes never left Sid's as he felt for a pulse.

"He's alive, but very weak," he announced. "Must have lost a lot of blood."

"Will he be all right?" Ceetra asked anxiously.

"I'm not a doctor, ma'am. But I know enough to be damn sure we'd better get him to the hospital fast."

"Use the helicopter." She looked at Sid. "There's room for him, too."

Phil Greene took a step toward Sid.

"I want you to follow me," he said firmly. "Is that clear?"

He didn't respond, but when the project engineer turned and started toward the helicopter, he followed.

Ceetra remained where she stood and watched from a distance as Sid gently placed Dan in the helicopter and climbed in behind him.

As the aircraft lifted off the ground, she experienced an intense sense of loss. It was a moment of déjà vu. She had felt it the last time her father held her before putting her aboard the plane that was to take her to a life of exile. She was beset by a sudden panic at being abandoned. It was heightened by the knowledge that now Dan was gone she must take his place. Fate had presented her with the opportunity to prove herself. It was the moment she'd been waiting for, but now that it had come her apprehension was so overwhelming she couldn't bring herself to act.

Finally willing herself to move, she approached a group of workers who were sprawled on the ground on a low hill near the main shaft. They were caked with mud, their eyes filled with a weariness that went beyond mere physical fatigue. Probing through the muck for the bodies of their friends had sapped some inner resilience and left them like zombies. When she neared them they looked at her with red-rimmed eyes.

"I know you're tired," she said. "But we've got to start cleaning this place up."

"You must be kidding."

She recognized the man who spoke as the same one who had been at the bar in Vanita's Place. He was broad-shouldered and thickset. She remembered his voice. He had accused her of lying about the explosion at the nuclear power plant in Saudi Arabia.

"This is no time to quit—"

"Fuck off," the man said. "Go and tell the reporters none of this happened."

Ceetra looked at the other men. None of them moved. It was hopeless.

"Hey!" The voice came from behind her. When she turned she saw Vanita Beth waving to her through the window of a beat-up pickup truck.

Ceetra crossed to the muck-spattered vehicle.

"What are you doing here?" she asked.

"Me 'n the girls figured we could help." She motioned to the back of the truck. It was loaded with crates of whiskey and a huge coffee urn. "We took some of the guys who weren't hurt down to my place," she said. "They're in the girls' rooms. Never thought I'd see the day when I'd allow a man in them beds without payin'." She laughed. "Poor bastards gotta sleep somewhere. Sure as hell ain't no place here.

347

Will ya look at that mess? What you need are a whole lot of them Quonset huts my old man—"

"I'll take all of them," Ceetra said. "Quonset huts, steel matting, fuel storage drums, telephone poles—I'll pay you top dollar for any of that surplus stuff we can use here."

"Honey, you got a deal." The other woman smiled broadly. "I been waitin' for years to get rid of that crap. You can have the whole kit 'n caboodle."

While they talked Phil Greene had joined them. Ceetra turned to him and asked: "Have we got any flatbed trucks?"

"There are some that weren't damaged."

"Vanita'll tell you where to send them."

"What the hell for?" the engineer asked."

"We're going to rebuild this camp and get this project back on schedule," she said.

"You're crazy. It'll take weeks to clear this debris and start building bunkhouses."

"That's why I'm bringing in Quonset huts. The men'll need somewhere to live while we keep the tunneling shifts going."

"It's impossible," Greene said.

"We'll see," Ceetra replied.

Suddenly possessed of an iron will to succeed, Ceetra plunged into the work. While Vanita Beth's girls distributed whiskey and food to the exhausted survivors, she toured what was left of the camp, making a detailed assessment of the extent of the damage. It was greater than she first thought; only a few buildings were left. But a lot of the heavy-duty equipment had escaped the deluge because it was parked beyond the furthest point the floodwater had reached. And the main shaft itself had remained completely untouched.

Using the project control center as her office, she drew up plans for rebuilding the camp with the same methodical attention to detail she would have used in scheduling the production of a new line of clothes. The raw materials were different, but the techniques were quite similar. The process involved bringing together a lot of disparate parts in a way that enabled them to integrate efficiently. Her only obstacle was the fact that now, instead of dealing with seamstresses, she was faced with spurring a group of hostile construction workers into action.

She decided her only hope lay in shaming the men into helping. With this in mind she led a group of Vanita Beth's girls into the deepest section of slime and started sorting through the rubble of debris for anything they could use. Pots, pans, dishes, chairs, iron cots, wooden beams, splintered wood for kindling. The trailers provided the best pickings. Although all of them had been tossed around like ping-pong balls by the flood, a few had remained sealed tightly enough to keep out the water. Their interiors were a scrambled mess of items thrown together in piles, but they were dry, and a lot of the stuff was still usable.

It was while they were trying to haul one of the trailers upright that the men who had watched their efforts finally offered to help. The first group were trainees. Ceetra recognized them from the union meeting she had attended the first night at camp. And when they pitched in, it wasn't long before the experienced miners followed.

The store of surplus military equipment from Vanita Beth's arrived in mid-afternoon. Ceetra arranged shifts and the men worked through the night. First they laid steel matting over the mud. Where it was too soft to support the weight of the metal they put down empty oil barrels and used telegraph poles to build platforms over them. Then they erected Quonset huts. While they worked, other men set up field kitchens, and Vanita's girls cooked hot food.

After her initial steps, Ceetra quickly learned how to take charge, and after a scant few hours was easily performing tasks she never dreamed she could do. Making on-the-spot decisions about the layout of the makeshift camp, issuing orders about areas to be bulldozed, redistributing workloads so miners were able to get some sleep before they went below to work in the tunnel.

Although Phil Greene helped by translating her decisions into technical jargon, and was on hand to offer his advice whenever she asked for it, she was the one in command. The men sensed it and responded automatically. Whatever doubts might have lurked in their minds were dispelled by the way she handled herself. When they rested, she worked on, and when they fell into exhausted sleep, she drank endless cups of black coffee to help herself stay awake.

The work also had a profound effect on the way the experienced miners and the trainees related to each other. The mud was a crucible. There were no experts; only men working together at tasks that were new to them all. The credential that counted most was a willingness to get the job done. Beyond that, no questions were asked.

By late the following evening the Quonset huts were up and furnished with iron cots. Latrines had been erected and chemical toilets installed. Field kitchens were operating at full capacity. Plumbing ripped out by the flood had been repaired, and water was available in the portable showers. It was cold, but nobody complained. Perishable debris had been burned, and areas where raw sewage had spilled had been saturated with gallons of strong-smelling disinfectant.

Ceetra's fatigue showed on her face. Her eyes were rimmed with red, and her skin had taken on a greyish pallor. Her whole body ached. She had broken all her nails during frequent sorties around the camp, when she had many times physically lent a hand to workers who needed it. Her hair was caked with mud and the yellow slicker she'd donned thirty-six hours earlier was torn in numerous places where it had snagged on splintered wreckage. There were blisters on the palms of both hands, and she knew from the pain that the soles of her feet were in a similar condition.

Yet she felt more fulfilled than at any other time in her life. She had confronted her own fears and conquered them. She had walked the darkness alone and emerged from it with a new respect for herself.

Numb with exhaustion, she sat with a group of other

workers around the stove of a field kitchen that had been set up outside one of the Quonset huts. The men were passing a bottle of whiskey. When it came her turn the person who handed it to her was the same man who had earlier told her to fuck off. Their eyes met and held.

"Go ahead," he said.

Still she hesitated.

"I reckon you earned it," he added. "You did real fine."

 **26**

YEARS AS A TOP Washington lobbyist had given Ed Morley a fine-
honed sense for knowing what
people were thinking, and every fiber of his body warned
him he was in deep trouble.

It didn't show on his smooth, freshly shaved face. He had
long ago learned the necessity of hiding his real emotions
behind a facade of breezy self-confidence that he now projected for the benefit of the three men seated in the library of
his elegant Georgetown mansion.

"Can I freshen your drinks, gentlemen?"

Beecher Curtis, who was standing at the window gazing
out at the beautifully manicured lawns, didn't respond.
Robert Grimwood merely shook his head. And Tyrone
Richardson merely put a hand over his glass. It was Curtis
who spoke first.

"I've got to hand it to you, Ed," he said. "This is a real nice
place you've got here."

"I like it," Morley answered.

"Must cost a fortune to keep up."

"It sure as hell isn't cheap," he admitted. "What is nowadays?"

"Pity you don't own it, what with the price of real estate
going up all the time."

"What's that meant to—"

The other man swung around and looked at Morley with cold, hard eyes.

"Don't bullshit me, Ed. This place is mortgaged to the hilt."

"How did—"

"There isn't much about you we don't know," Curtis said. "Including the fact that you spent that retainer we gave you keeping the wolves from the door. And the front money you told us you needed for the Rampling International deal. The question is, what do we get for all that dough?"

The lobbyist shifted uncomfortably in his chair. "Hey, listen," he replied, striving to sound confident. "These things don't happen overnight."

"We paid you a quarter million bucks—"

"As a retainer. To make my best efforts."

"And close to a million to guarantee us first crack at J. B. Rampling's share of the stock."

"It takes time."

"Yours is running out fast."

"How the hell did I know that crazy daughter of his would decide she didn't want to sell?"

"That's your problem, Ed. You assured us you could deliver. We believed you. Now it's time to deliver."

The lobbyist thought carefully before answering. These men had great power at their disposal. Grimwood in particular. His reputation for disposing of people who crossed him was legendary. There were rumors he had played a key role behind the scenes in Jimmy Hoffa's still unsolved disappearance. Morley was acutely aware that when men like these made threats they wouldn't hesitate to carry them out.

"The girl's under a lot of pressure from various banks," he said. "They were nervous enough about a woman taking over the company. The flood that wiped out the camp a couple of nights ago can't have made them feel any easier. It's bound to put the project behind schedule again. It's only a matter of time before they start calling in their notes. All we have to do is wait."

"We're through waiting." This time it was Grimwood, the big blunt-featured lawyer for the Teamsters, who spoke. "Tunneling on other sections of the VHST project is nearing completion. If we don't act fast it's going to be too late for us to take advantage of the situation. And that would be too bad—for us all."

He didn't have to spell out the consequences. Morley already knew them. But that didn't make finding a solution any easier.

"J. B. hocked his company to the hilt in order to come up with completion guarantees when he bid on the tunnel," Morley said desperately. "Believe me, I know. He hired me to get a syndicate of banks to underwrite the deal. And I've taken these guys a lot of other packages that paid off. They owe me. When I ask them—"

"You're bullshitting again, Ed." Tyrone Richardson shook his head like a disappointed parent. "I went along with this takeover deal because you suckered me into believing you could really deliver. Now I know better. You're all front. The stuff about who you know and what you can do is all just so much crap."

Morley tried to appear unruffled.

"How do you think I got where I am today?" he asked with an easy smile.

"By talking a fast line," Richardson replied.

"You're wrong," the lobbyist said. "I happen to have made it my business to know where the skeletons are hidden. There isn't a decision-maker in Washington, or a major figure in business, that I don't have something on."

"I heard all that stuff," Richardson said. "Damned if I didn't believe it for a long time, too. But now I know better."

"I can prove it."

"Why don't you?" Richardson asked.

Morley got up and crossed to the console of an IBM computer that occupied the whole of one wall.

"This is linked to two other computers in my downtown office," he said. "I've got tapes down there on damn nearly anybody of importance. Including all the dirt. Just give me a name."

"Let's start with mine."

The lobbyist hesitated.

"Go ahead," the other man said. "I'm not shy."

He punched the name "Tyrone Richardson" into the keyboard on the console, and waited for a readout. Seconds later the display scene flickered to life: INFORMATION ERASED.

"Well?" Richardson asked.

"I must have fed it in wrong," Morley said.

"Try these other guys." The oil man nodded at Grimwood and Curtis.

The lobbyist had an uneasy feeling they knew something he didn't, something that gave them a trump card. But he punched in the other names and waited for the computer to feed back the information. Once again the display screen flashed: INFORMATION ERASED.

"I don't understand—"

"He doesn't understand," Richardson repeated, addressing his two companions.

"Why don't you tell him?" Grimwood said.

"Well, if you say so." Richardson turned his attention back to Morley. "The explanation's simple enough, Ed. We hired a computer expert. He broke the security on your system and instructed the machine to erase all the information on those tapes of yours."

"But why, for chris'sake?"

"To show we mean business." He picked up a briefcase next to his chair and took out a roll of tape. "In case you're thinking about the duplicate you stashed away in your ski cabin up at Saranac Lake, forget it. We picked it up two days ago."

Morley's face turned ashen. It had taken him over ten years to gather the information on the tape the other man was holding. It contained every scrap of information Bonnie Oliver's girls had gleaned from the men they went to bed with. It was the key to his success as a lobbyist. Without it he was finished.

"What do you want?" he asked weakly.

"Only what you promised us," Richardson said. "Controlling interest in Rampling International."

"And if Ceetra won't sell?"

"That's a possibility we're not willing to consider," he said.

"Be reasonable, for chris'sake—"

"Reasonable?" Grimwood laughed. "When you've blown our dough and tried to make chumps of us?"

"I can't force her." Morley was beginning to whine.

"She's stubborn as hell. Worse than her old man."

"If she were dead—"

"She isn't, for chris'sake."

"Construction's a dangerous business," Grimwood said. "Accidents happen all the time."

"She's already survived a couple."

"Three's an unlucky number for lots of people."

The lobbyist didn't answer.

"I think," Grimwood added, "you should have a contingency plan ready. Just in case something unexpected happens to J. B.'s daughter. Don't you?"

 **27**

DAN BLAKE lay in a private ward at High Plains Baptist Hospital in Amarillo. He had been in a coma for three days. It appeared to the doctors and nurses who tended his needs that he was in a state of profound shock. It was either that or a serious concussion from a blow he had suffered while being swept along by the flood.

"Mr. Blake?" The voice was a woman's, faint and very far away.

"What's his pulse?" A man this time.

Dan felt a light pressure on his wrist.

"About fifty," the woman said. "Stronger than it has been."

He opened his eyes.

"Easy," the man's voice cautioned.

His vision was blurred, but he could see the vague outline of somebody wearing a white coat.

"Just take it real easy."

Dan murmured a reply.

"Feel pretty crummy, huh?"

This time Dan didn't even attempt an answer. But his vision improved to a point where he was able to see clearly the people at his bedside. The man in the white coat was young and black, with a stethoscope around his neck. The woman, also in white, put a paper cup to his lips.

"Swallow, honey. A little at a time."

Cool liquid spilled over his tongue, but when he tried to swallow his parched throat refused to obey and he began to choke. Strong hands grabbed his shoulders and raised him to a sitting position. A series of hard slaps on the back enabled him to get his breath.

"Jesus." He uttered the word in a deep-throated croak.

"Okay?" the doctor asked.

Dan suddenly became conscious of the intravenous feeding tube attached to a vein in his right arm, and dressings held in place by bandages on both legs.

"How long have I been here?" he asked huskily.

"This is your fourth day," the doctor said.

"What's wrong with my legs?"

"Severe lacerations."

"What put me out for so long?"

"Probably concussion. There's quite a bump on your head. You were in shock when they brought you in."

The nurse handed him three brightly colored capsules and another paper cup. This time he was able to swallow without choking.

"Hungry?" she asked.

He nodded.

"I'll ask the kitchen to send up some dinner."

"Is the television working?"

She handed him a remote control. The six o'clock news was just beginning on KAMR.

" . . . Cleanup continues at the site of the VHST tunnel project . . ."

The pictures on the screen were taken from a helicopter and showed a bird's-eye view of the camp. He barely recognized it. Quonset huts had been set up in neat, orderly lines, and large areas of steel matting laid to enable heavy-duty equipment to keep running in spite of the thick mud that was still clearly present.

" . . . Construction industry experts are applauding the prompt action taken by Ceetra Rampling, daughter of the founder of the firm she now heads . . ."

360

The announcer's voice continued over additional videotape that showed field kitchens in full operation, a network of walkways built over muddy areas, pontoons of oil drums and telegraph poles that provided foundations for temporary warehouses that had been created out of surplus aircraft hangars.

> . . . Using a wide range of surplus military equipment, Miss Rampling was able to keep the surviving work force intact by providing immediate shelter and food. Although the makeshift facilities are rapidly being phased out as more permanent structures are brought in from Dallas, experts attribute the fact that work on the tunnel has continued on schedule to Miss Rampling's ingenuity under incredibly difficult conditions . . .

When the segment ended, Dan switched the set off and lay back, thinking about Ceetra and what he'd just heard.

He was still deep in thought when she came into the room accompanied by the doctor. It was the first time he had seen her since the night she had visited him underground, and after the way he had treated her he was surprised that she would bother coming to see him.

"Are you okay?" she asked.

"I'm fine," he replied.

Ceetra's eyes caught the deep gash down the side of his cheek.

"You don't look so great."

"He isn't," the doctor said. "Lying around in that icewater all night didn't do his lungs any good. Right now it's pleurisy, but if he doesn't take care of himself it could become pneumonia."

"I'll be all right in a few days," Dan said.

The doctor shook his head. "It's going to take a lot longer than that. What you need is complete rest. Take a long vacation. Go somewhere you can lie in the sun and bake all that goo out of your lungs."

"I can't," he replied. "I've got work to do."

"The tunnel's on schedule," Ceetra said. "And we've started rebuilding the camp."

"I know. Saw it on television. Looks like a goddam military base."

"No wonder," Ceetra laughed. "I bought out a disused Air Force base."

"The guy on the news says everybody's pretty impressed."

"Don't believe everything you hear on the idiot box."

"You did fine by the looks of things."

"Coming from you, that means something," she said.

The doctor finished examining Dan's chart and turned to Ceetra. "Don't stay too long. He needs a lot more rest than he thinks."

"I had a call from the gnomes," she said when they were alone.

He looked puzzled.

"The bankers."

"I'm surprised they waited this long."

"Surprise," she said. "They're willing to extend their notes another ninety days."

"How come?" Dan asked.

"Guess they know a winner when they see one." Ceetra tried to make the remark sound flippant, but the blood still rushed to her face.

She changed the subject.

"That OSHA investigator—"

"Hunter?"

"He tells me the collapse of the dam wasn't an accident."

"He's right," Dan said. "Russ Edmonds blew it."

"Are you sure?"

"Saw it with my own eyes."

"My God, why?"

"Didn't Hunter have any theories?"

"He said Edmonds was under a lot of pressure. His mother died quite recently. He thinks he had some kind of nervous breakdown."

"That's close." Dan felt too tired to try to explain about the sacred burial grounds. "How's Gallagher?"

"He was badly hurt," she replied. "Internal injuries."

"Shit."

Again there was a silence.

"They're right about you needing to get away for a while," Ceetra said. "You've been working far too hard. The company owns a villa in Mexico."

"Puerto Vallarta," Dan said. "I know. I've been there a lot with your father."

"Why don't you go down there and take a complete rest. It'll do you a world of good."

"You say the banks gave us ninety days?"

"What's that got to do with it?"

"A lot," he said. "They're putting you on probation."

"I don't understand."

"They want to be sure they're betting on a sure thing."

"But the project's on schedule and we're rebuilding the camp."

"It's going to take more—"

"Than a woman can do?"

He hesitated. "What I'm saying is you're going to need all the help you can get."

There was another pause.

"Anyway," he added. "This sure as hell isn't any time to take a vacation."

"I'm not asking you," Ceetra said coolly. "I'm making it an order."

"You can't—"

"You're wrong," she interjected. "I can and I am. I need you very much, but not enough to risk your getting pneumonia."

Mule Barnes had been waiting almost half an hour by the time Ed Morley's limousine stopped at the corner of Fifth Avenue and 59th Street. Barnes was in New York when he

received Morley's call, and agreed to meet him on condition
that he bring Bonnie.

"Waiting long?" Morley asked as Barnes climbed into the
silver Lincoln.

"Just a few minutes," Barnes lied.

"Bonnie get there okay?"

The other man nodded.

"Some girl, huh?"

Barnes didn't answer.

"Something bothering you, Mule?" the lobbyist asked.

"Uh . . . uh."

"Sure?"

"Certain."

"It isn't like you to be down in the mouth after a good
fuck."

"I've been doing some thinking, that's all."

"About what?"

"All bets are off, Ed," he said.

"They're what?"

"Off," the other man repeated. "Ceetra isn't going to sell
the shares she inherited from Jake."

Morley jerked upright in his seat. "You said you could
handle her."

"I've tried. But she's a stubborn bitch. There's a lot of
Jake in her. The more I've pushed, the deeper she's dug in."

"We had a deal," Morley blustered.

"Can you squeeze blood from a stone?"

Morley's attitude underwent an abrupt change. "I'll level
with you, Mule. I'm between a rock and a hard place on this
thing."

"Welcome, friend," Barnes replied. "That makes two of
us. I've pressured that woman so goddam hard she isn't
going to think twice before firing my ass."

"I've got more than a job at stake," Morley said.

"Me, too," Barnes countered. "You know the bylaws. If I
get fired I have to sell my shares back to the company at a
price that's determined by whoever holds a controlling

interest. That means Ceetra Rampling. And I'm counting on those shares to get me through my old age."

"There must be something you can do," Morley persisted. "Hell, she doesn't know her ass from a hole in the ground when it comes to business."

"That's where we both made a mistake. She's sharp as a tack. Doesn't miss a goddam thing. And I'm not her all-time favorite. I'm gonna have to do a lot of ass-kissing to get back in her good graces."

"What about the banks? I don't imagine they're too thrilled by the idea of a dumb broad running a company they've got their money in."

"I was counting on that," Barnes said. "But it hasn't worked out that way. Seems they were pretty impressed by her handling of things when that flood wiped out the camp. Gave her a ninety-day extension. And my guess is they'll make it permanent unless—"

"What?"

"She'd have to fuck up pretty bad."

"That could still be arranged."

"Not by me," the lawyer said. "And if you've got plans I'd rather not know about them."

"Why not?"

"Because from here on in I'm doing whatever I have to in order to protect my own ass. And that includes warning her about any rumors I hear."

"You wouldn't be that dumb."

"Try me," Barnes said.

"Adopting an attitude like that could put you in a real bad spot, Mule. One that could prove fatal," Morley added coldly.

28

"CORRA, SEÑOR!"

The Mexican boy who had strapped Dan into the parachute harness signaled his partner in the speedboat that was rocking gently in the swell off the beach in front of the Posada Vallarta. The other youngster gunned the twin outboards, and the line linking Dan to the boat suddenly tightened. When it pulled at his harness he ran, and the parachute canopy caught the wind and billowed out at a slight angle behind him. He felt himself rising like a giant frigate bird, up and up until the 500-foot line was fully extended.

From his vantage point high over the ocean Dan could see the villa in a sandy cove. He had arrived there almost a week ago. At first all he'd wanted to do was sleep. Slowly his strength had returned enough for him to spend hours in the emerald waters, lying on a raft that was anchored offshore, or snorkeling around the rocks where fish of all colors abounded.

Now, except for some pain in his shoulder, he felt completely well again. He had phoned Ceetra in Dallas and told her he was ready to return, but she had insisted he stay another week, assuring him that everything was running smoothly. His first instinct was to argue, but she was now his boss and he had to accept the fact. Whether or not he could go on working for her was a different matter, one he had decided not to think about until he was healthy enough to make logical decisions.

But now that time had come. As he floated high over the

town, flanked on the east by the implacable Sierra Madre mountains, with the Islas Marietas little more than a shadow on the horizon, he realized the decision he must make was not whether he could work for a woman, but whether he could continue as a subordinate to somebody he loved. It was the first time he had ever felt this way about anybody since his father died. It was a totally new emotion, and he had no idea how to handle it.

He floated down to a landing on the beach in front of the Posada Vallarta, watched by a scattered handful of people sprawled on the beach. Even out-of-season, during July and August, the tourists still came to Puerto Vallarta. They watched as Dan unfastened his harness. Some, the older ones, were so wrinkled by too many seasons in the sun that their skin had turned leathery. They reminded him of iguanas. Their eyes had the same half-lidded, cold, unblinking disinterest.

When he reached the villa it was almost 6:30 p.m. Mario, the *mozo* who ran the house and supervised the work of the two maids, was waiting.

"Will you be eating in tonight, señor?" he asked in his heavily accented English.

"No, thanks, Mario," Dan replied. "But I feel like being around people."

"There are many good places," Mario said. "La Fonda del Sol—"

"It's too much like a satin-lined candy box."

"Bernardo's has very good red snapper Vera Cruz style—"

"The Garza Blanca's more my taste," Dan said. "Would you call and make a reservation for eight o'clock?"

"It won't be necessary, señor. Not at this time of year. The weather is too hot for most people."

When he walked into the thatched-roof dining room that was open to the sea, Dan realized Mario was right. The place was almost empty. Only about half a dozen couples sat at the candle-lit tables.

"Are you alone, señor?" the maître d' asked as he seated Dan.

"That's right," Dan said.

"Ah. It is a pity. The moon will be full tonight."

In fact, the moon had already risen. It hung like a huge orange-yellow ball over the ocean, turning the surface of the water into a shimmering mantle of palest gold. Dan moved his chair so his back was to it, and focused his attention on the menu. He was hungry for the first time in weeks, and ordered accordingly. Throughout the meal he drank Dos Equis beer. Afterwards he sipped Crema de Tequila Almendrado, and by the time he paid his bill, he was feeling good. Not drunk, but just high enough not to want the evening to end.

He got into his jeep and headed for Pitillal. It was a small village in an area that had been designated "zona rosa." Prostitutes were allowed to ply their trade there, provided they underwent frequent checkups for venereal disease at clinics in town. Dan had visited Pitillal many times before, and enjoyed the fact that he could get the kind of impersonal sex he liked best. Little talk, no commitments, and a good fuck. There was a lot to recommend it.

He parked his jeep outside a dilapidated adobe building with a thatched roof which was filled with holes. He was greeted by a swarm of dogs that ran yapping at his heels as he headed for the bar. They were all skinny creatures whose rib cages protruded under skin pocked with festering sores. And the children who came after them weren't in much better shape.

"*Por favor, señor,*" they cried, holding their hands in front of them as if expecting him to dispense a communion wafer.

He reached in his pocket and took out a handful of coins. Without looking at the denomination, he distributed one to each child. Their eyes fixed on the coins, then turned upwards to him with expressions of awe. But they scattered away into the darkness as a huge fat woman appeared at the door of the bar.

"*Bastardos!*" she shouted.

"It's okay." Dan said.

"You shouldn't give them anything, señor," the fat woman said, ushering him into the bar. "They bother the customers all the time."

"I didn't mind."

"You are a prince," the woman replied with a smile that showed a gold tooth. "Not all men are like you, Señor Blake."

He was surprised when she used his name. Then he remembered her from the last time he was in Pitillal. She was a madam who specialized in young, pretty girls, not the worn-out old whores most of the bars in the village offered. He ordered a beer and looked around the small, smoke-filled room. He was the only non-Mexican in the place.

"You want Teresa?" the woman behind the bar asked.

"I'd like to meet her first," Dan said.

"But you already know her, señor. Last time you were here—"

A girl with long dark hair sat on the stool next to him. She had huge black eyes and flawless skin.

"You do not remember me?" she pouted.

"Sure," he lied. "How could I forget a girl like you?"

"She talked about you a lot after you left," the fat woman said.

"I'll bet." Dan knew it was a put-on, but didn't care.

"Buy me a drink?" the girl asked.

"Give her a beer."

"But she likes champagne," the madam said slyly.

"Don't we all."

"Or tequila?"

"You want tequila?" Dan asked the girl.

"A margarita," she replied.

"You heard the lady," Dan said. "Give her what she wants."

The fat woman poured something Dan assumed was colored water into a cracked, dirty-looking glass and shoved it across the bar.

"How much?" Dan asked.

"Five hundred pesos, señor."

"Twenty-five bucks for two drinks?"

"And Teresa," the madam replied.

Dan looked at the girl next to him. She sipped her drink. He handed the fat woman the money and turned his attention to the small dance floor where a sex show was under way.

It featured a middle-aged woman and a girl about thirteen or fourteen years old. The girl was squatting on the floor while her companion, who was wearing a huge rubber dildo, went at her dog-fashion from behind. There was nothing sensual about the show. Both performers were as bored by it as their audience. A few of the men shouted comments in Spanish. They evoked laughter. The woman wearing the dildo withdrew it and waved it in the direction of the men who were seated at a table next to the dance floor. A dog wandered in from outside and began sniffing around the girl kneeling on the floor. The woman kicked it viciously in the ribs, sending it yelping back out into the darkness. The audience cheered. Nobody took what was happening with any degree of seriousness.

"Come," Teresa said.

Taking Dan's hand, she led him out through a back door and across a patch of dusty earth to a low adobe building. It was divided into small cubicles. There were no doors, only curtains made of plastic beads threaded on nylon cord. The furnishings consisted of an iron cot, two metal chairs and a table on which stood a jug in a large bowl. There was a faded bullfight poster on one wall, and a crucifix on another.

"Sit down." She smiled as she began to undress. "You look tired."

Dan perched on the edge of the bed. The mattress smelled musty and he noticed that plaster was peeling from the ceiling. He suddenly felt weary. There had been so many rooms like this in his life. He lay down and closed his eyes.

He could hear the girl humming and the sound of water being poured. Moments later she unfastened his belt and eased off his trousers. The movement of her fingers was almost mothlike as she washed his penis, but the water was cold and it turned his shaft flaccid.

"I'm not sure this is such a good idea," he said.

"You lie there," Teresa said. "I do everything."

The only light in the room came from a small kerosene lamp, but it was enough for Dan to see her body. It was lithe: small, firm breasts, narrow waist, good hips. Her long dark hair trailed across his belly as she leaned over him and began kissing the tip of his penis.

"Fuck me." The girl uttered the words with a fake passion that made them sound hollow. "Like last time."

But things had changed since then. He wasn't the same. He couldn't even get a hard-on. Suddenly he sat up and swung his legs over the edge of the bed.

"You don't like me any more?" Teresa asked, obviously startled by the abruptness of his movement.

"It isn't that."

"You want me to bring another girl?"

"No. Too much booze. That's the problem."

He stood up and zipped his pants.

"Maybe." Teresa sounded hurt. "Or another woman."

"You're crazy."

She lay naked on the bed looking up at him.

"It often happens," she said. "The penis knows a man is in love before he does."

Dan took out his wallet and peeled off two hundred pesos.

"Here," he said.

Teresa shook her head. "You already paid."

"This is for you."

"I did not earn it."

"Wasn't your fault."

She took the money. "I will give it to the church at the fiesta de la Virgen de Guadalupe."

"Looks like they're getting ready for it already," he said.

"That is just for the tourists. The people who come off the ships like to see parades. But in December it is real. And the last night is ours."

The pride in her voice was genuine, and Dan knew why. On the final night of the fiesta it was a tradition for prostitutes to walk in the procession through town. They wore their finest clothes and carried their heads high as the townsfolk cheered them all the way to the church. There they gave offerings that far exceeded anything ordinary working people could afford. Donations of a thousand or even two thousand pesos were quite often made by the girls. And the priest never refused them.

"If I'm in Puerto Vallarta I'll look for you," Dan said.

He strode back to his jeep and slammed it into gear. The rush of night air helped clear his head, and the effects of the booze had begun to wear off by the time he got back to town. The procession was still under way, and police had closed off the main streets. As there was no way of getting through, he parked and joined the crowd watching the parade.

It was a poor facsimile of the original, but most of the tourists didn't know, and were excited by what they saw.

"Did you ever see such cute kids?" a woman exclaimed. She was wearing a garish purple caftan to hide the fact that she was fat, and her straw hat was plastered with luggage stickers from hotels around the world.

"They're just darling," replied her companion, who was scarecrow-thin. "I'd just love to take one home with me."

Suddenly a pair of arms circled his waist.

"Guess who?"

He knew without looking it was Ceetra. She pressed her head against his back and hugged him tightly.

"I missed you," she said.

For a moment he stood without moving. Then he turned, took her face between his hands and kissed her.

"I had a whole speech prepared," she murmured, resting her face against his cheek. "All kinds of clever—"

He kissed her again. Then, putting his arm around her shoulders, he led her through the crowds to where he had parked the jeep. The police had opened the streets to traffic. In a matter of minutes they were on the road south of town heading toward the villa. Both remained silent. It was a calm quiet, the kind of restful ease two people share when they know they belong together.

When he made love to her in the master suite at the villa, each instinctively understood what the other was feeling. He was more tender than he had ever been. She sensed he was sharing himself with her for the first time. When he mounted her she clung to him with tears streaming down her cheeks.

"I love you," she whispered. "Oh, God—"

Her voice trailed away as their bodies merged in a rhythm that quickened until both of them climaxed together. She rested her head on his chest. They were both sweating. The film of moisture seemed to glue them together. His breathing was still rapid, and she could hear the quickened beat of his heart. Somewhere in the darkness outside a night bird cried out, a sweet, solitary call that was repeated again and again.

They remained in each other's arms for a long time. Then Dan released her and got up.

"Don't—" She checked herself when she saw he was only opening the curtains.

"What?" he asked.

She hesitated. "I was afraid you were leaving."

"Why would I do that?" he asked.

"I don't know."

"Tell me."

"You did in Paris and Rome." Suddenly she was afraid of saying too much, of spoiling everything.

"I guess it's time we talked," he said.

"Not if you don't want to."

"I do," he replied.

He remained a moment longer looking out over the shimmering sea, then turned and walked back to the bed.

"I tried to tell you in Riyadh," he said, "but it didn't come out right. For years it's been my job to do your father's dirty work. Cover things up—"

"Like the accident at Ju'aymah?"

"That and a lot of other things," Dan replied. "Paying bribes to people who could get us contracts was part of it, too. That's what I was doing in Paris and Rome. Your father trusted me—"

"Or used you."

"Either way, I let it happen. Nobody forced me to stay. It got to a point where I didn't think about what I was doing or why. In a way, it was like being in the service. I just did as I was told and didn't ask questions."

Ceetra cradled her head in his lap, and he stroked her hair.

"Jake was the kind of man you instinctively followed. He had that effect on everybody. Nobody bothered to ask where he was leading them. They had confidence in him. It wasn't until the last year or so that I realized he was flawed."

"In what way?" Ceetra asked.

"It's hard to put your finger on a thing like that. Like a bell that's cracked and just doesn't ring true. I guess it's what made him different from other men. Without it he wouldn't have achieved the things he did. I always thought he just liked to take risks. It took me years to understand that he sought out situations where the odds were stacked against him so he could test himself. Gamblers do the same thing. In a way they want to fail."

"Did he?"

"In the end, yes," Dan said. "He was under incredible pressure. It began getting to him. He became irritable. Seemed to lose all his energy. Couldn't sleep. Sometimes he'd work forty-eight hours at a stretch, and then collapse from fatigue. Or he'd just sit around for days unable to bring himself to do anything. Gradually he withdrew more and more. He didn't seem to care about himself. Wouldn't wash or shave. Went weeks at a time without changing his clothes. It got to a stage where he wouldn't meet people. I had to cover for him, make excuses, or take the meetings myself."

"It sounds like he was cracking up."

"He was right on the edge."

"Did he have a breakdown?" Ceetra asked.

"About a week before the accident."

"What triggered it?"

Dan paused. "Your brother was arrested."

"For what?"

"He was in a gay bar in Fort Worth. The police raided the place. They hauled Bromley in with everyone else. When your father heard about it he went crazy."

"Why, for God's sake?"

"Jake had tried to mold his son into a monument to himself. Discovering he was a homosexual shattered that image."

"A lot of straight men go to gay bars."

"He was there with David Seymour," Dan said. "And your father knew from his records that Seymour was a fag."

"It still doesn't prove anything."

"We know that. Jake didn't. Or he couldn't accept it. He was already in a very fragile mental state. Bromley's arrest was the last straw. He became convinced the boy wasn't really his son. Told me Ed Morley was Bromley's real father."

"Was that possible?"

"I don't know. Jake and Morley parted long before I joined the firm. Your father would never tell me why they split. Not until Bromley's arrest. Then he said Morley was having an affair with your mother during the time Bromley was conceived."

"Did you believe him?"

"He was half out of his mind. And it didn't matter what I thought. The point is he believed it." Dan was silent for a moment. "I really believe that if the two of them hadn't died in that cave-in, Jake would have found a way to kill the boy."

For a long time neither of them spoke. Ceetra remembered what Paul Mayhew had said the last time she'd seen him.

"This flaw of my father's," she asked, finally breaking the silence. "Did Bromley have it?"

"In a different way."

"But it was there?"

"Yes."

"So it could be inherited."

Suddenly Dan realized what she was driving at.

"Not a chance," he said. "It came from being around Jake."

"But my mother—"

"Her problems had nothing to do—"

"And you said I was crazy when I thought I saw Bromley underground."

"Stop it." He put his arms around her tightly.

"I'm afraid, Dan," she murmured.

"Don't be. I'm here."

"But for how long?"

"As long as you'll have me."

She pulled away and looked at him.

"You mean that?"

"Would marrying you prove it?"

"Is that what you want?" she asked.

"More than anything."

"Sure?"

"There's only one way I can convince you." He sat up. "Did you bring your birth certificate?"

"It's with my passport."

"Then all we need are blood samples, an application from the civil registry, and a judge who's willing to perform the ceremony."

"You're really serious, aren't you?"

"Would I kid about a thing like this?"

"Oh, Dan." She kissed him. "I think I'm going to cry again."

"I've got a better idea."

He made love to her again, this time with even more passion than before, and when it was over they lay in each other's arms until dawn.

The marriage took place at 4:00 p.m. in the chambers of Judge Enrique Perez in Puerto Vallarta. The hours before it had been a whirlwind of activity. Dr. Rojas, who had been supervising Dan's recuperation, took samples of their blood and signed the necessary documents certifying that both were free of venereal disease. Then he accompanied them to the civil registry, where he had a friend who cut through a lot of red tape to fill in the application. After examining their birth certificates and Mexican Tourist Cards, Judge Perez performed the ceremony in English. It was over in less than fifteen minutes. When Judge Perez pronounced them man and wife, she experienced an unaccountable shiver of apprehension. But it instantly dissolved. And by the time they returned to the villa she was floating on air.

"Know what I'd like to do?" Dan asked.

"I can guess," she giggled.

"We've got all night for that," he laughed. "Right now I'd like to go out in the yacht. We could take some wine and a picnic—"

"They seemed to have played a central part in our relationship."

"So what's more appropriate?"

He gave orders to the two maids and in less than half an hour they fixed a hamper of food. Mario loaded it aboard the yacht, and helped them aboard.

"If you swim," he warned, "be careful to stay away from the Islas Marietas. The current out there is very strong. Many people have drowned." He glanced at the horizon, where the jagged outline of the islands was silhouetted against the azure sky. "The wind is from the south. There may be a storm. If you see clouds gathering over the islands, come in quickly."

When he handed Ceetra a small ice chest containing two

bottles of local white wine, he addressed her as "Señora Blake."

"Señora Blake," she murmured, as if testing the sound of it.

"Like it?" Dan asked as he hauled the lines aboard and started the inboard engine.

"It has a certain ring to it," she replied.

"A gold one," he said. "All part of the package."

She laughed, and sat on the stern watching as he guided the boat out into the bay.

"Aren't you going to use the sails?" she asked.

He saluted. "Yes, ma'am. Or should I call you boss?"

She thought she heard the faintest trace of irony in his voice, but dismissed it when she saw he was smiling.

"Neither," she replied. "Not any more. Now that we're married you own half of everything I've got. That means we get equal billing."

"You promised to love, honor and obey."

"We both did."

"So why don't you help me with the sails?"

Although it was hot, there was a slight wind, just enough to puff out the sails. But it died when they were about a mile from shore. Dan switched off the inboard engine and threw out a sea anchor.

"Let's eat," he said. "I'm starving."

The hamper contained cold chicken, salad, cheese, bread and fruit. Nestled among the food were two small papier-mâché dolls. Both wore Mexican national dress: one male, the other female.

"Aren't they sweet," Ceetra said. "I wonder who put them there?"

"Probably the maids," Dan replied. "The only thing Mexican women like better than children are newlyweds."

Dan opened a bottle of wine and filled their glasses.

"To us," he said.

"Forever," she replied.

It was too hot to eat much, but because the wine was

ice-cold they finished both bottles. It hit Dan harder than Ceetra, and he could barely keep his eyes open.

"I must be getting old," he said. "I'm going to have to take a nap."

"Go ahead," she said. "Better now than later. I'm counting on keeping you awake all night."

"Again?"

"Bet on it."

He settled back on a canvas mattress.

"How about you?" he asked.

"It's too hot. I think I'll take the raft out for a while."

"Just remember what Mario said."

Ceetra looked at the horizon. "We're at least two miles away from the Islas Marietas."

"I still want you to tie that raft to the boat."

"Aye aye, captain." She tossed the long narrow raft over the side. It was made of rubber, and was about seven feet long and four feet wide, with a plastic panel for underwater viewing. It also had a thin nylon rope which she tied to a cleat before jumping overboard. She swam around for a few minutes before clambering onto the raft. The sun had disappeared behind a haze of low clouds. Looking back at the yacht she saw Dan rigging a canvas awning over the main boom. He waved, then disappeared from view as he lay back down on the deck.

Turning over, Ceetra peered through the plastic panel. She could see fish swimming in the emerald water. Quick flashes of silver and multicolored hues. There was something hypnotic about their darting and the gentle undulation of the raft on the waves. Her thoughts drifted.

Al Hunter had come to see her a few hours before she left for Puerto Vallarta. He delivered a copy of the OSHA report, detailing his investigation into the causes of the accident that killed her father and brother, as well as events surrounding David Seymour's death. He had concluded that neither was an accident. She hadn't had time to discuss the implications of his findings in much detail, and said she'd study the report on her return. But when she told him she was joining Dan in Puerto Vallarta, he'd warned her to be careful. When she asked why, he had hedged. "Just be careful, that's all," he repeated.

Now she remembered the probing questions Hunter had asked about Dan at the party celebrating the opening of Vanita's new bar. She'd had an uneasy feeling that he was trying to imply Dan was somehow suspect, but she hadn't stayed around long enough to find out what he was hinting at. Whatever it was, he was so far off base it wasn't worth speculating about. Hunter was going to have egg on his face when he learned they were married.

She closed her eyes and tried to remember all the things she must do when she and Dan got back to Dallas, but her fatigue and the wine combined with the gentle lulling of the waves to make her sleep.

It was dusk when she awoke. A wind that came out of the sun-baked peaks of the Sierra Madres blew offshore toward the Islas Marietas and the vast reaches of the Pacific Ocean beyond them. The sea had darkened and turned ugly. White-topped waves crested around her, their wind-whipped spume flecking her body.

She shivered and reached for the line holding the rubber raft to the boat. It hung loose in the water. There was no sign of the yacht. In the far distance she could see the lights of Puerto Vallarta. There was no way for her to gauge exactly how far away they were. All she knew for sure was that she had slept, that the line had come untied from the cleat, and she had drifted.

"Dan!" She shouted his name until her voice was hoarse, but it was useless. The wind tore the word to shreds.

Suddenly she heard a low roar. There was no mistaking the sound of surf crashing against rocks, and Mario's warning echoed in her head: "Be careful to stay away from the Islas Marietas. The current out there is very strong. Many people have drowned."

John Sherlock

Fear gripped her. She took a series of deep breaths, struggling to keep panic from overtaking her. But she could feel it rising in her gut as the sky darkened and the sea drove her mercilessly toward the jagged, saw-toothed rocks that were out there somewhere, waiting.

 **29**

HARRY GALLAGHER wasn't a religious man. Yet now he found himself outside St. Hyacinth's, a modern-looking Catholic church on West Hills Trail in the northwest section of Amarillo, trying to will himself to go in. He needed somebody he could talk to. A psychiatrist would have been a more logical choice, but Gallagher was broke, and priests came free.

He had tried confiding his worries to his doctor at High Plains Baptist Hospital, but anguish of the soul wasn't his specialty. He was only concerned with patching up bodies, and in Gallagher's case that proved to be enough of a challenge. Initially it appeared he had suffered relatively minor injuries in the flood: a couple of broken ribs, several deep lacerations, and undetermined internal injuries. It was tests for the latter that revealed he had a far more serious condition.

The symptoms were pain in the abdomen, a thready pulse, frequent spasms that set his whole body quivering. Suspecting an injury to one of his internal organs, the doctor had performed exploratory surgery, and discovered that he had a ruptured spleen. There was also something wrong with his liver. A biopsy showed he was suffering from chronic active hepatitis. The doctor had hedged when he told Gallagher. He had used a lot of medical double talk to describe how it differed from ordinary hepatitis. But the bottom line was clear enough. He had a year, maybe two, left to live. There was no cure. The only treatment they could offer was shots of cortisone. When the end came it would be from hepatic failure.

"How long will I be able to go on working?" was Gallagher's first question.

"Six months. Maybe longer," the doctor replied. "It depends on how effective the cortisone is."

"Does anybody have to know?"

"Not unless you want them to," the other man said.

A week after he was released from the hospital, Gallagher returned to his job as a powder man on the VHST tunnel. Midnight to 8:00 a.m. The graveyard shift. The only man he told about his condition was Ed Morley.

He and Morley went back a long way together. Morley had been Gallagher's boss at Brown & Root, and when Morley transferred over to become J.B.'s partner, Gallagher had gone with him. Despite the differences in their positions, the two men had remained close friends. After Morley split with J.B., Gallagher had considered quitting, but Morley advised against it. He told him that one day Rampling International would be the biggest firm of its kind in the business, and that he'd be a damned fool to give up that kind of job security. Gallagher's wife was pregnant at the time, and Morley's words hit home. Gallagher decided to stay.

Soon after Morley left the firm, Gallagher's daughter Jennie was born. She was a beautiful child, but before she was six years old it was discovered she was mentally retarded. His wife had been unable to cope with the situation, and had left for California, giving him custody of the child. He had placed Jennie in an excellent state-supported institution for retarded children, where he visited her as often as he could.

But Jennie had turned eighteen a few months ago, and Gallagher had to find another place for her. The private facility he wanted to transfer her to cost more than the union's insurance benefits would cover. He had very little savings.

Then he'd thought of contacting his old friend Morley. Morley had said he'd be more than glad to loan him the money he needed to send Jennie where he wanted.

The flood had occurred soon after. The lobbyist had called him in the hospital the day the doctor informed him of the diagnosis. When he heard about Gallagher's condition he offered to fly out to Amarillo to visit him as soon as he was on his feet.

But it wasn't until they met in Morley's room at the Hilton Inn that Gallagher realized friendship had nothing to do with the visit. Morley had come to collect his markers. This shouldn't have come as a surprise. Morley wasn't the kind of man who invested a dime without expecting it to pay off handsomely one way or another. But the demands he made were so horrifying that Gallagher had difficulty believing he was hearing them. He asked for time to think. Morley had given him twenty-four hours. They were due to meet again at 5:00 p.m. Less than an hour.

Gallagher went into the church. A man in his early twenties was standing on a pew changing a light bulb. When he heard the door open, he looked at Gallagher and smiled.

"I'll be through here in a minute," he said.

"Don't hurry," Gallagher replied. "I was looking for the priest."

"That's me," the other man said.

Gallagher had been expecting somebody old and frayed, with a white celluloid collar. This kid was young enough to be his son. He wasn't even wearing a cassock. Just a checkered shirt, boots and tight-fitting jeans.

"Listen, maybe I better—"

"Do you want me to hear your confession?"

"No." Gallagher hesitated. "I just thought—well, I wanted to talk to somebody."

"Why don't we go to my office?" he said.

Dusting off his hands, he climbed down from the pew and led the way to a small room at the back of the church. It was filled with Danish modern furniture, and the walls were decorated with brightly colored posters advertising the 1984 Olympic Games in Los Angeles. He felt the young man looking at him, waiting for him to begin.

"It's about this friend of mine—"

The priest nodded. He had thick blond hair and earnest blue eyes. It was the kind of face that belonged on a box of Wheaties. Gallagher felt uncomfortable. He suddenly wished he hadn't come.

"He was involved in this accident—"

"Were you badly hurt?" the young man asked.

"You're right," Gallagher said. "I am talking about myself."

Again the priest nodded, waiting for him to continue.

"I have a daughter," he said. "She's severely retarded."

"How old is she?"

"Eighteen. But she has the mind of a child."

"I'm sorry."

"It hasn't been easy," Gallagher said.

"Are you Catholic?"

"My parents were. I went to a Catholic school. But I don't believe in God."

The other man looked at his hands. They were deeply tanned, with fine golden hairs on the back of them.

"How can I help?" he asked.

"The doctor says I'm going to die. He says I've got a year. Maybe two."

The priest waited.

"I've worked in construction all my life. It pays okay, but I've never been able to save a dime. God knows how my daughter will manage after I'm gone."

"Prayer might help—"

Gallagher knew it had been a mistake to come. He got up. "I'm sorry to have taken up your time."

"Please stay—"

Gallagher didn't wait. He hurried back down the aisle. Now all he wanted was to get out of the place. He heard footsteps behind him but didn't turn. A cab was passing and he hailed it. As he climbed into the back seat he looked up and saw the priest standing at the door of the church.

"Where to?" the driver asked.

"The Hilton Inn."

"That's quite a ways from here."

"So get moving."

Gallagher sat back in the seat and wished to hell he'd never gone near St. Hyacinth's. He didn't belong. And what the fuck was he trying to say, anyway? The facts were clear enough: he was going to die. When he could no longer work, there would be disability. The union might come through with something, but it sure as hell wasn't going to come close to being enough to support Jennie. Ed Morley had offered the only solution.

He was waiting in his room at the hotel.

"Well?" he asked.

"I don't have a choice, do I?" Gallagher said.

The other man shook his head.

"Okay, I'll go along."

"You won't regret it," Morley assured him. "I'll set up a trust to take care of Jennie for life, and you won't have to worry about a thing."

"It's too late for that," the other man said.

"Damn right," the lobbyist agreed. "Now I'll tell you how I intend to put that tunnel so far behind schedule it'll never meet its deadline. By the time the firm finishes paying penalties and the bankers put on the squeeze, J.B.'s daughter is going to be begging me to buy the shares she inherited."

Ceetra shuddered. The wind had turned cold, and the spray from the waves wafted over her as she struggled to stay on the rubber raft. Her limbs were slowly turning numb, and it was increasingly difficult to maintain a hold on the rope loops around the sides of the raft. The panic she had experienced earlier had been replaced by a sense of utter helplessness. The Islas Marietas were now clearly visible against the darkening sky. She could see white water churning on the jagged rocks about a hundred yards offshore. The wind was blowing her inexorably toward them. In a matter of minutes they would rip the raft and herself to shreds. There was nothing she could do to prevent it.

Now she thought about Dan. Had Hunter's suspicions been right? Could Dan have deliberately untied the nylon rope holding the raft to the yacht? Or had it simply worked itself free, and Dan hadn't noticed because he was asleep? Certainly, he stood to benefit most from her death. He would automatically inherit her shares, and that would give him control of Rampling International. Was that what he'd wanted right from the beginning? Oh, God, please say it wasn't so.

She felt the motion of the waves change. The troughs between them were shallower, and there was a churning undertow that boiled the water up under the raft. She knew the reef was only yards away, but her brain was so numb by now that it failed to react.

"Ceetra!"

She heard the name, but no longer knew whether it was imagined or real.

"I'm going to throw a line. Try and grab it."

Was it a voice from somewhere deep in her subconscious, or was it close at hand?

"Make an effort, for chris'sake."

She felt something hit her back. Turning, she saw the hull of a boat outlined against the sky. Somebody was standing at the rail.

"Hold on."

A rope writhed wetly across her stomach. She grasped it, but it began to slip. Suddenly, she realized what was happening. Her lethargy was replaced by a frantic burst of energy. Fumblingly, she passed the end of the rope through two of the loops on the raft. It held. The boat got closer. Moments later she felt herself being hauled aboard. Dan had his arms wrapped around her.

"Jesus, let's get out of here," he said.

Lowering her into the cockpit, he grabbed the wheel and swung it around hard. The yacht responded. Its bow yawed. For an instant it seemed out of control. But slowly it turned and heeled over into the wind. The thunder of waves breaking on the reef slowly receded. Lights from shore appeared in the distance, and took on added brightness as they came closer.

"Drink this." Dan handed her a flask of brandy. She took a long swallow and felt the warmth of the liquor begin spreading through her body. Then he wrapped a blanket around her.

"I was asleep," he said. "When I woke up you were gone."

She didn't answer. Tears streamed down her cheeks.

"I'm going to get you back to the villa and into a hot bath," he said. "Then we're going back."

"I won't be sorry to see Dallas," she murmured.

"We're going straight through to the camp," he replied. "I had a call on the radio. They've got trouble. And it sounds real bad."

 **30**

IT WAS COLD, but Mule Barnes was sweating. His shirt was wet with fear-induced perspiration. Someone was watching him. He'd felt it from the moment he parked his car on the lot inside the main gate of the camp. The conviction was so strong that he had stopped two or three times as he hurried toward the project control center, but each time he looked around there was no sign of anybody. Only spirals of dust churned up by the wind.

This was the first time he had been at the camp since before the flood. It looked different. There was a military orderliness to the place. Trailers that had been scattered about the site in random fashion now formed neat lines in an area near the change sheds. There seemed to be a specified place for everything: piles of steel and concrete sets near the main shaft; skip buckets next to them; dump trucks and front-end loaders closer to the repair shops; mucking equipment and scissor platforms behind a row of forklift trucks. And a dozen bulldozers parked next to each other on a dirt area between the cafeteria and the project control center.

Now he understood why experts in the construction business were still talking about the way Ceetra had coped with the damage done by the flood. It was quite obvious she had considerable organizational skill in addition to a flair for improvisation. No wonder the bankers had been impressed. There was every indication that their investments were in safe hands. But he couldn't help wondering how they were reacting to the rash of incidents that had plagued the project during the last twenty-four hours.

The troubles began on the graveyard shift. First there had been a series of problems with the drill jumbo. The compressors which supplied it with power had suddenly quit operating. It wasn't unusual for one or two to break down at the same time, but the odds against all of them failing simultaneously were astronomical. Then the conveyor belt that carried muck from the work-face to skip buckets at the bottom of the main shaft had broken. At first it seemed like a routine blockage, but further investigation revealed the thick rubberized-canvas belt had been cut.

But the worst incident occurred just after the shift began. A charge of dynamite had been wrongly placed in a hole drilled into the main work-face. Either there was too much explosive, or the hole wasn't deep enough. Whatever the reason, it had resulted in a blast that brought down double the amount of rock it should have, and the consequences were disastrous. It had buried two front-end loaders, a bulldozer and five compressors. Fortunately, nobody had been killed, but two miners were seriously injured, and had to be flown by helicopter to a hospital in Amarillo.

Barnes was at the company headquarters in Dallas when he heard of the accidents. And when he heard that the powder man in charge of the explosion was Harry Gallagher, he knew the series of incidents were not coincidental. Gallagher was far too experienced to make that kind of mistake. He was also a longtime friend of Ed Morley.

Ever since their last meeting in New York, Barnes had known Morley would make his move sooner or later. The man was desperate. He had made it perfectly clear that he would do whatever was required to bring the VHST tunnel project to a halt. The attorney had considered warning

Ceetra when he returned from New York, but by that time she had left to join Dan in Puerto Vallarta. Also, he had no proof that Morley was intent on doing her harm. And even in establishing that he knew anything about the lobbyist's intentions, Barnes was aware he ran the risk of revealing his own collusion.

But the series of incidents on the graveyard shift gave him tangible evidence. It was the opportunity he had been waiting for: a chance to get back into Ceetra's good graces in a sufficiently dramatic way that she would be willing to overlook their past differences. He immediately called the villa in Puerto Vallarta and was put through to Dan on the yacht.

Their conversation had been brief. Barnes was reluctant to reveal his suspicions about Morley to anybody but Ceetra. She was the one who was in danger, and the person he wanted to impress. So he had limited himself to outlining the incidents that had occurred at the tunnel, and suggested that they get back as soon as possible.

Barnes had waited in Dallas, assuming Dan and Ceetra would return there, and it was late afternoon by the time he discovered they had flown in the company plane directly to the camp. As there was no other way of getting up to them, he had taken a regular commercial flight to Amarillo, rented a car and driven in from there. It was now almost 11:50 p.m.

Once again he had the feeling he was being followed. But when he turned there was nobody in sight. The floodlights around the perimeter of camp gave it an eeriness that added to his apprehension. He quickened his step. A wailing siren suddenly rent the night, and he saw a stream of miners pouring out of the man trip. Their faces were caked with muck, and their yellow slickers glistened wetly under the harsh illumination of the floodlights. But for Barnes there was a measure of comfort in their presence. For a moment he wasn't alone.

As he neared the main shaft, he saw miners boarding the man trip and guessed they were going below to work the graveyard shift. He wondered how they felt after what had happened last time they were underground. It took guts, he thought, to return to the scene of so many accidents.

Suddenly he saw Gallagher. He was standing in the man trip, facing outwards. He looked gaunt, and there was pain in his eyes. But what caught Barnes's attention was the man next to Gallagher. Although he was wearing a hard hat, slicker and rubber boots, somehow he appeared out of place. The steel door on the man trip slammed shut, but Barnes could still see through the bars. The man standing next to Gallagher was looking directly at him now. Their eyes held. Then, with sickening clarity, Barnes realized he was gazing into the face of Ed Morley.

On impulse, he ran forward, but long before he reached the man trip it sank out of sight. He stood numbly watching the cables of the hoist as they lowered the cage into the depths. He thought of his last meeting with Morley, at which the lobbyist had warned him not to get in the way of his plans to sabotage the VHST project.

For a long time he didn't move. His first instinct was not to get involved. Morley was in a corner, and a trapped animal could be dangerous. But if he got word to Ceetra about the danger she and the project were in, he could feather his own nest for a long time to come. Greed overcame fear. He turned and headed toward the steps that led to the project control center.

Separating him from them was a dirt area where the bulldozers were parked. They stood in a neat line, their huge blades resting on the ground in front of them. Like huge prehistoric animals. Dinosaurs and mastodons. Wind-swirled dust rose up around them. It hung in the night air, creating a haze that was thick enough to obscure vision. Barnes found it hard to see the machines furthest from where he stood. But it seemed to him that one of them moved. Not the machine itself, but the blade.

He stopped and strained his head forward in an effort to see through the veil of dust. Light glinted off the metal. The concave hollow of the blades focused it into a blinding glare. It made seeing even more difficult. The sense of another presence was almost tangible now. Every fiber of his being could feel it.

Suddenly he started to run. The bulldozers were parked in two lines, and the only path to the project control center lay along a narrow strip between them. He didn't look to either side as he hurried past the machines. Now all he cared about was reaching the steps. But the exertion proved too much for his corpulent body, and before he reached the end of the line he was out of breath. He tried to will himself on, but the pain in his side was agonizing, and he knew if he didn't stop for a moment he would vomit.

Putting his hands on his knees, he leaned his head forward, and took a series of deep breaths to help him overcome his hyperventilation. A creaking sound made him look up. He glimpsed the blade poised high in the air a split second before it fell. Instinctively, he leaped to one side, but not quickly enough. The blade missed his skull, but crunched into his right shoulder, slicing away part of his rib cage and severing his arm.

His scream rose on the wind. An atavistic sound that went on and on. Al Hunter and Phil Greene heard it in the project control center. They looked at each other, then ran for the door. It took less than a minute to reach Barnes, but by that time he was barely conscious. He was lying in a pool of blood. Intestines squirmed from the gaping hole in his side like serpents, steaming in the chill night air. There was a sweet, sickening smell which hovered for a moment before being blown away by the wind.

"Jesus," Greene gasped.

Hunter saw the injured man's eyes flicker.

"He's still alive, for chris'sake."

The men stood looking helplessly down at Barnes. They knew there was nothing they could do. When his lips moved Hunter knelt by his side and put his ear close to the other man's mouth.

John Sherlock

". . . Warn Ceetra." Only sheer will enabled Barnes to utter the words. ". . . Danger below."

He gave a deep sigh. Mucus bubbled on his lips. When his head fell to one side bile-green saliva trickled in a thread from the corner of his mouth.

"He's gone." Hunter shook his head and stood up.

"What did he say?" Greene asked.

"Something about warning Ceetra that she will be in danger if she goes below."

"Christ!"

"What?"

"She wanted to find Dan," the other man said. "I told her to wait, but she wouldn't listen. She went down with the graveyard shift."

 *31*

NEARLY A MILE underground workers on the graveyard shift trooped from the man trip to a transporter that was waiting to take them to the work-face. Gallagher was among them. There was a stabbing pain across his chest and each time he raised his arms the binding around his ribs chafed at his flesh. But his greatest anguish wasn't physical. It churned in his brain. Every fiber of his being protested the part he was playing in Morley's scheme to halt the project.

As the other men boarded the transporter, he hung back, deliberately providing a cover for Morley. The lobbyist waited until the rest of the workers were ahead of him, then ran at a crouch past a stack of concrete sets, and disappeared down a side tunnel. He hadn't confided his intentions to Gallagher. All he had asked him to do was equip him with work clothes, smuggle him aboard the man trip and make sure he had time to break away from the other miners. Now that Gallagher had fulfilled those obligations, he took his place on the transporter and tried not to think about what Morley had in mind.

Ceetra had come below with the first batch of workers, and was making her way along a narrow gallery that led to where she'd been told Dan was checking out the compressors. She moved gingerly, picking her way over a tangle of cables which lay half-buried in the tepid mud. The roar of air from the fan lines was deafening, and a steady stream of water trickled from where it had condensed on the ventilation ducts. There was a fetid smell to the air that made her feel sick.

Suddenly, the lights in the gallery flickered and went out, enveloping her in total darkness. She froze. The lights flicked on for a couple of seconds, then died out again. Her pulse quickened. She waited, deliberately taking deep breaths to quell the panic she felt rising.

She wished now that she had listened to Phil Greene when he urged her not to go below. It was unbearably hot. With the blowers out all air circulation had ceased. But the most oppressive thing was the total silence. She had become accustomed to the roar of fan lines, the chatter of hydraulic drills, the hum of compressors and the constant throbbing of diesel engines. Now they were absent it seemed as if life had suddenly gone out of the project. In minutes the tunnel had become a huge, vaulted sepulcher. She suddenly realized how it must have been for her father when he was trapped by the cave-in. Literally being buried alive. Or perhaps the flash fire had happened so fast he never knew this awful suffocating sensation.

She began to feel her way forward. In the far distance she could hear the sound of voices, and the clink of metal on metal. Instinctively she moved toward them. The gallery she was in led from the bottom of the main shaft to a cavern where the compressors were housed. It was linked by other smaller tunnels to where the main face was being worked. But as it wasn't a through passage to anywhere, it was little used. She had taken it because Gallagher, who was foreman on the graveyard shift, had told her it was a shortcut to where Dan was working.

Stretching her arms out in front of her, she began to inch forward, moving like a sleepwalker through the darkness. The air was becoming increasingly foul, and the heat was unbearable. Fear had created the taste of copper under her tongue. She closed her eyes tightly. Her heart pounded.

Each step she took enmeshed her feet in the tangle of cables. Only by keeping her hands pressed against the wall was she able to retain her balance. The rocks were filmed with slime. Water seeping through them ran down the inside of her arm. It was warm as blood. For a moment she thought the sharp edges of protruding stone had sliced through her skin, but when she put her palm to her tongue all she tasted was the brackishness of moisture tainted by diesel oil.

Then she heard breathing. At first she thought it was her own, but when she held her breath the sound continued. It was coming from somewhere very close. She stood perfectly still, pulse racing, struggling to control her urge to scream. Somewhere in the distance a voice echoed. There was an answering call, but it was very far away.

"Is someone there?" Her throat was dry.

There was no reply. But the breathing continued. It was impossible to determine the exact direction from which it came. The darkness had thoroughly disoriented her senses.

"Please, for God's sake—"

Her words bounced mockingly back at her from the walls. Now she could sense a presence. It was very close. She began to tremble. Something was moving toward her. She could hear the slurping sound of feet in the mud. The tangle of cables on which she stood suddenly moved, causing her to lose her balance. She reached out her arms to keep from falling, but instead of touching the rock, her hands came to rest on bare skin. She started to scream, but before her throat emitted a sound, a hand clamped itself over her mouth. An arm circled her neck, pulling her backwards against a body. It smelled foul.

A voice close to her ear murmured, "One word, and I'll break your neck."

The hand over her mouth was removed. She was too terrified to do anything but obey. Shaking uncontrollably, she remained rooted to the spot where she stood. A match flared, and she tried to make out the features of the menacing figure who held her arm in a fierce grip. The face was partially covered by a dirty, matted beard, but she could see it was badly scarred. His hair hung in stringy, shoulder-length rattails that were caked with mud. But it was his eyes that riveted her attention. Red-rimmed and bloodshot, they had the look of a trapped animal. It was an expression she'd sometimes seen in the eyes of her mother at the sanatorium: a terrible wildness that so often characterizes the insane. Suddenly Ceetra realized that the gaze which now held her mesmerized belonged to her brother.

"You . . ." she uttered, with a mixture of incredulity and terror.

The match went out. For a full minute the only sound she heard was his breathing.

"I wanted to die . . ." He spoke disjointedly, mouthing the words in a low monotone, ". . . always trying to measure up . . . all I wanted was my mother . . . you took her away from me. . . ."

His voice cracked and she heard the sound of sobbing. Suddenly the truth dawned. Pieces that had seemed scattered and unrelated now fit. Her brother was insane. But it wasn't the holocaust which had killed her father that had warped his mind. He had been cracking up for a long time before that. She remembered the half-finished sentence in Bromley's unmailed letter, and what Dr. Robinson had told her about the pressures Bromley had been subjected to by his father ever since birth. It must have finally all proved too much.

The realization triggered fear. Both attempts on her life had taken place while she was underground. For some strange, twisted reason only he understood, Bromley wanted her dead. And she knew reasons didn't matter. He lit another match. This time she saw him more clearly: pathetic, crazed, cowering, ashamed, and still capable of doing her great harm.

They looked at each other in the flickering light. It was an instant of frozen time, a moment in which she suddenly realized there was more of her father's substance in her than there had ever been in Bromley. Despite all the efforts Jake Rampling had made to deny her birthright, she still possessed a fibre that made her his natural heir.

Their eyes remained locked until the flame reached Bromley's fingers. It must have burned his flesh, because he suddenly winced and loosened his grip. She immediately twisted herself free, and ran headlong down the tunnel. Tangled cables and jutting rocks no longer mattered. All she cared about was getting as far away from her brother as possible. She stumbled and fell, but climbed back to her feet and stumbled on. All the time screaming. A terrible, atavistic shriek that picked up volume as it echoed down the hollow space ahead of her.

Dan heard it just as he managed to get the emergency generators working. As the lights flickered on, he ran in the direction from which the scream had come.

He found her in a corner next to a pile of concrete sets. She was rocking back and forth like a child trying to comfort itself. Her arms were wrapped tightly across her breasts. He saw they were badly gashed. Blood dripped from her elbows, but she seemed oblivious to it. There was fear in her eyes. For a moment it seemed she didn't recognize him, and when he came close she cowered against the damp wall.

"It's okay," he said gently.

At the sound of his voice her body relaxed, and tears streamed down her cheeks.

"God," she whimpered. "Oh, God—"

"Hey." He knelt by her side and put his arm across her shoulders. "It's all right now."

She shook her head violently from side to side.

"It was just a power failure," he said.

"No—"

"We've got the emergency generators going and—"

"Down there." She motioned back along the tunnel.

"What—"

"Bromley. He's alive!"

He cupped her face in his hands and looked steadily into

her eyes. Then he picked her up and carried her to the bottom of the main shaft.

"The man trip is on its way down," he said, setting her down carefully near the console which controlled the closure doors. "When it gets here I want you to go above ground. Don't wait. Do you understand?"

She nodded.

He took off his hat and used it to smash the glass of an emergency supply cabinet. Taking out a blanket, he wrapped it around her shoulders. Then he knelt and kissed her.

"I love you," he whispered.

She clung to him.

"I don't want you to get hurt," he added quietly.

"Stay with me," she pleaded.

He let go of her and stood up. "I can't. If my hunch about what is going to happen is right, I've got to move fast."

He set off at a run down the tunnel leading to the work-face. She didn't know whether he believed what she'd said about Bromley or not. Perhaps he thought she'd imagined it. Wasn't that what Mule Barnes had said when she'd told him she thought she'd seen her brother aboard the transporter?

Still shivering, she sat with her knees tucked under her chin, her arms wrapped around her legs, and tried not to think. She was too emotionally drained for her mental processes to be coherent. The past hour had seemed like a terrible nightmare, and now that it was finally over she didn't want to recall any part of it.

Then she heard footsteps, and another wave of apprehension swept over her. They were coming down the tunnel toward where she sat. Her brain told her to hide, but her body refused to move. The echoing steps got louder. Finally, she willed herself to crawl crablike toward some drilling bits that were piled near the bottom of the main shaft. But before she reached them the footsteps quickened, and when she looked over her shoulder she saw a man running toward her.

At first she thought it was Bromley. It wasn't until he was

almost on her that she recognized Ed Morley. The sight of him in work clothes puzzled her. The last time she'd seen the lobbyist was at the reception after her father's funeral and she'd been struck by the perfect cut of the suit he was wearing. For an instant she relaxed. Then she shuddered as light reflected dully from a knife he was holding in his hand.

He didn't speak. For a moment the two of them stared at each other, seemingly transfixed. Ceetra couldn't fathom whether he intended to do her harm or not. He had no reason to hurt her. Yet he kept coming closer, and instinctively she backed away.

"What—?"

Before she could utter another word he slashed at her with the knife. The movement was so abrupt it threw him off balance, and his feet slipped on the slime-filmed concrete. He quickly righted himself, and was raising his arm to strike again when a hand appeared from behind and grabbed his arm.

It was Bromley. Morley seemed as astonished to see him alive as Ceetra had been. As they grappled, Morley tore the younger man's tattered shirt away, and she saw her brother's body was a mass of festering sores. Huge burned areas on his back and across his chest had turned septic and turned to pus. His arms and hands were patterned by deep lacerations that hadn't healed. Yet he possessed a manic strength which enabled him to more than hold his own against Morley.

Neither man uttered a word. The only sound was an occasional grunt as one or the other took a blow. Even when Morley broke free and slashed Bromley across the chest with his knife, Bromley remained mute. He appeared oblivious to pain. If anything, the wounds Morley inflicted only made him come on, until he had the lobbyist backed into a corner on the opposite side of the console which contained the switches that controlled the closure doors.

Morley swung his knife in a wide arc. It missed Bromley's throat by less than an inch. Before he could try again, Bromley ducked under Morley's arm and got both hands on the other man's throat. The lobbyist hacked at him repeatedly with the knife, but Bromley didn't release his grip. Finally, the lobbyist's flailing weakened. He dropped the knife and tried to scream. The sound turned to a gurgle as Bromley tightened his hold on the other man's throat. Morley's face turned purple. His eyes bulged. Only after Morley's head had dropped grotesquely to one side and the last spasm of life had gone from his body did Bromley finally let him slide to the ground.

While the two men were fighting, Ceetra had edged her way back toward the gallery which led to the main work-face. Bromley saw what she was doing and started toward her. Then he hesitated, and turning back to the console that controlled the closure doors, he pressed a red, mushroom-shaped button. Immediately, a siren sounded. It echoed through the labyrinth of tunnels like the wail of an injured animal. Without pausing to think, Ceetra ran headlong into the tunnel.

Her brother came after her, and was gaining quickly when a flood of miners surged down the tunnel in the opposite direction, toward the bottom of the main shaft. After the accident that had happened on the last graveyard shift, they sensed this wasn't a dry run. They knew exactly where to go, and how long they had to get there. Eight minutes. Then the massive steel doors would automatically close, and explosive charges sealed in canisters suspended from the roof would be detonated.

Ceetra fought her way against the onslaught. But it was useless. She stopped struggling and allowed herself to be carried by the solid mass of bodies back toward the cavern at the bottom of the main shaft.

Dan was on a scaffold, attempting to reach a hollowed-out area high on the work-face that had been created by the intersection of two foliation planes which had broken away to form a natural peaked roof. Following a hunch, he had placed a ladder against the steel tubing and climbed up to take a look inside the collapsed section. He didn't know for sure whether Ceetra had imagined seeing her brother or not, but he was pretty certain that if Bromley was hiding anywhere this was the most likely place.

He had almost reached the hollow when the siren blared its warning. Miners drilling the main face immediately dropped their tools and ran. An operator working a front-end loader swung his machine around, swiping the ladder and splintering it. He saw Dan was stranded, but didn't stop to help him. Dan knew he'd better act fast. Grasping the struts of the scaffolding, he swung his body outwards and managed to catch the steel tubing below with his boots. Letting go of the strut he was holding, he let himself drop and caught hold of the tubing on the level below. It was a dangerous maneuver, but less so than staying where he was.

By the time he reached the ground, the main excavation chamber was deserted. Some of the men hadn't even bothered to turn off their equipment. The roar of compressors and diesel engines echoed from the glistening walls. A pneumatic drill writhed at the end of a length of rubber hose like an animal in its final death agony. Dan's body clock warned him that time was rapidly running out, and he hurried down the tunnel which he knew was the shortest route to the safety of the main shaft.

He was halfway down it when a figure emerged from a smaller side gallery. It was lit from behind, and Dan didn't realize until it was almost on top of him that the man blocking his escape was Bromley Rampling.

"Get out, for chris'sake," he yelled.

Bromley didn't move.

"If those closure doors shut, neither of us is going to get out of here," he shouted.

Bromley's mouth twisted into a crooked grin. The hate that filled his eyes was an accumulation of all the resentment which had built up over the years. Dan knew it was too late to try to reason with the younger man. He lowered his head and charged forward. But Bromley stepped aside at the last moment, allowing Dan to slam into the jagged rocks embedded in the wall of the tunnel. The impact stunned him. Blood spurted from a gash over his eye, momentarily blinding him. Bromley was on him in an instant, reaching for his throat. Dan tried to fight him off, but his badly blurred vision made it impossible for him to see well enough to get a hold on the other man. He felt Bromley's hands tighten on his windpipe. The more he struggled the tighter the viselike grip became. Dan had to fight for breath. Pain knifed through his lungs. Consciousness began slipping away. Then suddenly, unaccountably, Bromley let go.

It was almost a full minute before Dan saw why. He tried to sit up, but didn't have the strength. And when he was finally able to focus his eyes, it was just in time to see Sid holding Bromley at arm's length over his head. With the ease of a man tossing a sack of potatoes, he hurled Bromley against the opposite wall. His head slammed into the rock, and there was a sickening crunch. But he didn't fall to the ground. This puzzled Dan until he saw that bolts protruding from the steel liners had driven themselves into Bromley's back and skewered his body in the half-hanging position of a man crucified.

Sid turned and scooped Dan up in his arms. He ran down the tunnel with giant strides. The closure doors were almost shut. Lowering Dan to the ground, Sid wedged his huge body into the opening, bracing himself with his feet and hands against the rock wall and his back against the steel door. Even his great strength couldn't stop the closure, but he delayed it just long enough for Dan to crawl through the narrow gap. When Dan was clear, the big man made no attempt to follow. The steel door slammed shut and he was gone.

Ceetra saw Dan and ran forward. Grasping his arms, she struggled to pull him upright. Miners waiting aboard the man trip hurried to help.

"Let's get the fuck outta here," one of the miners yelled.

He grabbed Dan under the arms and hauled him into the man trip. Ceetra followed. The steel grille slammed shut, and the cage began its ascent.

"How much time have we got?" Dan murmured.

"Less than three minutes," the man next to him replied. "And it's gonna take twice that for this goddam rattrap to make it to the top."

Dan knew this was true. And he was also acutely aware that if the blast from the exploding charges caught the man trip while it was in the shaft they would be pulverized. There was an emergency switch on the ascent control lever. It automatically deactivated the controls on the hoist mechanism which governed the rate at which the drums turned. He knew from past experience that using it could be dangerous. The acceleration was so sudden it could easily compress a man's spine. He looked at Ceetra.

"Brace yourself," he said quietly.

She grasped the steel bars of the cage. The other men saw what was happening, guessed what Dan was about to do, and prepared themselves as best they could. He pulled the pin holding the emergency lever in a closed position, and yanked the handle down.

The effect was immediate. The man trip picked up speed at an alarming rate. The floor seemed to be trying to force them out through the roof of the steel cage. A few men shouted in an effort to relieve the unbearable pressure on their eardrums. The g-force molded the skin grotesquely against their cheekbones. Ceetra's nose began to bleed as the quickening rate of ascent forced blood from her head. Lights set in the shaft streaked past in a single, continuous blur. Then, just as suddenly as the jarring ascent began, it ended. The abrupt halt sent bodies careening into each other. And when the gate swung open, they tumbled out into the arms of those clustered around the main shaft in a heap that sent everybody sprawling.

Dan helped Ceetra to her feet.

"Quick," he said. "Let's get clear. When those charges explode that cage is gonna be blasted to hell."

They had started to run when there was a rumble deep underground. It was followed a minute or two later by a whoosh of hot air that rose up the main shaft with a force which hurled the man trip like a projectile high into the night sky. The sound of the explosion was the last thing to come. It echoed in the bowels of the earth like distant thunder.

"Is it over?" Ceetra asked when the noise finally died away.

Dan nodded. He put his arm around her waist and pulled her close.

"What now?" she murmured.

"We clear the debris."

"There can't be much left. Not after an explosion like that."

"You're wrong," he said. "It sounded a lot worse than it was. Thanks to those closure doors damage has probably been kept to a minimum."

"Can we still finish the job?"

"It's possible."

"And meet the completion deadline?"

Dan shrugged. "With luck. It's a gamble."

"Should we take it?"

"That's something only you can decide," he said.

Ceetra was silent for a moment. What would her father have done? Go forward, of course; take the gamble. But now *she* was president of Rampling International. It was her heritage, her birthright. She knew she could do it, but did she want to do it alone? Jake had always been a loner. Maybe that had been his strength—or maybe his greatest flaw. Perhaps things would have been different if he had not guarded the business so fiercely for Bromley; if he had given Dan Blake more authority, taken him on as a partner. Well, she would rectify that.

Ceetra looked up at Dan and hugged his waist. "Together" she said, "we can't miss."

About the Author

John Sherlock was born in England and attended private boarding school there until entering the Royal Air Force and serving as a Pilot Officer in Singapore. After his military service he was awarded scholarships which enabled him to earn his B.A. from the University of California at Berkeley, his M.S. from Columbia University (Pulitzer School of Journalism), and his Ph.D. from Oxford. He is the author of several novels, including *The Ordeal of Major Grigsby* (made as a movie under the title *The Last Grenade*), *The Instant Saint* and *The Dream Makers*. He has also written numerous magazine articles which have appeared in *Saturday Evening Post, Reader's Digest, TV Guide, Cosmopolitan,* and many other publications both here and abroad. He now divides his time between homes in the United States and Europe.